# LIME'S PHOTOGRAPH

Leif Davidsen was born in 1950. He spent 25 years at the Danish Broadcasting Corporation as a radio and TV correspondent, specialising in Russian, East and Central European affairs, and has been a correspondent in both Spain and Moscow. He published his first novel in 1984 and has written full-time since 1999. His novels are bestsellers in several European countries.

Leif Davidsen

# LIME'S PHOTOGRAPH

TRANSLATED FROM THE DANISH BY
Gaye Kynoch

VINTAGE

Published by Vintage 2002

2 4 6 8 10 9 7 5 3

Copyright © Leif Davidsen 1998
English translation © Gaye Kynoch 2001

Leif Davidsen has asserted his right under the Copyright, Designs and
Patents Act, 1988 to be identified as the author of this work

First published in Great Britain in 2001 by
The Harvill Press

Vintage
Random House, 20 Vauxhall Bridge Road, London SW1V 2SA

Random House Australia (Pty) Limited
20 Alfred Street, Milsons Point, Sydney,
New South Wales 2061, Australia

Random House New Zealand Limited
18 Poland Road, Glenfield, Auckland 10, New Zealand

Random House (Pty) Limited
Endulini, 5A Jubilee Road, Parktown 2193, South Africa

The Random House Group Limited Reg. No. 954009
www.randomhouse.co.uk

The publishers acknowledge the financial support of the
Danish Literary Foundation towards the publication of this edition

The publishers gratefully acknowledge the use of the following quotations:
Tom Kristensen, from *Fribytterdrøme*, Hagerup Forlag, 1920.
Sten Kaalø, from *Med hud og hår. 24 digte*. Sigvaldis Forlag,
Denmark, 1969.
Steen Steensen Blicher, from *The Diary of a Parish Clerk and
Other Stories*, The Athlone Press, London, 1996, translated by
Paula Hostrup-Jessen.
Markus Wolf, from *Man Without a Face*, Jonathan Cape, London, 1997.
Carsten Jensen, from *Jet har hørt et stjerneskud*, Rosinante Forlag,
Copenhagen, 1997.

A CIP catalogue record for this book
is available from the British Library

ISBN 1 860 46988 4

Printed and bound in Great Britain by
Bookmarque Ltd, Croydon, Surrey

*To Ulla, for love and for everything.*

# PART ONE

# PAPARAZZO

The term "paparazzo" was coined by the Italian film director Federico Fellini, who used the word as a description of a "gossip" photographer in the film *La Dolce Vita* in 1960. A paparazzo is a photographer who, like any hired assassin, lies in wait to capture the rich and famous in his viewfinder. Among paparazzi, the English term for a good and well-executed shot of a celebrity is the same word as hired assassins use about a contract – a "hit". A good hit can earn the lucky and ingenious photographer many thousands of dollars. Occasionally, several million.

# 1

There is no way of knowing when everything could shatter and your life be turned upside down – one minute secure and familiar and the next minute a nightmare in which you're running on the spot in slow motion, trying to wake up to reality. But the nightmare is reality. You feel safe by the time you've got halfway through your life, grateful that you managed to find love even though it came late, that you brought a child into the world to carry on the family name. Maybe that's an old-fashioned attitude, but continuity mattered to me as I approached 50 and had to acknowledge that I was now nearer to my death than my birth.

It began with my mobile phone beeping. I knew I shouldn't answer it, but I couldn't stop myself. You never know what lies in store. Good news, bad news, business, bills, bogus calls, death, maybe something significant. You don't know what you might be missing, and even though I was getting older, I wasn't too old to take on the assignments and opportunities that presented themselves. But with age had come disgust and conscience. I'm writing the words in Danish and there they are on my laptop's white screen and I'm surprised how easily they flow, considering that I've been speaking and in particular writing in English and Spanish for so many years. But it seems wrong to use a foreign language here, now that I'm trying to write more than just a brief article, a picture caption, a memo or a love letter.

I was on my stomach, the sun beating down on me. I was lying awkwardly on the weathered, rocky ground where, in spite of the distance down to the beach, little black grains of sand had been blown up by the wind and had found shelter in every cranny. I lay like a sniper in Bosnia, breathing calmly and slowly, conscious of the sun through my thin, pale t-shirt and blue jeans and on my neck below the rim of my white sunhat. Brown, parched mountains rose behind me. If you followed them further inland, you'd see how they increase in size, becoming high and inaccessible, but out here at the coast they were gentler, yet still burnished harsh and arid by the sun and the wind which blows off the Mediterranean in the winter, colder and more fiercely than you might think.

Down below me the little bay was deserted. It was one of the many small coves which over thousands of years the sea had cut into the Costa Brava. The French-Spanish border was a few kilometres to the north, to the south the tourist hell began, where over a couple of decades human greed had succeeded in destroying an area in which generation after generation had lived their lives without spoiling or altering their surroundings. The Spanish Mediterranean coastline has undergone a more radical transformation in a few years than in the previous two millennia. But up here near the border, the landscape was still relatively unchanged. The sea lay azure and glittering under the bright, golden sun, like a computer-enhanced postcard. I could see yachts tacking across the sea breeze and a couple of expensive speed-boats dragging white streaks through the water, but there was no sign of life in the bay below me. I felt like an explorer seeing it for the first time. It was one of many coves that could only be reached from the sea. The rocky coastline rose sharply, and an experienced mountaineer might be able to breach the overhang of the cliffs, but ordinary tourists

4

would be wise to keep away. The cove was what the holiday brochures promised: a private, beautiful and unspoilt spot on the bustling, efficiently run tourist coast.

I was lying at an angle, so I had a clear sightline both out to sea and down onto the cove's sandy beach, which was protected from prying eyes by the rugged cliffs. If you didn't know to look, you would never discover that there was a beautiful little cove beneath the overhang. Two jagged rocks a few metres out even hid the grey, powdery sand from the sea. Unless someone who knew what they were looking for took the trouble to use binoculars, the cove was hidden. It was a perfect place to be alone. Or for two to be alone.

The lovebirds had chosen a good spot. I was thinking in Danish, as I often did when I was waiting for a hit, concentrating my thoughts on the few hundredths of a second that separated me from success or failure, letting my mind wander and wind through the labyrinth of memory, thinking about my two loved ones; or recalling films and books and love affairs in an attempt to let time become nothingness. Become *nada*, a non-existent state, so that boredom didn't turn into impatience, leaving me unready when the moment, the moment of truth, arrived.

I kept an eye on the speedboats. One of them was streaking along the coastline, dragging a ruler-straight trail in its wake, but the other one changed course, slowed down and sailed into the little bay. It was a six-metre, gleaming white motorboat, with an elegant, svelte line. A young woman was lying on the foredeck, wearing black Ray-Bans and nothing else. They suited her. The man, naked from the waist up, was standing at the wheel, steering the boat in while he kept an eye on the echo sounder. There could be treacherous reefs and rocks this close to the coast, but either the white motorboat didn't draw a great deal of water, or he knew his way in between the two rocks. It was the latter, according to my informant.

I made my living from the public's insatiable craving to see the famous and rich disgracing themselves. Although I had 20 years' experience of our modern greed and lust for power, it still surprised me that so many high-ranking men were willing to sacrifice career, marriage and status for the sake of sex. They were so sure of their invulnerability that they took huge risks; just for the chance to prove that they were still men. Didn't they know that for every secret there was also someone willing to sell that very secret?

I had ended up here on the Costa Brava as the result of a tip several weeks earlier. It was always like that. The numerous informants and contacts that I had paid, nurtured, dined, praised, encouraged, buttered-up, massaged the egos of, were like an extensive intelligence network that kept me supplied with information about the affairs of the famous. A network that identified the target for me and gave me the essential raw material. Then it was up to me to work out the logistics, do a recce of the area and set up the hit. It had taken me the previous fortnight to get ready to strike this target who was now nearing the shore, blissfully unaware. My information had been extremely specific, right down to the name of the boat. When a new government takes charge after the old one has enjoyed the sweetness of power for many years, it ought to look over its shoulder more carefully. Especially if the new government is one founded on God, King and Country and hoists the moral banner so high that it has lost touch with dry land.

"Don't cast the first stone, my friend," I said under my breath in the Danish that still felt like my own language, even though for years I had spoken it regularly only to myself and then mostly in my own head. English was for business, Spanish for love and Danish for those innermost, secret thoughts which demand a profound understanding of the underlying nuance of each word; where it's not what is said that counts, but the way in which it is said and thought.

6

The man manoeuvred the boat steadily towards the beach. I heard the sound of the motor cutting out and the boat slowly drifted the last few metres before the man threw an anchor overboard and let the boat swing round against the tide. I lifted my new camera, a marvel of computerised technology. I knew I had made the right choice in selecting a 400-mm telephoto lens. I could see them clearly in the viewfinder. She must have been in her 20s, with a smooth, brown body, her black pubic hair clearly visible in the sunlight. She was neither too thin nor too fat, but shapely. She reminded me of someone, but I couldn't place her. There were immaculate female bodies like hers from St Tropez to Marbella. They attracted rich, middle-aged, powerful men as rotting meat attracts flies. With their seemingly flawless, perpetually young beauty they allowed men to forget their own decay. These young women had so little experience of that particular torment that they thought decay would never strike them.

I pressed my damp but steady forefinger on the release button, let the motor run and took a quick series, before zooming out a little so I got a clear shot of the young woman with the man's face in sharp focus behind her. He was in his late 40s, with dark, Latin looks, a cleanshaven face and thick black hair. He had strong arms and shoulders, but the beginnings of a paunch under his dark body hair indicated that he was no longer in tip-top condition. He was very tanned and through the viewfinder I could see his even, white teeth as he smiled down at the woman.

He said something and threw a pair of rubber sandals over to her, and the woman smiled and said something back as she put them on. Then she picked up a mask and snorkel and slipped naked into the water. There were lots of sea urchins on the submerged rocks, but the couple seemed to know about them and quite rightly had respect for the long prickly spines. I let the film run to the end and got a couple of shots of the woman's naked behind as it broke through the surface, before her legs stretched out straight and she disappeared under the water again as gracefully as a dolphin. She snorkelled in wide circles round the bobbing boat.

The man detached a rubber dinghy from the deck, lowered it into the water and rowed towards the beach. He was wearing red trunks and his legs were muscular yet elegant. Hadn't he once been a competitive swimmer? He paddled into the shallows and dragged the dinghy onto firm ground. He spread out a blanket on the sand and put a picnic hamper on it with a slender bottle sticking out of it. The woman swam to the beach and flung her snorkel and mask to the man, who caught them. She called to him and he threw himself into the water, breaking the surface with hardly any spray, and crawled with long steady strokes out to where the water was deep. The woman followed him. I changed the film and let the motor shoot frame after frame of the couple in the water. I had a momentary stab of conscience, or was it envy? They played like children and were beautiful as the drops flew off their bodies and sparkled in the sunlight with every colour of the rainbow. But there was no point thinking about that. Now it was a question of concentrating on the moment. Purely practical things like aperture, shutter, focus, definition. The woman pulled off his swimming trunks and let them float away like a red jellyfish. He lifted her right out of the water and kissed her breasts. The motor in the reflex camera whizzed like a flicking whip and instead of changing the film I changed the camera and took another batch. Sweat broke through the fabric of my t-shirt. I could feel a big wet patch spreading down my back. They were playing like puppies. He swam between her legs and lifted her half out of the water and let her fall over backwards, the spray encircling their bodies like a halo. Then she swam over to him and put her arms round his neck and wound her legs round his loins. It was a wonderful picture, full of love and eroticism and yet not revealing the actual act. Not being able to see the penetration made it more arousing. I also shot a couple of films as they finished their lovemaking on the blanket on the beach, although those pictures probably wouldn't find a buyer. It was no longer erotic, but pornographic, and I wasn't a pornographer.

Afterwards, the couple lay happily in the sun, as people do when they think they're safe in their nakedness. When they think they're alone in the Garden of Eden, forgetting to think about the serpent in the form of a 50-centimetre-long, sophisticated, high-tech, Japanese telephoto lens, which catches the moment and freezes it for all eternity and for everyone to behold.

The man rubbed her with suntan oil and I had enough experience to know that the best picture, the picture that would swell my bank account by as much as $200,000 over the next couple of years, was the least sexual, but at the same time the most erotic. It was when the Minister took his lover's feet in his hands and massaged them slowly and sensually. Maybe a sea urchin spine had found its way into the delicate skin of her small, shapely feet after all. She sat leaning back on her outstretched arms and gazed at a point behind his head. Her face was calm and satisfied and she smiled gently as he put her big toe in his mouth and then, as lovingly as a child with a sweet, sucked each one of her shapely toes.

"Bingo," I said, and was about to crawl away so as to give the couple at least a little time alone together before their happiness and lives were smashed for ever, when my mobile phone rang in the bag beside me. They couldn't possibly hear the weak beeping down on the beach. They were too far away and the gentle murmur of the sea would have smothered the sound even if the wind had carried it down towards them. But powerful men have become powerful men because of a sixth sense, a gut feeling for danger, for political minefields. It's as if they know in advance, maybe feel that something is niggling at their aura, nudging their self-confidence. He lifted his head at the very moment my mobile rang and squinted towards me, as if he fleetingly sensed danger lurking. Just as animals drinking at a water hole on the savannah know that a leopard is approaching even though they can't see, hear or smell their predator. We made the same movement. I thrust my hand into the bag and fished out my phone, while he pulled a mobile from the hamper and keyed in a number, looking up towards my hiding place. I crawled back from the cliff edge and flicked open my phone. I ought to have anticipated it. Of course he would have a bodyguard or two nearby. He might be reckless, but he was still vigilant and far from stupid.

"Hello," I said.

It was a woman's voice on the other end. She pronounced my surname the Danish way.

"Peter Lime?" Her voice was strong and clear, youngish and didn't have a dialect that I could pinpoint. The mobile phone is a remarkable invention. It has made life significantly easier for people like me, but it is also a curse.

In Denmark my name is pronounced like the Danish word for glue, but I always introduce myself using the same pronunciation as that of the small, sour, lime fruit. And, although the apostrophe isn't used this way in Danish, I put one after my name when referring to Lime's photographs. Sometimes when I'm abroad, I have to explain that I don't have any connection to Orson Welles and the Viennese sewers, but that the name has its origins in a little town in Jutland: Lime, between Ebeltoft and Randers.

When I was still quite young, I had decided to insist that my surname be pronounced in English. I didn't want a name that suggested sticky, made-in-Denmark glue. My name is all I have in common with that particular backwater, but I come from a place just like it. It's a speck on the planet, like I was a speck in the cities I called my own – those jungles where, more often than not, I've

10

hunted my quarry and bagged it when it thought itself alone and safe. I love the anonymity that cities wrap round us, but not round the famous people whose lives I ruined for a living. They couldn't stay inside their protective cocoons all the time, they had to emerge, and when they did I was ready. Perhaps they exposed themselves because, deep down, they liked the game of cat-and-mouse too. Because, when all's said and done, they were narcissists who needed affirmation of their existence. Maybe what they feared most was that no one was lying in wait for them, because that would mean they were no longer interesting, and their 15 minutes in the seductive glare of the flash-bulb was over. It's like a drug for thousands of people on our media-intoxicated planet.

"Who's asking?" I said.

"Clara Hoffmann, National Security Service, Copenhagen," she said.

"Where the hell did you get this number?" I asked as I crawled backwards until I was sure I could stand up without being seen from the beach and began walking down to the car. My t-shirt stuck to my back and the cameras jolted against my hip as I sped up.

"That doesn't really matter. Have you got a moment?"

"No. I haven't."

"It's rather important."

"I'm sure it is, but I haven't got time."

"I would like to meet with you."

"I'm not in Madrid," I said.

I had parked where a little dirt track leading down across a field came to an abrupt halt, blocked by two boulders. The shepherd I had seen when I arrived was standing pretty much in the same place, surrounded by sheep trying to find bits of rough grass between the scorched rocks. He was wearing a broad-brimmed hat which concealed his face. All I could see was the end of a hand-rolled cigarette sticking out from the corner of his mouth. He had an old knapsack on his shoulder and was leaning picturesquely on his crook. A large, shaggy dog was sitting at his feet. Another one was patrolling the perimeter of the flock.

"Where are you?" asked the calm, distinct voice coming through clearly from Copenhagen – if that's where she was.

"I don't think that's any of your business."

"It's important. If we could meet as soon as possible . . ."

"Ring in a couple of hours," I said.

"It's better if we meet. I'm ringing from Madrid."

"You're pretty sure of yourself, but I'm not in Madrid," I said, although she couldn't have known where I was, since she had rung my mobile.

"I'm sure you'd be glad to help your old country," she said.

"I don't owe Denmark anything," I said.

She laughed. Her laughter was melodious, like her voice.

"I'm staying at the Hotel Victoria," she said.

"OK," I answered. I closed the mobile and broke into a slow run down towards the car. It was a brand-new, four-wheel-drive jeep that I had rented a week before. I threw my gear onto the back seat and drove off, spraying gravel behind me. The shepherd turned his head slowly, as if it was a camera mounted on a tripod, and followed me with his eyes as the jeep bumped and lurched away from the coast. The sheep carried on searching for grass and weeds and only a couple of them lifted their heads and huddled together as I left in a cloud of dust which, I realised much too late, might be visible from down on the beach.

I had made my headquarters in Llanca, a little holiday resort about 20 kilometres to the south. I tried to press the jeep on the steep, narrow and winding roads, which meandered along the rugged coastline like an asphalt-black ribbon. The heat was making the asphalt steam. It was only the beginning of June, but it was already very hot. It seemed it was going to be yet another long, hot and dry summer. The tourist season had begun and it was difficult to find an opening to overtake the slow-moving cars towing heavy caravans, already making the long trek to the beaches of the south coast. I drove like a Spaniard, letting the jeep gather speed going downhill and braking hard just before the hairpin bend and the next slope. Now and then I got lucky and found room to overtake a holidaymaker or a stinking lorry emitting thick fumes that danced like a greasy sash around my face in the open-topped jeep. The sea was on my left, blue as the sky, and from time to time a little white town would come into sight down below. I felt good with the wind in my hair and the result of the hit in the bag on the back seat. I looked forward to getting home to Amelia and Maria Luisa, home to my city. And as usual the feeling of victory, of having accomplished a difficult job, was indescribably gratifying. I didn't actually need to take on as much work any more, but I wasn't sure how I would fill my days if I didn't. When pressed by Amelia I'd had to admit that the work, the hunt itself and bagging the quarry, gave me an almost brutal satisfaction. Even though I had lived in Spain for more than 20 years, my Danish Protestant background was probably a factor too. By the sweat of thy brow thou shalt earn bread. Without work you have no identity. Danes ask you what you do before they'll tell you their name.

It was slow going even though I pressed the jeep in and out of the hairpin bends. There was too much traffic and it took me nearly two hours to travel 20 kilometres. Twice I got caught in tailbacks because of roadworks. It was getting on for 3 p.m. when I drove into Llanca. The town had shut down in the heat of the siesta, or at least holiday-makers were still strutting around while the residents sat at home and had lunch and watched television. My hotel was down by the harbour, which had a lovely natural sandy beach. It was packed with families sunning themselves on the yellow sand or bathing in the tranquil green water. Voices sounded as if they were muffled by soft cotton wool. Gentle hands rubbed suntan oil into a bare back. A father was carefully helping a toddler with a bathing ring. A mother was scolding a boy for teasing his little sister. A teenager was doing crawl with splashing strokes, showing off to a couple of girls with braces on their teeth and hormones in every fibre of their bodies. A couple exchanged a kiss. A man lazily turned the page of a novel. A pair of infatuated lovers got up and walked arm-in-arm towards their hotel. Afternoon lovemaking awaited them.

I was thirsty, sweaty and hungry. There had been a time when I would have looked down my nose at happy families on the beach. At dad, mum and the kids, as they sat there all sunburnt, together and self-sufficient. There had been a time when I would have been a little bit envious, even though I would never have admitted it to anyone, or to myself. But now I felt fine about families with their joys and sorrows. I had a family myself. I had been known for saying, and considering it the only right way to go about things, that wolves live and hunt best when alone. That there's a difference between being lonely and being alone, and that I was alone and not lonely. But now I loved my life with my family and realised that I had been both alone and lonely before. Being indispensable – that others were dependent on me and that my actions would have an effect on those dearest to me – gave me great satisfaction. My family: just being able to say that made me happy now, as did the fact that the money I earned wasn't for me alone, but also contributed to the welfare and happiness of others.

I parked the jeep in a side street near my hotel. Before picking up my key, I stood at the bar and drank a large glass of freshly pressed orange juice and ate a tortilla with small pieces of potato and onion, which was light and delicate. The bar was next to the hotel. Like so many Spanish bars it was rather noisy, with a television blaring in one corner, litter and cigarette-ends on the floor, laminated tables, the smell of oil and garlic; and an agreeable chinking and hissing and clatter of cups, glasses and the espresso machine creating an animated wall-to-wall muzak. The walls were adorned with a couple of aged travel posters showing the Costa Brava's rugged coast and various Barcelona football teams from past years. A young Michael Laudrup was smiling confidently in several of them, from the days when he led the team to one championship after the other. Most of the customers were locals having lunch. I smoked a cigarette and drank a double espresso as the edge wore off my adrenalin and I settled down. I talked football with the bartender. He had read about Barcelona's collapse in his midday paper. The club wasn't top of the division any more, but third. In Catalonia that counts as a collapse. Barcelona has to win the championship, otherwise the team's a disaster. I'm a Real Madrid man myself, but we talked amicably as I tried to unwind. After a hit I always felt like I had done two hours with the Japanese in the karate institute on Calle Echégaray. I was refreshed, elated and exhausted all at once. So much planning, so much preparation, so many logistical considerations, and then the difference between success and failure was just a few hundredths of a second anyway. There could be a fault with the film or camera. A microscopic grain of sand in the shutter might have ruined the frames. For once my hands had shaken. The light calculation wasn't right. The victim was blurred and unrecognisable. Umpteen things could have gone wrong.

I showered and packed before ringing Madrid. The exposed films were in the locked camera case, my clothes in a handy bag that could be taken on a plane as cabin luggage. I travel light and get the hotel to do my washing en route or buy a new t-shirt.

Oscar usually turned up at his office around 4 p.m., whereas lots of offices in Madrid didn't open again until 5 p.m. That was changing. Their rhythm was becoming more and more European, but getting hold of people during the conventional siesta time was still difficult, especially in any kind of public administration office. The siesta hours were for business lunches, family, or for conducting affairs in secluded hotel rooms or in the small apartments of mistresses. I had the phone number of Oscar's current mistress, but just for emergencies. You could generally only reach Oscar at home with his wife on Sundays; that was how he and Gloria had arranged their lives. Gloria was a big woman and still very attractive, but she could no longer hide the fact that we were approaching 50. That didn't seem to bother her, and when she wasn't taking care of her flourishing legal practice, she saw to it that younger lovers confirmed her desirability. Spaniards are a pragmatic people when it comes to affairs of the heart and neither Oscar nor Gloria would dream of getting divorced. Not because they were Catholics, the law gave them the choice. But they were well matched and their private life and joint business transactions were so intertwined that the only people who would profit from a divorce would be the army of lawyers employed to unravel their assets.

They were both my friends and my business partners and we had known each other for more than 20 years. We had met during the chaotic, expectant years following Franco's death. Back then Oscar was a six-foot German journalist who wrote for a number of left-wing papers, and Gloria was a beautiful law student who carried her membership card of the outlawed Communist party as if it was one of the Tsar's missing crown jewels. We had a brief, intense affair, but everyone seemed to sleep with everyone in the days when we said "comrades" without blushing, and the affair ended quickly and without acrimony. Oscar and Gloria were another matter. They fell madly in love and had stayed together against the odds; not that fidelity had played a major role in recent years. We had been young, poor and revolutionary together, and we had become rich together. They were my second family. They had never had children. Gloria

16

had once had an abortion in England, back when it was forbidden in Spain, and after that she had regarded her illicit supply of the Pill as a revolutionary sword to be brandished in front of the Pope and all the other old, dyed-in-the-wool, reactionary, ludicrous men who tried to control her life. By the time she began to want children, it was too late. The clock had apparently struck. She couldn't get pregnant, but if it was a big disappointment she hid it well. Oscar was pretty indifferent – if Gloria wanted a child, he was happy to be a father. She couldn't, and without missing a beat they returned to life as normal, and after a couple of years stopped talking about it.

I thought about them as I packed my sweat-soaked jeans and t-shirt into the holdall and put on a clean shirt and a pair of light-coloured trousers. I drank a couple of cold colas from the minibar. Lately, I had begun thinking quite a bit about my childhood and youth. I was too happy and contented with my life to be experiencing a mid-life crisis, but maybe life ensures that you're more inclined to look back when you accept that your youth is definitively over, that life has passed its peak, that there are some things you can't do any more, even though you'd like to. Perhaps remembering the past makes it easier to cope with the years ahead, as you gradually slip into old age and hopefully an easy death.

I rang Oscar's direct number and he answered straight away. Oscar didn't speak Spanish when we first met, so we had used English from the beginning. Even though he now spoke fluent Spanish, we still used English when it was just the two of us. That's what came most naturally.

"Well, old boy," said Oscar in his husky, deep voice. "Fire away."

"It's in the bag," I said.

"And?"

"Almost a Jacqueline," I said. "So put the wheels in motion."

"You're a clever, cynical boy."

"It's a Minister, on the right."

17

"Just as well or you'd have trouble with Amelia," he said, and I could hear the amusement in his voice. He liked Amelia, but had never quite got over the fact that I was now married and was faithful to my wife, had become bourgeois in my old age, and listened to her and respected her opinions. But luckily all four of us got on well.

"I'll bring in the material tomorrow," I said.

"I'll make sure there's a technician waiting."

"I'll do them myself," I said.

"What about a lawyer?"

"They're taken on a public beach."

Oscar and I seldom said things straight out over the phone. Spain has an extensive and powerful security apparatus and there isn't always complete respect for the laws on protection from wire-tapping. Spain is a European country with terrorism, and blood and violence have a way of getting the better of constitutional rights.

"How public?" he said.

"Totally public. It's not private property. Anyone with a boat can use it."

"I'll put the wheels in motion. When are you coming home?"

"I'll change cars and drive to Barcelona now and get the first flight."

"OK, signing off, old boy," he said with the kind of satisfaction in his voice that these days was nearly only ever induced by the thought of making money.

"Give my best to Gloria," I said.

"Will do, old boy."

I checked out and walked over to the jeep with my holdall in one hand and the camera bag containing the negatives, which would fill Oscar's and my bank account with many, many thousands of dollars over my shoulder.

A black Mercedes was parked at an angle in front of the jeep. Two men were leaning against the car, their arms crossed. One of them wouldn't be much trouble. He was short and podgy, with a broad, heavy face below a bald pate. He didn't look very fit. He looked exactly like what he undoubtedly was: an expensive spin-doctor employed to pull unfortunate chestnuts out of the fire for his lord and master. The other one was 30-odd, with beefy arms bulging under his jacket and a cocky little smile below his black sunglasses, but he didn't have the air of a bruiser. He looked like a body-builder, not a fighter. It was a case of pumped-up muscles, not the sinewy toughness that you got from the gym I used. They were both in suits, despite the heat. Well-cut tropical wear, and they didn't seem to be sweating. The shepherd had talked. The shepherd could read and write, at least the numbers and letters on a licence plate belonging to Avis.

"*Oyes, hijo de puta,*" the heavy said. He straightened himself up, letting his hands hang down beside his body. He seemed relaxed, but I could read the signs.

The side street was deserted. The hum of the traffic starting up again drifted from the main street and I could hear the metallic sound of shop shutters being rolled up.

"Son of a bitch yourself," I said.

He took a step forward so that he was obstructing my access to the jeep.

"You're blocking my way," I said.

"Hand it over!" was all he said in reply and pointed at the camera bag.

"It's private property," I said.

"The films aren't. You'll get the cameras back, don't worry. Hand it over!"

I put the holdall down on the road. I could feel myself sweating, and my heart was racing. The noise from the main street grew imperceptibly fainter, as if it was filtered, while my concentration focused on the man in front of me. He wasn't quite as composed as he appeared. There was a frailty in his eyes and beads of perspiration on his upper lip. I shoved the camera bag round to my back and waited, hoping that someone might show up in the side street so he wouldn't be able to get violent, but he took a step forwards and made the mistake of sticking out his hand as if he was going to rip the bag from my shoulder. I grabbed hold of his hand, took a short step backwards, so I made use of his own momentum, found his little finger and twisted it while I wrenched his arm round and upwards. He gave a startled gasp, but the sound got caught in his throat as I jammed my knee into his testicles while still pulling his shoulder until I heard the joint crack. He crumpled in front of me with a hollow groan, numbed by shock and pain.

I picked up my holdall. The short, fat driver stepped away from the Mercedes and raised his hands in a warding-off gesture. It had all happened so quickly that I doubt he had registered what had taken place. His partner was on his knees, retching with pain. His finger would swell up and his crotch would ache for several days.

"No," was all the short fatty said as he stepped pointedly aside. I walked passed him, threw my bags into the jeep and drove off. My hands were trembling from delayed shock and the back of my shirt was soaked through. A family of holidaymakers with a couple of young children had come round the corner and stood gaping at me. The father put his arms protectively around the two youngsters. The woman had her hands over her face. It wouldn't make for a pleasant holiday, but that couldn't be helped.

I drove slowly and carefully down to the Avis office. It wasn't only the heat that was making my vision swim a little. I took three or four deep breaths to get my breathing under control.

At Avis I exchanged the jeep for a hard-topped, fast Audi, and it wasn't until I turned off onto the motorway and sped up that I calmed down, but I kept looking in the mirror to see if a Mercedes or a patrol car was pursuing me. I didn't feel completely safe until I was on the plane to Madrid. I put a Grateful Dead CD in my Discman and leaned back in my seat. The plane was half empty. I saw the Mediterranean disappear as we swung slowly round and headed inland across the vast, barren Spanish interior and the familiar, vicious craving for a drink overwhelmed me.

I thought about Amelia and Maria Luisa and asked the stewardess for a cola, as the plane carried me home to Madrid.

# 2

Luckily there was no reception awaiting me at Barajas Airport which was its usual busy self. I had no trouble getting a taxi into the city, enveloped in the blue-violet cloak of approaching night and the smog which, thanks to the heatwave of recent days, had settled over this large heap of stones on the Castilian tableland. Madrid had been my home on and off for nearly a quarter of a century and, since my wedding eight years ago, I had no intention of ever leaving it again. I was no longer a nomad, but a resident. I had always seen myself as an eternal wanderer, living wherever I hung my hat, but now I was like a farmer bound to my patch of soil. I had settled down and was so content with my life that now and then I feared retribution. Not in the form of violence or disaster – I couldn't really imagine that – but maybe the itchy restlessness would return with its old force and drag me away from that one spot in the world where I felt secure and happy.

A radio sports channel blared away as we drove into the centre, through the dense, honking, aggressive evening traffic. The taxi driver seemed to feel the same as I did – he couldn't be bothered to talk. He was a gaunt, lean Moroccan who most likely had neither a work nor a residence permit, but had crossed the narrow Strait of Gibraltar to seek his fortune in the rich and yet so crisis-ridden European Union.

Madrid's suburbs are among the ugliest in the world, Soviet in their monstrosity. They fan out in ranks from the centre, huge and dark, and it's almost impossible to imagine that they surround a vibrant city centre that I was always glad to come home to.

As usual after an assignment, I felt rather empty and depressed. Not seriously, just a feeling of the blues, that something was over and with it the knowledge that, with the passing of that particular second, I had taken a step closer to death.

The traffic snarled up completely when we reached the city centre, turned by the post office on Plaza Cibeles and drove towards Plaza Santa Ana. A few hundred metres from the plaza we ground to a halt, so I paid the driver and walked up the hill along Paseo de Prado, as the traffic, with belching exhaust fumes and honking horns, came to a standstill and the nippy motor scooters zigzagged between the stationary rows of cars. The scooters were driven by young men, their girlfriends riding pillion. The girls held on nonchalantly with one hand, their willowy legs placed elegantly as if they were sitting sidesaddle on a horse. Madrid is an affluent and elegant, yet at the same time brutal and oppressive city, but the young Madrileños outdid the young of both Rome and Paris in terms of elegance. In the heat of the night, most cities take on an aggressive tone which vibrates in the streets and bounces back and forth between the buildings and is absorbed by the inhabitants. Madrid was a nocturnal animal. A city which in the summer heat never seemed to sleep, seemed to be moving constantly, movement like that of a nomad, for its own sake, a journey with no real destination.

Plaza Santa Ana formed the centre of my *barrio*, my patch of the world. I had ended up there almost by accident when I was young, and had lived in various places in the neighbourhood ever since – when I lived in Madrid, that is. Teatro Real took up one side of the rectangular plaza, with the big white Hotel Victoria taking up the other side. The flanks were made up of tall, old residential properties with cafés and restaurants at street level. On hot summer days the trees provided cool shade. Children played on the white flagstones in the middle of the square, bathed in the soft violet dusk, while mothers and fathers sat on benches and chatted, keeping an eye on kids in their blue school uniforms enjoying their freedom before going indoors to eat their supper. Every time I came home from one of my trips, I liked to spend a minute with my back to the theatre looking across the square, the Cerveceria Alemana a fixed point of reference on my left. I felt a bit like the lead in an old film where the passing of time is shown by the white pages of a calendar, with their big black dates, flying off in the breeze. Standing here, I could watch the pages of the calendar running backwards, peeling off year after year of my time with the plaza, and the differences were in the details. In the length of hair, in the cut of a dress, in the make and shape of cars, in the conspicuously growing prosperity, in the women's make-up and, up to a point, in the children's games. But the overall picture was the same. The music of the voices, the humming of the cars and the roar of the motorbikes, the children's games of tag and skipping, the mothers' and grandmothers' murmured talk of children and love, the men's boisterous discussion of football and bullfighting as cigarette smoke coiled around them, the smell of petrol, and the aroma of garlic wafting from the cafés and restaurants. It was as it had always been and I wanted it to stay like that for ever, even though Madrid, under the impact of European integration and directives from Brussels about harmonisation, was imperceptibly but steadily changing and becoming less like itself and more like the others.

I looked for Maria Luisa and my wife. The new ingredient this summer was the appearance of smart rollerblades, making the children's feet look far too big. A couple of years earlier it had been skateboards. Each year had its new gimmick, but the old games of skipping or tag, familiar to me from my own childhood, were played by each new generation, here in the warm evening air of Madrid as well.

I saw my daughter first and the usual warmth filled my whole body. She had rollerblades too, but had evidently abandoned them. Instead, with that almost-seven-years-old fierce concentration, she was skipping, two of her friends turning the rope faster and faster. She looked like her mother, with black hair and olive complexion, but she had my blue eyes and long limbs. She had a delicate, round face and a mouth that was quick to smile and laugh. The rope hit her ankle and I saw her look of disappointment, but she accepted the rules of the game and took one end of the rope so that her friend could have her go. They were wearing school uniform and had ribbons in their hair. And, even though it was impossible, I was sure I could pick out Maria Luisa's voice above the cacophony of playing children. She was our shared small miracle. It had been a difficult birth. Amelia was 36 when Maria Luisa arrived and the doctors had thought she wouldn't be able to have any more children, and they were right. Amelia hadn't reckoned on having children at all. She hadn't wanted them with her first husband. She didn't talk much about him, but she had regretted the marriage almost immediately. He was extremely old-fashioned, at a time when Spain suddenly erupted after the dictator's death. She left him after they had been married for three years and, when the new laws were passed, she divorced him. The years passed and by the time we met one another it wasn't so easy. We were older and it was harder to conceive a child than we had anticipated. We tried unflaggingly for a year before we succeeded, and then no more children came along. So we were old and therefore molly-coddling parents. But no child has yet died of cosseting.

I spotted Amelia sitting on one of the benches, talking with the woman who lived in the flat below us. Amelia was the first miracle in my life, and she had come along late as well. We had been married for eight years. Her hair was beginning to go grey, but she tinted it. She was still slim and attractive in an indefinable way. She wasn't a classic beauty, but glowed in any company. She was at ease with herself and her faith in life, and I found the lines around her eyes and mouth enchanting, because they showed that she was someone who smiled and laughed at life. She was someone who had lived, and I was grateful she had chosen to share the rest of her life with me.

I hitched up the holdall and walked towards her. She caught sight of me and rewarded me with a smile as she stood up from the bench. I was polite and greeted our neighbour, Maria, with the traditional two air-kisses before I gave Amelia a hug and a kiss on the mouth. Although we lived in a modern society, she was still modest when it came to public displays of affection. I kissed her for longer than she really liked, but the memory of the Minister's bodyguards was still lingering. She pulled herself free and I let go of her and there was a moment of awkwardness while we tried to decide what should be said.

"Welcome home, darling," Amelia said finally. "Did it go well?"

"It went fine," I said.

"Where have you been, Pedro?" the neighbour asked. "Which exotic land have you been to now?"

"Catalonia."

"Ah, the Catalans. But they won't speak Spanish, so how did you manage?" she said with a laugh. She thought the Catalans were a peculiar people who insisted on speaking Catalan instead of Cervantes' beautiful language.

"It's not as bad as that, Maria," I said. Maria was a food columnist, married to a lawyer and no more than 32 years old. She had gone against the trend and already had three children playing somewhere out on the plaza. Most young Spaniards today stop at one or at most two children. Maria came from Andalusia and had kept her regional Spanish, clipped and fast with her "s" sounding like a soft "z".

I looked across at Maria Luisa. She was skipping earnestly again. "She's missed you a lot this time," said Amelia.

My daughter caught sight of me and stopped mid-hop. She broke into a run.

"Papa, Papa!" she shouted and rushed into my arms. "Papa, you're home!" I hugged her. She smelled clean and good. She put her hands round my neck and pulled the little ponytail I had grown years ago when my hair had begun to thin. I suppose it was because I didn't like getting older, but it was my little vanity, and my daughter thought it was fun and Amelia said it suited me. She liked me looking a bit tough. She didn't have anything against men who looked like rough diamonds, but she did have something against men who behaved brutally or callously and selfishly, especially towards women. Her first husband had been like that. He was of the opinion that the way to earn a woman's respect was via a few beatings. I might have looked a bit on the rough side, but Amelia knew that where women and children were concerned I was as soft as butter.

I put Maria Luisa down and listened to her outpouring, which within a couple of minutes got me up-to-date with stupid teachers, idiotic boys, not-to-be-trusted girlfriends and a knee that was dabbed with iodine because she had fallen over and bashed a hole in it. Amelia and Maria sat down on the bench again and I sat next to them, with Maria Luisa on my lap. She nestled against me while we talked about the good warm weather that had finally arrived, how my flight had been, and how Maria Luisa also wanted to go to the seaside and swim soon. Amelia was well aware that she shouldn't ask about my work in detail. She knew me well enough to know that, even though I said it had gone well, there was something that wasn't quite as it should be. After a while Maria Luisa jumped down from my lap and ran across to her friends.

"*Bueno*," said Maria. "I'd better go and finish getting supper ready.

Juan will be home soon." She called her children who protested violently about having to go in already.

"I'll bring them in," said Amelia. "We'll stay a bit longer. I'm only going to grill steak."

Maria left and Amelia leant against me, my arm around her.

"Well, my love. So how did it go?"

I told her about the day. She didn't interrupt. My job was probably the most ambiguous aspect of our marriage. I didn't know what Amelia really thought about my work, whether deep down she held it in contempt, but didn't dare voice this contempt because she knew that it was my work which enabled us to live as we did. She was aware of the large part my career played in my life, that I couldn't give it up. I loved my family, but I knew, and Amelia acknowledged, that they weren't enough to fill my days. I still needed the excitement I got from hunting my prey.

"Will this cause you problems?" she asked when I had finished.

"I don't think so," I said. "Oscar and Gloria and her lawyers will handle it."

"You could always not publish them."

"Are you taking sides with a right-wing Minister?" I asked, drawing her closer to me.

She laughed.

"No. No. They deserve what's coming to them, but I don't want you to get into any kind of trouble."

"I'm a big boy," I said.

"I know, but all the same."

"You don't need to worry," I said.

She straightened herself up.

"A Danish woman rang," she said. "She didn't speak Spanish, but good English of course. She said she was from the security . . . ?"

"Security police. Intelligence service. She rang my mobile. She's staying over there." I pointed at the Hotel Victoria, the lovely old bullfighter's hotel, looking like a sedate white ship in the streetlights at the far side of the plaza.

"What does she want?"

I shook my head and pulled my arm away, took out a cigarette and lit it.

"I don't know. I haven't got a clue what it can be about," I said.

"She said she'd ring again."

"I'll talk to her."

"Are you hungry?" asked Amelia. "Shall we go out? Have a few tapas?"

"I'm not particularly hungry. I'd rather eat at home. Let's give the kids ten more minutes."

We put our arms round one another and talked like good married couples do, about everything and nothing. Amelia was a teacher at a special school for children with learning difficulties. She was very poorly paid and in any case didn't actually need to work, but she wouldn't have given it up even if they stopped paying her altogether. She was the kind of person who got great satisfaction from even the smallest step forward. She told me about one of the children who could now spell his way through a comic. He was 15 and there was no real hope of improvement, but it was enough for Amelia that three years of work had enabled him to read a speech bubble. I wouldn't have lasted an hour in her job, but I enjoyed listening to her, feeling myself gradually relax.

A woman of about 40 approached our bench. She was wearing a blue skirt which came to just above the knee, with a matching blue jacket over a white blouse. She wore red lipstick and a trace of eyeliner. Her hair was combed back, making her look slightly prim and severe, but her blue eyes were friendly.

"Peter Lime?" she said.

She said my name the Danish way. Amelia sat up straight. She seldom heard my name pronounced like that.

"Clara Hoffmann," the woman said, and held out her hand as Danes do. I stood up and shook her hand. It was dry and slender, but her fingers were strong.

"My wife," I said in English. "Amelia, this is Clara Hoffmann. From Copenhagen."

The two women shook hands and took the measure of one another.

"We've spoken on the phone," said Clara Hoffmann.

"I didn't catch your name at the time," said Amelia in her slow, but correct English. "We Spaniards aren't very good with names beginning with h."

"Please excuse me intruding like this," the woman said. Her voice was light and young; it didn't seem to match her age. "I was going for a walk, it's such a lovely evening, and I saw your husband sitting on the bench . . ."

"How did you know it was me?" I said.

"I've seen a few photographs of you. True, they were taken when you were younger, but I could tell it was you."

Amelia looked from her to me.

"Why don't you go over to the Alemana while I get the children in, then you can speak in Danish?"

Clever move. Get it over with, and then I could go home for supper. It's always easier to get rid of someone once you've bought them a drink. But Amelia was also being friendly. It was natural for her to think that maybe we would like to speak Danish together. Amelia got terribly tired if she had to speak English, even for a very short time. She was a homebody who was reluctant to leave Madrid, unless it was to go to our holiday cottage in the green mountains of the Basque Country.

"OK," I said, and kissed my wife again. She looked a bit taken aback.

She didn't like that kind of show of affection in front of a woman she didn't know, but at the same time she was probably glad that I displayed my love openly. Amelia took my holdall. It wasn't very heavy. She knew that I never let go of my camera bag.

"This way," I said in Danish, and led Clara Hoffmann towards the Cervezeria Alemana on the other side of the plaza. She was wearing sensible shoes and only reached my shoulder. She smelled of a gentle, but classy perfume or lotion.

"It's lovely here," she said.

"Yes," I answered, walking towards the brown entrance to the café. It was nearly full, but miraculously three young people got up from a window table and I led Clara Hoffmann over, guiding her lightly by the arm. The tables were white marble. As in all old Spanish cafés, the noise level was high. Serrano hams hung from the ceiling over the bar, where two bartenders were preparing coffee, tapas and drinks for the waiters in their short white jackets and black trousers, who bellowed out their orders. The walls were covered with black and white photographs of old bullfighters such as Manolete and film and stage actors from the 1940s and 50s. A huge bull's head dominated one of the walls. The clientele was mixed, although mostly young people. The lighting was white and glaring, but the people and the smells of oil and garlic swathed the premises in a pleasantly mellow atmosphere.

"It's lovely here," Clara Hoffmann said again. "Well-lit and clean."

I laughed.

"That's nearly the title of a short story written by one of its very famous patrons."

"Who?"

"Hemingway. 'A Clean Well-lighted Place,'" I answered.

"Well, where hasn't he been?" she said, taking a cigarette from her bag, which was one of those flat practical ones, the size of a sheet of A4.

"You're not a fan?" I said.

"I don't think I've read anything by him. Not since my senior school days at least. He's sort of a bit passé, isn't he?"

I lit her cigarette.

"Perhaps you don't agree?" she said. Her eyes were almost grey. They held mine, you couldn't look away. She seemed confident, slightly cool and remote.

"I'm a big fan," I said, pointing down at our table and out of the window where throngs of pedestrians were on their way out for drinks and tapas before their late evening meal, which many didn't eat until 11 p.m. "It's even said that this was his regular table. He sat and wrote here while the fascists bombed Madrid during the Civil War. He usually stayed at your hotel when he was in town, along with the famous bullfighters of the time. Until some years ago, quite a few of the waiters here had known him and remembered him and had carried him home when he'd got too drunk to walk under his own steam."

She looked around.

"It's nice here," she said.

"But it's not Hemingway you want to talk about, Ms Hoffmann," I said.

"Please, let's not be formal."

"May I get you a drink? A glass of wine?"

"Yes, thank you," she said, exhaling her cigarette smoke.

Felipe came over and we chatted about this and that. He had been a waiter at the Alemana since my young days. He had been a promising young bullfighter when he was gored and had lost his balls, as the Spanish say. The injury was superficial, but the injury to his soul was fatal. He lost his nerve and didn't dare go in the arena again. The Alemana's owner, who was an aficionado, gave him a job as a waiter out of respect for the great courage he had displayed before that fateful day on which a bull had taken it from him. Now he was a small, thickset

32

man with mournful eyes and a red nose, but he didn't wear his bleeding heart on his sleeve. He lived alone in a little boarding house and every year he went to Ronda, where he came from, to stand all alone in the arena where he had made his debut. I have no idea what he did there. Maybe he cursed God. Maybe he just remembered his shattered dreams.

He stood with a cloth over his arm and took my order, a glass of red wine for the Danish woman, a lemonade for me and a plate of prawns in garlic and one of serrano ham. He bellowed out the order on his way back to the bar.

"I have a couple of questions," Clara Hoffmann said.

I looked straight at her.

"Just so everything's by the book," I said, "could I see some identification?"

"Of course," she answered, and handed me her identity card. The Danish police obviously didn't use the old badges any more. The photograph was a good likeness. So she was 43. I would actually have guessed her to be a bit younger, but it's hard to tell with women these days.

"Assistant Commissioner. Impressive," I said.

"My boss is only a few years older than me. She's a woman too. The Prime Minister's new permanent undersecretary is only 32. There's nothing impressive about it."

She didn't sound bitter, just a bit resigned, as if she knew that perhaps she had gone as far as she could, that her qualifications had given her so much, but the really big posts were beyond her reach. Or maybe she didn't feel like that at all. I gave back her card. Felipe slammed the glasses, bottles and tapas onto the table, along with the little white receipt. The prawns sputtered vigorously in the oil and garlic. The cured, wind-dried ham was arranged beautifully on the plate, cut in paper-thin slices, which could have been mistaken for flower petals.

"It looks delicious," she said. "What is it exactly?"

"Haven't you ever been to Spain before?"

"Majorca. Ages ago. I've been more – how can I put it – my attention has been directed more to the east."

"Catching Russian spies?"

"Something like that."

She smiled. Her face changed when she smiled. Some of the primness disappeared and her eyes lit up.

"Prawns in garlic. That goes without saying. This one is serrano ham. It's from a particular kind of pig which spends a pleasant life wandering in the mountains eating a special kind of root. The hams are cured and then hang in the bar for years just getting better and better."

She took a cautious bite and then ate the whole piece.

"I'll have to take some home," she said.

"Yes. It's good."

We sipped our drinks and picked at the food. Then she became businesslike. She leant across the table. I sat with my back to the wall so I could keep an eye on the door. There was a constant flow in and out of the café. I knew quite a few of the regulars, but they didn't come across and bother me.

"I won't keep you away from your wife for long. But if I might ask you a couple of questions?"

"Go ahead."

"You seemed quite dismissive on the phone."

"The timing was bad," I said.

"Laila Petrova," said Clara Hoffmann, watching my face carefully. After a moment or two I shook my head.

"Means nothing to you?"

"Absolutely nothing. Who is she?"

34

"She's 48 now. Chestnut hair, very likely dyed. Slim, 175 centimetres tall, average build. Often very tastefully dressed. An oval face, smooth after a little surgery. Sometimes blue eyes, sometimes brown, thanks to contact lenses. Photogenic. An art historian. Twice married. We don't know the name of her first husband. Most recently married to a Russian painter, they divorced ten years ago. Born Nielsen, or so we believe. The painter was, of course, called Petrov."

"Means absolutely nothing to me."

"Do you read the Danish papers?" she asked, eating ham and prawns in a very feminine and well-mannered fashion. She was hungry. Her stomach hadn't adjusted to Spanish mealtimes. She broke the bread into small pieces and used it to soak up the oil and garlic. She had slender, strong hands. She wasn't wearing a wedding ring, but a narrow gold ring studded with blue sapphires on her right hand.

"No," I answered. "Only if I come across cuttings."

"Cuttings?"

"I'm a professional photographer. You know that. My firm supplies photographs to the media all over the world, and so we employ an agency to make sure that we know who is using our photographs. In case they happen to forget all about copyright."

"I'm sorry. Of course," she said, and scooped the last piece of ham off the plate. She chewed carefully and sipped her wine before continuing.

"Then you don't know the story. Laila Petrova has disappeared. She was – is – director of one of Denmark's big, international museums of modern art. The cultural capital of Europe and all that. She's disappeared, and she's taken what was left of the exhibition budget with her. About four and a half million kroner."

"Not bad going, but why have you come to Spain to tell me about a clever little madam who runs off with the kitty? I've never heard of her. I could have told you that on the phone. You could have saved the taxpayer the cost of the trip."

"Yes, but I couldn't have shown you this," she said, and pulled a folder out of her bag. From the folder, which looked like it contained a number of other documents, she drew out a black and white photograph. She held it up in front of me, again watching my face carefully. It was a standard agency photograph, 25 x 36 cm. It was well defined, but obviously a copy from a photograph, not a print straight off the negative. The photograph was of a young, fair-haired woman who was looking a little to the right of the photographer, her eyes scrunched up. She had long, sleek, shoulder-length hair with a straight fringe down to her eyebrows. The photograph must have been taken around 1970. It was a Marianne Faithfull hairstyle which many young women had back then. She was wearing a floral shirt, the top few buttons undone. There was a narrow belt in her jeans and she was smiling. One of her front teeth was crooked, but that just gave her smile extra charm. The outline of a couple of fishing boats could be seen in the background. She was holding a guitar, the position of her fingers suggesting she was playing a chord. It was summer. It was a charming, happy photograph. To the far left, a bearded man was smiling admiringly at the woman. The direction of his gaze, coupled with a pennant on one of the fishing boats, divided the composition into a Golden Section, so that the observer was instinctively drawn to the woman's eyes and smile. I had a feeling that I had seen both her and the photograph before, but I couldn't place either.

I looked up at Clara Hoffmann.

"It's a lovely picture," I said.

Clara Hoffmann turned the photograph over. I could see from the copyright stamp that it was from POLFOTO. But that wasn't why she had turned it over. At the bottom, in sloping handwriting, were the words *Lime's photograph?* I looked up and Clara Hoffmann stared straight at me.

"Exactly," she said. "Lime's photograph. Question mark. And Lime, that must be you."

The photograph rang bells in my memory. I looked for the caption, but there was just a typewritten note: *Caption missing, but believed to be Denmark, 15 June 1970.*

"I've taken thousands and thousands of photographs in my life," I said, and took the photograph out of her hand. I looked at the handwritten words and the date: 15 June 1970. I knew the young woman in the photograph, but I kept my thoughts to myself. It's part of my nature to withhold information, at least until I know what the person seeking it wants it for. And it had been years ago after all.

"You just happen to have this photograph with you out on a walk in town," I said.

She smiled again, still watching me intently.

"If you're a single woman who wants to dine in peace at a restaurant in a city you don't know, experience has taught me that pulling official-looking papers from your briefcase and putting on reading glasses keeps the worst at bay."

"OK," I said. "Is it her?"

"Laila Petrova, yes. When she was young."

"She's not called Laila," I said, remembering. "She's called Lola. Nielsen. Jensen. Petersen. Something ordinary like that."

"Then it is your photograph?"

"I think so, yes. I think so."

I drank the last of my lemonade.

"But why is it a matter for the NSS? Isn't it more of a case for the Fraud Squad?"

"Who's the man in the photograph?" she asked. I studied him. He was also about 20, maybe younger. But he wasn't in focus, because that would have spoiled the composition. It wasn't by accident that he was a bit blurred, putting the principal subject in sharp focus. He had a full, black beard and a longish pageboy haircut. His teeth were even and white. He was wearing a dark, probably blue, anorak.

"I don't know," I said. "Is it him the NSS is interested in?"

"Let's just say we're interested and therefore also interested in Lime's photograph."

I passed it back to her.

"I can't help you."

"I wondered if you might have the negative. And if there are any other photographs from that place on the same roll."

"If it's my photograph, then I might have the negative. If I've got the negative, maybe I can find it. If I can find it, maybe there are other photographs. Who's the man?"

"He's been on the wanted list for over 20 years. He's German. One of his many names is Wolfgang. He was in the Red Army Faction. He's wanted all over the world for murder, arson, bank robberies and kidnapping. My German colleagues thought they'd got him when the GDR collapsed, but he disappeared. He'd been working as a mechanic in East Germany for 15 years. It's rather a notorious story, so the German tabloids have written about it. One of my colleagues saw your photograph in *Bild Am Sonntag*. He recognised our Wolfgang and got in touch with us. We had no idea that Wolfgang had Danish connections. Where was the photograph taken?"

Her voice had hardened, as though it wasn't a friendly conversation any more, but an interrogation.

"I've no idea. I'm not even certain that it is my photograph. It was taken nearly 30 years ago."

She handed me the photograph again.

"Keep it. I've got other copies. Think about it. Search your memory, look in your archives, Lime. Help us."

"OK. I'll see what I can do – Felipe!"

Felipe came over and I paid the bill and tipped him well, as usual. I got up.

"I'll ring you," I said. "In a couple of days. Enjoy Madrid in the meantime."

"Courtesy of the taxpayer," she said.

"I don't pay tax in Denmark," I said, hitched up my camera bag and left with a feeling of uneasiness which I couldn't explain or understand. But the period during which the photograph had been taken began to surface. I began remembering, and not all the memories from that time were worth hanging on to.

I put it out of my mind when I got home. I lived diagonally across from the café, in a top-floor flat I had bought many years ago and had extended several times by adding neighbouring flats. We had over 300 square metres, including my studio and a roof garden. We were constantly asked if we wanted to sell. It was a fantastic flat in the middle of the city, so we always said no. I let myself in and, as always, said hello to Jacqueline Kennedy who hung, life-sized and almost naked, just inside the door.

"I'm home," I called out to the kitchen, which is where Amelia and Maria Luisa would be at this time of day. I locked the undeveloped films in the safe and threw Hoffmann's photograph on my desk before washing my hands and sitting down to supper with my family. I was enraptured with my home, by the company of my two girls, which always filled me with a feeling of joy, mixed with a feeling of anxiety – that one day they might leave me. Amelia had made noodle soup, steak with salad and afterwards Amelia and I had manchego cheese and Maria Luisa had ice cream. It sounds banal to list the courses of an enjoyable meal, but it was in such banality that I had found my inner calm. My *wa* as the Japanese say. It's in everyday detail that the larger story is to be found. Amelia and I tried to talk, but we let Maria Luisa

39

steer the conversation. We listened to her chattering, and saw in each other's eyes how happy we were that she was the centre of attention at our table.

Sometimes after I had been away on a trip, Maria Luisa insisted that I read her bedtime story in Danish. I seldom spoke Danish with her. I had planned to when she was born, but it felt artificial, since we spoke only Spanish with friends and family. But I had read to her in Danish since she was tiny. She never answered me in my mother tongue, but it seemed to make her feel secure to hear me speak this foreign language. After supper it was time for her bath and then I read her favourite book about Alfons Åberg and his secret friend. Her eyes were heavy and sleepy by the time we reached the end, and I left her asleep with the bedside lamp on. I had a quick shower and crawled under the sheet where Amelia lay naked in the heat. Sounds of the city drifted in through the half-open window as we made love and became one.

Often I can't sleep, and I got up when Amelia moved her head off my shoulder and turned onto her side. As I had done so many times before, I went up on our roof terrace and drank a cola and smoked a cigarette in the warm night air. I had picked up the photograph which the Danish woman had given me and I sat looking at it, surrounded by geraniums, roses, eucalyptus, orange and lemon trees, listening to the throb of the city drifting up from the plaza below. The clip-clop of heels, the roar of a motorbike accelerating, a couple laughing, a drunk man grumbling, a taxi door slamming, a metal grille being locked up in front of one of the bars, the strident siren of a patrol car, a curse as a man stumbled, someone breaking into song from sheer joy, the late night symphony. This was my window to the sky with a view over Madrid. It was here that I could think and find peace. When I had first moved to Madrid in the mid-1970s, the night sounds had been different, the sound of flamenco as people clapped their hands rhythmically to call forth the *sereno*. The *sereno* was a man, a watchman, who walked around with a big gnarled stick and carried keys to the flats and boarding houses. People called him by clapping. He was often a disabled Civil War veteran. His pension was the small change, five pesetas – the *duro* – he received for unlocking the door. On mild summer nights the clapping echoed round the neighbourhood as if little gypsies were beating a seductive rhythm in the hours of loving between night and day break. The old *serenos* were gone now. Progress had swept them away. There were a few left, but they were on a fixed salary, museum pieces like the watchman in Ebeltoft.

I looked at the photograph. It had been taken in Bogense during a harbour festival and used by the local newspaper, which must have lent it on to a bureau. I had sold the paper a series from the festival, one of my first successful attempts at selling press photos. Lola was 20 years old and lived in the same commune as me. She wanted to be a folk singer, a female equivalent to Bob Dylan. We had slept together a couple of times. She had come into my room at night, but then she went to lots of rooms. The commune had been trying to cast off bourgeois jealousy. They couldn't of course, but Lola didn't seem troubled by it. On the other hand, she created problems because she was desirable and provoked a feeling of possessiveness in love-struck men. The man in the photograph wasn't called Wolfgang. His name had been Ernst. He was just 18 years old and came from Hamburg. Like everyone else, he wanted to be an artist. He wanted to write novels. He was left-wing, but I couldn't remember him flirting with bombs. He had taken part in discussions about the necessity of violence in the struggle against the bourgeois state, but others had been writing about that in magazines and newspapers. He had been madly in love with Lola and she had dallied with him, made love to him and moved on to my – or someone else's – bed. He had gazed at her with forlorn eyes and followed her around like a puppy.

I couldn't remember anything else. I don't think I'd given Lola a second thought in the intervening time, getting on for 30 years now. But on the terrace, in the darkness of night, I suddenly remembered that she had cried the last time we had been together. I think it was the last time. I thought she was lovely and sexy, but I wasn't in love with her. I knew I wanted to move on. I wanted out. It was as if, when she realised I was going to leave her, I took some of her power away.

I couldn't remember our lovemaking, but in night-time Madrid I suddenly heard her frail voice.

"Peter. My only talent is for seducing men. I have the talent to make men do what I want. Why don't you do what I want?"

I didn't know why I remembered that so clearly. I didn't even know if it had any significance. Memory can play the strangest tricks on you. I left the commune shortly afterwards. That's how it was. People moved in and out during that strange period when everything seemed possible, when the pain of life was suppressed and the world was changing. I tried to recall other faces from the period, but they were a blur of long hair and beards, flared jeans, mixed bathing, naked breasts in the sun, children left to their own devices, discussions about society and politics, parkas, identical t-shirts, unfiltered cigarettes and women wearing headscarves that looked like mauve nappies. As if we had been a bunch of clones who had been thrown together under the same roof.

I got up and went down to my studio to develop and copy the photographs from Catalonia, so that Oscar wouldn't be disappointed when he turned up, as he was bound to, first thing in the morning to admire my new scoop. It was something I could do better than anyone else: steal up on the prey and reveal it in all its nakedness.

# 3

Oscar came round at about 10 a.m.

As usual, I had prepared breakfast for Maria Luisa and Amelia at just after seven o'clock. Like most Madrileños we went to bed late, but we got up early. This was the rhythm of the city. We tried to take an afternoon nap. We led a very Spanish lifestyle, so we didn't eat much in the morning – a croissant and a big glass of strong coffee with milk for Amelia and me, and a glass of milk with a piece of white bread with mild cheese for Maria Luisa. She was in a bow-phase, her dark hair done up with pink or gaily coloured ribbons which contrasted with her sober, blue school uniform. From down on the plaza, we could hear the morning symphony – cars, the clanging of metal security grilles as they were rolled up, the roar of motorbikes and shouting and clattering from heavy lorries delivering supplies to the bars and shops.

Amelia drank her coffee in cautious sips. Each morning was new for me. Each morning it seemed like a small miracle that she was still there. She was wearing jeans and a shirt, a touch of make-up, her work outfit. She looked like what she was, an attractive, modern woman. Our eyes met and we recalled our lovemaking. We didn't speak much in the mornings, we didn't need to. We ate breakfast in the kitchen, in pleasant, sleepy silence with the radio's over-zealous traffic bulletins, sport and news in the background, and then my loved-ones set off

43

into the world. I often experienced an irrational feeling of loss when they left me in the morning. I dreaded losing them. They gave my life meaning.

Oscar thought it rather amusing and slightly incomprehensible that I had turned into this bourgeois family man, but he was probably a little envious too. He feared boredom, and needed stronger and stronger stimulants to combat it. I don't mean vast quantities of alcohol or drugs, although from time to time he stopped trying to avoid them, usually with catastrophic consequences, after which he'd dry out for a while. Speed and cocaine had both had Oscar in their clutches, but he got his biggest fix from challenges. He saw boundaries as lines to be breached, like a general always looking for the weak point in an enemy's defences. He constantly had to prove to himself that he was still young. Oscar had always been a Don Juan, and when he was younger I suppose this had its charm because he was so successful, but now that we were nearly 50 there was something desperate about his mania for conquests. He did admit that he no longer made such a big deal out of it, but that it was important for him to try his luck. He had been brought up short when he turned 40 and realised that many young women saw him as an old man. Yes, a dirty old man at that. Gloria had ridiculed him for weeks, until they had made their peace yet again. They couldn't do without one other. And also, of course, they had their joint businesses. Somehow or other they were joined at the hip. Without the one, the other would be useless.

I went down to the bar on the corner and read *El Pais* while I drank another coffee. The Basques were still at war with one another and the Spanish state. The previous evening ETA had killed a Spanish policeman in Bilbao. A young woman had been found murdered, shot through the mouth. The message was clear, she had grassed. A few weeks earlier they had murdered a young Basque local politician, a moderate nationalist, because the government had refused to release imprisoned members of ETA. The fury and frustration in the Basque provinces had been overwhelming. More than a million people had demonstrated on the streets of Bilbao. A couple of days later 30,000 ETA sympathisers had taken part in a counter-demonstration in San Sebastián. It was as if a civil war was raging. It seemed as if the killing would never end. At regular intervals a car bomb would explode on the streets of Madrid, causing a blanket of anger and fear to settle over the city. In my youth, during General Franco's dictatorship, I had regarded ETA as freedom fighters. Now they were only benighted youngsters who, at a time when Europe's borders were blurring and becoming lines in outdated atlases, were an anachronism. A hangover from the barbaric ideologies of the 20th century.

I took the newspaper home with me, to wait for Oscar who I knew would be anxious to see the photographs. I wasn't feeling too happy about them. Part of the secret of my profession was that officially no one knew that I was the photographer. The images were sold by the agency. But the Minister's bodyguards had seen me and the number plate on my rented car. I ran the risk of suddenly being thrust in the media spotlight myself, and even though I made my living from the public's ferocious thirst for knowledge of other people's lives and misfortunes, I guarded my private life more zealously than if it were a royal household.

Oscar rang the intercom. I knew it was him from the insistent way he pressed the buzzer. Money had become just as powerful an aphrodisiac for Oscar as a shapely behind had once been. Money could turn him on.

I lifted the receiver.

"Yes, Oscar," I said, and pressed the button that released the lock so that my old friend could come up.

Oscar and I went way back, to that extraordinary spring of 1977, when Spain had changed so dramatically. The changes in Spain that year were just as radical as those that swept the whole of Europe in 1989 when the Berlin Wall came down. In 1977 there were only two countries in Europe that didn't participate in some form of European collaboration – Albania and Spain. That spring, barely two years after General Franco died in his sick bed, Oscar and I had met in the middle of the night in a bar on Calle Echégaray, where I was living in a little boarding house. It was one of Madrid's really old bars and Oscar seemed to fill the little room. The walls were covered with yellow decorative tiles and the tables and chairs were small and made of hard wood, so you sat very awkwardly, but they served fantastic wines and stayed open till dawn. Three down-at-heel Andalusian gypsies were attempting to sing flamenco songs. The lead singer had two front teeth missing, the rest were gold. They sang *No te vayas todavia* with hoarse smoker's voices, while clapping out the arrhythmic, seductive beat. I noticed Oscar straight away. He was huge and cut an oddly clumsy figure as he sat, holding a large glass of beer, on one of the low seats that resembled a milking stool. Like most people at that time, he had a long, pageboy haircut and a bushy beard. I was with a colleague from Reuters who introduced us.

Oscar was a West-German freelance journalist. I was a Danish freelance photographer who had been hired by a Swedish journalist to take photographs for his articles on the democratisation of Spain, and to translate for him. The communist leader Santiago Carrillo had just returned home and was going to hold his first public rally in Valladolid, and we invited Oscar to join us in our rented car so he could get a story for his German newspapers and journals. He worked hard, but the small left-wing publications he wrote for paid small fees for very long articles.

That's how it began – by chance – but most of life is made up of a series of chance occurrences which only afterwards, when they're looked back on, make sense and form a pattern. This is how we try to create a whole out of the fragments of our lives, just as historians try to create an overall picture from the pieces that are left. Age brings with it a desire to see the whole, a desire to believe that there was a pattern, that it wasn't all just a matter of chance. That life is actually like a big jigsaw in which all the pieces fit together perfectly.

I let Oscar in and we gave each other a hug, as we always did when we hadn't seen one another for a while. We were real friends. I was extraordinarily fond of Oscar and the feeling was reciprocated, even though we were so different. Back then Oscar and Gloria had probably leaned more to the left. I was more inclined to go with the Zeitgeist, whereas they genuinely believed in the new social order, in the revolution. Today we tend to laugh at the revolutionary fervour of the 1970s. Call it romantic, belittle it. It's as if we don't want to acknowledge that lots of people actually believed that the revolution and socialism were just around the corner. In words, at least, Oscar and Gloria, like so many others, flirted with the potential of violence, but I'm sure they didn't follow up words with action. They looked up to the heroes of the time, such as Mao and Ho Chi Minh. When the atrocities of the Chinese Cultural Revolution began to become apparent, Gloria was disappointed and genuinely shocked, but Oscar was less troubled. Their more radical political beliefs gradually disappeared, replaced by concern for things closer to them. But once they had been as devout as Jesuit priests. We didn't talk about the past much. In a way that was the most remarkable thing about our youthful conviction. Now it was as if it and the Berlin Wall had never existed. That Marx, Engels, the Soviet Union and the GDR had become mirages in the twilight of the 20th century.

We began earning money and that has a way of changing people. We weren't alike, but we liked the same music, the same films and the same books, and we were hardly puritans. We thought that life was there to be lived. I had lived too hard, but Amelia had helped me put that behind me, even though the craving would never disappear.

We no longer thought about revolution.

Oscar was a very big man, but he kept himself trim. He had a bit of a belly, but it wasn't too pronounced, his broad shoulders were imposing and counterbalanced the bulk of his girth. He had a broad face, clean-shaven now, and peculiarly small, brown eyes. He was always elegantly and nonchalantly dressed in tailor-made suits with silk shirts, but no tie. He had a ready, loud and infectious laugh and a poised, confident gait, which announced that he was a successful man. He dominated a gathering and could charm most people. He was a born salesman and had the ability to sell in such a way that the customer felt honoured to be allowed to do business with him. He loved selling. He was essentially a manipulator of people. And, like all great seducers, his moral code was a little dubious. I was glad he was my friend and not my enemy.

We went up to the studio and I showed him the photographs. I had made ten colour and ten black and white prints. It was a nice short story in pictures. The speedboat appears in the cove, they bathe naked, maybe they make love in the water, they lie down together on the beach, the Minister sucks the girl's toes. The last photograph was the best, but their faces were easiest to see in the shot of them on the speedboat. The Minister leans over his lover. His face is perfectly in focus and his eyes gaze down at her naked breasts. She's moistening her lips with her tongue. I had managed to get so close that I hadn't needed the big telephoto lens, which makes for grainy photographs. The details were clean and sharp, as if I had been invited along on their excursion. I had selected the ten prints knowing that most of the world's celebrity magazines or newspapers would be able to use at least one of them, depending on where each nation and its press featured on the piety scale, what was acceptable practice. As he was a politician, even the broadsheets were bound to use a photograph in articles on the political implications. This would give them a pretext for showing naked breasts, but it would have to be one of the less erotic shots. Just for the hell of it, I had made a single print of their intercourse on the beach, but it was, as I had anticipated, far too pornographic and Oscar didn't give it a second glance. He knew there wasn't any money in it.

"Nice work, Peter," was all he said as he slowly and carefully looked through the series again. I could almost hear his brain calculating which customers should have which photograph.

Oscar, Gloria and I were partners in the agency, which we had named OSPE NEWS. My name had never appeared under a single one of the exposés and other paparazzo photographs that I had taken over the years. I was unknown beyond my professional circle, but a photograph copyrighted to OSPE NEWS featured practically every day in a magazine or a newspaper somewhere in the world. And the money came rolling in. Even my famous photograph of Jacqueline Kennedy was still selling. We had branches in London and Paris and supplied many other photographs, not just of the famous. The agency represented conventional photojournalists, and one of our photographers had won awards for his coverage of the war in the former Yugoslavia, and we also had some excellent sports photographers on our books, but the really serious money came from photographs of famous people in private situations.

Oscar took the photographs and sat down at the white table in the middle of the spacious room where I drank coffee with business associates, or with the clients who sat for me when I was engaged on the other side of my trade. I took portraits of the famous, who paid me a fortune, or of faces which suddenly caught my interest on the street, in a café or a waiting room. I did those free of charge. My own name appeared on the portraits.

Oscar looked at me. "They're worth even more than you think," he said.

"He hasn't been a Minister for long enough to be particularly well known outside Spain," I said.

Oscar smiled his wolf's smile. "Peter, old boy. It's written all over your face. You don't know who she is!"

I waited. Oscar read celebrity magazines in 17 languages. Not because he was an inveterate voyeur, but because it was part of his job. He studied the international jet set with the same sensitive barometer that a skilful speculator uses to study stocks and shares, balance sheets and foreign news. To be at the cutting edge, to keep one step ahead of the market, the new God of our times. To keep abreast of who was hot right now, in the limelight and thus vulnerable and marketable.

"Italy," was all he said.

I picked up one of the photographs. The attractive, smooth face was just like any other pretty young female face, but then again not quite, because it rang a bell. The pouting mouth and the large, slightly slanting eyes. I tried to imagine her wearing make-up. Make-up can change a face so radically that it's almost unrecognisable, but before I could place her, Oscar told me who she was.

"It's Arianna Fallacia. It has to be her."

I looked at the photograph. It was true. She had just missed out on an award at the Cannes Festival. She was a hot newcomer in Italian film. That in itself wouldn't be enough to make her a household name in Italy or anywhere else, but before she'd started in films she'd been a scantily-clad hostess on one of Italian television's idiotic game shows – and that made her most definitely profitable.

"You're right," I said. "Where the hell would they have met each other?"

"The old lecher has interests in one of Berlusconi's television

50

stations. Besides, he's rolling in it. He'll have seen her in a newspaper and sent his private plane to pick her up. Lovely girl. She'll be even more famous now. It won't do him any good, but her stock will rise once Lime's photographs clear the front pages in Italy and Spain. Who do you think should have exclusive rights to break it first?"

"Do you want a beer or a coffee?" I said.

"Cola."

I fetched two colas from the fridge and put them on the table. Oscar looked at me.

"What's on your mind, Peter?"

"Maybe we should forget about it?"

"Could be a million or more. Undoubtedly more. You must have a pressing reason."

"I have."

I told him the story. He listened carefully. Oscar could flit about, be garrulous, superficially cheerful, but it was a façade he wore for the outside world. He was a sober businessman through and through, and he knew me well enough to respect that if I had misgivings there would be good reason. I had taken thousands of photographs in my life, and hundreds of photographs that people would prefer I hadn't, so Oscar was well aware that it wouldn't be moral scruples that led me to have misgivings.

"We'll bring Gloria in on this one," he said. "But I can't see a problem. It's a non-starter. It can't be substantiated. You haven't done anything wrong. They were in a public place. Your name won't be mentioned. It's always like that. And anyway, anyone who knows anything knows that often when OSPE runs really revealing photographs they've got the Lime signature, right?"

It was true, so I nodded.

"It's just a hunch," I said.

"I respect that. Gloria can snoop around a bit."

"OK," I said, but I had the feeling that we should leave it alone, although I had complete confidence in Gloria's and Oscar's ability to assess the situation. They knew all about the minefield, the borderline between the legal and the possible. They knew how to make the most of people's instinct for gossip, but they also knew that if we broke the law our profits would soon be eaten up by lawyers' fees. That's simple arithmetic, as Gloria was wont to say.

"We'll give it a couple of days," said Oscar, and got up to use the telephone.

He rang Gloria. I heard him putting her in the picture. He was standing next to my desk and I saw him pick up the black and white photograph that had turned up from out of the past. He glanced at it and put it down again. We had known one another for so long that he wouldn't think he was poking his nose in my business. Then he picked up the photograph again and stood holding it as, suddenly preoccupied, he responded to Gloria in his slow, heavily accented, but correct Spanish.

"Four o'clock?" he said at the end of their conversation.

I shook my head. I had an appointment with the Japanese. I needed it. I had that strange uneasiness in my body, tingling fingers, shivers down my spine, churning stomach, dry mouth. All the danger signs. I needed to get physically tired, and maybe I should think about going to a meeting again soon. I had hoped that it wouldn't be necessary any longer.

"Peter can't," said Oscar. "What about now?" he suggested.

I shook my head again. Oscar was holding the photograph in both his hands, the receiver clamped under his chin. I had a sitting in half an hour, with a 56-year-old diva from the Royal Spanish Theatre who had decided to give her latest lover a portrait, which I had promised would make her look as enigmatically beautiful as the Mona Lisa.

"Six?" said Oscar. He looked at the back of the print before putting it on the desk again. I nodded and he blew kisses down the telephone. They were a couple, those two. Either in love or living separate lives. He turned round so that his backside was resting on the table, and lit a cigarette.

"Who's the mystery woman?" he said, pointing at the photograph.

"I'm not entirely sure." Actually I was, but I couldn't be bothered to explain. I wasn't surprised that he asked. Oscar had been born nosy, which was one of the many reasons that he was so good at his job.

"What's it doing here?"

I told him about the woman from the National Security Service in Copenhagen.

"Have you got the negatives then?" he asked.

"Why are you so interested in an old photograph? Do you know her?"

"No. But she's beautiful. In an enigmatic, mysterious sort of way. As if she's saying 'I have many secrets. Only a strong man will be able to find the key to them. It's difficult to unlock me, but if you do the reward will be considerable.'"

I laughed. It was typical of Oscar. That's how he viewed women. He conquered them, discovered their secrets, and as soon as he thought he knew their bodies and souls, they began to bore him. Only the unpredictable, astute, sexy Gloria had held onto him long enough for a separation to be too inconvenient. Besides, he loved her in his own peculiar way, and periodically he would be madly in love with her, as if they had only just met and there were still secrets to be revealed. That usually happened when he had been away on business for a while.

"Have you?" he repeated.

I pointed at the fireproof steel cabinets along one wall.

"You know I never throw a negative out. They'll be here somewhere or other. The photograph doesn't ring any bells, but I dare say it's around. Maybe up in the attic."

"So you're going to dig it out?"

I shrugged.

"It's not at the top of my list," I said.

"It's a real Lime photograph," he said. "It's got everything: proportion, tension, mystery, disquiet, danger, joy. You were good right from the start."

"Goodbye, Oscar," I said.

He gathered up the photographs of the Minister and the Italian actress and put them in an envelope, patted my cheek and left.

I switched on my mobile phone. When I wasn't out on an assignment I often let its answering machine act as my secretary. There was a message from Clara Hoffmann asking if I would ring her. I decided I wouldn't just then. Instead I walked over to the steel cabinets and opened the first one. It contained a huge part of my life in small squares packed in grey, soft negative paper. The negatives were arranged by year. I had written the date and subject of the shots on each roll. There were thousands. I had travelled around a lot during my life, but had always been systematic about organising my photographs. Even during the most chaotic periods, when I had teetered on the brink of an abyss, I had kept my negatives in good order. It was as if I knew that once my pictures got into a mess there would be no going back and I would be dragged down into a pit, which would be impossible to climb out of. In the first few years, when I didn't really have a permanent address, they were stored in cardboard boxes in the basement of my parents' house. Later, when I moved into my first little flat, which was now the kitchen and family room of our large flat, the boxes came with me. The images which froze time in a thousandth of a second were now to be found in the steel cabinets, beautifully organised.

But not all the negatives.

This particular one might be in my secret archive, which even Oscar didn't know about. I had not only always taken great care of my negatives, I had also considered the best and most controversial ones to be both a life insurance and a pension, plus creating a portrait of my life. I had been in the habit, since I was young, of posting these special images to my parents. I would put the negative inside a letter addressed to myself, which I then put in an envelope and sent. They knew that they just had to look after the letter until I came home. When I dropped in during one of my irregular visits to Denmark, I opened the letters to myself and put the contents in a suitcase. There had been various suitcases over the years, increasing in size, and now my archive was a big, white, steel Samsonite case with a combination lock. Only one suitcase was allowed. That was part of the ritual. Of the myth of my own making which involved a good deal of superstition. I put the negatives in order, filed them and listed the subject matter in a black notebook. It may have been an eccentricity, but I didn't trust centralised archives and I didn't trust computers. I didn't store just negatives of my famous photograph of Jacqueline Kennedy sunbathing naked and other images that had earned me a fortune. There was also a landscape that meant a lot to me, or had done once. There were the first photographs I had taken with my first Leica, or with my first camera. There was a really rather banal tourist shot from the Red Square in Moscow in 1980 alongside a little portrait of my first girlfriend taken with my old Kodak box camera. The first photographs I had developed and printed myself were in my suitcase. There were negatives from Iran, from Denmark, from my childhood and adolescence, of half-forgotten lovers and girlfriends, from my lifelong project of taking photographs in all of Hemingway's drinking-holes, and then there were the million-dollar-negatives like the one of the "Minister and his Mistress". There were the first photographs of Amelia and Maria Luisa just after her birth. But there were also love letters from a long life, letters from my father and mother, my first letter to them written when I had been away on a summer holiday, a couple of school reports, a couple of essays and my clumsy attempts at writing poetry, sketches and hastily scrawled diary entries and thoughts. The odd newspaper cutting, but only a few and all from my childhood and early teens – the Kennedy killings, first John F. and later Robert; the first man on the moon. The photograph I took of the Vopo laughing on the crumbling Berlin Wall. It was more than just a suitcase. It was a safe place for nostalgia, in which I had recorded my life's adventures, for my eyes only. My will stated that after my death the suitcase should be taken, unopened, to the public incinerator and burnt. Throughout my unsettled existence, the suitcase, which I used like a diary, had been a secure berth, somewhere in which I could store my life's secrets and innermost thoughts. After my parents died, I had a solicitor store it and receive my post for a while, but for the past five years it had been looked after by Amelia's father. Being a former intelligence officer, he could keep a secret and, even though we saw things very differently, I knew that he trusted me and respected me, yes, was fond of me because he could see how unconditionally I loved his only daughter and grandchild.

I picked out the negative of one of the more pornographic shots and put it in an envelope, along with a note of the time and place, and addressed the envelope to myself before putting it into a larger envelope with a short message to Amelia's father. The photograph of the mystery woman could quite easily be in the white suitcase in Don Alfonzo's pleasant house near Madrid.

I checked my emails and replied to a couple of letters. They were mainly from sources telling me about possible hits. Rumours and hearsay about where the famous were planning to go on holiday or were holidaying already. They didn't have to be sensational photographs. Every picture of someone well-known in a private, informal situation where his or her vulnerability was on display was worth a fortune. I decided I wouldn't follow up any of the tips, but I thanked my sources and transferred the $1,000 that I thought one of the informants had earned. I emailed a tip to a young photographer who worked for us as a freelancer in London and who deserved a break. I had been there too once, jostling for position in the heaving crowd of photographers waiting outside a restaurant in Kensington, because word was that a royal was having lunch there. Hours of waiting for that thousandth of a second. The photographer's lot: hurry up and wait!

The diva arrived with her dresser, and I spent an enjoyable hour while the old poseur sat for me in my studio, chatting about men past and present and affectionately telling indiscreet tales from behind the scenes. She was from a bygone era, but she had a marvellous face and, being the great actress that she was, she knew how to employ every one of her hundreds of face muscles. I tried various kinds of lighting. She wanted to look mysterious and enigmatic. She also wanted to appear 20 years younger. If the photograph was good enough, she would insist that the theatre used it for their publicity. I also had a number of authors on my client list. It had got to the point where the photograph on the back cover was more important for sales than the content of the novel. We lived in a media-driven age where image was everything and substance nothing. Everyone in the spotlight wanted to play the role they had chosen. They would claim that they were just being themselves, but I knew better than anyone that they really wanted to play a role, and that they were miserable if they weren't able to perform it through to the finale. Even the tragic, beautiful Princess Diana was both actor and victim. She hated us when we lay in wait, but loved us when we could be used in her power struggle with husband and Palace. She couldn't live without the media, and she ended up being devoured by it. She thought she could choose, but once you've invited the media in, the guests won't leave until they're ready. If you live by the media, you die by the media. Either abruptly, or that slow, painful death when no one points the viewfinder at you any more. When you're no longer a story, just a memory. When emptiness strikes and the flashbulbs go out. Fame can be both a drug and an aphrodisiac. I made my living from today's narcissism and insatiable appetite for gossip. I was the man sitting in the middle of the global village square, passing on gossip about the famous. By making visible their sorrows and joys, infidelities and loneliness when they were abandoned, I both mythologised and humanised them at one and the same time. But I needed something more. So I took portraits, because in a photograph of a face I could, if I was lucky and skilful, lay bare the individual's soul in all its fragile nakedness as I peeled away their chosen persona without their realising what I was doing. They couldn't hide from me in a portrait. I revealed the depths of their being.

Afterwards, I spent a few hours in the darkroom with the diva's portrait, but I still didn't think we had hit exactly the right expression, so I decided I would have her to sit again. I was happy in the dark-room. The outside world disappeared. The darkroom was soundproof, and light-proof so nothing disturbed me as I created my own world and saw my art emerge under the red light. The chemical processes were simple, but it was my precise attention to detail and my ability to combine them in the right order with the right timing that made the result uniquely mine. I said goodbye to the young woman who looked after Maria Luisa during the midday break, ate a quick sand-wich and went out into the afternoon summer heat, round the corner to the Japanese karate institute. They were old friends and had been my trainers for 20 years. When the institute had first opened, I had done the publicity shots and helped them through the tortuous Spanish red tape. They didn't have any money, so they had paid me with lessons. Now they had loads of money, as did I for that matter, but I still regularly took photographs for them and they let me train at the institute when my body needed the restlessness knocked out of it. Karate training kept me fit, and I enjoyed talking with the old trainer, Suzuki, who had the ability to look at life from a distance and put it into a perspective, which reached beyond the everyday. Talking with him was a bit like talking to the priest I could never believe.

Oscar had thrown himself into golf with the passion which only middle-aged men are able to invest in a new vice. He was far too tall to be particularly good, but he worked at it as if it was a matter of life and death. He had taken me out on the course a couple of times, but it didn't really appeal, even though I suspected that I might have been better suited to it than he was. Oscar had more than enough money, so he invested in expensive coaching and he had improved a lot over the last couple of years, but I stuck to karate and the discipline it demanded. That self-control which Suzuki drilled into me on the mat and in our conversations afterwards.

The Madrid heat hit me in the face as I stepped out of the door and was instantly enveloped in the smells and sounds of the city. The boisterous song of the streets. The smell of freshly boiled squid emanating from a big bluish-red creature hanging over a steaming copper pan in a restaurant window. The blind lottery ticket seller's keening chant as he promised to plead to the goddess of fortune in the next big Los Onces draw. The clattering rattle of a three-wheeled delivery scooter and the quiet hum of a Jaguar. Madrid's and Spain's ceaseless and conspicuous cacophony of contrasts, of old and new.

I walked past the Viva Madrid café and a few metres on to Calle Echégaray, one of the oldest streets in Madrid. I posted my letters and walked on feeling quite content. Bars and little boarding houses sit side by side. The pavement is narrow, so you have to press yourself against the buildings when the cars clatter past. In my young days I had lived at Pension las Once, halfway down the street opposite the Hotel Inglés and the Japanese karate institute. They had opened the year that I had moved in, renting a small room on the fourth floor from señor Alberto and his señora. Their Galician domestic help, Rosa, was 30, maybe a virgin, illiterate and so sharp-tongued that I told her she could marry only a member of the Guardia Civil. Rosa couldn't be called beautiful. She had regular but coarse features and a clumsy, round body. She looked like what she was: the daughter of a poor day labourer and a mother who was worn out because, like so many other poor Spaniards in those days, she had to grind and toil to keep the home together. Rosa always wore a pink overall when she cleaned and cooked with the señora. She came from a small village far away in green and hilly Galicia, born into a large family of poor farm workers. Her father had lined up every morning along with the other men on the village square, in the hope that the landowner's foreman would give them a day's work. Poverty was widespread, exploitation gross and the class barriers high. Rosa had been in service since she was seven, but I never discovered how she had ended up in Pension las Once in Madrid. In the evenings, the señora would sit with the *ABC* newspaper and try to teach her to read. It was a red-letter day when Rosa finally managed to read the headlines by herself. Old señor Alberto had fetched a bottle of special sherry which he had been keeping for 25 years, and we ceremoniously raised our glasses to Rosa who'd solved the mystery of how random letters put together in a particular order make words, which make ideas, which in turn shape dreams. It was easy to be a socialist in Spain in those days. The exploitation and oppression under Franco's dictatorship were plain to see. The wealth created along the coast by the tourist industry benefited only a few. There is no reason to romanticise the past, so why do we do it all the time? Spain had come a long way and, whereas a generation ago there had been lots of Rosas, now there were only a few who didn't go to school and learn the basic requirement to be a member of society – to read and write.

I wondered, as I often did, about Rosa and what she was doing now. She had eventually married, not a civil guardsman, but a small-holder from Andalusia. Had she slogged herself to death in some godforsaken Andalusian olive grove? What did she make of modern Spain with its computers, cars, materialism, small families, abortion, contraception, democracy, liberty and postmodern modernity? Had any of us imagined that the country would change to such an extent? I don't think so. And somewhere along the line we probably regretted the changes too. Hadn't we loved Spain precisely because it was differ-ent and out of date, non-European, almost African in its colours, lifestyle and expression? Now it was like every other European country. Bound together by the European Union, it still had its own cultural expression, but, in essence, this expression was the same from Stockholm to Madrid. At least where the young were concerned. And it was American. It was only in the bullring that the old Spain survived as a kind of museum for a lost individuality. The rest was moulded by the incessantly grinding, global media machine, of which I was a prosperous cog.

Maybe it was my age that made me increasingly question my profession. Maybe it was just my subconscious preparing me for the catastrophe. Maybe that's just the wisdom of hindsight.

In any case, I was walking along lost in thought, surrounded by the reassuring life and hubbub of the city, when two men blocked my path. They were tall and trim, mid-30s, in well-cut suits.

"Señor Lime?" one of them said.

I stopped.

"You're under arrest," said the other, while the first one, with the unerring hands of the expert, pulled my arms behind my back and snapped on the handcuffs.

# 4

They drove me the few hundred metres along Calle Alcalá to the headquarters of the security services and the police, a massive, old red building on Puerta del Sol. The centre of Spain, where the distance marker reads zero and the walls in the looming building have absorbed the forgotten screams of the condemned and the tortured. They were firm but polite when they took away my mobile phone and the little Leica I always carried and put me in the back of the car, one of them holding my head to make sure I didn't bang it on the doorframe. The car was a big, white Seat. There were no handles on the inside of the doors, but I was placed securely between the two plain-clothed officers anyway. I sat like a child wedged in tightly between two adults. My shoulders pressed against theirs, which felt confident and fit and muscular. The driver pulled away without a word and without turning round. Like the other two, he was close-cropped, elite corps style. They didn't answer when I asked why I had been arrested. Spain is a constitutional state, but with plenty of violent crime and an active terrorist movement like ETA, the security forces and the police are not quite as subtle as they are in Denmark. The State's reponse to the violence, and the consequent erosion of the concept of justice, lowers the threshold of what is acceptable. Only 20 years earlier I would have been terrified. At that time the police still beat confessions out of people they didn't think they could secure a conviction against, or who they had already decided were guilty. Even though the Basques maintained that the Guardia Civil still did it, I wasn't worried about outright physical abuse. I asked again why they had arrested me and didn't get an answer. The handcuffs were cutting into my wrists and digging into the small of my back and it was uncomfortable when the car accelerated or turned a corner and I couldn't cushion myself properly. The security officers smelled of tobacco, garlic and a rather cheap men's eau de cologne. It was depressing to be sitting there between them, watching the radiant and anarchic Madrid life going on outside as if nothing had happened. As if life could just carry on without me. I wanted to shout out to the pedestrians carrying their belongings, to the lovers walking hand in hand, to the frantic businessman with his attaché case, to the road sweeper in his yellow waistcoat with his little cart, to the well-dressed women on their way back to work after the siesta, to the school children in their blue uniforms, to the motor scooters, to the cars, "I'm stuck here. Help me. Stop the traffic. How can you carry on as if nothing has happened?"

The driver hadn't switched the siren on, and the traffic slowed us down. The windows were tinted, so even if someone I knew had walked past they wouldn't have spotted me. I tried to get my rapid breathing just a little under control and told them that I wanted to ring my lawyer, but they ignored me. I was sufficiently well-versed in the law to know that if they wanted they could find the right loophole in the anti-terrorism legislation which would allow them to keep me in isolation for 48 hours at least, maybe even for three days. I wasn't a terrorist, but perhaps an examining magistrate wouldn't worry about a little detail like that if the right Minister pushed the right buttons. As we drove into Puerta del Sol and I saw the familiar yet suddenly so remote newsstands, lottery ticket sellers, the swarm of people teeming out of the metro exit, maybe heading up the hill to the El Corte Inglés department store to do something as everyday as the shopping, my brain began to function again. I breathed slowly and deeply, in the way Suzuki had taught me so very long ago.

There was a Minister who would go to great lengths to prevent his happy home life and political career as a respectable Christian Democrat from being destroyed by a series of photographs taken by Peter Lime. He had reacted swiftly, but a politician today who doesn't appreciate that the media acts at lightning speed wouldn't have become a Minister in the first place.

The Seat turned left and drove alongside the ponderous building which housed the police headquarters, swept past two guards armed with machine guns, who looked as though they were pregnant in their bulky, brown, bulletproof vests, and drove into the courtyard. There were several parked patrol cars, a water cannon and a number of white Seats in which the riot squad thought they drove around inconspicuously, but I didn't get to see much else. They pulled me out of the car, grasped hold of my elbows and led me through a low side door into a dark corridor. We went down a staircase, made a right turn down a long corridor and down another flight of steps that led into a large room with a shabby, stained desk. A warder in a grey uniform was sitting behind it. A sports newspaper was lying open on the table, the headline announcing Real Madrid's latest triumph. There was an empty coffee cup next to it. The warder didn't say a word either, but he had clearly been expecting me. He walked in front of us down another long corridor lit by the glaring light of naked bulbs encased in wire netting. The corridor was lined with blue cell doors. He stopped at the fourth door and opened it. My handcuffs were unlocked and wrenched off. I gasped and was just about to protest when one of them grabbed hold of my ponytail, yanked backwards, then let go and shoved me violently between the shoulder blades so I stumbled into the cell.

I fell down flat. My hands were numb and not much use. I hit the floor with a hollow sound and lay winded on the cement trying to rally myself as the door clanged shut and I heard the harsh, horrible sound of a key being turned twice in the lock. I was incarcerated.

I lay there for a while trying to pull myself together, the blood tingling in my hands. The corridor was silent, as if the cells were soundproof. I got a creeping feeling that they had put me in the old torture cells used during Franco's dictatorship. If their aim was to frighten me, they were succeeding. I would happily have done a barter, my freedom for 20 photographs of a horny Minister, but his henchmen didn't know Oscar and Gloria. To them the police were still fascist pigs and the lackeys of those with vested interests. They would move heaven and earth to get me out. They would use every legal means, but they also wouldn't hesitate to use the pornographic photographs of the Minister and his mistress as blackmail, should that prove necessary in order to free their friend from the claws of the bourgeois state.

I took comfort in that as I got myself up off the floor and sat on the narrow bed covered with a thin blanket. I also took comfort in the thought that all this was probably just a clumsy attempt at intimidation. They didn't have a case at all. They didn't have any evidence. They hadn't even gone through the usual routine of taking a mugshot and fingerprints.

A glaring lightbulb, also covered with heavy wire netting, hung from the ceiling about three metres over my head. The walls were a dirty yellow and bare, painted with a smooth thick paint which didn't look like the kind you could scratch messages on, as we like to imagine prisoners doing. A hole in one corner passed for a toilet. There was a wash basin, with rust stains running down to the plug-hole, and a little table bolted to the wall. The door sported its little peephole like a piece of jewellery. You could look in, but not out. They hadn't taken away my belt, nor my comb or shoelaces. Maybe they couldn't care less if I committed suicide. Maybe they would be pleased if I did. My knees hurt and my wrists hurt, so I drew my legs up under me, placed my hands on my knees, closed my eyes and looked inward, as Suzuki had taught me to do, until my mind was blank, my breathing calm, the pain eased and a small, bright dot between my eyes was the only thing my consciousness registered. I found my way into the *nada* that Suzuki had taught me to find, and which he called *wa*, when it was necessary to stop time. Then seconds pass slower and slower until they almost stand still, vibrating and bright, and the only point of concentration is the small, luminous dot, which Suzuki described as the innermost chamber of the soul. My luminous dot emerged from the faces of my two loved ones, who smiled at me and gave me peace of mind.

So when they came to get me later in the evening, I was hungry and thirsty, but I was feeling composed and in fighting spirit. The same two men and the fat warder entered the cell. They didn't handcuff me again, but made do with taking a firm hold of my elbows. I demanded again to be allowed to ring a lawyer or home, but they didn't respond. They took me up to a small room and made me stand against a white wall. Then the rituals started. They took my photograph and fingerprints, still without saying anything more than was absolutely necessary, and led me into a small courtroom.

The examining magistrate was a heavily built, middle-aged man who looked down at me over the top of a pair of narrow reading glasses. He had big, bushy, grey eyebrows and a receding chin. The stenographer was a woman. She was wearing a blue skirt and blouse and didn't look at me.

During the first stages of a criminal case in Spain, the magistrate acts as both magistrate and investigator. He has to establish whether or not an offence has been committed and if there are grounds to proceed with prosecution, or whether the accused should be released. This magistrate looked like someone who could quite easily be one of the Minister's friends. He had tried to conceal his weight under a well-cut suit. His tie was dark and muted. He looked like a funeral director whose business was doing very nicely.

The two silent officers made me sit on a chair in front of the magistrate, who exercised his right to look down on me. They positioned themselves behind my high-backed, uncomfortable chair. The magistrate rummaged through some papers and asked if my name was Peter Lime, if I had residence permit number such and such, and if I lived on Plaza Santa Ana in Madrid. And if I understood the Spanish language. I answered yes to everything, while making every effort to remain calm. After we had established that I was who I was, I spoke.

"I haven't had the chance to speak to a lawyer. I've been given neither bread nor water since my wrongful arrest. My family must be frantic with worry and terrified because they don't know where I am."

The magistrate didn't appear to have a sense of irony, or any other human qualities.

"You will speak to the court when you are questioned, otherwise you will remain silent."

He looked down at his papers and then again over his reading glasses at me.

"On the 3rd of June you were in Llanca in Catalonia."

I couldn't hear the question mark, so I didn't answer.

"The accused will answer the question," said the magistrate. It was terrifying. I was dependent on the decisions of one single man. The Minister had long tentacles. It couldn't be anything else. During all the ups and downs of my adult life, I had clung to the fact that I was a free man, not at the mercy of the authorities or the capricious whims of a regular employer.

"It is correct that I was in Llanca," I said.

"Using a form of martial art, you physically assaulted an officer from the Justice Department and threatened another?"

"That is not an accurate interpretation of the facts," I said.

"And the correct interpretation is?"

"I defended myself against two men I didn't know, who were attempting to steal my cameras and wreck my job," I said.

"What is your job?"

"I'm a photographer."

"What were you taking photographs of that day in Llanca?"

"I am not obliged to disclose that or anything else. I want to speak to a lawyer," I said, my anger mounting.

"The criminal investigation department in Llanca have witnesses," said the magistrate. His face was expressionless and his eyes were as cold as a dead fish.

"I would like to confront them face to face," I said.

"They live abroad. It will take a little while to locate them."

"My lawyer?"

"All in good time."

"Then I'll be happy to come back at that time."

He looked over his glasses again.

"It is alleged that you have trained in karate for many years. One could say that your body is a weapon, a lethal weapon."

Again, I couldn't hear a question, so I kept silent.

"Is it correct that you are a black belt in karate?"

"That is correct."

That seemed to please him immensely. At any rate, the suggestion of a smile slid across his face. He rummaged through his papers again. I realised that he was having difficulty thinking of anything to ask me. The case was flimsy. He was doing a friend a favour that had to be given a thin layer of judicial varnish.

But then he dropped the bombshell that made me really nervous. He looked down over his glasses.

"It is alleged that over the years you have had contact with members of the terrorist group ETA. Numerous contacts?"

"Alleged how?"

"Is that correct?"

"No," I said.

"Reports of recorded conversations, marked confidential, have been submitted to the court. Surveillance reports, marked confidential, have been submitted. There has been contact."

"What year?"

"That is immaterial."

"No. The former members of ETA with whom I have had contact, and only professionally I might add, were all granted amnesty in 1977," I said.

The magistrate remained poker-faced, but I could tell he was ill-prepared. The whole case was. They were using intimidatory tactics and they hadn't had much time. They'd got my file from their extensive secret archives and quickly concocted something which they assumed would hold water for a couple of days. He extricated himself from his predicament by bringing the preliminary hearing to a close.

"That will have to be investigated. You will be held for three days in isolation, as permitted by law, while inquiries continue. Thereafter you will be brought before the court again. On that occasion your lawyer will be present."

*Incommunicado* was the Spanish word he used for isolation. It was used often in the Spanish judicial system. It gave the police three days in which to find and submit additional material so that the custody order could be maintained, and it could be months before there was an actual trial or the charge was dropped. I was beginning to get seriously worried. Even in democratic Spain, the clan-like fellowship between those in power still meant a lot. I had wreaked havoc in very powerful circles, and they were prepared to use every available contrivance and loophole in the system.

"I insist on being allowed to ring my wife and my lawyer," I said with mounting desperation in my voice. My mouth was dry and the palms of my hands wet.

The investigating magistrate turned to the court stenographer who looked as if the whole affair was boring her to tears. He wasn't a complete idiot. At least I hoped not. I clung to the fact that he must know he had a very flimsy case that wouldn't hold water, and would safeguard himself against reprisals by making sure that the formalities were as they should be. At any rate, he dictated:

"Enter in the record! The accused will be held in isolation for three days as of now, in accordance with Article 189, Section 4 of the Criminal Code. The criminal investigation department will notify the accused's wife of the said detention. The accused may consult with his lawyer for two hours before the next sitting of the court, scheduled for five o'clock in the afternoon three days from now. The first preliminary hearing will be heard in camera and may not be reported in the press. Until the appointed meeting with his lawyer, the accused may not receive visitors. The accused is entitled to 30 minutes of outdoor exercise every day, on his own. The accused will be offered the Bible or other religious literature as reading material, but will not be allowed access to radio, television or newspapers. The accused will be provided with normal provisions and hygiene as applicable for those held in isolation. The preliminary hearing is closed."

He stood up, and the rest of us did too, and I was led back to the cell, the door slamming behind me, a sound that now was rather more sinister. The system had just shown me that I was a very small human pawn in a game manipulated by the powerful. But as one of the powerless I was grateful for small mercies, and I found myself thanking the chilly magistrate for letting the police get in touch with Amelia. She would be beside herself with worry by now, but once she had given it some thought she would ring Oscar and Gloria.

This improved my frame of mind a little, and half an hour later the fat warder brought me a bowl of hot vegetable soup with two pieces of fresh bread, a piece of chicken with sautéed potatoes and a bottle of mineral water. He looked like someone who indulged in the richer fare of the Spanish country kitchen. His small eyes were almost completely hidden in pockets of fat and his smooth, stretched skin gave him the expression of an aggrieved child. I wasn't really hungry. I would rather have had a shower, but I ate anyway. "It's important to preserve your strength and health," I could hear Amelia saying. I would rather have had a cigarette than the chicken, but they had taken away my cigarettes and lighter along with my keys and wallet. The fat warder came to fetch the grey plastic plates and brought me a bar of soap, a toothbrush, toothpaste and a small thin towel, plus a copy of the Bible. He also threw a rough grey blanket on the narrow bed. It seemed it was bedtime for prisoner Lime in solitary. I asked him for a cigarette, but he didn't answer.

"Goodnight," I said to his back, but he still didn't answer. The cell was as good as soundproof. I couldn't hear any other prisoners. I couldn't hear any sounds from the street. I couldn't hear jangling keys or shuffling footsteps. It was silent and peaceful. It was a strange feeling in Madrid, which is always noisy and never completely still. The only sound was the blood throbbing in my head and a faint humming from a pipe in the wall. I used the stinking hole in the corner, washed, brushed my teeth and lay down on the bed. I'm a bad sleeper. I don't sleep much at all, and now it was impossible to relax and fall asleep. The light was on and the quiet set my nerves on edge. I missed Amelia and our little miracle. I forced myself to think about the good times we spent together. I understood how people could

71

become very vulnerable and even lose their minds when isolated from their fellow beings. I had always seen myself as a lone wolf who was comfortable, and maybe even happiest, in his own company, but I already missed to the pit of my aching stomach the company of my loved ones and other people, even if just strangers in a café. The Minister's people knew what they were doing. If they kept me here long enough I would agree to anything. Almost. Because, along with my anxiety and fear, I was also angry and stubborn and felt deeply violated in body and soul. I lay on my back and kept this little flame of anger and chagrin burning. I needed a cigarette. I wanted to hold on to that sense of injustice, which would help me put up a fight. I knew it wasn't any use meditating, so I just lay there as time stood horribly still and my thoughts raced erratically. I shivered and sweated alternately, even though the temperature, like the black silence amid the bright light, remained constant.

I must have dozed off finally, because I woke with a jolt when the door swung open. The two henchmen from Llanca came in, the small fat sweaty one and the big heavy. The big one glowered at me, and his expression told me that he hadn't forgotten that I had nearly broken his wrist and his testicles were probably still black and blue. The small one attempted a smile. They were wearing suits, but the time of day was reflected in the rough, dark stubble on their chins. It was nearly 4 a.m. They looked exhausted. They'd come early, knowing that this was the time when defences were at their lowest, but actually they looked more tired than I felt. I had napped and was feeling quite fresh.

The big one leant against the door, covering the peephole. He had a habit of rubbing his left hand across his chin and then sliding it up and carefully twisting a finger in one of his nostrils. It was a strange kind of tic. As if he was nervous, while the rest of his body seemed menacingly composed. The small one leant against the wall. He had dead, grey eyes and a very narrow nose, and his eyes were deep-set as if they had been shoved into place a little too forcefully when he was born.

I sat up and prepared myself for the beating they had undoubtedly come to give me. But instead the small fat one threw me a packet of Chesterfields and a disposable lighter. I lit up, inhaled deeply, felt my body tingle all over and a pleasant dizziness made the room swim momentarily. A few lines from an old poem by Sten Kaalø drifted into my mind.

And here in the kitchen in Skåne with the radio on the blue
    wax cloth
the sun has just risen above the hilltops
and a little dizzy from the first morning cigarette
I sit enthralled and listen

Years ago a local eccentric called Sigvaldi had sold copies of the poem from a pram he pushed around Copenhagen. I had been fascinated by poetry when I was young. Perhaps I had wanted to be a poet. This memory appeared out of the blue, as if I was losing my mind and could picture the past quite clearly, while the present remained enveloped in a fog. My detachment baffled them. They read it as anxiety, which probably wasn't so wide of the mark.

"Calvo Carillo," the man by the wall introduced himself. "My colleague is Santiago Sotello. There's no reason to be afraid. How about talking business, Pedro? Surely this can be sorted out in a civilised fashion. We are, after all, mature and experienced men. We're used to making our way in the world and leaving rash behaviour to the young. That being the privilege of youth."

I smoked and didn't say anything, just watched his strange doll-like eyes. Eyes like Maria Luisa's teddy bear. Stuck on with a blob of glue.

"This could take a serious turn," Carillo continued.

"You haven't got a case," I said.

"Serious in the sense that we can make life uncomfortable for you. Maybe you'll be out in a couple of days. But then you'll be back in again. The terrorist angle is flimsy, but every time there's a killing we'll haul you in for questioning. The assault charge is maybe a bit slim too, but the state has large resources at its disposal, and should we so wish we can find the witnesses to your brutal attack on a man in the service of the King. We would have to lock you up again, for further interrogation. For an identification parade. Do you get my drift?"

I nodded. I knew he was right. They could give me a really hard time. As if reading my thoughts, he continued with the list of harassments available to a modern, civilised and strong state when dealing with its citizens, or perhaps more specifically those people who are not its citizens.

He took a step forward.

"You are a foreigner in our country, but a foreigner who has learnt our language, understands our culture and I believe I can say has a certain love of the life here, right? It can be difficult to get a residence permit extended. At least, the process can take a long time and in the meantime we would have to withdraw your work permit. Wouldn't we? Then there are the tax authorities. They can be exacting too, and they can also be very slow. They can ask for all manner of documentation, receipts, accounts. Insist on meetings, auditing checks, search warrants; delve into the past, contact business associates, demand payments, impose fines, embark on drawn-out court cases. Do you understand what I'm saying?"

"And the church could always excommunicate me, I suppose?" I said.

Carillo smiled. The heavy glowered. He pulled his hand out of his pocket and rapped his thigh slowly and rhythmically with the baton that must have been there all the while, and which he now indicated could be put to use if I didn't listen to reason. A thick, vicious-looking cosh which he had obviously made himself. A solid rubber tube undoubtedly stuffed with lead and iron. These men were about as subtle as bulldozers. They were evidently in a hurry.

"No. There's not really much the church can do, but the investigation could of course involve family and friends," he said, without a trace of irony.

"Keep my wife out of this," I said.

"When the wheels start turning, then the wheels start turning."

"But they can be stopped?"

"They can."

"How can I be sure they won't start turning again?" I asked.

He looked at me, relieved. Now we had a negotiation under way. He was a politician's lackey and he would rather solve problems through honourable compromise, both parties thinking they had come out of it without losing face.

"Nothing gets into print. We get the photographs and negatives, but of course we'll have no way of knowing if you've kept the odd one or two."

"No, you won't," I said.

"It's of no matter. In a modern society it's important to have an insurance policy which covers the unanticipated as well."

"You're a wise man," I said.

He didn't register the sarcasm, or else he didn't want to hear it. I knew that he knew that I would accept the offer. What did the whole business actually mean to me? It meant a good deal of money, but I had all the money I needed. It meant that I would have to swallow a fair share of pride, but it wasn't exactly a case that learned lawyers with expertise in freedom of speech legislation would study for years to come. They were hardly the kind of photographs that ideologists would use in defence of freedom of the press. They were photographs taken because they would excite people's curiosity and appetite for scandal. They were photographs which would fan the flames of righteous indignation, but they wouldn't change anything one way or the other. And, personally, I couldn't care less which politicians were in power. I thought it over while the little bureaucrat waited patiently.

"When can I get out?" I asked.

He hesitated. So there were certain complications.

"In 24 hours. Maybe sooner."

"Why not now?"

"We should at least make it look as if the formalities have been observed, and that means getting you released by the judge. Frankly, we've leant on him a bit to get you in. I don't think we'd be doing ourselves any favours by putting more pressure on him."

"You mean he takes his responsibilities seriously?" I said.

"Perhaps."

"I think it smells fishy."

They had, all things considered, found me with amazing speed.

He paced the cell for a few moments. Watching him, I realised just how little space I actually had. A few steps back and forth. I knew I would go mad if I had to sit alone in a tiny cell for months.

"The business with the judge is genuine. But then of course we might want to have the photographs and negatives in our hands before we, as it were, drop the case. We don't want any, and I mean not any, press coverage," he said.

"I'm in solitary."

"It can be arranged. You'll be given access to a telephone tomorrow morning. You can have newspapers, a radio, a television, whatever food you choose, all the exercise in the yard you want, but the detention order remains in force until, let's say, appropriate authorities appreciate that the case is bound to be thrown out because of the nature of the evidence."

He flung his arms wide. What he was saying was: "This is the deal, I haven't got anything else to offer, I can't go any further. If I have to go further, then I'll need to go and get new instructions."

"OK," I said.

"We've got a deal?"

He was surprised, but what else could I do? What had he expected? That I would shout and scream? Demand immediate release? I was familiar enough with the world he and I operated in to know that although he might be presenting me with a proposal, the bottom line had already been calculated and the figures had to add up.

"We have."

"It's a pleasure to do business with you," he said, and held out his hand.

I shook it. He let me keep the cigarettes and the lighter. They left, wishing me a good night and saying they would see me again in the morning, and I smoked one more cigarette before lying down on the bed and falling asleep. I didn't feel completely comfortable with what I had agreed to, but it was probably the best solution. Oscar would be a little disappointed about the money, but of course he would understand that photographs of an old lecher and a beautiful Italian actress were not worth all the hassle we would have to face if we put them on the market. We had lost a battle. We had lost battles before, just never to the powers that be. We would win others. Against the powerful, too. This was my reasoning, but I was kidding myself. Deep down I was cursing myself for having given in so quickly, and at the same time pleased because I could see my decision as the first step towards quitting one aspect of my job.

I had been thinking about it for quite a while, ever since my daughter had begun to talk. These days I felt something like shame at lying in wait to trap people at their most vulnerable. I'd already thought about stopping in order to concentrate on my portraits and perhaps

77

do some photojournalism. The money wouldn't be the same, but did we really need more money, my little family and I? I had a nice portfolio of securities. If I sold my share in the firm, and if I found a good financial adviser, I would barely have to lift a finger for the rest of my life. Deep down, wouldn't I like my daughter, in a few years' time, to be able to look at me with pride and be able to talk about her father's job without embarrassment? I felt rather relieved. I wasn't exactly going to make a definitive decision that night in the cell, but I took a step or two in the right direction. People are fools. They think they can make decisions, but then discover that fate has shuffled the cards again.

But I managed to fall asleep, which is always a small miracle for me. I knew that things were up and running. I understood Spain well enough to know that it was a rich, civilised and modern country, but the Spanish still laboured under traditions and bureaucracy and everything took its time, so if I was given a telephone tomorrow I could just look at the next day as a day off.

And that's what I did.

A new, younger warder appeared the next morning. He brought coffee and milk, bread and butter and the morning papers plus a radio. And not least a mobile phone which was fully charged and worked. This meant that the cell couldn't have been completely insulated, unless it had been secured with an electronic filter which, in this day and age, they had been able to remove during the night. Because now I thought I could hear sounds: tapping, buzzing, clattering, a voice. It was as if I was no longer completely cut off from the world. Or perhaps it was a special telephone. It wasn't mine, at any rate. It had a ringing tone, but neither a menu nor a memory like my phone, which also showed who had called and the name of the phone company. It was a straightforward, modern device from which you could ring out, but couldn't pass on the number. It occurred to me that perhaps it wasn't a mobile phone at all, but a cordless, so that somewhere a pair of large, state ears were listening in. The new warder said that it was against all the rules, but that he had been instructed to let me have it for 15 minutes, then he would come and fetch it again.

I immediately rang Amelia. She picked up the telephone on the first ring and started crying when she heard my voice, but I calmed her down. I don't think she had slept a wink. She was generally a calm and robust Spanish woman who was not easily unsettled, and she stopped crying so we could talk. I assumed the line was tapped, but they were welcome to hear me saying how much I missed and loved her and how much I looked forward to seeing her and Maria Luisa again. I was fine and would be home within 24 hours. I had a lump in my throat, but spoke in a calm voice and called her only Amelia and not Sugar, our little pet name for each other. She was the daughter of an intelligence officer, so she knew not to grill me. I explained the situation and the deal that had been made.

"The Danish woman has asked after you," she said at one point.

"Who?"

"I can't remember her name."

"Oh, her," I said.

"She asked about . . . yes. You know."

"I've got other things to think about right now," I said, sounding more irritated than I actually felt. Amelia shouldn't have borne the brunt, in any case.

"Is there anything you want me to do?" she asked.

"Talk with your father. I'm fine. See you before long. Kiss the little one."

"I've sent her off to school. I thought it was best. I said you were away on one of your trips."

"You could just have told the truth. I've nothing to be ashamed of."

"Well, I didn't."

"OK."

There was a short silence.

"Pedro," she said.

"Yes, my darling."

"I understand. I love you."

"I love you too."

"Come home soon."

"I shall. Don't you worry. Kiss the little one!"

"Will do."

"*Adiós*," I said, and pressed the button, breaking the connection.

Time was nearly up, so I rang Gloria's direct number. Oscar would be in a state; Gloria would take it calmly. Oscar was in Gloria's office. I could hear him muttering and banging around in the background as I told Gloria what had happened.

"We've got three or four lawyers working to get you out," she said in her familiar and pleasant voice. "But they're using the anti-terrorism legislation, and so are of the opinion that they aren't obliged to say anything. We've gone to court to challenge your detention under that legislation in the first place. It's not looking good, Peter."

"What does Oscar say about it?"

"Oscar is pacing up and down talking about fascism and is of no use to anyone. He's listening now."

"Hello, Peter. Keep your chin up!" I heard him shout.

I explained to Gloria, and an interjecting Oscar, about the offer from the remote powers that be, and I remembered to say that the press had to be kept out of it. Oscar protested in the background and talked about freedom of speech and not giving in to force, but that's easy said when you're not in a cell and won't feel the repercussions, while Gloria was, of course, thinking practically.

"We don't need that kind of harassment. It would damage the business in the long run and we've got to get you out now. I can't bear

80

the thought of you rotting away in some cell. It makes me so damned furious. Do shut up, Oscar! We're based in Spain and don't need the antagonism of the authorities here. Let's get Peter out. What shall I do, Peter?"

I gave her the telephone number of the Minister's lackey, which he had given to me as he left the cell the night before, and asked her to hand over the photographs and negatives to him.

"What about a guarantee?" said Gloria.

"You don't have to bother about that," I said.

"OK, Peter. Anything else?"

"How's Amelia?"

"OK. She's not easily thrown. But of course it's hard. You've got yourself a treasure there, Peter, but then I suppose you know that."

"OK. Thanks."

"Take care of yourself, *carino*. I haven't given up on getting you out today."

"That would be nice."

The line went dead. They must have had some central way of doing that. It was a cordless phone which they could "hang up" somewhere else. A little while later, the new warder came to fetch the phone, and I watched with mixed feelings as he took away my lifeline. I had made contact. There was a world outside. There were friends working to get me out.

It was a boring day, but actually rather relaxing and peaceful as well. Perhaps because it was only a question of time before I was free again. Amelia and Maria Luisa knew that I hadn't come to any harm. Everything had been put in motion and now the cogs were turning calmly and steadily and predictably. It was like waiting for the quarry during an assignment. You had to dig deep inside yourself and make time stand still.

I read the newspapers, slept a bit, smoked cigarettes, exercised in the yard for half an hour and ate again. Chicken soup, this time, followed by a grilled trout, *trucha a la Navarra*. I asked for some coffee and was given it, and lay on my back gazing at the ceiling and actually can't remember how the evening passed. I drank water, read the newspapers again, listened to the radio – they never brought the television – and thought about my family. I watched scenes played out on my inner cinema. Good scenes with Amelia, Maria Luisa and me in the house in the mountains above San Sebastián. Maybe you would expect a day like that to be spent reflecting on life or other profound issues. But that kind of contemplation doesn't just emerge because you've got time. Time simply existed and it passed slowly and laboriously, but a day only has so many seconds. I did a sequence of push-ups and sit-ups and lay down on my back and waited for sleep which, as usual, was a long time coming.

But at last I fell asleep, with a more or less easy mind, not knowing that during these very same hours my world was being completely smashed. That my journey to hell had, without my knowledge, already begun.

# 5

I had a nasty dream just before they woke me up. I was on a camping trip, as if I was a boy scout again, but the camp had been made in a strange, surreal landscape with artificial mountains, fake snow and a delicately burnished, ultra-blue light which could have been created by the Hollywood dream factory or computer generated. It was darker out on the horizon, as if thunderclouds were gathering. The camp fire was a gas-burning contraption in the middle of an open cave with slimy, grey walls. I was bent over a pot which was bubbling like a hot spring in Iceland. In the distance a bird was screeching, over and over again. It sounded like a mixture of a woman's desperate laughter and a death rattle. Oscar was there. He stood with his back to me, wearing one of his impeccable suits. He was taller than usual and was holding a book. It had a black cloth binding. He was wearing a white shirt with a lilac tie. Gloria was standing next to him. She had turned into a red-head. At first she was wearing a long kaftan, like the ones women used to wear in my youth, but suddenly she was naked, just her pubic area covered with a red square like the ones newspapers use on moral grounds. Oscar held out the book to her and she reached out to take it, but her hands were gnarled and aged, with long nails which had grown to different lengths. Oscar said, "Take the book of accounts. Everything has been entered and audited."

Gloria thought better of it and didn't want to accept the heavy black book. "I asked for the hour of reckoning, not the book of reckoning," she said.

I wanted to turn to them and say that Oscar had got hold of the right book, but I knew I had to stir the bubbling pot and I didn't dare move my head, but I saw it all anyway. I was very, very frightened. I was also full of regret because I didn't dare tell Oscar that he had found the right book.

I struggled to wake up, because in the dream an inner voice told me that my own face would soon appear in the diabolical devil's brew and it would be covered with running sores. The whole scene was bathed in opalescent, dark lilac light speckled with silvery, virulent streaks.

I woke with a start.

The fat warder was standing in the doorway. He had a peculiar expression on his face. I was drenched with sweat, my heart was hammering and it felt as if electric currents were running through my head as I struggled to wake up and send my subconscious packing. I sat up and swung my legs out so quickly that I became dizzy and everything went black for a moment.

"I'm sorry, señor Lime, if I startled you," said the fat warder. It was the first time I had heard him speak. His voice didn't go with his body at all. I had expected such a big man to hold a deep guttural bass with the Madrileños' hard consonants, but he had a thin, light voice and from his accent I guessed that he came from Badajoz in Extremadura. I knew the town. One summer I had photographed the storks sitting in their nests on the old, parched, tiled roofs, just like their ancestors had sat there as the conquistadors had set forth to murder, rape and plunder the new world. The image conjured up by his mellow dialect, and the stately white birds on the roof ridges, calmed me and my heart stopped racing.

"That's all right," I said, rubbing my eyes and out of habit gathering my hair into its ponytail.

"May I kindly request señor Lime to come with me?" he said.

His courtesy made me suspicious.

"What's the time?"

"A little after seven o'clock."

"So you're releasing me now? The judge is up early."

"If you would just please come with me, señor Lime," he said.

"What for? Where?"

"Señor Lime. Please. Just come with me. A couple of friends are waiting. Nothing will happen to you. Of that I can assure you."

There was a kind of desperation and at the same time sincerity in his fat face, so I believed him.

"Give me a minute alone," I said pleasantly.

He went out of the cell, but left the door ajar. I had a pee, splashed water on my face and put an elastic band around my ponytail before pulling on my jeans and putting my shirt on over my t-shirt. I was still a bit dazed, as you feel when you've had a stupid dream and have been woken up before it reaches a resolution or you've fallen back into a dreamless sleep.

We trudged along the corridor. It was still quiet in my cell block, but as soon as we started to climb the stairs I heard the intoxicating strains of Madrid's morning symphony. My spirits rose at the thought that I would soon be seeing my wife and child. We reached a wide corridor. It was bustling. That's the word that struck me, because there were several people walking this way and that. I had been alone for so long that seeing several people at once had an overwhelming effect. The sound of their hurrying feet could be heard above the distant turbulence of Madrid's heavy morning traffic, as pleasantly recognisable as one's own face in the mirror. Some nodded, others looked away. I hadn't been isolated for all that long, but it felt like an eternity. I realised what a terrible punishment solitary confinement is. I realised why people who endure weeks

85

and months of it finally crack. The human being is a social animal.

We went into a big office. The judge was sitting behind a desk. Gloria and Oscar were sitting opposite him. They looked as if they had encountered Death. Gloria was red-eyed. It was years since I had seen her like that. Without her usual meticulously made-up face, she suddenly looked older. Her make-up looked as though it had been put on in a hurry. But it was more her expression. It seemed drained of the energy which her beautiful, mature face always radiated. Oscar appeared to be in a stony trance, but still agitated with his usual pent-up energy.

"About time too," I said with cheerful irony. That was our usual tone. "I thought you were going to let me rot in here for ever."

"Sit down, Peter," said Oscar stiffly.

Apprehension made the bile rise in my throat.

"Has something happened to Amelia?" I said.

"Just sit down, Peter!" Oscar repeated.

Gloria came over to me and took my hand and pulled me down onto a leather sofa against the wall. There were two leather chairs to match in front of the examining magistrate's desk. It was a very masculine, but also heavy room which said that rigour and order prevailed here, and possibly justice. There was a transparent plastic bag on the desk, with my things in it: wallet, keys, Leica, mobile phone, lighter, cigarettes.

"What's happened to Amelia and Maria Luisa?" I was shouting now. I don't know why I was so certain. I just knew. But the shock still hit me with a vicious intensity when Gloria, quietly and with tears in her voice, uttered the worst words I have ever heard in my life.

"Amelia and Maria Luisa are no longer with us, Peter. They are dead, Peter. They died in a fire last night. It's so damned unjust and so damned wrong and so damned dreadful."

Then she burst into tears and even though I vomited down her back she kept on hugging me and holding me in her arms.

*

Time evaporated. I don't know how long I was out, but there's a hole in my memory like the empty nothingness of the universe. They told me later that I hadn't fainted, but vanished behind my own eyes as if the light had been switched off and, like a robot, had ground to a halt. I don't know if it was an unpleasant experience because I can't remember anything about it. Just darkness and silence. It lasted ten minutes. Ten minutes as if in a deep sleep. They were afraid that I would never return to the living, but linger among the living dead. They feared that I was turning into a zombie before their very eyes. In a way that's probably what I really wanted, but we cling to life. I look back upon the episode as my body's back-up. Like a computer, when the programme crashed, it closed itself down in order to save fragments from the wreckage and protect the vital parts. I died a little, is how I think of it.

When I came back to unmerciful reality, I was sitting on the sofa with a glass of water in my hand. I swallowed the contents in one gulp. It was cold, but my mouth and my throat remained dry. They stood round me like a tableau of wax figures, set rigid in time, frozen in the moment of eternity. Gloria looked completely depraved. Like a woman who had been startled by her husband while indulging in foreplay with her lover. She was half-naked to the waist, wearing only her black bra and her jacket. I could smell myself and my vomit that was lying like a foul shadow on the floor. Someone must have wiped it up. Gloria's blouse had been stuffed into a plastic bag.

I was given more water.

"Are you OK?" Oscar asked.

"For heaven's sake, Oscar!" Gloria said.

"No. I'm not OK, Oscar. But I'd like to know what's going on," I said.

My voice was unnaturally composed. It was as if I was standing outside my own body, listening to myself speak.

The judge cleared his throat. He sat stoutly with an aloof expression on his face. He had small pig's eyes.

"Señor Lime," he said, and nudged a piece of paper in front of him as if it was unclean, as if it had been used to wipe up my vomit. The smell surrounding me and inside me was like the manure heap on my uncle's farm when I was a boy. I could feel my face going red then pale then red again, but the judge didn't bat an eyelid. Gloria sat down beside me and took my hand while the judge intoned:

"My condolences. Here are your release papers. And your belongings. No further action will be taken. You have the right to seek compensation for wrongful arrest and detention from the State of Spain. I will leave you the use of my office so that you can confer with your friends in peace and quiet. Again, my deepest sympathy. Please sign the receipt before you leave."

He edged out from behind the desk and slid out of the room.

"What's happened?" I asked again. I sat quietly and listened to the story. There were no tears. I was empty and silent inside. Gloria did the talking. Matter-of-fact and precise, like a lawyer quoting a police report, she put cold words to my life's tragedy.

At 1.30 a.m. there had been an explosion in our flat. It had been so forceful that the windows had blown out. The explosion was followed by an intense blaze, which had spread through the whole building. It was gutted. The roof had collapsed. All the flats were burnt out. Only a couple of hours earlier the fire brigade had got the blaze sufficiently under control to be able to send in firefighters equipped with breathing apparatus. Thirteen bodies had been recovered so far, eleven people were injured. The two families on the ground floor had managed to get out, along with the families on the second and third floors. The bodies had been taken to the central

88

institute of forensic medicine. The police had opened an inquiry. Their preliminary theory was that there had been a gas explosion caused by a leaking pipe in the kitchen or bathroom of our flat or the flat below.

She might as well have been a newspaper reporter, and later it appeared just like that in the broadsheets, while the tabloids spread it on thicker, writing about a tragic blaze and following up with leaders about the antiquated, hazardous gas fittings still to be found in Madrid's oldest neighbourhood. Plus all the gossip, of course.

"Are you sure they were home?" I asked.

"Absolutely, Peter," said Gloria. "I'm afraid they're already quite sure."

"I want to see them," I said.

"Of course," said Gloria.

"We can go there right away," said Oscar. "But it won't be pleasant."

"It can't get any worse," I said.

Oscar wasn't good at expressing emotions, but he coped very well. He was visibly shaken, white as a sheet and stooping, as if someone had put a huge boulder on his shoulders. He dragged his feet as he walked across to me, lit a cigarette and stuck it in my mouth. He put his arm round me and there we sat, not saying a word, his strong heavy arm on my shoulders and Gloria's hand in mine, and I smoked my cigarette and tried to comprehend that Amelia and Maria Luisa had been taken from me. I couldn't bring myself to think the word: dead. It didn't seem right. It was too detached and almost normal. People die at some time or other, but my two had been taken from me. Stolen and carried off. I can't describe the sense of emptiness, grief and irrational anger at their having deserted me. I was also filled with guilt at not having long ago had the gas fittings removed and electric heating installed. But gas water heaters still hissed and reeked in thousands of kitchens and bathrooms in the old parts of Madrid.

I had been sad when first my father and later my mother died. But they were both nearly 80. They had lived long lives. It was only natural that they had passed away and left the stage to my older brother and me. They had both died after long illnesses, so we had the impression that they were tired and had enjoyed their fill of life. Maria Luisa and Amelia had been snatched away. It was so damned unjust.

Oscar's big Mercedes 600 was parked in the yard and he helped me into the back seat next to Gloria. The police sentry in his ungainly bulletproof vest lifted the barrier and we drove into what could have been freedom, but freedom for what? To be unhappy? To take my own life? To go back to the bottle? Two television crews and a small group of photographers and reporters were waiting. Cameras were hoisted onto shoulders the moment the mascot on the bonnet of the black Mercedes came into view.

"What is it, Oscar?" I said, when he braked hard so as not to drive into the waiting pack.

"You know what it's like. They get to know about these things instantly," he said.

"How can they?"

"You're part of the package. Of course the rumour spread that you'd been arrested as soon as we began ringing round. Damn it, they knew where you lived. They can put two and two together. There are rumours about the photographs. I had the feelers out, for God's sake."

His voice was hoarse and angry.

"Oscar. Give it a rest. Peter's not a fool," said Gloria.

The television cameras and camera lenses approached the tinted windows as if they were going to nuzzle them. Or penetrate them. Rape the people sitting inside. I could hear the reflectors in the equipment working and heard the journalists shout out, asking how I was feeling, if I had a comment, say something Pedro. It was strange to be sitting on the other side in my grief, when I really ought to have been

90

alone and private. It was strange to be on the other side of the lens. As a young man, one of the waiting wolves outside the restaurants used by the famous and royal in Kensington in London, I had elbowed my way forward to reveal and unmask a human face in all its vulnerable nakedness. Had my face been just as distorted, my mouth open like a fish gasping for air, my eyes the same blend of schadenfreude and excitement? How many times had I seen the victim trying to shield their face even though there may have been nothing to hide? As if an infringement of privacy was both painful and, in itself, created a sense of guilt. I was too desolate to be angry. I just felt so heart-broken.

"Drive me up to Santa Ana, Oscar," I said.

"The whole pack's there, Peter," he said.

"Just do what Peter says," said Gloria.

"OK."

Using the horn, he edged his way through the pack of reporters which parted like water in front of the sharp bows of a large ship. The most persistent ran behind the car for a short distance. When he was clear of them, he accelerated and turned up a side street and drove across the Puerta del Sol and the short stretch up past the office for the bullfights, and negotiated the half kilometre to Plaza Santa Ana via the back streets.

The square was cordoned off. We were stopped, but when Oscar told the policeman who I was we were allowed through. He parked the car on the pavement and we got out. There were four large fire engines in front of my building. *Bomberos* was written on the side of them, a Spanish word which I had always had difficulty connecting with the emergency services. The blue flashing lights were like the twinkling of fireworks in the greyish-white morning. I noticed that it was overcast and a little chilly. There were several parked patrol cars and the flagstones in the plaza were running with soot and water. Firefighters were still hosing the neighbouring building with water. And, like shadows in hell, several firefighters were working in what had been my home just a few hours before. I had covered blazes too. I had stood as a cool observer, thinking only about light, aperture, distance, angles, long shots, close-ups, the story. As a professional you can only live with disaster if you keep it at arm's length.

They were putting out the last flames. The air was thick with soot and smoke and an indefinable stench of death. There was clanking and hissing, crackling radios and the murmuring chorus of voices which you always hear at the scene of a disaster, when people are first silent and then elated at the realisation that they are alive, while others have lost their lives. It could have been me, they think. But I've been spared this time. A tragedy always reminds people that they are only here on borrowed time and that death awaits us all.

I walked towards my burnt-out home. The reporters caught sight of me. Even though I never signed my photographs, I knew most of them from Madrid's Press Club. They started running towards me as I walked in their direction. They pushed and elbowed to reach me first, following that mysterious, all important commandment: you must be first and must not let your competitors get past you. They came to a halt. The lenses pointing at me felt like loaded bazookas, but I kept walking straight ahead and, for a moment, it was as if they felt sorry for me and I managed to squeeze through and reach a cordon from where I could see inside the gutted building.

The stench and the heat hit me in the face, making it burn, and I knew that the photographers got their shots as tears began running down my cheeks. They were tears of grief and despair – perhaps. Or was it just the smoke scorching my eyes?

Everything had collapsed and was drenched with water and giving off little wisps of smoke. There was nothing recognisable. Everything was jumbled together and tangled up. Sooty, white-singed beams lay criss-crossed in all directions. The bathtub was no longer white, but streaked with black. The bathtub was actually the worst thing I could see, because it was recognisable. It was as if a bomb had blown the guts of my house to smithereens. I could hear voices around me. Asking questions and wanting a comment. I couldn't make out one from the other. But they were idiotic questions. How was I feeling? What was I feeling? What would I do? What was I feeling? Repeated in a never-ending stream. As if my feelings could be expressed in words. As if this abyss of emptiness inside me could be described in sentences.

Then Felipe Pujol came right up to me. He stepped in front of me, squeezing himself between two television cameras. I knew who he was. He was a small thickset Catalan, the crime reporter on *El Mundo*.

"Pedro? How are you? Why were you arrested?"

I didn't reply. I looked over his head into the grimy hell that mirrored the hell in which I found myself.

"Pedro? We're old friends. Why were you arrested? Give me a comment."

"Piss off, Felipe," said Oscar behind me. He hadn't got through the press corps as easily as I had. He stood behind me and I sensed, rather than saw, that we were encircled by reporters, by police, by onlookers who had been attracted to the scene of the disaster like flies to a dog turd on a hot summer day.

"Shut up, Oscar," said Felipe. He stepped right up to me, so he was practically standing on my feet, tipped back his head and looked me in the eyes. I could smell him. He had drunk a brandy this morning along with his coffee.

"I hear you've dumped on a Minister. And that's the reason. I hear you've got naughty pictures. And that's the reason. Come on, Pedro. Damn it. You know the score. Give me your story. It could help you. Is it true that you've taken a series of photographs? *El Mundo* would be happy to pay for the exclusive rights."

I rammed my knee into his balls and he collapsed in front of me without a sound, just an agonised, flabbergasted expression on his face. I couldn't have cared less. I turned on my heel and, with Oscar leading the way, pushed through the clamouring pack of photographers, reporters and television cameras. One of them was from morning television. They were undoubtedly transmitting live. They lived off disasters, gossip, scandals, recipes and traffic bulletins. Oscar was big and ploughed straight through and I walked behind him as if in a stupor, as if it was all a dream, blurred and milky white, from which I would wake up in a moment and reach out my hand, grasp Amelia's hand and she would turn and nestle her soft buttocks into my crotch and we would slowly wake together in the snug darkness of the bedroom.

The police finally got their act together and formed a ring round us and steered us over to the car where Gloria was behind the wheel. Oscar sat in the back next to me and the uniformed officers cleared a passage so we could get out of the plaza. It helped when they pulled their truncheons half out of their holsters to indicate that now their patience had run out.

"Damned vultures," said Oscar.

"We're part of the pack ourselves, my dear," said Gloria tonelessly.

What happened next is a bit hazy. As if the nightmare continued. As if it wasn't really happening. I can remember only one exchange of words on the way to see the remains of my beloved ones.

"I want a drink," I said.

"OK," said Oscar.

"No," said Gloria.

Then I was standing in front of two covered bodies in a sterile tiled room. The doctor or policeman pulled the sheet down only a little way. Their hair was covered with something that looked like a bathing cap. But there wasn't any hair left. I could barely recognise Amelia. Her face was charred, but Maria Luisa was hardly burnt at all, as if she had suddenly fallen through the ceiling and had been covered with some kind of protective material. Her eyes were closed. She was a bit sooty and there was a blister on her tiny delicate cheek, but it was the missing eyelashes that made me weep silently. The tears ran down my cheeks. I felt both guilty and ashamed.

"Are they your wife and daughter?" asked the man wearing a white overall.

"Yes."

"I would like your permission to perform a post-mortem."

"Why?"

"It is at my request, señor Lime."

The voice belonged to a middle-aged man wearing a tailored suit. He was standing in the corner of the room, but I hadn't been aware of him. Gloria and Oscar were standing just inside the door, pale as death. Gloria had aged visibly and Oscar was crushing his hands together. Gloria must have had a spare top in the car because she was wearing a simple blue sweatshirt. I hadn't noticed her pull it on, but she was so beside herself that she hadn't fixed her hair afterwards. It swirled around her head as if she had just got up.

"Rodriques, criminal investigation department," he said and held out his identity card. He had slim brown hands and was wearing both a little diamond ring and a wedding ring. Gloria stepped forward to protect me, but I raised my hand and stopped her in her tracks.

"I can't make a decision about that right now," I said.

"You have to," he said. "Your family must be laid to rest."

That was true, of course. In Spain people are buried very quickly. They don't wait up to a week like in Denmark. Perhaps it's a custom which dates back to the old days when bodies couldn't be left for very long in the sweltering heat. Perhaps it has something to do with

Catholics not attaching as much importance to the flesh as we do, but more to the soul.

"But why?" I asked.

He stepped forward and pulled a pair of surgical gloves onto his elegant slim hands and carefully turned Amelia's damaged head. I felt sick, but there was nothing left in my stomach. Small bright dots danced before my eyes.

"Look at this, señor Lime," he said. He pointed out two indentations. With an almost gentle gesture, his thin gloved forefinger followed them round her slender neck below her small, delicate ears. I was dizzy and had trouble focusing. The disfigured neck right in front of my eyes vanished and was replaced by pictures of Amelia's tender white throat when she threw back her head and laughed at something I had said or at one of Maria Luisa's quaint remarks.

"Can you see? I don't understand, and my pathologist doesn't understand, why your wife has these contusions. You can't see what they are?" Rodriques continued.

I must have shaken my head because he continued in the same courteous neutral tone of voice.

"They resemble strangulation marks. As if your wife was choked. And we would like to know if it happened before or after the fire. Do you understand what I'm saying? Whether she was dead when the fire broke out or whether she incurred her injuries afterwards. Possibly got caught on a flex. Whether this is an accident or the murder of 13 people. If it is a case of arson leading to loss of life, then I don't need to tell you that it's a very serious matter indeed. Therefore, we would kindly request permission to perform a post-mortem. You can refuse, but then we will have to go to the courts."

Time stood still. I turned to Gloria and Oscar.

"Sell the photographs," I said and then everything went black.

# PART TWO

# TIME HEALS NO WOUNDS

The greatest grief on earth, I fear,
That is to lose the one you hold dear.
                    – *Steen Steensen Blicher*

# 6

The idea that time heals all wounds is a fallacy. Time heals no wounds, but time dulls the pain like a pill dulls a bad headache. The pain is still there, but it no longer jabs like sharp nails. Time blunts the spiked nails, and the pain that makes you want to scream your grief to the whole world is replaced by a constant, gnawing torment that won't leave you alone, not even at night when sleep is impossible.

The period that followed the death of my family was chaotic and bewildering and, for the first time in my life, I wasn't in control of what was happening to me. It was as if I was a child again and dependent on grown-ups' care and supervision. Well-intentioned people took charge of my life and led me out of the tunnel of darkness to a pallid, sickly sunshine. Gloria and Oscar took care of the purely practical things with their usual efficiency. Insurance, the compensation claim against the authorities and the sale of the ten photographs which Oscar had removed from my flat and which went all round the globe and earned us a fortune. I didn't want to be involved in rebuilding the block and sold out to the insurance company. The compensation payments were considerable, but money couldn't make up for the loss of my negatives. The steel filing cabinets had been neither explosion-proof nor fireproof. Gloria took legal proceedings against the manufacturer and the insurance company. They had to compensate for the unquantifiable, artistic value of the negatives. The potential fortune which had built up over the years every time I had captured a split second of reality on film. My tragedy filled thousands of working hours for many zealous lawyers. I let Gloria and Oscar do as they pleased.

For the first few days after the disaster the media went crazy. Two factors intensified the hysteria which swept through the city. The photographs of the Minister. And the official statement that the fire was being investigated as a murder case. Amelia had been strangled before the blaze. Maria Luisa had been killed by smoke fumes and hadn't burnt to death. The other fatalities were a direct consequence of the fire. Evidence of explosives had been found. The media speculated like mad about why someone would want to blow up my flat. They hinted cautiously at the Minister. He, of course, denied everything, but had to resign because of the erotic photographs. They made his position untenable in a government with family values as its core principle.

Detective Superintendent Rodriques called by now and then to keep me informed. He had nothing to go on. They had only one witness, who had seen two men leaving the flat shortly before the explosion blew out the windows. They were burly, had black hair like millions of Spanish people, and had disappeared down towards the Puerta del Sol. And that's where the trail went cold. Rodriques wondered whether it was an ETA action that had targeted the wrong person. There was a woman with a false identity living in one of the flats, under the witness protection system. She was a Basque and had given evidence against ETA ten years earlier. As had so often been the case, rejection by a lover had made her go to the police and turn informer. One of the leaders had dropped her in favour of another woman. The banal tends to play a bigger role in life than novelists think. She had revealed the identity of one of the underground ETA units in Barcelona and had been given witness protection in return. A new identity and a new life in big city Madrid. Anyone could vanish there.

"Maybe they finally found her, señor Lime," said Rodriques. "The past always catches up with us."

We were sitting at Hemingway's table in the Cerveceria Alemana, drinking coffee. The old waiter, Felipe, watched over me as if I was a fragile piece of porcelain. I don't know why I kept going back to the Alemana. It was just across from my former home, which was now an open sore in the row of houses, demolished, boarded up by a high fence painted green, waiting while applications for planning permission fought their way through the intricacies of the municipal government's red tape. Apart from that, the plaza looked the same as usual in the late afternoon light. The old men and women sat talking or reading newspapers and the children would soon be coming home from school to begin playing their games. It hurt, but the Alemana was my first haunt in Madrid and, even though it grieved me to look across at what had been my house, the place was also a lifeline back to a past that I had started thinking about more and more. I didn't want to forget Amelia and Maria Luisa. The memory of them was both joyful and painful, both melancholy and piercing, but it was all I had left.

"So that's your theory?" I said.

"It's the best there is. The terrorists are very active again. They never forget and they especially never forget an informer. Colleagues in counter-intelligence have heard that they had found out where she was and were going to eliminate her. The explosive used was Semtex from the former Czechoslovakia. There's lots of the old stuff in circulation. Maybe they got it from the IRA, or from their old friends in the GDR. All the other lines of inquiry fizzle out."

He threw out his arms in a gesture of regret.

"How could they get it so wrong?" I said.

"Carmen Arrese shared certain traits with your wife, señor Lime."

Carmen had lived with her husband in the flat underneath ours. Married to a lawyer. Both perished along with their daughter who was the same age as Maria Luisa. The couple had been in their mid-30s.

"Carmen Arrese spoke with an Andalusian accent," I said. "She didn't sound Basque in the least."

"Her parents came from Seville, even though she was born in Pamplona. We re-taught her the language of her childhood. It was one element of her new identity. Of her new story. Her new life. It's not just a question of altering looks. We gave her a completely new life. Even her husband didn't know."

"She was ten years younger. How could they get it wrong?"

"Señor Lime. I can see from the photographs that your wife was a beautiful woman. May God protect her soul. She could easily pass as being ten years younger. Carmen looked older. And actually she was older. We made her younger. Maybe the terrorists made a mistake. Went into the wrong flat. Strangled the wrong woman before they planted the explosives."

"Why blow up the house?"

"We think they planted too much. We think they were inexperienced. ETA has problems recruiting the best today. Maybe a gas leak had something to do with it as well. But we think that your family was killed by mistake. It wasn't aimed at you, but at the woman downstairs. I'm sorry."

"But why explosives?"

"Why spread terror? Anxiety, fear is at the very core of terrorism. Not rationality."

"So the case has been shelved," I said.

He straightened up in his chair.

"By no means. But other, more qualified agencies will be involved.

The State uses huge resources in the fight against terrorists, as you know. The work will be stepped up. My job is to expose murderers. To find killers who commit murder from quite obvious human motives such as sex, greed, jealousy, drunkenness. I have more than enough to do in this city alone. Other people will have to take care of national security."

He looked at me apologetically. He didn't really have anything to apologise for. It wasn't his fault that we had lived in the wrong place. But I was angry anyway, because they had placed a ticking bomb in our immediate vicinity without telling us. Somewhere along the line it was the fault of the State authorities, but my anger was still directed at the unknown assassins who now seemed more real.

Rodriques stood up, shook my hand, thanked me for my cooperation and expressed his condolences again. I stayed for a while and drank another coffee, watching the light outside on the plaza fading into blue. The Alemana slowly filled up with students from the various institutes in the neighbourhood, with their notebooks and their youth and optimistic belief in the endless opportunities the future held. I sat by myself next to the window, knowing that Felipe would make sure I could sit there in peace.

I had stayed with Oscar and Gloria for the first week. My father-in-law and I had arranged the funeral once the bodies had been released after the post-mortem. We had always been courteous and pleasant with one another, but had never shared confidences. It was as if grief brought us closer together without our having to talk about it. That wasn't Don Alfonzo's style. He had served the old Caudillo for 25 years as an officer in the Guardia Civil and commander in one of Franco's numerous security services. He was over 70, a shrunken little man who now looked like Franco had when old. Like so many others, he had gone from serving the dictatorship to serving the transitional government and then democracy. If his hands were stained with the blood of torture victims he didn't show it, and he had never been investigated. In the Spain of reconciliation following the Caudillo's death, there were matters that were best left unmentioned.

The funeral was meant to have been private, and Don Alfonzo, Oscar, Gloria and I were indeed alone with the priest, the altar boy and the gravedigger in the cemetery, but outside the camera lenses were trained relentlessly on us, kept at a distance by the police. It was as private as a television news bulletin. The only thing that spoiled the pictures for my colleagues was the pouring Madrid rain. Or maybe not. The brooding black clouds could have been designed as the stage setting for the final scene of a tragedy. The thunderstorm had gathered dramatically over the mountains and, as we stood next to the coffin, the skies opened. Huge bolts of lightning like blasts of flashbulbs could have symbolised the day ahead. I had been a paparazzo all my adult life. I hated the label, but I suppose it was fitting for my job, even though I had always referred to myself as a photojournalist. Now it was my turn to be hunted down by the paparazzi wherever I set foot.

It had begun on the morning of my release. In a live broadcast on the morning show, the television-watching population of Madrid had seen me flooring the reporter from *El Mundo*. My tear-stained face had been on the front page of all the tabloids and in a prominent position inside the more serious broadsheets. I had been stalked to Gloria and Oscar's flat, to my interviews with the police, to restaurants, to the office. For a week I had the feeling that there was a camera trained on me constantly. That it was unpleasant goes without saying. Did I empathise more with my own victims? Not particularly. I had no feelings other than guilt, anger and grief, thinking only of myself. We hoped to be left in peace after the funeral, but even here, on the way to the cemetery near my father-in-law's house, the pack was after me. Like shadows in Hades' underworld, they followed me wherever I went. They pleaded for my understanding. Begged for my cooperation. Promised me money for a one-to-one interview, and illustrated their broadcasts and articles with pictures of my distraught face in front of the scene of the fire, and the Minister kissing the Italian actress's shapely toe. My own words, spoken to other celebrities, echoed in the cacophony of voices which buzzed around me now.

I can't remember what the priest said. I can hardly remember the funeral at all. They were buried in a shared coffin, and I threw a flower down onto it and walked away arm in arm with Don Alfonzo. Neither of us had any tears. I can actually remember only the drumming of the rain on the white coffin and the priest standing under a black umbrella held by a young altar boy, while the words *earth to earth, ashes to ashes, dust to dust* were intoned in Latin. I didn't believe it for a second. I was angry with God, so I must have believed in him, but everything was still dark and clouded, like the sky from which the rain was pouring down.

Afterwards all I really wanted to do was drink, but Gloria made me take a sleeping pill and tucked me up in bed like a little baby.

Now it was nearly two months later. A mild May had passed into a warm June and a hot July, and when the August sun made the city seethe it wouldn't be long before Madrid closed down. I moved in with Don Alfonzo in the comfortable, roomy villa he owned in a little village outside Madrid. In the shadow of the mountains, he was spending his retirement reading about the Spanish Civil War and growing tomatoes, orchids and other flowers. After a while I couldn't stand Gloria fussing around me any more, so I had gone out to my father-in-law who gave me a room in one of the gables of his house, with a view across the plain which was abruptly interrupted by the grey-green mountains in the distance. I sat staring at them for hours, while I thought about nothing and everything. He made sure that I got something to eat, but otherwise left me in peace.

Some days I went with him on his expeditions in the surrounding countryside where he was exploring the old trenches from the siege of Madrid in 1937 and 1938. He had been just a lad at the time, but child soldiers are not an African invention. They had fought on both sides during the bloody, savage confrontation when General Franco rose against the legitimate government of the Republic. We found old weapons and pieces of rusty barbed wire and helmets shot to pieces and other relics of the bloody fratricidal wound in the history of Spain. Alfonzo made a note of everything and drew meticulous maps of where he thought the lines of trenches had been when the fascists tried to capture Madrid. Huge passenger planes flew lazily above us on their way to and from the airport. They were a conspicuous sign of change, of a Spain that had forgotten the grand overture to the slaughter of the Second World War.

We didn't say very much to one another. We found a slope where we sat and shared a loaf of bread and some cheese and ham from one of the small local farms. Don Alfonzo drank wine. I couldn't bring myself to address him as Juan or just Alfonzo. He was an old-fashioned man and it came naturally to address him with the formal *Don*. I drank cola. I felt that I must keep my promise to Amelia. Mostly we sat in silence and then I would tell him that I could hear the grasshoppers in the shimmering heat of the plain. He liked to hear me say that. It was one of the things he missed. Hearing the vibrating tune of the grasshoppers, the monotone melody of summer. We never talked about our loss. There wasn't anything to say. It was simply too unbearable. Don Alfonzo would say something like, "As long as there's a fine little wine, fresh-baked bread and a good piece of cheese, it can't all go wrong," as if he was quoting Graham Greene who he had undoubtedly never read, but I didn't tell him that. I would reply, saying something like, "They're singing loudly today, the grasshoppers." He would cup his hand behind his ear and try to listen. Using his hand to form an ear trumpet to try to catch the high-pitched quivering sound just once. He was looking very old, with paper-thin skin covering his narrow cheekbones. Older than 72 anyway. He had looked ten years younger than his age in the past. Now he just kept his precise little moustache ruler-straight and he dressed every day in clean clothes, which his housekeeper put out for him. She was a 60-year-old widow from the neighbouring village who came every morning and cleaned, did the washing and the shopping and prepared his meals. The fullness of his body faded. He wasted away a little more every day, as if he was being slowly airbrushed out of the picture before my eyes. I had the impression that he enjoyed my silent company, our occasional words hanging in the parched midday heat. He would point at a stork's nest, saying:

"That was there during the war too. I remember it. I was lying over there, shooting in the direction of the city. The Republicans wore red scarves round their necks. It was stupid of them, but they were anarchists after all, so it was a kind of uniform for them, even though they were actually against uniforms and badges of rank. That's why the communists loathed them. They devoured one another. They were easy targets in those scarves. But I didn't hate them."

It was a conversation with neither point nor substance. Everything we did had just the one purpose, to pass the time. To let the slowly ticking seconds of our lives pass, without losing our sanity.

It was for this very reason that I took photographs of ants. Otherwise, I didn't take photographs any more, at least not of people. But I bought some new equipment and photographed the big anthill at the bottom of my father-in-law's garden. The garden covered almost 4,000 square metres on a gentle slope, and was well-kept, with cypress trees and large red geraniums and my father-in-law's two greenhouses where he pottered about looking after his flowers and tomatoes. The ants were large and reddish-black, working and struggling from morning to evening. I took long shots of the anthill, medium shots and sharp close-ups of the formidable beasts. I studied them intimately and was impressed by their talent for organisation. Their progress to and from the anthill made me think of the construction work of a Roman legion. The worker ants were just like legionnaires as, in marching step, they took waste products from the mound and food and building materials home to their queen. Time stood still, but moved on anyway, as I scrutinised them for hours on end. It was the same sensation of timelessness I'd had as a child, sitting on the toilet watching the myriad of patterns and squares on the terrazzo flooring. I used to imagine that it was a town inhabited by small creatures who reported to me on their lives, and their victorious campaigns. The stone floor became a whole world populated by these creatures who I controlled and yet didn't control, because my imagination seemed to wander at their bidding along the paths they chose. The same daydreams came tumbling into my mind at night, as I stood in the bathroom and developed prints from the negatives. It was like beginning again. I had my Leica and some equipment which I set up every night. I could have been a child again. I took photographs that were of no use whatsoever. Which had no purpose other than to kill time.

In order to get back and forth between Don Alfonzo's house and the city, I had bought a motorbike. Now I paid for my coffee and left the Cerveceria Alemana, driving out of the city along with millions of others. It was a powerful Honda 750 that I rode swiftly and recklessly, moving in and out of the lanes of cars. Oscar had muttered something about a subconscious death wish, and maybe he was right. But maybe it wasn't all that subconscious. I drove fast and I took risks, but I also enjoyed the feeling of the wind in my hair as I left the suburbs behind and could glide through the twists and turns along the small back roads leading to my father-in-law's house.

He was pottering in the garden as usual. I could see his bleached straw hat as he nipped the tomato shoots and watered the plants. I fetched a cola and a glass of chilled rosé for Don Alfonzo, and sat out on the terrace. It was very warm and very quiet. There was a droning sound in the distance, a plane lazily banking and beginning its approach. The cicadas were singing and I could see a donkey in the neighbour's field. Apart from the airport it was as if time had stood still just 40 kilometres from Madrid. There was something eternally Spanish about the evening. The shimmering heat slowly rising into the clear, gleaming firmament and the little lights emerging in the twilight out towards the mountains on the horizon.

He sat down with a formal *buenas tardes*, took off his hat and mopped his tanned forehead. We sat for a while in our usual, comfortable silence that never felt awkward. Then I recounted my conversation with Rodriques. He listened without interrupting. I often forgot that this taciturn old man had been one of the Franco regime's astute intelligence agents, with many important contacts all over Europe. Franco's Spain may have been officially abhorred and isolated by the rest of Western Europe, but Franco was, above all, anti-communist and harboured American air-bases even though at the time the country wasn't a member of NATO. Franco's Spain was the USA's friend because he was the enemy's enemy, and the CIA worked in close collaboration with the Spanish security services.

When I had finished, he waited a moment and then began to speak in his usual, drawn-out manner. The sentences came slowly, punctuated by pauses. He was a man who had all the time in the world.

"Yes, Pedro. It sounds plausible. But my life has taught me that intelligence work is like an iceberg. Most of it is hidden beneath the surface. Information is a currency with no fixed exchange rate. Its value fluctuates, and words cover both lies and the truth. People want confirmation that a piece of information is important. That it is significant. That the very thing you and I can tell them is crucial, that it is the one thing that counts. People and organisations have in common the need for solutions and explanations. The equation must work out, otherwise we get uneasy."

"You don't believe it, then?"

"It certainly sounds very logical and reasonable. It has ETA's finger-prints all over it. Mistakes happen, but the whole thing bears the stamp of that ruthlessness which is at the heart of terrorism. It would be good for you and me too – it would give us a little peace if we had an explanation. Perhaps it would heal our wounds if the senselessness of their deaths made illogical, absurd sense. If there was a reason for our loss. Perhaps."

We were getting close to what was usually left unsaid. So I sat quietly for a while before I spoke.

"I thought I'd go to San Sebastián."

"Of course. It might be a good idea. Try to do something. But Rodriques is right – the State will leave no stone unturned. It will use all its resources to obliterate the malignant tumour in our society."

"Well, I've got some old contacts there."

"I know, Pedro. But the police know them too."

"They're clean today."

"Nevertheless," he said.

He knew what I was talking about. In 1977, before the first free election in 40 years, Spain had given full amnesty to all members of ETA who renounced the use of weapons. Political prisoners had been released, and the slate wiped clean. The vast majority of the old members of ETA had given up arms and now lived normal, lawful lives in the Basque Country, which had achieved a degree of self-governance under the old Basque name of Euskadi. But a new generation of young Basques kept up the armed struggle against the Spanish State, and they surpassed the old partisans in ruthlessness.

"They're Basques, above all. They've laid down their weapons, but they're still reluctant to talk to the police. They don't want to be informers. Maybe they'd talk to me?"

"Maybe. It will give you something to do, Pedro. I understand."

"I'd like your help."

"I understand."

"You're in a position to make inquiries, to ask."

"Let me give it some thought. I'm an old man."

He took a careful sip of his rosé. I went in to get our supper. The food would be ready and waiting, I just had to add the final touches. The villa was well-planned and sparsely furnished, but there were more than enough books. It was two-storied, with an open-plan ground floor and a large, comfortable kitchen. The tiled floor and bare white walls made the interior feel cool. There were four rooms upstairs; one of which was mine. In the living room, under a picture of the Virgin Mary holding the Infant Jesus, Don Alfonzo had placed a photograph of Amelia and Maria Luisa. I had taken it one summer's day two years earlier, in the garden, in front of his beloved tomato plants which were weighed down with ripe, red fruit. Amelia and Maria Luisa were laughing at the camera and there was a glow like a halo around their light summer frocks. It was a beautiful and happy photograph and it made me ache every time I saw it, but Don Alfonzo refused to put it away. There were two candles next to the framed photograph and I knew that he lit them when I wasn't home.

I made a tomato salad using his sun-ripened fruit, and fried some lamb chops in oil with garlic and basil from the garden. Doña Carmen, his housekeeper, had also bought fresh bread. I put everything on a tray and poured a glass of red wine for the old man, found another can of cola in the fridge and arranged it all on the terrace table. We ate in silence. We didn't eat a lot and I don't know how much we enjoyed the meal, but we had to eat. I washed up, made coffee and took it out to him with his evening brandy. He smoked his second cigar of the day. It was completely dark now. A soft and lovely darkness that enveloped us and muffled all the sounds around us and made the distance appear clearer.

"I used to believe in life," he said. "I actually believed there was some point to it. I lost my faith in God in the trenches outside Madrid. But, then again, many of us did. I regained my faith when Amelia was born. A person can't live in a void. A person who can't pray is an unhappy person. When my dear wife died in childbirth, I was unhappy, but it was fate and I didn't blame God."

There was another long pause, before he continued.

"This century has been one long violation. But on the eve of the next millennium, we have cause for certain optimism. If I disregard the commandment about not being conceited, I can even feel a certain pride on behalf of my generation. We overcame Nazism. We overcame communism. Two ideologies born in blood and lived in blood. We overcame fatal poverty here in Europe. My own country? Maybe you won't believe me, but during those years under Franco, I felt that although the means we used weren't always sound, their objective was to make Spain civilised. The country I was born in over 70 years ago was a poor, underdeveloped and isolated country, rife with destitution and illiteracy, hatred and cruelty. A million people lost their lives in the fratricidal war. Deep wounds and scars split the country for 40 years. Such terrible hatred. Spain today? Look around. We are a civilised, democratic country. That makes me happy. It makes me happy that once again a king is protecting my native land. It makes me happy that the new generations take it for granted. That was the whole purpose, after all. That living in peace is taken for granted."

Another pause and then he continued in a low voice.

"When Amelia and Maria Luisa were taken from us, God died for the second time in my life. This time I don't think He will be revived again. But I have hope, and if I damn Him, then I must believe that He's there. Why damn a being that doesn't exist?"

He paused, and in the stillness of the warm night his words were like an echo of my own thoughts at Amelia and Maria Luisa's funeral. Don Alfonzo went on.

"I go to Mass, I hear the familiar words, I close my eyes, I fold my hands together, and nothing happens. I still can't pray. My prayers have dried up, like this garden in August. I can't go to confession. My sins are not as great as His negligence, so why should I confess them to Him and ask Him for forgiveness? Therefore I can't receive the Sacrament either. This time He is dead. He is as dead as my daughter and my grandchild. I do so want to believe again in the Resurrection and eternal life, but I can't."

His eyes shone in the yellowish light spilling softly from the living room and across the terrace. I had never seen him cry. I had never seen him express great emotion, at least not in words. I had seen, on countless occasions, the special expression of happiness that spread across his face when he looked at his granddaughter. He was a product of his times and his life. A punctilious man who had lived according to a code of honour. I put my hand on his and squeezed it tight. It was dry and cool despite the evening heat. We never touched one another, and for a moment I thought he would pull his hand away, but instead he put his other hand over mine and clasped it. I think he was weeping. But inside. There were no tears, and his voice was as calm and steady as usual when he spoke.

"I'll help you, Pedro. Not because I think it will be of any use. I don't even want revenge. What use would that be? Do I believe in justice? Hardly. Then why? Two reasons. Because it will dull the pain that I can see you trying to conceal from me and from yourself. Perhaps revenge will help to purge you. Or at least the quest for revenge. To show that one is doing something. And secondly, because I owe it to you. A deficient and all too late thank you for giving my daughter her happiest years – and an old man a few years of happiness in the radiance of his only grandchild."

# 7

I went to the office the next day. Madrid was groaning in the heat. The asphalt was bubbling, the leaves on the trees were dusty and dry, and the flowers – which the municipal authorities failed to water with the plentiful supply from the mountains – hung their heads in just the same way as the few tourists queuing up outside the Prado. The vibrant, white light shimmered between the buildings and the sluggish, tooting traffic. Drops of water evaporated into gleaming rainbows round the fountains, ice clinked in drinks under the shade of pavement café parasols, and tempers were short. The sun beat down over the rocks on the plain. The millions who living in the concrete pile wheezed through the long, arid day, but air conditioning in the offices ensured that the business of earning money could continue with cool efficiency.

Our office was on the fashionable Paseo de la Castellana. Oscar and Gloria owned the whole building, occupying the penthouse flat with the same aplomb with which they dominated any gathering they chose to grace with their presence. On the floor below, we had broken down the walls between the small, old flats and created two large spaces. OSPE NEWS was on the left when you stepped out of the lift, Gloria's law firm was on the right. Efficient young lawyers and their secretaries tapped away on computers and whispered into telephones, fired off emails and churned out important faxes. They were the lungs of modern society. They were equally predators and spiritual advisers, sheriffs and jailers. Lawyers had their fingers in every pie, and each telephone call meant more money in the bank. Time was money. Money was God. For tax reasons Gloria's firm and OSPE NEWS were independent of one another, but in practice they were intricately entwined.

Gloria was successful. She could pick and choose from the annual clutch of newly qualified, talented lawyers who would happily work 70 hours a week for a few years in order to be in the running as one of the select few who, after years of well-paid servitude, were made partners in her firm.

As a fledgling lawyer during the twilight of the Franco dictatorship, Gloria had made a name for herself by taking on political cases. She defended socialists and communists, liberals and trade unionists, student activists and ETA or GRAPO terrorists. She fought like a lioness on their behalf in the courts and the press. Television loved this young, beautiful, dark-eyed lawyer with wild hair and an unwavering commitment.

These days she still took on a few of the more sensational criminal cases, either waiving her fee or accepting the modest legal aid paid by the authorities to a defence counsel. Most often they were cases in which the accused was poor or female. Particularly important to her heart were women defendants who had murdered a violent husband in order to protect themselves and their children. She frequently won, securing an acquittal or a very light sentence. These cases attracted a great deal of media coverage. She took them on both because she loved the battle in court against men who were no match for her and because she got to be on television. The people didn't forget her, and the publicity attracted clients like my ants were attracted to an open honey pot. Money also poured in from property cases, copyright disputes, actions for damages – and the sale of my and the agency's photographs. I had a good shareholding in both companies. The three of us were so inextricably entwined that, even though we had our ups and downs, we were as good as forced to stick together like a long-standing ménage à trois – till death should us part.

OSPE NEWS had eight permanent employees in Madrid alone, dealing with the administrative side of the business, and a network of freelancers all over the world to supply photographs and check that our copyright was protected. In recent years, we had also started making videos and had set up a successful media suite on the floor below, renting out equipment and crews to television reporters, but we made the serious money from the burgeoning television advertising market. Young men with crew cuts worked with powerful editing software, manipulating sounds, words and images to create the modern version of the sirens – the seductive, bogus message that happiness can be achieved only by the purchase of this, and only this, product.

We were standing by the window in Oscar's spacious office with its modern, pale Scandinavian furniture. I was drinking cola. Oscar and Gloria were drinking water. The air was dry and cool, in sharp contrast to the grimy, shimmering heat lying across the city outside. My office was opposite Oscar's, with the secretaries sharing an open-plan area in between. I had an old desk, a new computer, a telephone, a shabby Børge Mogensen sofa I had picked up in Madrid's Rastro market, and an old Spanish-made, 20-inch television. I didn't have the meeting table for twelve, new furniture, modern Spanish art hanging on the walls, high-tech swivel chair behind a large desk and Danish Bang and Olufsen multi-media system that Oscar had installed as tangible confirmation of his success. I had spent time at the office only intermittently before "the incident", as I called it. I had preferred to work at home. And over the last couple of months I had more or less stayed away completely.

We were comfortable, yes, rich actually. I listened with only half an ear as Oscar told me how well business was going. They were pleased to see me and had immediately instructed the secretaries to field their constant telephone calls and postpone and cancel meetings, but not their lunch appointments. They knew I wouldn't stay that long. They fussed around me as usual and hugged me and said kind words. Their well-meaning concern irritated me. I wished they would return to their usual sarcastic, ironic manner and quick-witted repartee, but I loved them anyway. Somehow or other they were my family. And all I had left now.

I looked at my old friends. We were each pushing our half century, but we didn't look it. We were tanned, well groomed and, on the surface, bristling with arrogance and confidence. We kept ourselves trim and fit. We were closer to death than birth, but faced up to that fact only in our nightmares. We counted on getting the better of the Grim Reaper, just as we had got the better of most things so far. Oscar was wearing one of his pale, lightweight Armani suits, Gloria an elegant, floaty summer frock which accentuated her cleavage with its hint of a black lace bra, and stylish sandals on her feet that revealed red varnished nails. And I was wearing a t-shirt and a pair of jeans which had cost as much as a farm worker's monthly board and lodging. I was casually dressed, but from my handmade boots to my expensive t-shirt, I knew that quality cost what it cost.

We had come a long way, we three, old left-wing rebels who had met in this city so very long ago. Back then we had been poor and idealistic. We had believed in the future. With the invulnerability of youth we had seen everything in black and white. There were the others. And then there was us. We were a generation who had wanted to build a new world on the ruins of the old one, and the first step towards a democratic, socialist republic had been taken when the shrivelled old Caudillo had rotted away on his sick bed. When had we changed? Not on any specific day. Not suddenly, but gradually we had become different. Before long we were no longer in our 20s, but in our 30s and couldn't, without a self-conscious, silly grin, say along with Bob Dylan that we didn't trust anyone over 30.

It would be too ridiculous to maintain that we were rebelling against "the establishment" when we ourselves were now an integral part of the elite of modern society. Lawyers living off injustice, tax evasion, impenetrable laws, the cryptic clauses of contemporary life, the EU's jungle of splendidly incomprehensible regulations – and a photographer who provided breakfast entertainment with his telltale pictures of the peccadilloes of the rich and famous. A constant diet of fresh scandals, tragedies and happy couples on which to feast.

We were successful and rich, but were we happier than when we were young? The question was ridiculous. Being young is about being free from responsibility and having no fear of death. We had been happier then because we didn't yet have anything to lose. It wasn't until we experienced the pain of loss that we discovered we were no longer immortal. Once we had realised that one day we would die, we lost our innocence, and life was never the same again.

They didn't think it was a good idea for me to go to the Basque Country. They didn't think that my playing private detective was a good idea at all.

"Well that's not really what I intend to do," I said. "I need to get away. I'll have a little chat with Tómas and some of the others from the old days and stay in the house for a while. I'll feel like I'm doing something."

I had yet to visit the holiday cottage Amelia and I owned outside San Sebastián. The neighbouring farmer looked after it. I still dreaded seeing it again. The fire had effectively wiped out all the material reminders of my family that had been in the flat, but in the house there would be clothes, photographs, toys, books, smells – physical and mental mementoes.

"I've got a better offer for you," said Oscar. "I've got a tip-off that Charles is going to have a weekend tête-à-tête with that horsy woman – but with the children. Just picture it. Those poor children with the bad fairy and the chilly prince. You could get a photograph that would go round the globe, Peter. It'll need some planning to get close enough, but you can do it. Your mind will be on something else. You'll be moving on. You'll . . ."

He dried up. He didn't usually. Maybe he could see from my expression that he was going into territory that he should avoid. I didn't respond. Gloria gave him one of her looks and smiled sweetly at me.

"Maybe it's a good idea, Peter," she said. "But you'll fly, won't you?"

She had always been mistress of the ambiguous statement. What was a good idea? Oscar's or mine? I chose to think that she meant mine.

"No. I'll take the motorbike," I said.

"I hate that dangerous contraption. And you don't even wear a helmet."

"You're getting too old to play at Easy Rider," Oscar said.

"I'm not going to throw away my watch, but otherwise it's pretty close to the mark. I don't own anything any more. I'm actually back to where I was when we met. No worldly goods. A rucksack with some clothes, just the one camera. Lots of memories."

Oscar laughed.

"Old fool," he said. "There's quite a big difference. You've got three or four credit cards and rather a lot of money in the bank and even more in the form of a most profitable business which you share with your two dearest friends. If you're anything, you're an old champagne-hippie. It's not quite like when you and I met, with just a *duro* between us. When we didn't know where the next meal was coming from and we couldn't have cared less either."

This was the Oscar of old. It made me laugh. For a moment Gloria looked as if she thought he was going too far, but he spoke it in his disarming, charming manner which made you laugh at yourself and at him and with each other. His broad face and high forehead were wrinkled now, but it was easy to see the lad in the adult face. He had always been able to resolve a situation with a string of words using cadence, body language and his big smile to make his point by means of the unsaid. Under the words. Like the iceberg in Hemingway's writing.

"OK, OK," I said. "I've just got to get away."

"And Don Alfonzo?" said Gloria.

"We help each other."

"You'd be better off leaving it to the authorities. They're going through the city with a fine-tooth comb. They won't give up. The State will not tolerate terrorism," said Gloria.

Her face was smooth, with a few attractive wrinkles round her eyes. She was a big woman and worked hard to keep her ample figure under control, both in the gym and courtesy of the most skilled plastic surgeons. There had been no need for major surgical intervention yet. Just a few specific corrections to face and breasts in order to counteract the unfair ageing process.

The morning radio, television news and the daily papers had reported that the crimes had been the work of ETA. That the criminal Basques had done it again. The press carried almost daily reports about the murder of one or other innocent right-wing politician, but this time it was considered really vicious, the worst for a very long time. The people of Madrid groaned in exasperation. Now they not only had to endure the heat, but also police cordons, checks, searches, sniffer dogs, warnings to be vigilant. But I knew the Madrileños well enough to realise that this story would be forgotten within a couple of days too. I had already had several reporters on the line that morning. I preferred being the hunter to being the hunted. Magazines and television talk shows rang every day and my secretary turned them down with patient composure. Now I was being asked to be interviewed for a strange series on grief management. Do photographers have a moral responsibility? Does God feature in your daily life? Did I want the death penalty introduced for terrorism? Which is the best book of the year? My opinions were interesting because I was interesting. I had suffered. I was a celebrity. The entertainment business was grinding out its never-ending diet of opinions on this, that and everything.

I said no to all of it.

"They haven't claimed responsibility. They usually do," I said.

"Not if they've made a terrible mistake."

"I'll have a chat with Tómas. And a couple of the others. But you know them! We're bound to end up just talking about the old days," I said.

"Well then, at least take this with you. You've got to get back to living in the modern world," said Oscar. He handed me my mobile phone and its charger. I hadn't switched it on since the police confiscated it. Oscar had apparently brought it back to the office. I took it hesitantly.

"We'd like to be able to get hold of you," said Gloria. "We care about you, Peter."

Now they were getting sentimental again. I keyed in my PIN number and the telephone came to life, beeping peevishly. There were, of course, numerous messages via the answering service. I sat down and listened to them. A couple were from sources, a couple from business associates and more casual friends expressing their sympathy, and the last one, just before the tape had run out, was from Clara Hoffmann. Her cultivated, lilting voice, speaking the Danish I wasn't used to hearing any more, came across clearly. There was a faint background noise, which could easily have come from below on the Plaza Santa Ana if she had rung from the balcony of the Hotel Victoria, and I tried to picture her as she had looked the day we went to the Cerveceria Alemana.

"Peter Lime. I am so terribly sorry to hear of your tragedy. I feel for you and send my deepest sympathy, even though words have little meaning at such a time. I'm returning to Denmark today. I won't trouble you with my inquiries; however, I have to say that we are still interested in learning more about the woman and the man in the photograph. If you can help in any way – when the time is right for you, of course – if you want to get in touch with me, please ring me in Copenhagen. Otherwise, I'll be getting back to you at some point. And again, I'm so sorry. More than words can say."

She gave me two telephone numbers and, out of habit, I waved my hand in the air for a pen and wrote them down on a slip of paper which I stuffed in my pocket before clearing her message too.

"Who was that?" Gloria asked. I must have had a strange look on my face.

"Something I'd forgotten about. A woman from the National Security Service – Danish – who contacted me just before, yes, just before, you know. About a photograph from the past."

"Oh right, that," said Oscar.

"What are you talking about?" said Gloria.

"Nothing. It doesn't matter," I said.

"Presumably it's lost like all the others," said Oscar.

"It'll probably be in the suitcase," I said.

They looked at me again.

"What suitcase?" said Gloria.

"Nothing," I said. "Forget it."

Gloria became businesslike, putting on her lawyer's voice, the cut-glass, sharp tone which loosened the stomachs of her male opponents in court.

"Have you got negatives and prints that have survived? Because if you have then I, as your lawyer, would like to know. We are in the middle of a massive action for compensation against the insurance company. We're basing it on the fact that you've lost your professional foundations, your professional assets, and that you should thus receive compensation. I'm not going to stand up in court, Peter, and plead your cause if the other side could suddenly pull valuable photographs out of the hat. The case rests on the fact that everything, and I mean everything, was lost in the fire. So what's this all about?"

Oscar's secretary stuck her head round the door.

"London," was all she said and Oscar left the office, giving me a long, hard look.

"Out with it, Lime," said Gloria.

"Over the years, I've put aside some negatives and prints and kept them separate from the rest."

"Why?"

"I don't know. Some people write diaries. My photographs are my diary. Some people collect stamps. I collect moments in time."

"What kind of photographs?"

"Professional, personal, important, inconsequential, ugly, beautiful. My photographs."

"You mean Lime's photographs? The Jacqueline Kennedy negative, for instance?" she asked.

"For instance."

"It won't stand up in court. That one alone is worth a million. Where are they? I want them valued."

"Out of the question."

"Peter!"

"Forget it. It's not important."

"Where are they?"

"I'm saying it doesn't matter!"

"You're making things difficult, Peter."

"Then drop the case."

"Certainly not. We've got every chance to screw those arrogant men in their tight-fisted insurance companies."

It was the battle. It was the brawl. It was the chance to take arrogant men down a peg or two that motivated her, and not really the money at all. I didn't say anything and we stood in awkward silence, which was unusual for us. Tobacco is a saviour, so we each lit a cigarette and blew the smoke away from one another, managing to break eye contact without making it too conspicuous, but Oscar could sense the tension in the air when he came back into the office.

"Well, well," he said. "And which angel might have passed through here while I was out?"

"It doesn't matter. I can tell you later," said Gloria. "Go on your trip, Peter. We'll talk again when you come home. Nothing will happen before October at the earliest, anyway. Go on your trip on that infernal machine of yours. Get the shit out of your system."

Oscar seemed to want to say more, but Gloria's look silenced him, and they went through the ritual, saying that all three of us should go out for lunch, and that they could clear their diaries. But I released them from their torment, letting them go to one of their American-style power lunches or perhaps a rendezvous with a lover, while I drove in the midday heat to the Danish Embassy, where I picked up my new passport, and then home to say goodbye to Don Alfonzo. Madrid suddenly felt like a straitjacket that threatened to suffocate me. The buildings leant in over the congested streets like gravestones, as if they were about to topple, making my head swim.

Gloria and Oscar had seen me out with cheerful talk of holiday plans. Madrid's unbearable August was knocking on the door. Gloria wanted to go to her beloved London. Oscar wanted to spend a couple of weeks playing golf in cool Ireland and then meet up with Gloria in London. I sort of promised to join them at some point. Business and pleasure. If we were going to meet in London, we might as well check up on our British operation which, like everything else Gloria and Oscar touched, purred like a fat cat skimming off the cream. But I got the feeling that what they really wanted more than anything was to have their old friend Peter Lime back, and for the incident never to have happened, or at least be forgotten.

Don Alfonzo wasn't home. He had left a note saying he had gone to the city and anticipated staying in a hotel for a couple of days while he looked over our case, he wrote, and he wished me good luck on my trip. He had put one of his most beautiful orchids in a small blue glass vase next to the note. I understood, because while he knew that I found no comfort in visiting the cemetery, he was encouraging me to say goodbye.

I often forgot to eat, but Doña Carmen had made a salad with serrano ham that I ate in the shade on the veranda while I watched the shimmering heat over the mountains. I felt empty and miserable, as usual, and I missed my wife and my child with a force and pain that was physical, and which I wouldn't have imagined possible. I missed them constantly. Day and night. At regular intervals the monster raised its head with a force so painful that I thought I would go out of my mind.

I made some coffee and then packed a rucksack with a change of clothes and strapped it onto the motorbike. The air vibrated with the droning buzz of the grasshoppers. The smell of dust and tomato plants and a gentle coolness drifted across from Don Alfonzo's garden, which he had undoubtedly watered before he left. I locked up the house, swung my leg over the Honda and drove slowly to the cemetery, the orchid resting in my lap.

The white crosses and tall marble headstones were beginning to redden in the early evening sun. We had chosen a simple stone with their names and their two decisive dates: birth and death. And that was all. Don Alfonzo's orchid was on the right. I put mine to the left of his and then rested on one knee for a while, wishing with all my heart that

I could pray or weep, but nothing ever came. There were no voices, no God, no revelation, no transfiguration, no inner conversation with the bereaved. There was just a gnawing guilt and a smouldering, irrational rage at them for leaving me, for leaving me alone and lonely. It should have been rage directed at their murderers, but that wasn't how I felt that day.

I followed the traffic round Madrid and opened the throttle when I reached the old main road north. I chose it in preference to the motorway. It was as familiar as an old glove. I had driven along it hundreds of times. As photojournalist on my way to the big Basque demonstrations for autonomy at the end of the 1970s, and with Amelia and Maria Luisa on our way to the holiday cottage near San Sebastián.

Evening fell, and the sun sank on my left in a profusion of reds which crept down over the mountains and across the plain in a slow red tide. It was always a thrilling and strange feeling to leave a big Spanish city and get out into the countryside. In the middle of Madrid you could forget that Spain is a big empty country where the horizon is constantly pulled further and further into the distance and ends in mountains or undulating hills and parched fields. The traffic thinned out. It consisted mainly of small cars and reeking, old lorries whose drivers didn't want to pay the motorway tolls, but the Honda purred its way past them in smooth curves. The sun set, and I felt an increasingly pleasant, cool wind on my face as the blush of the sun turned into a deep crimson fire, making me feel as if I was driving through an ocean of blood.

# 8

I drove through the gentle, warm darkness, stopping only when I needed to fill up the tank. Driving at night is a journey in stillness, with the monotonous rumbling of the motor in your ears, and a loneliness shared with pale, young men in hushed petrol stations, wordlessly pushing coffee across the counter. If one wasn't preoccupied with one's own wretched life, one could invent all sorts of tales from their monosyllabic replies to a request for coffee, a soft drink, or 18 litres of high-octane petrol. Perhaps they were here in the solitude of the night because they had gone through a divorce, couldn't find any other job, couldn't sleep, had a broken heart. But I didn't think about them. I just drove on. I became one with the Honda. It hummed between my legs, first sending my buttocks to sleep and then making them ache. I put on my helmet after midnight when the starry night sky began to absorb the warmth of the earth. My only company were the belching old lorries, a holiday-maker who had got lost, speeding north with snorkel and beach towels in the back window, and a few other solitary night travellers who for God knows what reason chose the old, free main road instead of the anonymous, deserted and efficient motorway. I was exhausted and therefore extra vigilant, and I was actually sorry when, 20 kilometres or so before San Sebastián, I had to turn off the main road and the motorbike carried me up and up along the gently curving mountain road to my and Amelia's little refuge. The journey was the most important thing, movement. The destination was rather a disappointment.

The house was bathed in a morning haze, as if we had said goodbye to it together only a week before. The mountains in the distance arched massively like the backs of elephants in the glimmering dawn. Our house was up on a ridge, but the green hills were more reminiscent of Austrian summer pasture. It was an old stone house that had once belonged to a medium-sized Basque sheep farm, but the times had taken their toll on both the farmer and his life's work. I had bought it in a fit of passion at the beginning of the 1980s, but had never done anything to it. Amelia fell for it on sight, at a time when I still wasn't quite sure that she loved me. She came from the town and therefore loved the countryside. I came from the countryside and loved the anonymity and rhythm of big cities.

She had left the solid, rectangular outer walls of grey-beige Basque granite standing, but had ripped out most of the interior; only the old kitchen range had been allowed to remain. Then she had rebuilt the inside and created a home, with an open-plan kitchen as the natural focal point and enough rooms to put up 20 people. Running water was installed, electricity and heating, but everything was kept in rustic, natural materials. Oscar had said it was the kind of house every Madrid architect dreamt of showing off in *Hola* or some other magazine, and we were happy in it. We had created it together. It was up in the hills and you looked down through the valley to the Bay of Biscay, the mountains behind providing shelter when the winds came from that direction. It had two storeys and a generous cellar for wine and cheese. But when just the three of us were staying, we used only the ground floor and lived more or less in the kitchen, the reassuring presence of the big black range radiating warmth in the cold Basque winter or the unreliable summer when the heat of the sun was smothered by a chilly mist if the wind brought in a sea fog from the Atlantic.

I was worn out as I drove the last few hundred metres up to the house, the gravel crunching loudly under the tyres. The neighbouring house, where a Basque sheep farmer called Arregui lived, was a couple of kilometres further on up the mountain. In defiance of every EU resolution, regulation and efficiency measure, he went on tending his sheep, made his cheese from their milk, cured meat and made enough to live on. He would have earned more if he let the whole place lie fallow and rented out his farmhouse to summer holidaymakers, but sheep had been his way of life for 60 years, along with the Basque cause, and he would die for them both. He had started as a shepherd at the age of ten and that same year one of his uncles had been shot in a clash with the Guardia Civil. Sheep and nationalism went hand in hand for him. I sent him an envelope every month, money for watching over the house, making sure there was dry firewood and keeping robbers away. He would have done it without payment, but I got him to take it by saying that I could claim it against tax and thereby cheat the central authorities out of a bit of revenue. He saw it as being free for me and expensive for the Castilians, and so he was happy. He was Catholic, a conservative and ardent Basque nationalist and spoke Spanish only when absolutely necessary. But since I was a foreigner, and he'd fallen for Amelia and later for Maria Luisa in a big way, he accepted that we would never learn Basque. He was an anachronism in modern-day Europe – a dinosaur who still, despite his years, lifted boulders, split logs and played *pelota* with bare fists at the annual summer contests. His elder son had been garrotted in 1972 by the state authorities under Franco. His other son, Tómas, who had become my friend, spent three years on death row before the amnesty of 1977. His daughter, the youngest child, was serving a life sentence in a prison south of Seville, convicted for the murder of a captain in the Guardia

Civil five years earlier. Arregui thought that he had bred good Basque children who had done him credit. It was hardly surprising that the Basque issue continued unresolved.

I parked the motorbike and got off with stiff legs and a burning backside, not unlike the early sun that was creeping up in the humid, misty morning. The clicking hiss of the engine as it began to cool was the only sound in the growing morning light, the mist lying like a grey rug over the reaped pastures. The key was in its usual place under the pot by the back door, and I let myself in. The house was still warm from the heat of the day. In the silence I thought I could smell Amelia and Maria Luisa. There was some knitting on the kitchen table. As if Amelia had just popped upstairs or walked over to visit Arregui. Maria Luisa's doll's house was in the corner and a pile of children's books lay on the table by the fireplace. I could see their raincoats and favourite umbrellas and the calendar that Amelia used to make a note of birthdays and other anniversaries. There were postcards, notes, one of Maria Luisa's drawings and a photograph of her best friend in Madrid fixed onto the fridge door by little magnets with animal faces. We had bought them in a kiosk down in San Sebastián last summer.

I went outside again, got my sleeping bag from the motorbike and unrolled it on the wooden veranda that we had built right around the house. I fell asleep at once, my mind full of loss and the dark country road and the labouring motorbike, as relentless as a chain saw in a condemned forest.

I woke in the middle of a nightmare in which Amelia and I lay next to one another, like silver spoons in a cutlery case, and her soft, warm body slowly turned into a liquid skeleton, but I couldn't make myself take my arms away, even though I was terrified.

Arregui was squatting in front of me. One of his big, shaggy sheep dogs was sitting next to him. The other one was looking after the flock grazing up on the hillside. I could hear the tinkling of the rams' bells.

131

Arregui had a broad, almost square face, criss-crossed with fine wrinkles. His skin was leather-brown and his hair was white, thick and cut short. His eyes were completely black, as were his teeth, which were discoloured by the hand-rolled cigarettes he smoked all day long.

"*Hola!* Pedro," he said in his deep, rasping voice.

"*Buenos días*, Arregui," I replied, sitting up. I was still dazed by the dream.

"There aren't any ghosts in that house," he said.

"Maybe."

"The dead don't harm anyone. I kept vigil in the house one night. Their souls, thanks be to God, are at peace."

"Maybe."

"Let's have coffee," he said and went into the house, where I could hear him lighting up the stove. We had an electric kettle, but he was an old-fashioned man. The dog came up to me and I scratched absent-mindedly behind its ears, as I watched the sun rise above the highest mountain tops and cast a warm, golden glow down over the black and white sheep grazing so peacefully. The dew twinkled on the Honda's chrome and lay like tiny pearls on the grass.

He brought out coffee with sugar and hot milk in two big mugs, and some bread with his own sheep's milk cheese, and we ate while he talked about his animals and the weather which was never quite how he would like it to be. Farmer's chat that calmed me and soothed my frayed nerves. I asked after Tómas and his daughter in prison. They lived, as he said, the life that God had chosen for them. One had fought his battle, and he accepted that he would fight no longer. His daughter was just one martyr among many in the struggle for Euskadi's freedom. I had never discussed the issue with him, and didn't intend to start now. Both children, he said, were fit and healthy, and with patience and God's will he would have them both at his side again. He bid me a dignified farewell and picked up the rucksack that he had left on the veranda. It contained bread, wine and cheese, and I assumed that he would be sleeping higher up the mountain as he often did when he let the sheep and dogs move on to fresh pasture. With a whistle to the dogs, he was gone. I remained sitting, watching them shrink into small dots high up on the green mountainside which led up into the huge massifs of the Pyrenees.

Then I burnt all the mementoes on a bonfire in the garden. Amelia and Maria Luisa's clothes, the photographs of them, the calendar, the knitting, the toys, the doll's house, the photograph of the friend. I couldn't burn the scent or the memories of them, but I couldn't bear the thought of sleeping in a house so full of physical reminders. I didn't care what Arregui said. He was wrong. There were ghosts in that house.

I drove down to San Sebastián, on the La Concha bay, to meet Tómas. The town disappeared and reappeared as I swung through the bends at a leisurely pace. It was a hot day and the esplanade and beach were full of people. It was a white, lovely town and I was very fond of it. The Basque Country was going through a recession because of the terrorism, but there were no outward signs of this in San Sebastián. People were well dressed, and the bars and restaurants in the town centre were buzzing with life. Basque people love food, and the sea supplies them with an extensive cuisine which combines the French and the Spanish.

Tómas hadn't arrived yet, so I stood at the bar and ate tapas and drank a cola. Pieces of squid, prawns with egg, sardines and slices of ham were served on small chunks of freshly baked bread. I stood at the corner of the bar, near the open door, and caught sight of Tómas before he saw me. He was only a little younger than I was, but the years had been kind to him. He always said that it was good for the health to do time in prison. You got lots of exercise, a low-fat diet and no alcohol. He had his father's broad face, but his body was slim, and his hands were elegant and long. There were touches of grey in his short, thick hair, and the smart, titanium frames of his glasses made him look like a polished, well-to-do banker. In fact, he earned his money as a computer programmer for finance companies and large businesses. The same brain which during the 1970s had made him ETA's pre-eminent tactician now provided him with a good income as a troubleshooter. Tómas could always see the bigger picture and was often three or four moves ahead of everyone else. I had met him in 1972, a few years before he went to prison, and the Franco dictatorship sentenced him to death for terrorist activities. We had met by chance on the street in San Sebastián and the chemistry had been instant. He was a good source of information, but I hadn't been aware of his deep involvement with ETA until I read about his arrest. I visited him several times in prison and helped him when he was granted amnesty along with other political prisoners.

We had been friends ever since. He had witnessed my ups and downs. His broad face lit up in a smile when he saw me and we gave each other a big hug before going into the back of the restaurant to eat a late lunch.

I drank cola. Tómas drank wine and, while I picked at my food, he ate with a hearty appetite, first a big salad and then *merluza a la vasca* – hake in a subtly seasoned sauce with vegetables. We chatted about one thing and another, but avoided the incident. We had exhausted the subject on the telephone a long time ago. Even though he was a bachelor, he understood my bereavement. He had suffered many losses himself during his life underground, but he had made the right choice when he laid down his weapons and started afresh. I knew that he despised the new generation of ETA activists, but being a Basque through and through, he could never bring himself to condemn or denounce them. He thought their politics and methods were wrong. But they were fellow countrymen first and terrorists second. And I knew that although he was no longer active, he still had his connections and sources. He could be trusted. I knew there had been discussion of the possibility of him becoming an unofficial, secret mediator between the old socialist government and ETA, to try to work out a solution. He had put out feelers and made contacts. First, imprisoned members of ETA would be moved from Andalusia and other distant places to prisons in the Basque Country, in return for a cease-fire. The next step would be to work out a conclusive peace agreement, with the possibility of a partial amnesty. But the new, right-wing government would not negotiate with terrorists under any circumstances. The violence had flared up again, the eternal, evil spiral of violence. Now, however, it seemed as if there was change in Northern Ireland, Tómas said, and this could possibly help to resolve the situation. He didn't harbour any great hope, but if the Irish could find a way, why not the Basques?

We had reached coffee before I asked, "Tómas. Was it them? Was it a terrible mistake?"

Tómas plucked at his napkin while I smoked. Like so many, he had long since given up smoking, but had taken up fiddling with things instead.

"It wasn't them, Peter," he said. "It wasn't them. I'm not saying they wouldn't have done it, but it wasn't them. They didn't know the traitor was living in that building."

"Who then?"

"I don't know. I don't understand it. It doesn't make sense."

"Then why haven't they disclaimed responsibility? Said it wasn't them?"

He looked away and drank from his *café solo* even though there were only dregs left in the bottom of the tiny cup. Then he spoke quietly, but with anger in his voice, an anger that I sensed was directed at himself.

"To create fear is at the very core of terrorism. They get a fear-inducing element handed to them on a plate, free of charge. Why shouldn't they make use of it? A traitor was eliminated. Others will hesitate, because they've shown that the avenging arm is long. We didn't spread terror back in Franco's time. We went for military personnel, members of the oppressive police network, the regime's top people. We were soldiers in a dirty war. But we were soldiers, not murderers of innocent civilians."

I had never heard him take issue with the morals of his successors. There was truth in what he said. ETA had begun using violence – what they called the armed struggle – back in 1968, when he had been just a teenager. Like cowboys escaping across the Rio Grande, they had taken refuge in France after carrying out their actions. And France, like other European countries, had considered them freedom fighters struggling in a just cause – seeking to overthrow the fascist Franco dictatorship.

"I need to make some sense of it. I need to know," I said.

"I understand. But maybe the authorities are behind it. Maybe it was an attempt to get rid of the photographs of the Minister. Maybe it was simple revenge. They've done it before, during the dirty war. And that was a socialist government! Have you thought how opportune it is for the Spanish to say that it was ETA? It's rather convenient, the way ETA's become active again. Maybe ETA's just a smoke screen. What do they call it in English – a red herring?"

Under the Social Democrat government the authorities had sent death squads to both the French and Spanish Basque Country to liquidate alleged ETA members. Brutally execute them without trial. Violence breeds violence. The issue was being dealt with by the courts now, but so far all efforts to discover which members of the governments of the 1980s had known about the death squads had been in vain.

"I want to hear them say it," I said. "That it wasn't them."

He sat thinking.

"It's very risky, Peter. Risky for me, for you, for them. They're being pressed from all sides. They're divided, anxious, edgy, aggressive."

"I want to hear them say it."

He sat for a while. Then he made a decision and left. I stayed and ordered another coffee and paid the bill. He came back 20 minutes later. I didn't know where he had phoned from or what he had been doing, and I wouldn't dream of asking.

He sat down. He was sweating, as if he had been walking too fast in the afternoon heat, but it could also have been nerves. Even though he was a free, law-abiding citizen, he had to assume that for the rest of his days the intelligence and security services would be keeping an eye on him. He also had to be on guard constantly, in case the other side became suspicious that he was playing a double game, might turn traitor, and by so doing sign his own death warrant. In effect, he lived the agonising, edgy and stressful existence of a double agent, where you could end up frightened of your own shadow.

"There's a bench. The underground car park next to the Londres, eight o'clock. Carry an evening edition of *Diario Vasco*," he said in a quiet, nervous voice.

"Thanks, Tómas," I said simply. "I'm in your debt."

"Friends are never in debt to one another," he said. But I could tell that I had pressed our friendship as far as was humanly possible. Perhaps it had been them after all, and he had a bad conscience. Maybe it was for Maria Luisa's sake. For Amelia's. Or for all the years we had known one other, or because he knew that I was working through my grief. We said a slightly cool goodbye with a firm handshake and I watched him disappear round the corner by a shuttered camera shop in the deserted, siesta-time street.

I wandered around the town for a couple of hours. It did me good to walk. The straight, narrow streets in the town centre slowly filled with people after 5 p.m., when the shop shutters were rolled up with a rattle that echoed like the sound of castanets. The promenade by the park was buzzing with people again after the siesta, and the traffic was back to its roaring intensity. I bought a copy of *Diario Vasco* and, at 7.45 p.m., went and sat on the bench opposite the pedestrian entrance to the car park under the plaza. The town hall was on my right and, on my left, the Hotel Londres where I had stayed several times in my younger days when some newspaper was picking up the bill. I could see the statue of Christ up on Monte Egueldo. The tide had gone out, exposing the yellowish-grey sand below the esplanade. There were people in the water. Young men swam out to a raft anchored in the mussel-shaped bay, from which it took its name. The raft always made me think of Hemingway. Other youngsters had marked out football pitches in the sand and played with a lot of shouting until the sun went down in an orgy of red and darkness stopped play. The beach, which gradually grew narrower and narrower as the tide came back in, emptied.

A young mother pushing a small child in a pram came and sat down next to me. It was a warm and gentle evening and she held out an ice lolly which the child licked in delight. She chattered to the infant in Basque. The child waggled its hands and knocked the little bonnet that had been lying on its tummy out of the pram. I bent down and picked up the bonnet and handed it to the young mother. She smiled, but only with her mouth. Her brown eyes were anxious.

"Thanks. Go down towards the harbour when I've left," she said in Spanish, turning her head and held out the lolly for the delighted child again.

My heart was thumping. She sat calmly and let the child finish eating, but I saw her hands tremble a little as she wiped the infant's mouth with a paper napkin. Then she got up and pushed the pram towards the crossing by the Hotel Londres. I stayed where I was for another five minutes, one tourist among many, and then walked slowly towards the little fishing harbour where blue cutters were moored below the grey stone walls adjoining the town centre. I tried not to look around, but the palms of my hands were sweaty.

There were lots of people strolling down by the harbour. I stood at the quayside and looked out at the blunt-nosed cutters. A young man came up beside me. He looked at me and I followed him, walking a few paces behind. I knew what they were up to when, like all the other people out for an evening walk in San Sebastián, we wandered, apparently aimlessly, around the town centre. Others would be watching to see that no one was following me. We returned to the harbour. Loud rock music was blaring from a bar, which the young man entered. His place was taken by another young man wearing the same kind of outfit, jeans and a short-sleeved shirt, who walked up to me, took a firm hold of my arm and pointed at a white BMW parked by the kerb with its engine running. I got into the back seat and the car drove off smoothly.

There were two men in the car. They were wearing baseball caps and sunglasses, despite the fact that it was dark, and they took care not to turn round. Again we drifted aimlessly with all the other young men in their shiny cars. The modern, motorised version of the Spanish *paseo*. To see and be seen before dinner. Up and down the boulevards and up in the direction of one of the headlands and back again before driving out to the industrial suburb of Renteria, leaving fashionable San Sebastián behind us. It was replaced by tenement blocks, the flaking walls appearing in the car's headlights, burnt-out cars along the kerb looking like modernist sculptures. I could see scrawny human shadows hunched between the piles of rubbish and rubble. Junkies and junkie prostitutes on their way out into the dark night. ETA could be safe here too. Not because they loved the fiery young terrorists in Renteria, but because they hated the police and authorities even more.

The BMW turned off into a wasteland. Two big rats ran alongside a derelict building which had once been another squalid tenement block, housing the Andalusian workers who had come here during Franco's time to participate in the Spanish economic miracle. In the glow of the headlights, I could see a gas cooker and a rusty fridge lying in one corner. The nearest streetlights had long since been smashed.

"Out, Lime!" said the driver.

I got out, and the BMW slid away. My heart was hammering. I could hear cars on the nearby motorway interchange that sliced through the neighbourhood like a luminous scar. I had the feeling that there was someone inside the ruin, but without the light from the BMW's headlights, everything was in total darkness. Adrenalin was pumping through my body, and I took a couple of deep breaths, clenched my fists and slipped into combat stance. Ready for action, as I had learnt at the karate institute in Madrid.

But they didn't come from the derelict building. Another car pulled in and stopped a few metres from me, so I turned and stood with my back to the ruin. It was a black Seat and two men got out from the back, while the driver stayed in the car. The engine was running and the headlights dazzled me, but that was the whole idea. They stood next to the car, so they could get in again quickly. I stood in the glare of the lights, but I could see their silhouettes. They were sturdy young men, wearing jeans and dark windcheaters. They had turned up the collars and pulled their caps down over their foreheads.

"We haven't got long, Peter Lime," said one of them.

"Why did you murder my family?" I said hoarsely and took a step forward. My mouth and throat were dry.

"Don't move, Lime," said the same man.

"Why?" I said.

140

"It wasn't us. We understand that you want to hear it from us. You're hearing it now. I swear on Euskadi's soil and by the blood of the martyrs, we had nothing to do with it. We didn't even know the traitorous whore had been housed in that building. It wasn't us."

I didn't know what to say. I didn't have a second's doubt that they were who they appeared to be. They exuded danger and desperation, and the possibility that Tómas might have conned me was completely out of the question. It was obviously important for them to have it put on record that they weren't responsible. They wanted to tell me – perhaps because they owed Tómas a favour.

"I am grateful for the information," I said tonelessly.

One of them got back into the car, but the other one stayed where he was.

"If you find out who was behind it, then perhaps we can help you to take the revenge you apparently want," he said.

"Why should you help me?"

"Because you once helped one of ours."

"That was many years ago."

"We never forget, Peter Lime. Remember that. We never forget."

He got into the car and, before he had even slammed the door, the driver released the clutch and accelerated round the corner, churning up a shower of grit and sand. I couldn't see a thing in the total darkness. I was gripped by fear and broke into a gasping run out of the wasteland, down a side street and onto a main road. I don't think anyone was following me, but anxiety drove me to keep running until I reached a well-lit road. I stood catching my breath. San Sebastián's golden sheen lay before me and I walked calmly now, looking over my shoulder for a taxi with a green light that would drive me back to my motorbike.

It was where I had parked it, outside the Hotel Londres. I drove home slowly. I was exhausted and my mind was filled with conflicting thoughts and emotions. It was the answer I had been expecting, but perhaps I had hoped they would claim responsibility so that I would have had a convenient target at which to direct my anger.

The house was in dark and quiet. There was a faint smell of smoke from the bonfire. I didn't look at it as I took out the key to the front door. I let myself in. He must have gone to wait in the alcove just inside the door as soon as he heard the motorbike, because he struck me squarely on the neck with a cosh. Everything exploded in a shower of fragmented light.

# 9

When I came to again, I was sitting on one of the narrow-backed kitchen chairs. They had moved it out onto the floor against the low wall leading into the kitchen and tied my hands tight behind my back. My neck hurt, but not unbearably. My assailant knew the effect of his cosh. He had struck neither too hard nor too soft, just the right touch to knock me out without fracturing my skull. They were professionals and they terrified me, making my heart beat wildly. There were three men, in their late 30s. I was even more scared to see that they weren't wearing masks. Two of them were of medium height and built like small, stocky rugby players. The third was bigger and taller. They were wearing jeans and open-necked shirts. Two of them were wearing leather jackets; the big one was in his shirtsleeves. He was holding the cosh, a fat little rubber sausage that he patted lovingly against the palm of his hand. He had a narrow, sly face under a high and pockmarked forehead. The other two stood opposite me, just to the left of our dining table. One of them had a narrow moustache and slicked-back, greasy hair, the other one's fair hair was fashionably cropped. They surprised me by speaking English, with an unmistakable Irish accent.

"Well, my friend. Welcome back to the land of the living," said the big man with the cosh. "Now we're going to have a nice little chat.

Apologies for not introducing myself first, but we know about your Japanese talents, so we thought it best to get you nice and settled first. Before our little chat. Don't you think? You should sit comfortably when you're having a friendly little chat, don't you think?"

"Three clowns in my house," I said.

They reacted fast. Three steps and moustache was standing behind me and yanked my vain ponytail, pulling my head back with a crack, while the cropped one jabbed me twice, precisely and sharply, in the liver, racking my body with pain. Everything went dark again.

"Well, well, well, Mr Lime. Mr fucking-funny-name Peter Harry Lime of movie-fame," said the big one with the cosh. "Not a good idea to be a naughty boy at night."

"What's the IRA doing in Euskadi?" I said when I had got my breath back. I probably appeared quite calm on the surface, but I was terrified.

"We've got a lot in common with our Basque comrades," said the cosh. "They're good nationalists and Marxists. Like us they're oppressed and kept in chains by a fucking king who they don't acknowledge. Like us they're nationalists first and Marxists second. Like us they have a just cause in an unjust world."

There had always been connection between the IRA and ETA. I knew that they had collaborated on arms deliveries and the purchase of Czech Semtex. The IRA could call on American sympathisers for money and weapons. ETA could buy weapons from the IRA, financing their purchases by collecting protection money, which they chose to call a "revolutionary tax", and other activities. I understood why Tómas had been so nervous. Friendship was one thing, the issue apparently another. If he hadn't been given the choice between betrayal and death, that was. Now I couldn't make it all fit. I simply couldn't see what they were after. If they didn't want me snooping, they could just have liquidated me and left me at the side of the road with a bullet through my mouth. Then they would have sent yet another clear signal.

That was probably how this was going to end anyway. They weren't wearing masks because they didn't count on me being around to describe them.

"Fuck off," was all I said, and tensed my body, but it didn't help, the pain was still intense as the cropped one belted me on the jaw and I tasted blood as he hit me hard and accurately in my side again.

"Mr Lime," said the cosh. "It's not worth it. I know you're a tough guy, but it's not worth it. We won't let up."

"I don't know what you want," I said hoarsely.

"Mr Lime. Please accept my apologies. I had quite forgotten to say. What do we want? We want to know where you've hidden the suitcase containing a photograph or two which we would like to have for our photo album."

"I've no idea what you're talking about," I said, and tensed every muscle again, but it didn't help of course.

When I came round my mouth was full of blood, and the small of my back and my stomach were aching and it felt as if they had cracked a rib. One of my ears was swollen and my lips and one eyebrow were split. At first I thought my t-shirt was soaked with blood, but they'd thrown water over me when I fainted. Spots of light danced before my eyes and I had that nauseous feeling that accompanies slight concussion. The cosh was sitting at the kitchen table now and they had dragged my chair up close to the edge of it. I could sense the other two standing right behind me. The smaller one held me up. My arms had been untied, but they were numb, and my elbow was burning. They must have finished up by overturning the chair. I rested my arms on the table. They started tingling. My ankles had been tied to the chair. My eyes focused on the bottle of whisky in front of the one I thought of as the cosh, and the two tumblers next to it. He poured a small shot for himself and filled the other tumbler to the rim. The golden brown liquid stirred almost sensually as it caught the light. The aroma of malt and peat filled me with a mixture of lovely memories and awful nightmares.

"Let's be friends, Mr Lime. Let's have a drink together instead," said the cosh. He smiled, but his strangely colourless eyes were completely dead in his acne-scarred face.

"No," I said.

"But yes, Mr Lime. Friends should have a glass together."

"I don't drink," I said.

"In Ireland it's very impolite, well almost an insult, to say no to enjoying a drink with a friend. It's sissy too. Only fairies and sissies don't drink. Real men like their whisky the same way they like their women – unadulterated. Have a glass, Mr Lime!"

"I don't drink," I said, and swept the full tumbler off the table. The liquid ran along the brown wood and the glass smashed onto the stone floor and shattered into pieces. I waited for the punch, but none came. Instead, he shook his narrow head that seemed at odds with his large body. He got up and fetched another glass and half-filled it. The cropped one took hold of my arms and wrenched them back so I sat rigid. The other one held my head back with my damned ponytail in one hand and pinched my nose together with his other hand, as the cosh got up slowly, as if in slow motion, holding the glass. He came closer, the glass grew larger before my eyes, my mouth gasped for air. The glass with its rippling, golden and compelling liquid dominated my field of vision. I could smell the oak casks and the malt and the smokehouse peat. It was a fine Irish malt. It was both compelling and repulsive. He tipped a mouthful into me. It tasted like fire and I was about to vomit, but he waited patiently until I had regained my breath, and then the rim of the glass bit into my battered lips again. Most of it ran down my chin, but I instantly felt the effect of the little that stayed in my mouth. It was impossible not to swallow, despite the coughing fit provoked by the strong drops seeping down towards my lungs. It was as if every cell in my body rejoiced and wept at the same time, but opened up like flowers after rain and sucked in the alcohol. A beautiful, white light infused my brain and the pains in my body were soothed in a second, as if I had been given a shot of morphine.

I hadn't touched spirits for nearly eight years. Before that I had drunk heavily for 20 years. Most of the time I could control it, but there were many occasions of which I had no recollection whatsoever, when I had been on one of my grand benders, disappearing into an alcoholic haze for days on end. Amelia had put up with it at first, even though the first time she saw me with a complete blank about what I had been up to it had frightened the life out of her. But when Maria Luisa was born, she had given me a choice. The bottle or them. She loved me, but she didn't want to witness, or let our child witness, my slow self-destruction. We lived in an alcohol-soaked culture, and Oscar and Gloria had never so much as mentioned my problem, but they backed Amelia up. I realised for the first time how they saw me. It seems so simple to write about that period, but it was hell. Going to my first meeting at Alcoholics Anonymous was one of the hardest decisions of my life. And then slowly, with an air of unreality, walking through the rows of chairs, up to the rostrum and turning to face the gathering and say "Good evening. My name is Peter. I'm an alcoholic." It was a difficult time, but the choice was actually no choice at all when I looked at Amelia and Maria Luisa. The karate institute was my physical salvation. Meetings at AA a vital crutch. I could keep the demon at arm's length by pressing myself physically to the limit. But I could never walk past a bar without hearing that tempting call, like a siren promising me good fortune and joy if I followed her and stepped inside, putting myself in her hands once more. Just once. Just a single glass. But I had kept the image of my two miracles in my mind's eye and gradually it became easier. I had been on the verge of succumbing several times after their deaths, but somehow I felt that my promise to Amelia had even greater significance, meant even more, now that she was no longer here.

He put the empty glass in front of me and poured another measure. He nodded, and they let go of my arms and my nose.

"Let's have a drink together, Mr Lime. Like real men," said the big Irishman in his peculiar, almost comical accent.

I swept the glass onto the floor and it shattered with a loud crash as the wonderful aroma of whisky filled the kitchen.

But I was just delaying the agony. He fetched a new glass, filled it, and the procedure was repeated. They managed to force a few more mouthfuls into me. My body began to relax. After the third dose I realised that I was beginning to swallow voluntarily. My throat and stomach were burning from the unaccustomed, pure spirits. My body hadn't forgotten. The alcohol was received like an unexpected gift. It went straight to my head which became light and airy and the longed for, familiar feeling of pleasant drowsiness and relaxation set in as if it was only yesterday that I had stood at a bar with my *una copa*. It wasn't the taste, even though that was also instantly recognisable, but the effect. It was like a comfortable glove which wrapped itself round my body and soul and warmed me up on a cold winter's day. It was like coming home to a reassuring place after a long and perilous journey. It was so horribly familiar and pleasant.

The cosh fetched another glass. The others were lying on the kitchen floor in a sea of whisky, along with the smashed bottle which I had managed to knock over during the last dosing. My throat and nostrils were burning and my battered body was hurting. My head was buzzing and I was dizzy. In my drinking days, I had been able to take copious quantities of alcohol, now it was as if I was 15 years old and drinking my first strong lager. He fetched a new bottle and filled the glass again and nodded. They let go of my arms and I lifted up my right arm unsteadily to sweep this one onto the floor too, but my arm had ideas of its own. As if it didn't belong to me any more. It was as if I was standing alongside watching it approach the glass. I told my hand to hit out hard and sweep it away, but instead it closed around the glass and picked it up slowly, guiding it almost sensually to my mouth, and poured in a little of the liquid which lay like a soft membrane on my tongue and then slipped down my throat like a gentle, yet firm caress, down to my stomach and out into my bloodstream and on towards my consciousness, as if carried along by a beautiful, calm river. Tears came to my eyes, but not because of the whisky. They were the tears of self-contempt. I was a pathetic sight – snot, blood, tears and whisky all over my face and down my t-shirt. I drank again, emptying the glass, and slammed it down on the table.

"Arsehole," I said. "Fucking arsehole!"

"Cheers, Mr Lime. It's pleasant drinking with a friend, isn't it now?" said the big Irishman. He emptied his own and gave us a refill with a cocky, scornful expression which should have made me throw my glass in his face, but instead I watched my hand move downwards, grasp the glass and guide it to my lips, switching on the familiar light behind my bruised eyes.

"Why are you interested in that suitcase?" I remember asking at some point. I have only fragmented, foggy memories of what we talked about. I can see only that pockmarked face and the narrow mouth, and the glass in front of me from which I'm drinking.

"We ask. You answer," he said.

"It's nothing more than memories, you fucking arseholes. It's nothing other than my own lousy, trivial damned memories of a wasted life," I said, and began swearing in Danish from rage and self-pity.

I can't remember what else I said. I can't remember what I told him. At some point I began singing in Danish too. I rambled on and on and must have talked in a big jumble about my suitcase, Amelia, Maria Luisa and Don Alfonzo, about Oscar and Gloria; and about the time I was on a Greek island and quite by chance noticed Jacqueline Kennedy walking along with a bathing towel over her arm, accompanied by a woman of about the same age. Jacqueline Kennedy Onassis was in shorts and a thin blouse and still had a lovely body. She was wearing large sunglasses and a white hat, and no one seemed to recognise her without make-up. Or was this unspoilt island paradise still a place where people minded their own business? There were very few tourists there.

I had gone to the island to escape the horrors that had chiselled themselves into my mind after a tour in the hell that was Beirut. My nerves were in tatters. I was finished with putting my life in danger to take photographs that none of the newspapers would print anyway, because the media in the West had long since lost interest in the unending Lebanese civil war. The island had been recommended to me by a young stringer from A.P. who, like me, was tired of sending reports home which few sub-editors could be bothered to read, let alone publish, while we spent our days lying in the dust, caught in the crossfire between the warring factions.

Jacqueline was walking along, vulnerable and private with a friend, in a place where she clearly felt at ease. I followed them down to a little sheltered cove a kilometre from the village. She removed her shorts and blouse. She wasn't wearing a bikini, and as she rubbed suntan oil on her naked body, I lay behind a rocky outcrop with my Nikon and took the series of photographs that turned Oscar and me into million-aires and OSPE NEWS into an internationally renowned agency. She didn't realise I had been there until she saw herself in magazines all over the world. It was so easy and so lucrative. Why run around taking journalistic photographs which give prestige among colleagues, but hardly butter on your bread, when the world is craving photographs of the rich and famous going about their private business? I became a paparazzo by chance and over the years I became one of the best, the most proficient and the wealthiest, because I never showed any mercy. I didn't look at my victims as people, but as commodities.

I know that I rambled on about that story, because I remember the cosh saying:

"We're not interested in rich women's bare tits, but in another photograph, Lime. We're interested in the whole suitcase. We'd like to choose for ourselves, like when you choose which negatives you want printed. So where is it?"

He asked over and over. I can't remember if I told him, but I must have done, in light of what happened. I remember that I talked and drank and that then there was an enormous crash, and a huge stone flew through the glass door leading to the garden, and that the door smashed into the wall, and two greyish-brown shadows with bared teeth leapt in and went for the Irishmen's throats. My chair toppled over and I fell into the whisky and broken glass and, from a strange distorted angle, I remember seeing Arregui come in behind his dogs and swing his stout shepherd's crook, smashing it into the skull of the cropped one who was pulling a gun out of his holster. There was snarling and yelling and swearing in English and Basque and then I went out like a light. It was getting to be a nasty habit.

I woke up on the sofa where we used to sit to watch television. I hurt all over, but I was also still very drunk, so the pain was strangely distant and unreal. The sofa and the room reeled when I tried to get up, and I couldn't get the face in front of me into focus. It was Tómas, gently pressing me back down. He handed me a glass of water. I was terribly thirsty and drank it in one. I could smell myself.

"Lie still, Peter," said Tómas.

"Where are they?"

"Two of them have gone. I've dragged the third outside. He's dead.

Suddenly it came back to me.

"You shit," I said. "You lousy shit."

He let go of me and stepped backwards. His face began to sharpen up. I could feel the alcohol pumping round my body, but it was more like having a skin full in the old days. My head was clear, and I was bristling with whisky-induced belligerence.

"It's not what you think," he said.

"You got hold of your IRA terrorist chums, you fucker," I said.

"It's not what you think," he repeated.

I tried to sit up, but that wasn't a good idea. The room and Tómas whirled round and landed again. Then I remembered some more snatches.

"I've got to ring," I said.

"Just stay where you are. They really worked you over."

"Telephone."

He gave me his mobile, but I couldn't hit the right keys, so I dictated the number and he called Don Alfonzo in Madrid.

"No one's answering," said Tómas.

"What is it with that suitcase?" I said. "Why are you all interested in that suitcase?"

"I don't know what you're talking about. It's not what you think, Peter."

"How long have I been lying here?"

"A couple of hours."

"Shit," I said.

"Yes," said Tómas. "Just be glad that my father decided to come down from the mountain with a sick sheep. They'd parked their car down by the bend. The dogs were restless so he came up to see what was going on."

"He could just have asked you, couldn't he? You knew what was happening all right," I said.

"It's not what you think," he repeated.

"Call that number again," I said.

He rang, but Don Alfonzo still didn't answer. He helped me up and out to the kitchen table. The kitchen stank, but it had been cleaned up. One of the dogs sat in the doorway, its yellow eyes following my every move vigilantly. It was its usual placid, slightly lethargic self. I don't know where Arregui had got to. At some point I heard a whistle and the dog disappeared from the doorway.

"Where's Arregui?" I asked when Tómas had got me onto a chair.

"He's getting rid of the trash," he said with a coldness and nonchalance that I hadn't noticed in him before, but he couldn't have got to where he had in ETA without a very brutal streak.

He put a big mug of black coffee in front of me.

"I'd rather have a proper drink," I heard myself saying.

"Later. Come on, drink," I heard like an echo from the nightmare.

"Why are you interested in my suitcase, Tómas? Why didn't you just ask me? Why did you set IRA thugs onto me? I thought we were friends."

I could feel self-pity, my old companion in the land of the drunk, tapping on my shoulder, but I didn't want it back. I took a gulp of the hot and sweet triple espresso. I was still drunk, but at least I would be an alert drunk.

"It wasn't the IRA," said a voice behind me. A younger man was on his way down the stairs from the first floor. He must have been listening from the landing. I recognised the voice. He had spoken to me on the wasteland in Renteria. He wasn't much more than 25 years old, with an angular, pale face below his crew cut. He was wearing a thin black leather jacket over a grey t-shirt. He had slender, olive-coloured hands and his pallor suggested that he spent a lot of time indoors.

"So you're here too. Are we going to carry on in Spanish now?" I asked.

"Tómas rang us. We'll see to it that one of the shitbags disappears in the mountains. He won't be missed. The other two won't get out of Euskadi. They carry the scars of Arregui and his dogs. You'd better think about what you'll tell the police, for Arregui's sake."

"I hadn't reckoned on talking to the police. Who did Arregui kill?" I asked.

"They weren't carrying any identification. He was fair-haired. Does it bother you?"

"I hope he rots in hell. I'd just hoped it was someone else," I said thinking about the big Irishman with the cosh. But I was rather surprised that I felt nothing, even though someone had lost their life. Just disappointment that it hadn't been all three of them. We all wear a civilised coat of varnish. It might be a thick layer, but if you're pushed far enough, it peels off, and naked aggression raises its ugly head.

He came to the bottom of the stairs, sat down at the table and took the little cup of coffee which Tómas offered him. He leant across the table and spoke insistently.

"Peter Lime. I've said it before. I'm happy to repeat it. We had nothing to do with the death of your family. Nothing. We have nothing to do with the three Irishmen who were here this evening. They're not IRA. I can't tell you where my information comes from. But they weren't from the Republican Army. They're freelance. We've heard about them. They've shown up in Euskadi before and let it be understood that they were part of our Irish brothers' and sisters' struggle, but they're common criminals. They're hitmen. Their guns and fists are for hire to anyone who asks. So, señor Lime. What is this suitcase you talk about? I have no idea. You do, so you should ask yourself why someone is so interested in it that they would kill you.

And who else knows that you have the suitcase. We didn't know. How could we? Tómas is your friend. He came immediately when Arregui rang. They're good patriots. In a couple of hours every trace will have disappeared. Every trace!"

It was a long speech. I believed him.

"Who says they were going to liquidate me?" I said. "They gave me a beating and got me drunk. I've been there before. Just a long time ago."

He looked at me and smiled.

"The others who've seen them without their masks on are no longer alive to tell the tale. You are, Peter. So I'd look over my shoulder in the future. Until we get them. At some point we will. We'll keep an eye on Arregui. Besides, he's not afraid of anything on this earth."

I wouldn't bet money on that. His organisation was divided and under pressure and more or less driven underground. But, like every self-proclaimed revolutionary, he had to believe in his cause and his potential for victory in order to survive the double life he lived.

"And the fair-haired one?" I said.

"He'll disappear. You don't need to know."

I finished the coffee. My body ached all over and I was tanked up like I used to get in the old days before running amok and drinking myself senseless. The alcohol also deadened both the physical and mental pain. He got up, and so did I, but I had to sit down again. It hurt too much and I was too dizzy, but I took his outstretched hand and shook it.

"It's not us. You should be looking elsewhere. If we hear anything we'll contact Tómas. We keep Euskadi's soil tidy. We remember our friends," he said.

"OK," was all I said, and he slipped out into the early dawn, like a shadow that could exist only at night.

I tried to get up again, unaided, and this time I managed. I was drunk and the worst thing was that, although I was in agony, I was enjoying the sensation of alcohol in my blood. I got dizzy again. I could smell my own vomit and piss and tried to pull off my soiled t-shirt, but I couldn't keep my balance. Tómas put my arm round his shoulders and helped me up the stairs to the first floor. I had shooting pains all over my body, but we reached the bedroom. Tómas helped me to take off my t-shirt and without embarrassment unbuckled my belt and pulled off my sodden jeans. I leant on him while he pulled off my socks, but I took my underpants off myself. I put my arm round his shoulders again and he helped me into the bathroom and held me up under the shower. I had difficulty keeping my balance, but he took it in his stride. He had seen beaten-up people before, of both sexes. He held me up and soaped me gently. My right side was completely livid, and I caught sight of my face in the mirror looking like a swollen mask, a boxer's beaten face after 15 fruitless rounds.

He helped me into clean clothes and then back into bed. I could still smell vomit and whisky. Cool night air drifted in through the open window.

Tómas fetched some iodine and cleaned my wounds. There was a nasty gash under my right eye. It stung, but not too badly. I asked him to ring Don Alfonzo again, but there was still no answer. He helped me into the double bed and sat on the edge as if I was a sick child who was afraid of the dark. Which wasn't that far off the mark. I told him about the suitcase. That it contained the most significant photographs I had taken during my life, but there was nothing secret about them. Jacqueline, the Minister and snapshots of my childhood dog. It was my own private world. What could it have to do with anyone else?

"The answer's in the suitcase," he said. "Otherwise it doesn't make sense."

"I'm sorry," I said.

"Forget it," he said. "I'd have thought the same in your shoes. Forget it."

"You're taking a big risk, Tómas. It could have repercussions for your new life."

"You once took a risk with me, and hid me and helped me and closed your eyes and kept your mouth shut."

"Then we're even," I said.

Tómas smiled. His face was blurred.

"I've told you before, Peter. Friends don't keep tabs."

My alcoholic haze was beginning to turn into a hangover. My head was aching and throbbing and my stomach seething and rumbling. Tómas calmly fetched a bucket and put it next to the bed and handed me a couple of pills. They would be of no help whatsoever, but I took them with a glass of water without making a fuss. I knew I ought to get up, but I couldn't.

"I can't drive the bike. Could you take me to the airport tomorrow? I mean today. I've got to go to Madrid. I've got to talk to Don Alfonzo."

"Of course. I'm not going anywhere. Sleep a bit first. Then I'll drive you to the airport later today."

"Wake me if you get through to Don Alfonzo."

"Of course. Now just keep quiet for a while."

I was more battered and exhausted than sleepy, but I fell asleep and dreamt about Amelia. She was lying in state in the bedroom of our burnt-out flat. The room looked as if it had been rebuilt just as painstakingly and reverentially as the Poles had rebuilt the centre of the old Warsaw. Every single thing was in its usual place. The bedroom was now a museum. Lots of people were wandering around looking at her clothes and jewellery and the photographs of Maria Luisa that we had as good as papered one of the walls with. I couldn't understand why in death Amelia was suddenly so interesting that people would pay to see her mummified body, and inspect her things as though they were works of art. There was a queue going along the corridor and down the stairs and out onto the street, where it wound across Plaza Santa Ana just like the one I had seen in front of Lenin's Mausoleum in Moscow many years ago in the days of the Soviet Union. An ebony-black man was lying next to Amelia, his arms crossed over his chest. At first he was completely still, and I couldn't understand why he was lying next to my sleeping wife. I wasn't really jealous, but thought he ought to explain himself.

He lifted his head and looked at me. He didn't have eyes, just two even blacker holes in his black face. None of the visitors seemed to have noticed him. He got up. He was completely naked, hairless and sexless. He looked like a finely carved statue given life by an unseen God. He rose and slowly dissolved in the air, and I realised that Death had slept with Amelia.

# 10

I woke with the impression of two shadows standing by my bed. I had slept for much longer than I wanted to, and now it was mid-afternoon. A low sun shone through the window; soon it would disappear behind the western mountain range. I ached all over. My body hurt from the beating, my mouth was dry but slimy, my head was raging and my stomach burning as it struggled with all the poison that had been poured into me. It was difficult to focus and the thought of sitting up made me nauseous.

One of the shadows turned into Tómas, the other one was a stooping, middle-aged man with a little grey moustache under a pointed nose and dishevelled, thin hair. I tried to sit up.

"Stay where you are, Peter," said Tómas gently. "You look dreadful."

"Thanks. Who's your friend?" My voice was husky and rasping, and my lips hurt when I spoke.

"Doctor Martinez. He's a friend. You were completely out of it," said Tómas.

I was naked apart from my boxer shorts. One side of my body was blue, mixed with various shades of red.

"May I take a look at you, señor Lime?" asked Martinez. His voice was light, almost like a woman's, and his slender, white hands were effeminately soft and cautious as he examined me. My face was swollen and I had an ugly gash under one eye and a badly bruised rib, but he didn't think he could detect any internal injuries. He wanted me to go to hospital for further tests, but I refused. He sighed, but didn't argue. I doubt I was the first patient he had seen who didn't want to be written up in case notes.

"Then I'll have to stitch you here," he said.

He filled a syringe and injected my cheek, and we waited for the anaesthetic to work.

"Don Alfonzo?" I said.

"He's still not answering."

"Try again."

"I keep trying," said Tómas, and punched in the number. He held the little black mobile phone against my ear so I could hear it ringing.

"I've got to go to Madrid," I said through the fog of my hangover.

"Not today. You've got slight concussion on top of everything else," said the doctor and pricked my cheek cautiously. It felt numb and alien, but it still hurt as he inserted five small stitches with fine thread and covered the gash with a plaster. Then he gave me a handful of painkillers and a sleeping pill.

"You look like someone who heals well. Rest and sleep assist the process better than anything else," he said, and left the room nodding briefly in my direction and shaking hands with Tómas. My old friend Tómas still had connections in many circles. I tried to sit up, but couldn't. I noticed that the bucket by the bed had been emptied and rinsed out. I vaguely remembered throwing up at some point. Maybe it was the indignity of it all that made me accept what Tómas said, and so I didn't insist on being driven to the airport. He handed me a big glass of water, which I drank. It nearly came up again. He fetched more water and I took the pills he gave me. They must have contained some hard-hitting substances because I fell into a dreamless sleep and woke to a grey darkness with just the beginnings of shimmering light.

My headache had gone and, although it hurt down my side and across the small of my back when I got up to go to the toilet, the pain was bearable, like when I was young and got knocked about playing football. It hurt, but was all part of the job. I couldn't tell whether the faint light indicated that we were starting a new morning or if I had slept only for a couple of hours and dusk was bringing the day to a close.

I put on my bathrobe without too much difficulty, went down the stairs and saw Tómas, asleep and fully dressed, on the sofa. The kitchen was clean and tidy and I couldn't smell the whisky or my vomit any more. It was as if they had never invaded my life and beaten me up, got me drunk and made me talk. Tómas lay on his back with his mouth half-open, looking like a young boy. The glass in the door had been replaced and I looked out at the dawning, grey light creeping in from the east. I heard the tinkling of bells from Arregui's sheep and realised that I must have slept for the better part of 12 hours at a stretch; that now the third day after the attack was about to begin. I looked across at Tómas and felt touched by his friendship. He was taking care of me as if I was a child. I went to the telephone and dialled Don Alfonzo's number. There was still no answer, but the sound woke Tómas and he sat up with a start.

"Good morning, señor," I said. "And what would the gentleman like for his breakfast?"

He laughed in relief and ran his hand through his hair.

"A shower. I didn't want to disturb you, so . . ."

"Breakfast will be waiting on the table when sir has finished his shower."

"You must be feeling better, even though you still look like a brawler," he said.

He went upstairs and I wasted no time before rummaging through the cupboards looking for the booze, but if the Irish thugs had left

161

anything then Tómas had thrown it out. My hands shook slightly and my throat was dry, but water didn't help, even though I swilled down three glassfuls. I brewed coffee, found some ham that Tómas must have got from his father and made two omelettes, which I knew he liked. While I was preparing breakfast, I saw Arregui coming up the hillside with his sheep. He looked just like every other elderly Basque shepherd whose way of life was slowly vanishing, and his small, compact frame gave no hint of the strength it harboured, the ferocity which could seize it. The two dogs worked the sheep briskly, but still in a strangely lazy fashion, rounding them up and driving them towards better pasture. Maybe the human race could do with some kind of dog to lead the way forward.

I thought about the last few days and knew that now there was no going back. I couldn't let the matter drop, but I had no idea how I would get enough answers to know which questions to ask. I just knew that I had to look in the suitcase, even though its magic stemmed precisely from the fact that I never had. That it existed, that it contained my life's secrets, joys and mistakes. But that I couldn't remember exactly what was in it, because I never inspected the contents when I put in a new photograph or note, wrapped in white paper or in an envelope. Its essence and mystery came from the very fact that it was secret even to me, but I knew that now I had to violate that secret. I had to look at Lime's photographs.

Tómas came downstairs and we ate my omelettes and drank coffee and the juice he had been out to buy. Maybe Arregui had watched over me while he'd been gone. We didn't say much, just ate in amicable silence. There was no trace of the two Irishmen – we didn't mention the fair-haired one – they had apparently vanished from Euskadi. Tómas cleared the table while I had a shower. I still looked like a boxer after a tough fight, but the gash seemed clean when I pulled off the plaster. I put on a fresh one. I was battered, but not incapacitated.

It hurt when I raised my arms to wash my hair, and the shaver had to be used with caution, but with a fresh blue t-shirt, my ponytail in place, clean jeans and my old leather jacket, I was ready to catch the plane back to Madrid. I normally looked like an ageing bruiser in many respects. Gloria said that I dressed like a tough guy and Oscar like an affluent fop because we had to compensate for our youth in the mixed-up 1970s, when everyone had looked like each other, irrespective of gender. Now I just looked like a battered, ageing bruiser, and Gloria would say it gave me an enigmatic tinge of danger and romance – or she'd probably say that it fitted the image I tried to project. Another Indiana Jones just home from a dangerous expedition. Image and role were everything in the confused me-culture of the late 1990s. I felt euphoric and cheerful in some way, as if they had knocked both the despair and the common sense out of me. I hadn't thought about Amelia and Maria Luisa since my dream, and when I realised this, the gaping void opened instantly, but not quite as overwhelmingly as before. As if Amelia was asking me to remember that I had to carry on living. To carry the memory of our short life together as a gift of joy and sorrow, never to be consigned to oblivion, but to remain deep inside, so it would no longer gnaw at my mind like a cancer.

Tómas commented on it when my flight was called in San Sebastián's little airport. I was lucky. We arrived just in time for the next plane and there were empty seats.

"You look ghastly, but you seem to be in an amazingly good mood."

"Gallows humour," was all I said, and handed him the keys to the motorbike. "Take a spin. Fresh air will do you good. I'll pick it up later."

"Arregui will keep an eye on the house, I'm sure."

"Thank your father."

"Will do."

"And thank you. For everything," I said, and there was a brief, awkward silence.

163

"I'll make sure your motorbike gets the occasional airing. Be young again, right? Put a girl on the pillion and drive up and down the streets of San Sebastián like in the old days."

"Yes. They were good."

"Not really, they improve in the remembering," he said.

I gave him a hug and he patted me cautiously on my back. It hurt, but felt good too. As did the double vodka which, with neither trembling voice nor trembling hand, I ordered on the plane once we were headed south towards Madrid, and the green Basque hills, the high grey mountains and the Bay of Biscay's green-blue water and foaming white horses had disappeared below the wings.

From the air, Madrid looked like a scorched heap of yellow stones, an enormous desert fort in the shimmering midday heat. I walked straight out into a sauna, and my t-shirt had stuck to my back before I had reached the taxi rank. It was the stagnant, sweltering heat that drove every Madrileño with the time and means out of Madrid when August struck. I had rung Don Alfonzo from the airport terminal and his phone had been engaged, and I had rung again from a taxi and his phone had still been engaged. A white Policía Nacional patrol car was parked outside his house, and sweat poured off me until I saw Don Alfonzo standing at the veranda door talking with one of the police officers. I paid the taxi with a rush of relief. I had feared the worst. However much I tried, I couldn't remember what and how much I had said to the three Irishmen.

Don Alfonzo looked at me and held out his hand in a formal greeting.

"You look like my house," he said, and stepped aside.

Everything looked normal on the outside. Inside, all was chaos.

A uniformed Policía Nacional officer, in a short-sleeved shirt, with a heavy gun and baton hanging from his belt, was writing in a notebook, but it looked as though they were nearly finished. It was a banality for the police, just another break-in among the thousands that took place every day. With unemployment running at 25 per cent and thousands upon thousands of junkies, homeless people and illegal immigrants, burglaries in and around Madrid were just as common as the hordes of flies in the August heat. The house looked as if a hurricane had blown through the rooms in the wake of desperate thieves' search for cash or easily sold goods. Everything had been turned insideout, randomly but efficiently, with no attempt to cover their tracks. Drawers had been yanked out, cupboard doors ripped off, mattresses pulled off the beds, the kitchen cupboards emptied roughly onto the floor, clothes, CDs, books, knick-knacks and pictures strewn all over the floors. The same chaos reigned upstairs. Don Alfonzo was taking it calmly, but I could see the pallor and exhaustion under his fragile, old-man's skin. Fortunately he had Doña Carmen. Other women would probably have wrung their hands, sighed and wailed, but she was of the generation that had been through a bit of everything. She was already armed with broom, bucket and cloth, and stood waiting impatiently for the police to leave so that she could get going. She had called in reinforcements from the neighbour, whose two sturdy daughters in pink smocks stood behind her, at the ready with vacuum cleaners, a tiny platoon of combat soldiers waiting for their sergeant's order to launch a clearing-up offensive. Don Alfonzo had always had a talent for getting things done for him. I was just relieved that he hadn't come to any harm.

One of the officers stayed by the door. Like the women, he scrutinised my battered face, but Don Alfonzo had simply told them that I was his son-in-law and I was staying with him for the time being. They were too polite to ask, but they probably recognised me from countless television features about the incident. The police stared discreetly, the women openly.

"We're off now, Don Alfonzo," said the officer by the door. "An inspector will be along later, but the case seems clear-cut. They got in by forcing open the veranda door. So presumably it's just another burglary."

He handed Don Alfonzo a form.

"Here's a copy of our preliminary report. For your insurance. You'd better start trying to see if anything's missing."

When the police had gone, we could see that Doña Carmen and her two cohorts were itching to get started on putting the señor's house back into shape. Don Alfonzo fetched a beer and a cola from the fridge and headed towards the terrace.

"I'd rather have a beer," I said.

He glanced at me, but didn't say anything. Instead he put the red and white can back in the fridge and took out another beer.

We sat under the parasol. I was sweating in the oppressive heat, but Don Alfonzo in his white, short-sleeved polo shirt and light, summer trousers was his usual serene and cool self, appearing untroubled by the heat. The weak, pale-green, cold Aguila beer tasted bitter and refreshing and surprisingly different. It was my first beer for eight years and the taste was more singular than actually pleasant, like it had been when I first drank beer at a young age. I had got used to the sugary taste of cola. I downed half the bottle in one go and could feel the effect almost immediately. I liked it, yet at the same time I despised myself for my weakness. I pushed my thoughts from my mind and told Don Alfonzo about the last few days. I left nothing out, admitting that I didn't know what I had told the three heavies, but it was obvious that I had mentioned his name and told them about the suitcase.

"Where on earth could they have heard about the existence of the suitcase, anyway?" I concluded.

He emptied the last of his beer and fetched two more.

"Who knows about it?" he asked.

"You, Oscar, Gloria . . ." I said and stopped short at the thought.

But he carried on regardless, in his subdued voice that made me keep my wits about me.

"You're fooling yourself, Pedro. I've known of its existence for years. Even before you asked me to look after it."

"Impossible," I said.

His eyes held mine.

"Drunks have few secrets," he said.

I felt myself blush, like an adolescent boy caught looking at the schoolmistress's breasts. He was right. I could recall boisterous conversations in the small hours, me bragging about my well-hidden suitcase, my life insurance. What I had never told anyone was that it was my private diary, that I considered it to be a Pandora's box, that once I opened it, it could never be closed again, and all its secrets would escape. That it was part of my superstition, my atheist's shrine, which couldn't be explained rationally. It was my mystical fifth dimension in a godless world. A talisman which worked like a rabbit's foot in my pocket.

I remembered that Gloria had seemed astonished when she heard that I had hidden some of my photographs. So she couldn't have known of its existence earlier, could she? Had Oscar? Oscar and I had spent so much time together that it would stand to reason I had talked to him about it at some point when drunk. But sitting there in the scented, scorching garden it struck me that I hadn't done that at all. I had bragged to strangers, especially women I wanted to get into bed, but I had never bragged to Gloria and Oscar. We knew each other too well. We couldn't pretend. We wouldn't pretend. We didn't have any secrets from one another, or so we thought, and therefore they were the very people from whom I had kept a secret. But not from Don Alfonzo – unless he had heard about it somewhere else. Unless it was because I had been under surveillance.

"Was I kept under surveillance in the old days?" I asked.

He looked at me with his wise, melancholy eyes. He hated disclosing secrets, even today.

"We kept all potential risks under surveillance."

"Was I one?"

"You were left-wing and mixed with left-wing elements."

"Elements?"

"Elements is a better word than others that were used."

It suddenly dawned on me.

"You checked me out when Amelia and I got serious?"

"I did what any responsible father would do with regard to his only child."

"And that was?"

"To take a thorough look at my future son-in-law."

"Not a very pretty sight at the time."

He smiled again and surprised me by placing his dry, delicate hand on top of mine.

"Pedro. Sometimes in my greenhouse I see an orchid that looks like a straggly weed, but underneath I can see the beginnings of a flower, perhaps not of extravagant beauty, but still with a strength which I, with love and care, can nurture."

"Yes, yes, that's all very well, father-in-law," I said. I never used the term.

"You turned out to be a good son-in-law."

"And you gave me a going-over with a fine-tooth comb and heard about what I'd said, among other things, about my suitcase. You found that although I might be a drunk, I was neither communist nor poor."

"I found that ultimately you were suitable for Amelia."

"And if you hadn't?"

Now he laughed out loud.

"Then my love-struck, headstrong daughter would have taken you anyway. Even then the old days were long over."

"Yes. The old days are gone," I said.

We sat in silence with our memories. There was nothing to say. We had said it a hundred times before. It all came rushing back.

"Did they get it? The suitcase?" I said instead.

"No. They didn't get it."

"Where is it? Where are my photographs?"

"We'll get back to that," he said.

The vacuum cleaners started up inside the house and we could hear rattling and splashing, clinking and clattering as the three women cleared up and threw out and put things away. Doña Carmen's high-pitched voice barked orders at the two young girls and we could picture them jumping-to. Pleasant and yet nerve-jangling domesticity.

"It keeps coming back to the Minister," I said. "It's not the Basques. I'm convinced of that. So who is it? And why? The Minister? The photographs have been printed. The photographs of him and the Italian woman are in the hands of editors all over the world. So why is he still after me? And I'd reckoned on doing a deal with him. So why should he order a break-in at my home? And kill my wife and child? It doesn't make sense, and yet . . ."

I stopped short. A shadow had passed over the old man's face when I had mentioned his daughter and grandchild, and I felt the familiar, acute grief jabbing at my heart too. The deep sense of loss that was unbearable, more physically painful than all my bruises.

"Revenge, maybe," said Don Alfonzo. "Maybe a case of good old revenge taken by a proud Latin man whose honour you have tarnished."

I couldn't help smiling at his old-fashioned words.

"Don Alfonzo. Spain is a modern nation. The old days are gone, you said so yourself. It's not Sicily after all."

"Pedro. There is still a great deal of the Sicilian or the Moor in the Spanish male's psyche. And this man has the means. If they can send

169

out clandestine groups to execute Basque terrorists, then they can also take revenge on a foreign photographer who has insulted a señor's personal honour, wrecked his home life, damaged the government and degraded Spain."

"Is that what it is? Is that what you've found out over the last couple of days?"

"No. That was my starting point. I'm an old man from a vanished era as you say, so to me it also made moral sense. I wanted to understand the incentive even though I condemn it. Perhaps I was a good investigator in the Caudillo's days because I always tried to understand the offender's incentive, his motives, and by thinking like them I often succeeded in thwarting plots against the security of the State."

"So you don't think it's that?"

"I know it isn't."

"Then what is it?"

"The terrorist was right when he said that the answer is to be found in one of your photographs. Let me put it a different way. We have asked the wrong questions because we have focused our attention on the present instead of the past. Because our shared distress is here in the present, we have assumed that the cause is to be found in life as it is now, but is that the case?"

"I've no idea what it's about," I said, and lit yet another cigarette.

"I don't know either, but every investigation is a matter of elimination – in order, if one is lucky and resourceful, to reach the truth of the matter. You have eliminated the Basque terrorists. I have eliminated the government, the State."

"Then we're back to square one?" I asked despondently.

"On the contrary. We've come an incredibly long way in a very short time."

"So what now?"

He got up and went into the house and came back with a blue ticket

170

to the Las Ventas bullring for the following Sunday. He brought a cola for me and a soft drink for himself. I would rather have had a beer, but I had too much respect for him to say anything. Or perhaps it was because I saw Amelia reflected in his eyes. I looked at the ticket. It was an ordinary *corrida*. The names of the *cuadrilla* were unfamiliar. In my youthful infatuation with Hemingway and the dream of Spain, I had once been an aficionado and knew the bulls and the bullfighters but for many years now the game with death in the afternoon sun had left me cold. Amelia, like the majority of well-educated Spaniards, found the whole business archaic, repulsive and barbaric, but there were large sums of money involved and it was still mostly Spaniards who filled the arena during the season.

"During the third bull the seat next to you will be taken by a man of your age. He'll be carrying the *El Pais* Sunday supplement. Listen to what he has to say," Don Alfonzo said.

"Who is he?"

"Let's say that he works for the State. Let's say that he was once my apprentice. Let's say he has some information that only he can tell you. Let's say that he can take us a step forward on the long path of elimination."

"Why so furtive?"

"Because he is bound by his professional pledge of silence. He's settling a debt that has been on the books accumulating interest for some years. He has access to the archives, but this particular archive doesn't formally exist. The new democracy declared publicly that it should be shredded, but it wasn't, it was just locked away from all but a select few. It's an archive like your suitcase. It contains stories and photographs from the past, and there are many people who don't want it opened because they fear what it would bring to light."

"Why?"

"The past has a habit of catching up with people when it's most unwelcome, when what has been and gone looks incomprehensible and meaningless in the modern world. Because what once made sense doesn't necessarily make the same sense today. When we have enough distance from the last 50 years, there's an archive that can shed light on Spain's turbulent history. The secret agreements that Franco entered into with the USA in the name of anti-communism. He was guaranteed survival, whereas Hitler and Mussolini fell, and America got its military bases and a southern bulwark against Bolshevism. The dirty war against those people who would overthrow the state. The King's role in the attempted coup of 1981. The military's inner-most thoughts when the Caudillo passed away. Portraits of people who have visited our country over the years and stayed here."

He was a cryptic old man, but it was in his blood. All those years in the dark corridors of the secret service had destroyed his ability to be straightforward about anything. Information was like a pension. You must use the funds sparingly and not all at once, in case the good Lord should let you live on for years. It was not to be scattered freely, but piece by piece. Information was not for common ownership, but for an inner circle that survived by exchanging secrets. That was how he saw it and nothing would change his mind. He had spent too many years in a war on an invisible front where secrets existed for others to seek to uncover and then hide again.

"Where's my suitcase?" was all I said.

"Come. Let's go into the garden," he said. "The sun is beginning to die off a little. It's rather sad for an old man – that yet another day has drawn to a close and there won't be many left to count."

# 11

He had opened all the windows and ventilation slats in the green-house, creating a bit of a breeze, but even so the heat and humidity were more intense than the baking oven outside. The scent of the flowers was sweet, but also rather cloying when mixed with the heavy smell of soil and compost. The spacious greenhouse was stocked with a variety of flowers, all of which were unfamiliar to me, miniature lemon and orange trees which Don Alfonzo cultivated, and in the middle there was a long chest which he used as a potting bench with all the para-phernalia necessary for the meticulous gardener. Don Alfonzo removed buckets and watering cans, trowels, some string and scissors, and then he removed the whole table-top and stood aside. At the bottom, next to a couple of empty buckets and a broken spade, I saw my suitcase, pretty as a picture, its combination lock glinting in the light.

"You're stronger and your arms are longer. So please help yourself," said Don Alfonzo.

I reached down and tugged at the solid metal suitcase. It was heavier than I remembered, or else I was still weak after my beating. At any rate my ribs hurt as I pulled it out and carried it over to the veranda. Don Alfonzo asked if I would stay for supper. Doña Carmen and her cohorts would soon have the house back in shape and then she could cook us a meal, but I didn't want to. I wanted to be alone with my secrets.

"I don't like it being here any more," I said instead. "I'll take it to my bank."

"As you choose," he said.

"They might come back."

"It's up to you," he said simply, but I think he was a little disappointed. I realised that he was probably lonely in his quiet, solitary life and perhaps I was the only person he had left. He seemed to be perfectly content on his own, but maybe cultivating beautiful flowers and searching for tangible fragments of memory in the crumbled, forgotten trenches around Madrid was a way of compensating for human company.

I rang for a taxi, threw the suitcase onto the back seat along with a bag of spare clothes and then I got in next to my worldly goods and asked the driver to take me to Madrid. He was a local minicab owner who had driven me before, a stocky little Catalan who smoked black cigarettes as he switched between sports channels on the radio. There was a *supermercado* on the outskirts of the village, where we had often done the shopping for Don Alfonzo. I asked the driver to stop and I bought a bottle of vodka and six colas. I got in again, opened a cola, drank half and poured vodka into the can. The driver looked in the mirror, but he made no comment. What could he say? He knew that I always paid and tipped well, so if I wanted to mix cola and vodka in his taxi it was my own business. I rang the office on my mobile and asked for Oscar, but his secretary told me that he was playing golf, and should have finished with his 18 holes any minute. His club was virtually on the way, so I asked the driver to take me there first. He was rather pleased. It would be a good long trip. The fare meter ticked over merrily while I drank vodka and cola and felt it working on me, and I was disgusted with myself and at the same time didn't give a damn.

Golf had become a very popular sport over the last ten years and there were courses everywhere. A new one seemed to be laid out every day. Oscar had elbowed his way into one of the more prestigious clubs in the area, not the very grandest, but near enough, as I had gathered from his boasting. The clubhouse, with restaurant and bar, was an old château attached to a vineyard at the end of an avenue of erect cypress trees. It was almost unbearably white in the late, low sun that threw the first shafts of red across the tawny-coloured tiles on the sloping roof. It had bay windows and spires and was built from greyish-white stone. The outside terrace was crowded with people sitting on yellow wicker chairs at white tables under multicoloured parasols. They were drinking aperitifs after their 18 holes, still wearing their polo shirts, caps and strange, checked trousers, while they discussed bogey, birdie, par and handicap just as they had once discussed share prices and love affairs.

I asked the taxi to wait. My suitcase and bag were safe with him. He had his afternoon newspaper, his radio and cigarettes and promised not to leave the car. Every click of the meter made him happy. I looked for Oscar on the terrace, but couldn't see him. His mobile was switched off. I remembered him telling me that it was a breach of etiquette to have your phone switched on while playing, so I knew he must still be out on the course, but darkness would fall soon, suddenly and quickly. I asked a waiter where the last holes were and he pointed across the vineyard's old garden, having first sized up my battered face and inappropriate attire. I drained the cola can and threw it into a rubbish bin. Beyond the far end of the garden there was an impressive view across the course, which was pretty and undulating and strangely verdant in the parched landscape. Its heavily irrigated green made it look fake, as if the lush golf course was an alien construction in central Spain's arid countryside where the sun scorched everything white. It was a big playground for adults who, in their modern pursuit of thrills, ignored the fact that they were playing on a course that used the water consumption of a largish village simply to keep the grass succulent.

The flag marking the 18th hole was straight ahead. The first hint of an evening breeze stirred the pennant gently. Oscar came walking along with two other men. They were wearing checked trousers which came down to just below their knees, expensive plain-coloured polo shirts and baseball caps, and each pulled a trolley with a bag of clubs. Oscar refused to use a golf buggy. I liked that. I could see two white golf balls on the closely mown grass of the green, but Oscar stopped and I spotted his ball 20 metres or so out on the fairway.

Oscar took an iron from his bag, went over to the ball and took a couple of practise swings. I had been caddie for him on several occasions when we had been on work trips. I didn't play, but golf courses are attractive and it was a good way of spending a couple of hours together, so I was familiar with the game and its rules and jargon. Oscar was an aggressive player who attacked the ball with woods and irons as though he were killing a menacing snake with a machete. I didn't really understand why he was so fascinated by the game, he so often got furious with himself when he sliced the ball and it flew across the grass like a startled hare. He grumbled for days after I had compared him to a destroyer escorting a convoy across the Atlantic during the Second World War, zigzagging back and forth to avoid German submarines.

He was too aggressive this time as well. He tried to chip the ball onto the green with a short, sharp stroke, but he hit it too hard and it dashed past the hole like a mouse chased by a cat, and rolled down through a bunker behind the green before coming to rest not far from me, where I was standing behind a tree watching him. I could hear him swearing. I knew I shouldn't, but I couldn't help myself. I picked up the ball, as he stalked round the green on his long legs and came in among the cypresses. I stepped forward and held the ball out on the palm of my hand.

"Are you looking for this, Oscar?" I asked in English.

"Fuck you, Lime," he said. "You know you're not allowed to touch the ball."

I threw it down at his feet.

"Just take the shot from there," shouted one of the other players. Oscar scrutinised me.

"What the hell do you think you look like?" he said.

"I ran into a couple of problems or three."

"Begun diluting the cola again have we? Well Peter?" he said. He knew me far too well.

"There's just something I'd like to ask you about," I said.

"Gloria will kill you."

"It won't take up much of your time," I said.

"You don't have to make an appointment with me," he said amiably. "We could always have a drink together, just like the old days."

"We could indeed," I answered.

"Gloria will flay us alive," he said. He turned round, took up his position and, without a practise swing pitched the ball effortlessly in a gentle arc, out onto the green where it came to rest just half a metre from the hole. He gave me a satisfied look, and stomped off to get his putter, basking in the other players' praise for his fine stroke.

Oscar settled up with his golfing friends, and after some painstaking arithmetic, he signed the scorecard and we went and sat at a table at the edge of the terrace. We had a beautiful view across the golf course, tinted red by the sun as the scorching day finally gave way to the mellow, pleasant evening warmth.

The waiter came across to us and Oscar looked at me quizzically.

"Two gin and tonics," I said.

"She'll kill you," he said.

"It's my business," I said.

"OK, Peter. You're an adult. Who got you into that state?"

I gave him a broad outline of what had happened, and a very brief sketch of my thoughts. I began to calm down and the restlessness in my body vanished as I drank the cool, fizzing drink with its tang of juniper and lemon. It was as if we had never been apart. It was hard to give up drinking; it was very easy to begin again. Oscar listened without too much interruption, other than to commend the efforts of our friends Tómas and his father and to curse the Irishmen.

"I've said it before. Stop playing amateur sleuth. Come back to work. Listen to your inner voice. Listen to what Amelia would have said. She would have told you to pull yourself together, live your life and do what you're good at, taking photographs," he said when I'd finished.

He was undoubtedly right, but that didn't make it any easier.

"I miss them terribly, Oscar," I said.

"They're not coming back, Peter. I know that sounds brutal, but it's not meant like that. I've got only your best interests at heart. Work your way out of it, my friend. Come back to us. We're your friends and we miss you."

"There's something I've got to straighten out first. Let's just see the summer through."

"OK. Besides, we're shutting down soon. It's too hot and everyone's away anyway. But we want you back. In good shape. As audacious as usual."

We sat there. The cicadas were singing and there was a pleasant, noisy chatter going on all around us. The Spanish are a vociferous people, but I liked that.

"Have I ever spoken with you about a suitcase full of Lime's photographs?" I asked after a while.

"Gloria said something about it the other day. That you had set your best negatives and prints of some of your photographs aside. And that this was both good and not so good. Good because you've saved some fine photographs. Not so good because it weakens her action for damages. She'd intended to milk the insurance company for every last peseta they've squirrelled away for a rainy day."

"Have I ever talked to you about it?" I said.

"You mean have you ever blabbed when pissed in the old days? Is that what you mean?" he said brutally.

"Yes."

He leant across the table.

"No. I heard about it for the first time the other day. You've talked about how you kept a box of old photographs in the loft, but I thought you meant photographs from your childhood. You know, the nostalgic shit we all lug around. But otherwise you've been damned orderly with your photographs. It's always impressed me. Even when your life's been total chaos, you've sorted, selected and catalogued your photographs in that fancy filing cabinet. Why do you ask?"

"About my photographs?"

"Yes, about your photographs."

"I think that's where the answer lies."

"Peter. I don't think there is an answer. Why torment yourself? Leave well alone. Come back to us. You've got many years to look forward to. We can't bear seeing you so wretched."

"You're a good friend, Oscar."

"Then listen to what I'm saying, damn it!"

"OK. After the summer."

He looked like he was going to say more, but instead he sat back in his chair. And then, without really knowing where the idea came from, I said:

"You knew the girl in the photograph, didn't you?"

He looked at me in surprise, but his eyes flickered.

"Which girl?"

"Cut it out, Oscar."

179

"I thought I'd seen her before, but I can't place her. It was 30 years ago."

"Why didn't you say that you knew her?"

"I wasn't sure I did."

"But you do?"

"I think so. At least, she reminds me of someone. But what the hell . . . all the chicks looked the same in those days. No make-up and hairy armpits. Big mouths, bloody fanatical. That's just how it was back then, man!"

"It's still odd though, that we'd known the same woman before we even met each other. Don't you think?"

"Not really. We might have thought that we revolutionaries were in the majority, but we were really a small band who were always bumping into one another at demonstrations, meetings and god knows what else. We gossiped about each other just like all groups do. It wasn't exactly completely by chance that you and I met. It would have been more surprising if we hadn't. Both working for the press. Both regulars at the same bars. Both members of the same international press association in Madrid. What's so unusual about it?"

"Did you know the man in the photograph?" I asked.

He shook his head and emptied his glass.

"I've never seen him before," he said, and I believed him. There was some truth in what he said. Over the years I had run into lots of people who I had known during the 1970s and who had been part of the revolutionary milieu which cut across all boundaries. Radical students from West Berlin's Free University, American draft dodgers, writers and other budding young artists who wanted to try their luck in inexpensive Madrid which back then seemed to have it all, just as Prague was the place to be after the fall of the Berlin Wall. Major upheavals always attract the young and adventurous.

"It's just a weird coincidence, Peter," he said, and looked at his watch. He asked if I would come home with him, so we could go out to dinner with Gloria, but I said no and refused a lift into the city. He walked away, exchanging greetings right and left, and I ordered another gin and tonic and drank it before getting the taxi to drive me to the Hotel Inglés in Calle Echégaray, just round the corner from Plaza Santa Ana. Maybe it was strange and masochistic to have chosen a hotel a few steps from the site of the fire, but it was a small family hotel with large rooms and I had often stayed there before I got my own flat. It was unassuming and it was in my neighbourhood, where I felt at home, and where I felt somehow that I had to make a fresh start if I was to prevent the desperate emptiness turning into a lethal depression that would lead to suicide.

I got a double room for the cost of a single. I had often provided them with customers when friends or business associates wanted to spend a few days in Madrid at a good hotel for a reasonable price. Carlos in reception knew me and didn't want to see my passport or identity card. Besides a double bed, there was a table and high-backed chair, a telephone, a minibar and a television. The room was decorated with faded wallpaper and reproductions of Goya and Picasso etchings from the blood-stained sand of the bull-ring. This was, after all, Madrid's old bullfighting district. The bathroom was clean and spacious, like they used to be, and there was a pink bath tub. I put the suitcase on the floor just inside the door and threw my bag on the bed. No one knew where I was. Somehow I sensed that the suitcase was secure as long as it was in an almost public space.

I left the hotel and walked to Suzuki's institute just a few metres further along the narrow street. I knew that I was putting off the moment when I would have to look through my photographs, but I needed the old man's soothing, consoling hands. The air was warm and young people were strolling along arm in arm in the middle of the street, as they had always done, on their way to *copas* and *tapas* in a city that seemed never to sleep.

I removed my shoes and returned a bow to Suzuki's youngest son.

"My father has been expecting you, Lime-san," he said in his impeccable Spanish.

I undressed, admiring the colourful bruising on my chest, now going yellow and brown, had a shower, wrapped myself in a towel and lay down in the inner room. It was like a little piece of Japan in the middle of the capital of Spain. Thin *shois* decorated with calligraphic characters served as walls. The floor was covered with soft mats and there was a fragrance of jasmine. I could hear sounds of training from the big hall, the rasping sound of bare feet in attack, defence, feint, lunge, and the Japanese terms shouted with a Spanish accent when the blows registered. My bruised rib and stitched gash hurt, and a headache was tightening its grip at the nape of my neck.

Suzuki came in, dressed in his white kimono. He bowed and I got up and bowed respectfully to him. He was a small, sinewy Japanese man of about 70, but he didn't seem to have changed at all during the 25 years I had known him. His close-cropped hair was still jet black.

"Welcome to my house, Lime-san," he said in his slow, heavily accented Spanish.

"Lie down and find peace in your soul. I have heard about your misfortune and I can see the pain in your eyes."

I lay on my stomach and his strong, yet gentle fingers began their mystical journey across my body. He squeezed, pressed, massaged and stroked, from my feet all the way up to my neck. It was as if he was pushing both the physical and mental pain forward, like a snow plough pushes snow, and the pain gradually drew together and gathered at the nape of my neck, disappearing into thin air as he massaged my neck firmly and lightly. At first I had difficulty relaxing, but eventually his magic worked its usual trick.

"You have filled your body with poison again, Lime-san," he said. "You have filled your soul with bad thoughts. You must seek your *wa* again. Otherwise you will be lost. You are full of evil spirits and negative thoughts. You must stop abusing your body and your soul. You must look into the very core of your soul again, even though you have lost the fixed point in your life. You must find a new one. You owe that to your family, Lime-san."

It might have been nothing more than an old man's rambling, but it revitalised and relaxed me, both physically and mentally. His heavily accented Spanish had always had a strangely soothing effect on me. He had a deep, hoarse voice and I think he employed many of the methods hypnotists use. Whenever I was tense and on edge he succeeded in making me look into an empty, comfortable darkness where there was neither sorrow nor joy, only nothingness. It was better than taking pills. And for many years it had been better than alcohol.

In a way it doesn't really matter what helps, as long as it helps, I thought before I felt my headache break free and vanish into the subdued light in which the calligraphic characters seemed to come to life, and I slept like a little child.

He let me sleep for an hour and then woke me with strong, sweet tea that we drank squatting opposite one another. I had borrowed a kimono and we sat in silence. His youngest son came in and greeted his father and then me with a respectful bow. He sat down on the floor and shared the tea with us. It was a signal that we could talk about everyday things. I hadn't been there for a while, so I asked politely about their business and life in general. Both were going well. The institute was thriving and Suzuki had become a grandfather again, to a healthy little girl.

I got dressed and they followed me out to the door where we bowed once more. It might be exaggerating to say that I felt like a new man, but I felt cleansed and the pain from my injuries had eased and the restlessness in my body and my mind had faded. I knew that this wouldn't last, considering the state I was in, but the little peace that Suzuki had given me would last long enough to give me the courage to begin looking for the photographs which I knew existed, but which I really had no desire to see again.

# 12

I spent a couple of days in the hotel room with my mobile phone switched off. One day thinking exclusively about myself. One self-centred day when I took myself back to my childhood with my affectionate parents, which hadn't been at all problematic, and then on to my very difficult adolescence. I often wondered whether my own restlessness was due to my parents' stability. They were born, fell in love and died in a little village on the island of Fyn, and I think they met their deaths happy and contented with the quiet, bourgeois lives they had lived. Of course I can remember them, but the memories lose focus and become hazy. There's a slightly remote father who goes to work. And a perpetually kind mother who stays at home and is there for you when you need her. It's as if they were always old and yet ageless, and for a short period before they died very quickly, one after the other, it was as if they suddenly aged in front of my eyes and withered away within a couple of weeks, so that I no longer saw them with the eyes of a child.

It was two days spent delving into myself, trying to rediscover the crucial events of my life. Going to the depths of my subconscious, where I was the prosecutor, defence counsel and judge. I slammed on the brakes when the pain became too intense, but for the first time in my 50 years, I spent hours trying to find out who I was and why I was that person. I didn't find as many answers as I might have, but I found an understanding of my life, and came out of the process a more whole person. I went right in to the heart of my grief and while I couldn't extinguish the despair, I managed to isolate it somehow, get it more under control.

I was alone. I could laugh and cry without being seen. A good, low-key hotel is the most anonymous place in the world. I could pace up and down. I could sit cross-legged on the floor or on the bed. I could eat and drink when I wanted. I didn't have to shower. I didn't need to shave. I could sit in the heat of Madrid naked as a baby or just in my underwear. The only thing I couldn't do was shout. The hotel didn't have air conditioning, and if I had bellowed out my pain, the police would have turned up. I could hear sounds from the street, but the people walking along Calle Echégaray couldn't hear me. My conversations with myself were mumbled under my breath, a dialogue between two parts of my mind trying to speak of the wordless.

I ordered food a couple of times, but barely touched it, although I soon began emptying the bottles in the minibar. I didn't get completely drunk, just mellow and sentimental as I delved into the suitcase and into my past. It was a bit like surfing the internet. I didn't know what I was looking for, I just sifted randomly through the bits of paper, old notebooks, half-finished diaries and photographs taken over the 40 years I had lived with a camera fixed in my hand as if it was an extension of my body. In a way it was a purging process. I faced up to the past and drew a line under it, so I could begin again, alone and without the family that had been my foundation for the past few, vital years. The sense of loss never left me but, as pictures and words surfaced and took me back to my childhood or adolescence, there were moments when I forgot Amelia and Maria Luisa.

You can't really remember who you were; you think you can, but there's a fine line between memory and oblivion, and a photograph doesn't help to unravel the thoughts and the feelings of a particular time. All that's left is small, vibrating echoes from the past, like what I'm writing now – can I really recall how I felt, all alone in Hotel Inglés? Or do I just think I can remember the atmosphere – a strange euphoria mixed with deep melancholy in the knowledge that time passes and death approaches step by step, day by day.

I thought about this as I took photograph after photograph out of the suitcase. It was all very organised. Photographs and notes were in chronological order. The photographs from my childhood were beginning to yellow – a picture of a stray dog, a tree I had climbed up to carve my initials at the very top of the trunk, my parents looking young and reckless in front of their first little Volkswagen. I had forgotten that they had been young once. That's not how I remembered them. But there they stood with the world at their feet, a happy sight. An image of my mother hanging out washing on a clear, frosty winter's day called to mind frozen trousers which stood up by themselves when they were brought in from the clothesline. Old-fashioned words and phrases surfaced: copper kettle and wash day, coalman, delivery boy, baker Bosse who brought round the bread in his little handcart. Here were the fishermen pulling a big wooden boat through the streets at Shrovetide, their familiar faces painted like clowns, trying to steal a kiss from the girls, who must put a coin in the fishermen's collection boxes if they succeeded. The money went to widows whose husbands had been taken by the sea. I was born in the middle of the 20th century and have never really considered my lifetime as being anything other than modern, but in reminiscence the past becomes alarmingly old-fashioned. A little photograph with blurred background, thanks to the poor optics in my box camera, and my large, solemn handwriting describing the event on the back: *Me on the beach, January 1958.* Twelve-year-old Malene in her swimming costume and, four years later on the same beach, without any clothes on, the sun beating down across the photograph. A friend from my teenage days whose name I'd forgotten. The first photograph of Oscar and Gloria. They're standing on the street with their arms round one another during the San Fermín *Feria* in Pamplona. Their white outfits are spotted with wine stains and Oscar is holding a wine skin over Gloria's head as if he's about to anoint her. I know they're wearing red scarves round their necks, even though the photograph is black and white. Gloria has an untamed mane of black hair. And Oscar's shoulder-length hair is curly and his beard is as wild and luxuriant as a Viking's. It's a glorious photograph, bursting with youth and vitality, filled with the belief that the world is our oyster and life will be good. A photograph full of *joie de vivre*, a declaration that dreams can be realised. It's a photograph that symbolises our conviction that we were the first generation that could and would change the world for the better, that the old order would collapse and be replaced with love and equality. We were in Pamplona together for the first time and we ran in front of the bulls in the morning and partied at night with the Navarrese and the Basques and the thousands of tourists who spent seven days cheering and drinking in the capital of Navarre, a copy of Hemingway's *The Sun Also Rises* in their pockets.

And then the first photograph of Amelia, wearing a white blouse and a blue skirt, squinting in the sunlight in front of the fountain on Plaza Cibeles in Madrid. The sight of her beautiful, dainty feet in gold sandals made me weep. Her twisted face as she gives birth to Maria Luisa, whose curly-black head can just be seen on its way out. The two of them together, naked in the sunshine at a cove near San Sebastián. And the last photograph I ever took of them. They're sitting side by side on a bench, feeding the pigeons. I hate those rats with wings, but Maria Luisa loved them, and I've captured the moment, the birds like a halo round their heads, the eye drawn towards the child's laughing face and the woman's joyful eyes. I studied them for a couple of hours, my grief like physical pain.

Box after box. Envelope after envelope. Photographs that meant something only to me, and photographs which had made me famous and rich. There was one image that I studied for a long time. It was taken in 1971. It showed a group of paparazzi outside a restaurant in Kensington. I'm in the photograph too, I must have lent my camera to a colleague. We're young and the way we're posing makes us look as if we're a football team. There's rain in the air. I could recall the smell of damp clothes and Virginia tobacco and hear their jovial voices. We're laughing, most of us have got a fag in our mouth or hand, and our hair is long, cut in a pudding basin style. We're wearing jeans and leather jackets. Our cameras, with their telephoto lenses, hang round our necks, like ancient talismans worn by a mystical tribe. We're waiting for John Lennon and Yoko Ono to leave the fashionable restaurant after their lunch. When they appeared our noisy bravado and camaraderie would vanish, and we would charge forward and point our lenses at them, each of us hoping that we would be the one to get the shot that would put food on the table that evening.

We stood there in cold and wind, sun and rain. Waiting for our prey like a pack of wolves. We hunted in packs, but only the strongest got the big pickings. We knew where the famous ate, exercised, walked their dogs, visited lovers. We knew the habits of the royals better than we knew what our own families were up to. We were predators, pursuing our quarry on familiar terrain. They tried to dodge us, but we tracked them down and bagged them if we were lucky. They also sought us out when they thought they could use us in a power struggle, or because they feared being forgotten more than they feared the lens. I was part of the regular pack but, like so many others my age, I left the group when I thought there were photographs to shoot and money to be earned elsewhere. In Moscow, Beirut, Tehran, East Berlin, New York, Madrid. News coverage or sports coverage. The world was my playground and my workplace. I spoke the international language of the photograph, and it could be understood by everyone, everywhere. The 20th century is the century of the photograph, moments captured in a split second that recorded history, usually to be forgotten two days after the photograph had appeared in the newspaper. But not Jacqueline Kennedy's picture. My lucky break. My ticket to the big money.

I sat looking at the photographs, sentimental and drunk and despondent because I could see how the years had vanished, time blown away like the pages of a calendar in an old American movie. Childhood, adolescence, manhood. Captured on perishable photo paper or brittle, crackling negatives and yet inescapably over. I never gave my age a thought when I had Amelia and Maria Luisa. Didn't fear growing old. Now, holding my photographs in my hands, I could almost feel the physical decline in my body, the laboured beating of my heart. I began calculating the number of times my heart had beat over nearly 50 years, and grew dizzy at the thought of the huge task it had accomplished. I pictured the grit forming in my kidneys, the black coating on my lungs, the fragile brittleness of my bones and suddenly I was afraid of dying, furious with time and with God who let it pass without our noticing. Without our understanding that every second has gone once it's been.

Eventually I returned to the photograph lying on the top of the pile. I don't know what drew me to it exactly, probably a sense that it harboured a secret, that the photograph was somehow closely linked to the incident. I studied that photograph of Lola Nielsen, the woman with Marianne Faithfull's hair, and the man behind her.

Clara Hoffmann of the Danish security service had put the

photograph in front of me in the Cerveceria Alemana and life had not been quite the same ever since. So now I put it on the floor in the Hotel Inglés, looked at it and remembered.

There was one more print from the same period. A colour photograph, taken in a living room. Lola Nielsen was pictured with another woman whose name I couldn't remember, and three men, all sitting round a low table. There were two large, brown pottery ashtrays on the table and a chillum left carelessly alongside an old-fashioned pipe. That famous poster of the era was hanging on the wall – Che Guevara with his stubbly beard and gentle eyes below his beret, contemplating the evil capitalist world. There was also a poster denouncing the imperialist war in Vietnam that galvanised my generation. Like so many other things, it's forgotten now, a distant conflict in a faraway country. The chairs and sofa looked like they had come from a flea market. Lola is playing her guitar, and the men are looking at her. Her fair hair half-conceals her face. One of the men is Ernst Strauss who had arrived that summer from Berlin with two other Germans. They look alike, young men with beards and long hair.

I remembered that they had stayed in the commune for a couple of months early in the summer. I could picture them: intense and committed, discussing the revolution. They were dogmatic, insisting that a peaceful, social revolution was no longer an option.

"Through the work of small, disciplined groups organised as independent cells, bourgeois society will be forced to reveal its true fascist face. The bourgeois state must be forced out of its repressive tolerance through violence and terror. The Palestinians have proved that the international community won't listen until words are accompanied by force, until hijackings or the taking of hostages put the cause on the front page of newspapers all over the world. We must strike at the very heart of bourgeois society via the armed actions of the people."

It was then that I realised that Ernst wasn't West German, but East

German. At least he had been born in Halle. "Did you escape over the Wall?" I'd asked him, but his answer was evasive.

Quite a few of the Danes in the commune agreed with the young Germans, while others opposed the use of violence. The discussions were heated, but mostly Lola and I kept out of them. Lola thought only of her career as a songwriter, while my thoughts revolved mainly round my photographs – how I was going to be the Robert Capa of my generation, getting Lola or some other girl into bed and smoking hash. I knew the right phrases, but I didn't really believe in their Marxist and revolutionary talk. West Germans and Danes had it too good.

I studied the photographs, remembering more. We had all earned some money picking strawberries on the flat fields that encircled the town. We got up at 4 a.m. and cycled out to the place where a tractor towing a trailer was waiting to take us to the day's picking area. The money was good if you worked hard, and no one asked for your tax code or your social security number. I suddenly recalled the feel of the heavy wet plants and the taste of the big, sweet berries, the cool morning breeze and the smell of salt and mist from the sea nearby, and I could see the bent backs and the raised bottoms in the grey, morning light and feel the biting stiffness in the small of my back.

And then suddenly I remembered something else.

I had left Lola's room early one morning. She didn't feel like picking strawberries that day. Usually she didn't feel like it. She counted on men providing for her. She spouted all the feminist theories but, as so often with her, they were mostly empty words. She would rather be waited on hand and foot, preferably by men.

As I came out of her room at the very top of the building and went downstairs, I saw a shadow sort of pull itself back, and then half-run down the stairs ahead of me to the kitchen. The commune occupied the large, old, main house of a disused farm and people were always coming and going, so you often encountered someone you didn't know. Many had believed that a commune really did mean communal living, and that if there was a spare bed you could just move in. I went down to the kitchen to have a cup of coffee and some breakfast with the others but I was too late. They had already left. A woman was standing by the sink with Ernst. She was holding a mug of tea and talking energetically but quietly in German, while Ernst listened intently. I said good morning and the woman turned her face away and Ernst asked me to make myself scarce in a strange, harsh tone of voice. I didn't reply, just got a cup of coffee and some bread and cheese. It was as much my kitchen as theirs. The woman stood with her back to me. She had a rather slender, attractive back under a baggy sweater that hung outside her faded jeans. Her hair was short, in a simple cut, and I got a glimpse of a pale, severe face and peculiarly fervent, intense eyes when she glanced at me. The two of them stayed where they were and I went out into the yard and sat in the early dawn and ate my breakfast, drank my coffee and smoked a cigarette.

That evening I asked Ernst about the girl. He was standing in the old garden behind the farmhouse, his ardent gaze following Lola as she wandered around in the evening sun, her fair hair loose down her back, her body naked under a flimsy, striped cotton dress. She was holding a three-year-old by the hand, the daughter of one of the people who lived in the commune. I knew Lola had slept with Ernst, but it didn't bother me. I liked Lola's indolent nature and sensual, leisurely lovemaking, but I wasn't in love with her. Not so it hurt. Not so I got jealous. We aimed to drop words like jealousy and infidelity from our vocabulary. No one could own someone else's desire, or their right to satisfy that desire with other people. I knew what she was like from the outset. After all, she had left someone else's bed to get into mine. But Ernst wasn't coping too well with the new, revolutionary openness.

Ernst had looked at me, even though it was hard for him to take his gaze from Lola moving sensually in the lovely, Danish summer evening. Insecurity was written all over his young face, and he blushed slightly. Half in fun and half in earnest, I said to him that the mysterious woman who had been in the kitchen wasn't as pretty as Lola, was she? He turned on me in a rage, snarling that I should mind my own business, that I would be wise to forget I had ever seen her. He left the garden, furious. And I never saw him again. He vanished, along with the woman. They might have come back later in the summer, but a week later I packed my rucksack and hitched to Copenhagen to seek my fortune.

It wasn't until a few years later that I learned the name of the woman when I saw her face on wanted posters in West Germany. Her intense eyes, alongside Ulrike Meinhof's intense eyes, stared out from the poster that stated that they were wanted for murder, kidnapping, robbery and other terrorist activities. But I didn't think much about it. I can remember only that when I saw her photograph, I realised that my suspicions had been right. The commune near Bogense had sown the seeds of terrorism, but they were being sown in many places back then. Most of us didn't overstep the mark. Just look at Oscar and me, and some of the others who lived there at the time. One is a successful advertising executive. Another is a Secretary of State, known for his robust, effective handling of his ministry in the right-wing government of the 1980s.

I studied the photograph again, looking carefully at one of the three young men. Suddenly I remembered his name – Karsten Svogerslev. He had a lot of curly hair and a big beard and sat farthest to the left, looking across at Lola. I didn't really keep up with Danish politics, but now I realised that he was a member of parliament, part of a far-left alliance of old communists, anarchists, Trotskyists and Maoists. All the political parties from the 1970s that called themselves something containing those words: Worker, Communist and Party. Otherwise most of the people from those days had left their pasts behind. When the Berlin Wall fell, their convictions crumbled with it.

I had left both the commune and Denmark behind long ago, and Lola was just one woman among many, a pleasant memory, but nothing more than that. It wasn't until I was sitting in that hotel room nearly 30 years later, seeking to retrieve the fragments of the past from the recesses of my mind that it all came back to me.

I spent the night before I left the commune with Lola. Her room was small, with sloping walls. The only piece of furniture was a wide bed which she had found in what had once been a bedroom in the farmhouse and painted deep blue, and some old wooden beer crates painted dark red and covered with velvet. The walls were bare and white, decorated only by her guitar, which she had hung up on the wall. It was very hot, and the warm summer evening air drifted in and out through the curtainless window, carrying away the smoke from our joints. We were naked and had made love and she was lying on her side tracing patterns on my chest. Her breast brushed my arm and I felt warm and light-headed from sex and marijuana and I was both sad and happy at the thought of leaving. Feet were made to roam and I would pursue my restless instincts. I thought of the nomad as a romantic figure and I saw myself as a modern nomad with the whole world as my domain. I was never going to own more than I could put in my rucksack. Others could sing. I would take photographs, since photographs could be sold anywhere. I was 20 years old and hopelessly romantic. I had my secondary school leaving exam. I had worked for six months spray-painting cars and put money aside. I had done my compulsory military service, giving a year to the nation. Considering the circles I moved in and the spirit of the times, I should really have refused and done the 16 months of civilian work that was the alternative, but I really couldn't be bothered. Next I had worked as a labourer. I had earned enough to do a bit of travelling, and I hadn't told the others at the commune about my savings in the bank in Odense. I called it my freedom fund.

Now I remembered that I had taken a photograph of Lola that night or rather early morning, as it had begun to get light outside. I searched for it in the suitcase, as memories rolled like a film in my intoxicated mind. I could see it quite clearly. She's sitting up in bed, naked, and is pulling her long hair up above her head, raising her breasts. Her long legs are bent slightly to one side in a Little Mermaid pose. It must have been a lovely photograph, but I hadn't kept it. It wasn't in the suitcase. For a moment I felt huge disappointment, but then I sat back down cross-legged on the floor and studied the photograph of Lola and Ernst by the harbour in Bogense, remembering our last night together.

"Where do you come from, Lola?" I had asked.

"From nowhere," she had answered.

"We all come from somewhere and we're all on the way somewhere."

"I grew up in Vordingborg in a military family, but I'm from England originally. I'm adopted. I think I'm a member of the aristocracy. Something tells me there was a big scandal," she had said.

She reinvented herself constantly, giving herself new roles, new identities and backgrounds, she wrote her own history and didn't worry about tangling herself up in lies and inconsistencies. Each time she created a new myth, she became convinced that it was true. Once she had told the commune that she was the daughter of an unmarried mother who had taken to drink in Copenhagen. I knew that she had told Ernst that she was the eldest of a family of six children and had grown up on an impoverished farm on the west coast of Jutland. Her Danish didn't give her away. You could tell that I was from Fyn by the way I spoke, even though I was already trying to make it sound like standard Danish or even working-class Copenhagen. Her voice was elegant and mellow, rather like an actress in an old black and white film from the 1940s, with a delicate, nasal tone that flattened the "a" sound as members of the upper classes from north of Copenhagen did.

I didn't contradict her. She kissed my chest and caressed me with her tongue and further down with her fingers and I could feel my desire swelling again between her hands.

She kissed the tip of my nose, my chin and my mouth.

"You've got so many talents, Peter. You're a talented lover, you're a talented photographer, you're a talented poet, you're a talented seducer, you're a talented liar, you're a talented cheat. All that talent will be your undoing, and do you have to leave now?"

I pushed her gently onto her back and entered her.

"Peter. I don't have any talent. My only talent is for seducing men. I have a great ability to make men do what I want. Why won't you do what I want?"

Her voice echoed across 30 years, loud and clear, as if she lay naked on the bed in the hotel room, so close that I shivered, as if in a trance in my very own, private world.

I both remembered and experienced. It was like being on a psychedelic trip. It was hard to tell what was real and what was fantasy. As if in a film, I saw Peter Lime leave that morning, a rucksack slung over his shoulder, walking away from the farm, along the deserted dirt track that led up to the road. I had the scent of Lola's skin and sex in my nostrils and on my skin. It was one of those glorious, early summer mornings in Denmark and the light on the salt meadows was so beautiful that it could only have been painted by a celebrated artist, and the few drifting, fragile clouds could only have been created by the most talented stage designer in the world. A damp grey morning mist crept along the ground. I walked along the country road feeling euphoric, partly because I was stoned, but mainly with a sensation of total freedom. Of joy at the unimaginable opportunities life held for me, and a feeling of invulnerability in my young, vigorous body.

And I don't think I have ever, before or since, been so happy and light-hearted, without a single worry. Just naïve, completely carefree happiness at being alive at precisely that moment in history.

The world lay at my feet and was there to be conquered.

# 13

Las Ventas, Madrid's bullfighting arena, stood burnished, round and scorching in the late afternoon sun as the taxi dropped me off just before 5 p.m. on Sunday. The usual throng of people milled around outside the arena and there was that familiar, infernal din of honking horns, shouting street vendors and traffic officers blowing their whistles in an attempt to bring some kind of order to the chaos. Sweet-sellers stood alongside stalls selling beer and soft drinks, carts with toys and posters, ugly toy bulls and imitation swords and capes. There was that buzz of expectation in the air that always precedes a bullfight and which, although I had forgotten it, instantly infected me. It was as if I had just woken from a long hibernation. I could feel the life around me, not just the chill within. Holding their brightly-coloured tickets, the crowd moved towards the entrance that towered up into the afternoon sky. It must have been like this in Rome when people were on their way to watch the gladiators fight. The electrifying proximity of death which you could experience without personal danger. I spotted the odd tourist, but most of the people thronging round the gates were Spanish. I didn't know the bullfighters on the poster. I didn't keep up any longer, but I heard a couple of aficionados saying that one of them was a young Andalusian beginning to make a name for himself. The bulls were from the Miura ranch down by

Seville, big strong animals. The true aficionados really came only because of the bulls; to see this half ton of beast, bristling with aggressiveness, attack with explosive speed anything that got in its way. I began to look forward to it, became wrapped up in the ritual again, and very nearly forgot why Don Alfonzo had sent me there. A man with the *El Pais* Sunday supplement under his arm would approach me when the third bull charged across the sand in the sun and dust to its inevitable death.

I had slept on the floor at first, then on the rumpled bed, protected by a Do Not Disturb sign on the locked door of my hotel room, and I had woken up with a clear head, but pains in my bruised ribs and the gash under my eye. I had tidied up and had a shower and had gone down to the restaurant and eaten my first proper meal for several days. Afterwards I had gone to Suzuki and surrendered myself to his intoning, melodic voice and healing hands. I felt that I had reached a turning point, even though I couldn't specify what had changed. Suzuki told me that I was breathing better, that he could feel the beginnings of *wa*, of a balance in my physique and my mind. As if I had been cleansed. I felt in control and the desire to sit and drink had receded, but I knew it was still there. It wouldn't take much to knock me back again. I had switched my mobile phone back on. The answering service was full of messages from Oscar and Gloria, telling me off for not being in touch. They had recorded the last message together, saying that they were going to Ireland and London and looked forward to my return to work. They hoped I would have a good summer. They were taking their mobiles, and they assumed they would hear from me. In fact, they insisted that I ring them!

Don Alfonzo's ticket was one of the expensive ones. I had a place on the fourth row on the shady side, just under the President in charge of today's *corrida*. The seats gradually filled up. Cigarette smoke spiralled with the buzzing voices straight up into the blue sky above

Madrid. Soon, nearly all the seats were taken. Mass and bullfighting start punctually in Spain. There were two empty seats on my right and another empty one on my left. Four men sitting in front of me were busy discussing the bulls they had seen that morning at the drawing of lots to determine which of the six bulls the three bull-fighters would confront, and in which order. They were experts and wouldn't be interested in anything except the bullfight. There were four women, American tourists, sitting behind me. I could tell from their voices that they were apprehensive at what they were about to see, but perhaps they didn't want to go back to the US without being able to talk with indignation of the cruelty of the Spanish bullrings. Their main topic of discussion was how aggravating they found the cigarette smoke, even though we were sitting in the open air, that it was just too bad there weren't any smoking areas in the arena. They were all of the opinion that Europe smelled.

I placed the brown cushion on the concrete, sat down and breathed in the smell of the men's fat cigars and eau de cologne and the Spanish women's discreet, expensive perfume. Beer and soft drink vendors ran along the rows of the stands, others were offering cognac and whisky or wine. I bought a cola and a packet of peanuts and inhaled the smell of sand and wood and animals and savoured the buoyant sound of expectant voices. Looking over at the cheap seats on the sunny side was like watching a ballet, as the spectators fluttered their fans rapidly in the sluggish air. Hats or folded newspapers were used to shade faces and scalps from the burning sun which made the raked sand glow yellow.

The band signalled the start of the bullfight with a bugle call and I saw the three bullfighters with their troop of *cuadrillas* prepare to march to salute the President. They crossed themselves, the band began playing the *pasodoble*, and they walked across the sand to start the ancient dance with death.

The first bull came out of its dark stall at great speed, its head held high. It stopped for a moment in the sharp sunlight, surprised by the huge crowd, the smells and the noise. Then it caught sight of the bull-fighter's assistant, the *banderillero* with his yellow and red cape, who had stepped forward from the barrier. He would make the first moves, allowing the bullfighter to inspect his opponent. The bull pawed the ground, tossed its head and bellowed, and the crowd began to whistle. Marking out its territory was a sign of weakness. The bull should attack immediately. The assistant got it to run after the cape that he dragged along behind him and then the bullfighter stepped forward to take up combat. He flourished his cape a few times and the bull attacked, direct and fast, but jerked its left horn upwards when the bullfighter drew the huge, black beast round him in a couple of beautifully executed *verónicas*. On his third attempt, the bull's forelegs buckled as it tried to turn and a sigh of disappointment surged through the crowd. Weak legs, the big problem with the Spanish fighting bull today. They were bred too fast. There was a signal from the band and the horses came trundling in. They looked like large, prehistoric lizards or ungainly dray horses with bulky protective padding round their bellies and flanks and blinkered eyes. The *picador* sat erect, holding his lance, and leant over the bull after the bullfighter, with a movement of his wrist, had lured it away from the cape so that it faced the horse. The bull attacked immediately, the *picador* thrust his lance down into the huge, distended hump of muscle on its back, and the blood began to gush. The spectators whistled in contempt as the *picador* pounded the lance into the bull's back to stop the animal from jerking its left horn upwards. But the bull pressed against the lance with such power that the hefty horse was crushed against the wooden barrier until the capes swirling around the bull's eyes lured it away. Now it knew that there would be no mercy. Not until all its enemies had been removed from this hot sand would it be left in peace.

The bull was given another dose of the lance before the President, deferring to the audience's deafening whistles at its being unduly weakened and exhausted, signalled for the animal to be released. It stood in the middle of the arena, breathing heavily, red blood streaming from the wounds on its back.

The spectators applauded when the bullfighter saluted the crowd with his *banderillas*, the short, colourful darts. He was going to place them himself instead of letting one of his assistants do it, as was normal. He ran across the sand towards the bull, the animal caught sight of him and started to run too, and for a moment it was as if man and beast merged into one when the bullfighter effortlessly went up on tiptoe and then spun away, deftly placing the two darts in the right-hand side of the hump of muscle. The bull roared and tossed its whole body as it tried to shake off these irritating, painful things. The audience applauded both the perfectly placed darts and the bull's new-found courage. The next two *banderillas* were placed in an equally elegant manner, but the third pair fell out when the bull's weak legs gave way and it sank to its knees.

It stood alone and bleeding in the middle of the arena, awaiting its fate. I looked down at the bullfighter in front of me. He took a sip of water, crossed himself and picked up a red cloth – the *muleta* – and a lightweight sword that he folded into the cloth, pulling it taut. His face was pale under his olive-coloured skin and his dark eyes were frightened, but he saluted proudly by taking off his hat and throwing it to a woman a few rows up, dedicating the bull to her. I took a couple of quick shots with my Leica. I should have used a telephoto lens. I wanted to capture the stark fear on his face, the blank eyes with their tiny pupils. It was the first real photograph that I had taken since Amelia and Maria Luisa died, and I lifted the camera, adjusted the focus and assessed light and distance with my usual proficiency, acting almost unconsciously, but with that unerring instinct. It was a fantastic feeling, an indescribable moment. I was suddenly active again, and responding to my surroundings by doing my job – capturing and freezing the instant. It felt like a moment of truth of the same intensity as the one that awaited the bull down on the blood-sprinkled sand.

The bullfighter was older than I had thought, with his boyish, slight frame in its close-fitting yellow and red outfit, but what I remember most was the fear in his aged face as he stepped out alone on the sand to confront the bull. He knew that now, when weakened by loss of blood, the bull's rage and cunning were at their peak and he would have to kill it quickly. He had placed the *banderillas* himself to over-come his fear, and because it looks braver than it actually is. The real skill lies in the critical moments when he stands alone with the bull in the middle of the arena and again his reluctance was clear. He drew the bull over towards the barrier, so that his assistants would be close at hand if anything went wrong, and then he finished the job as fast as he could without being seen to be a coward. The bull kept tossing its left horn, and when the bullfighter tried to pull it round in a pass with the *muleta* its weak legs gave way again and it sank to its knees. He had trouble making it attack. It just stood snorting, red blood caked in its black pelt, looking more like a despairing cow, and the bullfighter had to get very close to make it come forward. When he saw the way things were going, he pulled out the death-dealing sword, poised himself ready for the moment of truth and killed the bull without further ceremony. At least he was professional. He saluted the crowd, bowed to his woman and the President, and the mules entered and dragged the dead bull out to the sound of sporadic applause. A Sunday afternoon like any other all over Spain. Memorable experi-ences in the arena were few and far between – when you were no longer fascinated by death itself, when the colours of the costumes, the atavistic mystique of the drama being played out and the ritual had lost their attraction. The minute you began to feel sympathy with the bull, the magic of the bullfight vanished. I realised why I had stopped following the Sunday killings. The show no longer made any sense.

It didn't make sense to the American women behind me either. I had listened to their outraged exclamations throughout, and when the team of mules dragged the huge dead beast across the bloody sand they left, protesting loudly about cruelty to animals. It was worse than they had imagined. They would write to their local newspaper. It had made them feel physically sick. Now they had something to talk about back home in Iowa.

I ordered a cognac and a beer and drank them while the second bull was killed in much the same way. The bull was stronger but the bullfighter was worse, and he let his *picador* weaken the huge, powerful animal, so it finally fell to its knees. He was a bad killer and made three attempts while the spectators whistled and jeered their contempt.

I ordered another cognac, and when the bugle signalled the third bull call, an elderly man sat down on the empty seat next to me. He was carrying a copy of the shiny Sunday supplement of *El Pais*, a whole magazine in itself, which he put on his lap.

"*Buenas tardes*, señor Lime," he said.

"*Buenas tardes*," I replied and looked at him.

He was a small man with a high, rounded forehead. His hair, still black and pomaded, was combed straight back and he wore a pencil moustache above a small mouth. He was smoking a big Havana cigar. Despite the heat, he was wearing a pale suit with a meticulously knotted tie. He spoke in a dry, slightly rasping voice, hardly moving his mouth, as if afraid of lip-readers.

"Are you enjoying our *fiesta brava*?" he said.

"Not particularly. The bulls just fall over, to put it bluntly, and the bullfighters seem to be thinking more about their bank balance than their art."

"Quite. Could apply to most things these days. Money is raised above art or the traditions which make Spain a civilised country. But you are, of course, well aware of that. Don Alfonzo has said that you know and understand our country and only wish the best for it."

"That's correct," I said.

"This was not always the case," he said.

"What do you mean?"

"You were once part of a group that wanted to create disorder."

"If you mean I was an opponent of Franco's dictatorship, then you're right."

"That is an oversimplification, señor Lime. The Caudillo, blessed be his immortal soul, was a man of vision. He understood our torrid blood, our brutality, our capacity to kill, our fascination with death of which the *corrida* is but one example, our lack of tolerance, our machismo and our uncompromising pride. He saw it as his mission to heal the wounds inflicted by the fratricidal war and turn Spain into a modern European nation. And he succeeded."

"I'm sure those who were tortured and executed are grateful for the undertaking. Spain was an abscess on the map of Europe. A strange relic of fascism, where Nazism survived long after it had perished in Germany."

He didn't get angry, but continued in the same subdued tone of voice.

"The alternative was chaos. There were powerful forces which wanted Spain to perish. Forces within and outside the country. The Caudillo's vision was right. Spain had to follow its own course for many years in order to emerge from its past unscathed."

You could hear the echo of servants under other dictatorships. From Stasi informers in the former GDR to fascist executioners in many Latin American nations. They did it in service of a cause. They were just following orders. They bore no personal responsibility, and they defended their actions until death caught up with them, because otherwise their lives made no sense. Sometimes it was hard to grasp that dictatorships could function only because thousands closed their eyes and thousands more participated in maintaining the oppression.

"Are you an historian?" I said.

He laughed.

"Of sorts. But we're not going to discuss politics or history. I'm here to repay a debt to a man I respect."

I was going to say something else about Franco, but the crowd began yelling and whistling so loudly that we couldn't make ourselves heard. It was time for the third bull. This one was lame. It stood in the middle of the arena and when the bullfighter began working it with his cape it was clear that it limped badly on its left hind leg. The bullfighter looked up at the President in entreaty and soon afterwards a herd of steers entered the arena. The huge, angry bull turned into a meek cow, allowing itself to be lured out of the arena by the steers it recognised from the wide open spaces of the ranch where it had been reared. Now, as placidly as a sacrificial lamb, it left the arena in order to be killed by an electric shock to its forehead, administered by an efficient slaughterer waiting in the passageways under Las Ventas.

"One believes there is a way out, but all routes lead to death," said the man at my side.

"You know my name. I don't know yours," I said.

"For the sake of convenience, you can call me Don Felipe."

"Don Felipe. If you're not an historian, what are you?"

Like my father-in-law, he preferred to talk in riddles. I couldn't place his accent, but he sounded as if he came from somewhere in the south. I knew that he must have been an intelligence officer under General Franco, who had more secret services than medals. But he was slightly more loquacious than Don Alfonzo.

"Please don't misunderstand," he said, leaning towards me so that

I got the full aroma from his cigar. "I'm a supporter of democracy. The real purpose of our work was to combat communism and anarchism, so that Spain would be ready for democracy. It succeeded. We had many enemies. Bolsheviks, terrorists, separatists. Foreign agents attempted to undermine the authority of the State and the social order. There was great pressure during the 1970s as the Caudillo's strength began to fail. Our enemies saw a breach in our defences and sent agents to incite those forces that desired chaos. I helped to monitor and stop these subversive forces. My speciality was the KGB."

"Together with Don Alfonzo?"

"Don Alfonzo had his duties. I had mine."

"Which were?"

"To defend the State and its institutions. To ensure that good citizens could sleep peacefully at night."

"I thought that was my father-in-law's task too." I used "father-in-law" just to remind him who I was.

"Your father-in-law concentrated on the enemy within. My job was to endeavour to stop the foreign agents who infiltrated our nation."

"The Russians?"

"Among others. The Soviet command liked to use Cubans. They fitted in better with the – what shall I say – the milieu."

"OK," I said and drained my glass. I would have ordered another one, but the substitute bull was sent in and the sale of drinks stopped as the ritual followed its established, predictable course. Now I understood that Don Alfonzo had worked for the internal security network, while Don Felipe had been employed in counter-espionage.

"You were one of the people who featured in certain reports," he added.

"Reports?"

"Normal intelligence operations. Bugging, surveillance, covert searches of places of residence, material from informers. You know what goes on."

A buzz went round the bullring and I looked down at the sand as the band struck up the *pasodoble*. We were witnessing one of those moments of great beauty when bullfighting becomes art, and beast and man merge in a deadly embrace, when the bullfighter's suit of light and the beast's dark, blood-drenched pelt become one. It was the young Andalusian, not yet old enough to realise he was mortal. He used the red cape to draw the bull towards him in tighter and tighter circles so its blood stained his tight-fitting costume. The bull went straight for him, eager to attack, as he lured it with calls and small flicks of his wrist. You could tell that he wanted to stretch the moment for as long as possible, to continue his macabre, exquisite ballet for ever, the music and the rhythmic shouts of *olé* from the spectators a drug which drove him on. But common sense finally prevailed. With each pass the bull learnt a little more, and soon it would realise that behind the red cape there was a man, and you could see that its eyes no longer focused exclusively on the *muleta*, but that it sensed a soft body on the other side. The bullfighter executed a series of three passes, to the spectators' noisy delight, and then fetched his sword.

"May the killing be elegant," said Don Felipe respectfully. He was obviously an expert, an old aficionado.

The young bullfighter walked into the open arena, bowed and presented the bull to the ecstatic crowd. He positioned himself and drew the bull across in a couple of tight passes which I remembered were called *manoletes*, named after the legendary *matador de toros* from the 1920s. Then he lifted himself onto the balls of his feet and sighted along the blade while locking the bull's eyes with the red cloth so it raised its bleeding hump of muscle, exposing the spot where the blade could penetrate to its inner organs. A hush fell over the arena, the bullfighter flicked his wrist and the instant stood still, frozen, for a long time. And then man and bull attacked simultaneously and the bullfighter passed in over the horns and thrust deep, severing the artery in its neck. The bull sank to its knees, motionless for a moment, spewing blood, and then falling on its side as the assistant came in and delivered the final blow with one thrust of his short-bladed knife.

I got to my feet, joining the ovation for the young man standing with his fallen quarry, proud with the arrogance of youth. The scarves came out and, with the President's permission, the two ears and tail were cut off and given to the bullfighter as a trophy before the mules dragged the bull round the arena to the sound of deafening applause, in tribute to the beast for its courage and bravery. I had forgotten how this barbaric spectacle could suddenly appear to be sublime, making you momentarily suppress your sympathy for the animal.

"Let us thank God for our good fortune," said Don Felipe.

"Or Don Alfonzo for the tickets," I said.

He laughed.

"Yes. And now we ought to leave. We were fortunate to witness one of those rare moments when art is born and dies before our eyes. That is unlikely to occur again today, or possibly ever."

"I thought you had something for me."

"I have. But we don't need to sit here any more. Now it will only be disappointing, and I've checked that we're not under surveillance."

"And you're sure about that?"

"You are going to have to trust me a little, señor Lime. Seeing as how I trust you. Let's go!"

We went up the stairs and into the building. There were only a few people in the wide passageway under the sweeping arches. He hurried along to one of the many bars and bought two cognacs, and we went over to one of the arches from where we could look down through the opening to the square in front of the arena which was still swarming with people. The buzz of voices had become more intense.

"They expect our young Andalusian maestro to be carried out shoulder-high after the level of artistry he achieved," said Don Felipe and handed me the *El Pais Suplemento*. We could hear the music starting up again inside the arena.

"I've put a surveillance report inside. It's from an archive that doesn't exist – officially, that is. I've removed the archive number, which could identify the report should it fall into the wrong hands, but you have my word that it is bona fide. I'm repaying a debt of honour. I'm breaking the law, I'm breaking my pledge of secrecy, I'm breaking my oath to the Caudillo never to divulge secrets about my work, but I feel for Don Alfonzo and mourn for his loss, which is your loss also."

"What's in it?"

"Read it. There are two men talking. One is called Victor Ljubimov. He was the cultural attaché for many years, but his real employer was the KGB. His area of responsibility was the Spanish Communist Party, the PCE. He was an agent, couriering money for the party, and helping to organise the PCE. As you know, the party was illegal before the transition."

I nodded. He had used the word *transición*, which the Spanish used to describe the peculiar, dangerous years between General Franco's death in 1975 and the first free parliamentary elections in 1977. Shortly before his death, Franco had authorised five executions. No one knew whether the King or those within the old regime would opt for democracy. The younger forces in the only party permitted by Franco would have to relinquish their own monopoly voluntarily and take Spain from dictatorship to democracy. They would have to do so without antagonising the army and vast security network, which would have resulted in a classic, Latin-American-style military coup. It was a heady and exciting period, and a dream to be a reporter in Spain at the time.

"Do you understand what I'm saying?" Don Felipe asked.

I nodded again and he continued.

"The PCE was under careful surveillance, but it was the Americans who found Victor for us. He speaks fluent Spanish and English. He was the KGB's main contact with the PCE."

"OK," I said. "Who's the other one?"

"Please, be patient with an old man," he said. "The PCE – *Partido Comunista de España*. A large number of the party leaders lived in France or in Moscow, but in the 1970s a new generation was in the process of re-establishing the party within Spain. The PCE was extremely active in the universities and the trade union movement, and we lost access to parts of their underground organisation because the new, young communists were difficult to infiltrate. Of course, we knew that Moscow was trying to maintain control and influence, both through agents and by financing the party. I remember that time so well. Spain was in a state of revolution. There were many foreign agents operating here. Our own revolutionaries sensed what was coming, but many on the left didn't think Soviet communism was what should replace Franco's regime. Moscow was worried about that too. That's the background you need to understand the transcript."

"OK," was all I said, and this time I waited patiently. He took a sip of his cognac and I did the same from my glass. My fingers tingled as I felt the soothing effect of the alcohol.

"We had Victor under surveillance. We collaborated closely with the Americans, of course. Were we not a bulwark against communism? Did we not accommodate their bases? When it came to the fight against the Bolsheviks, the Americans would have been willing to collaborate with Satan himself. The identity of the other person talking is, however, unknown to us. We gather that he is of German origin. That he is from the GDR and that he works for the Stasi. His assignment was to infiltrate the PCE. We don't know the exact nature of his role – or if he recruited you, señor Lime."

I looked at him astounded. I had not expected that.

"Me? I've never been a member of a party. He didn't. I've never been asked by either the one or the other," I said.

"Well, it's of no consequence today. But Don Alfonzo considers it of significance."

"I've worked as a photographer in the GDR, but I don't know anyone and didn't know anyone from the GDR here in Madrid."

I knew Oscar of course, but he was from Hamburg and, as far as I knew, had set foot in East Germany only once as a very young man, when he went in on a one-day visa just to see what life was like on the other side. I didn't regard Oscar as German at all, he had long since renounced everything to do with Germany and he had talked incessantly about becoming a Spanish citizen for years, always mocking me for refusing to consider giving up my Danish passport. He often said that we had made our homes and lived well in Spain, so we ought to go the whole way and become citizens of the country that had treated us so well. What did I think I owed Denmark?

I looked at him questioningly and after a pause he continued.

"I've got friends from those days. Contacts. Some active, others, like me, who savour the tranquil pleasures of the pensioner. I know the Soviet agent is still alive, but he left the service when the Soviet Union collapsed and he's now a so-called businessman in Moscow."

"Mafia?"

"He calls himself a security consultant."

I could tell from the buzzing sound coming from down in front of Las Ventas, the music and the cries of *olé* drifting up from the sand, that the young Andalusian had been successful with his last bull, and I realised that Don Felipe, or whatever he was called, had timed it so that he would leave the arena at the same time as thousands of others. And now it looked as though the crowd would pour out of the main gate with the bullfighter carried shoulder-high, a rare honour – an honour that would create total confusion.

Hearing the spectators' ecstatic applause, he stood up, leaving *El Pais* on the table.

"Thank you for the remarkable experience," he said, raised his glass and drained it. "Don Alfonzo must have second sight. Asking me to arrive specifically at the time of the third bull was a stroke of genius. It is seldom that *el arte de torear* really is an art. Goodbye, señor Lime. It has been a pleasure talking to you."

He left, trailing a plume of cigar smoke, a small, stooped man with big secrets. The elated, satisfied crowd began pouring out of the exits and swept him along, and he vanished as if I had never sat talking with him. I looked through the window and watched as the throng gathered by the main gate and shortly afterwards a group of men came out with the young Andalusian on their shoulders. He looked happy and alarmed, as if the mass of people posed a greater threat than the two bulls he had killed with such honour and courage that afternoon. He held the ears and tails proudly above his head, shook them and then threw them into the air. How simple and straightforward life was for him. He didn't fear death, he had been carried aloft by the discriminating aficionados who frequented Las Ventas, he was on the threshold of his life and took it for granted that youth, beauty and good fortune would be his for ever.

I raised my glass and drained the last drop of cognac, wished him good luck and carefully opened *El Pais*. I was standing in my little alcove as people streamed past, paying no attention to me. A few sheets of white paper, carefully folded in half, had been slipped inside the middle pages. I was itching to read them, but I put them back and, when the crowd began to thin out, I left with *El Pais* under my arm to find a quiet place where I could delve into yet another strange aspect of my past.

# 14

I went to our Sunday-quiet office on Paseo de la Castellana. For most of the year, the office was busy even on Sundays. The insatiable appetite for photographs of the rich and famous didn't let up, but in August we put operations in Madrid on the back burner and let the London office deal with business over the weekends. Most of our employees spent their holidays far away from the stifling, smoggy heat that enveloped the city day after day. On the short taxi ride from Las Ventas to the office, my body stuck to the imitation leather of the back seat as if glued to it  and when I got out, the back of my t-shirt was soaked through.

I let myself in, and met the dry coolness of the air conditioning that hummed faintly. I pulled my t-shirt out of my trousers and flapped it like a girl at dance class, and fetched a cold cola from the fridge in the kitchen. Apart from the humming, the office was completely quiet, and the computers sat covered and silent. I wandered through the empty rooms and had a quick look in Oscar's office. His cluttered desk – usually covered with dozens of copies of photographs, glossy magazines, coffee mugs, long computer print-outs and full ashtrays – was tidy and polished. The telephone and computer looked abandoned, although I could see the light flashing on his answering machine. The large cupboards in the archive room were stuffed full of negatives and copies of photographs, but the ones that were most in demand were stored digitally on computer, ready to be transferred when a newspaper or a magazine needed a particular photograph. We dealt mostly in photographs of famous people, but we were also able to provide a good picture of a Goya in the Prado if needed. We could send a photograph round the world via the telephone network in seconds. The magic touch of the information age.

I put off reading the report for a while, and pottered about savouring the calm and the cool air, but eventually I sat down in my office. I left the door open so I could look out across the big, open room where the secretaries and assistants worked and on into Oscar's office. I felt at home and yet a bit like a guest who shouldn't have the key to the domain of these diligent people. The rooms were still part of my life, I owned a share in them, and yet I didn't belong there any more. I put the sheets of paper in front of me, lit a cigarette and began to read with growing fascination and astonishment as the stark words took me back in time.

Surveillance Report PCE/13/05 March 1976. 14.45.

Prepared by (blanked out). Translated from English by (blanked out).

Participants in conversation: Victor Ljubimov, approx. 40, cultural attaché at the Soviet Embassy in Paris, entered on a Cuban passport via the Portuguese border 23rd February 1976, staying at Hotel Victoria (see enclosed copy of hotel registration). Unknown man, mid-20s, tall, bearded, hippie-type. Conversation took place in English. Some interference noise, otherwise technical equipment functioned excellently. However, first four minutes of the conversation missing. Surveillance group PCE/13 is of the opinion that this part of the conversation took place in the entrance hall beyond the range of microphone 3. Surveillance was also restricted by a TV set in the sitting room broadcasting a film. After processing the tape, the major part of the conversation has been deciphered. Having studied the recording, the service's language expert A/24 reports that the subjects speak good and grammatically correct English, but it is not their first language. The hippie speaks English with an accent defined by language expert A/24 as German despite his attempted use of some American jargon. Ljubimov's English is fluent with British pronunciation, reports language expert A/24 having listened to sections of the tapes without prior knowledge of the subjects' identities.

Ljubimov arrived 15.45 at the cover address on Calle Princesa no. 12. In accordance with Directive 11 with authorisation from Classified Court Division 6, in agreement with the owner of the neighbouring apartment, a good patriot with many years membership of the Movement, electronic surveillance equipment had been installed.

The cover address is owned by (name blanked out), whose connection to the illegal underground trade union, Comisiones Obreras, is well documented. In the light of current investigations, the recommendation remains to refrain from arrest and questioning of (name blanked out).

15.58, interlocutor arrived at Calle Princesa no. 12. As the identity of the subject is currently unknown, the transcription designates the subject Hippie because of his long hair. Surveillance group C/3 was unable to obtain a photo of Hippie as he apparently left the building via another exit. Surveillance group C/3 will continue investigations in an effort to establish his identity and official business in Spain. Gives the impression of being a tourist, but is athletic and clean despite the long-haired appearance.

Obviously they hadn't succeeded in establishing Hippie's identity. "Tall and long-haired". That could describe thousands of young Westerners who swarmed to Madrid, enjoying the good life in the 1970s when the dollar and Deutsche Mark bought a lot of pesetas. I looked out across the Madrid rooftops and thought about how, at the height of the cold war, bureaucrats all over the world churned out report after report like this one. Could they be trusted at all? Hadn't it always been the case that the reports of secret agents were often completely unreliable, because it was in their own interest to turn each little triviality into a suspicious element, into a sinister piece of a larger pattern. This was the way in which the secret services ensured that their budgets, and therefore their staff, continued to grow. It's expensive to run a police state.

But the conversation must be genuine. Or was it? There was no way of knowing. I lit another cigarette and read on. At least now I was spared the bureaucratic, tortuous phrasing of the preamble. The conversation was presented like the dialogue in a screenplay. All it needed was the shooting directions.

> Ljubimov: . . . have you any idea if Comisiones Obreras will get the workers out on the streets on the 1st of May?
> Hippie: The comrades are doing great work and it looks like they're following the strategy which the Central Committee in Moscow supports too. It's a question of mobilising and forcing PSOE onto the defensive.
> Ljubimov: What about the strikes next month?
> Hippie: All the indications are that they're going to be nation-wide. Virtually a general strike.

Ljubimov: Have they got enough funds?

Hippie: There's a shortage of funds. No doubt about that.

Ljubimov: I can get more. I'll need a couple of days. We'll have them transferred here via Paris, through the usual channels.

Hippie: Then there's the student movement. The anarchist groups are strong and are pushing the Party into the background. We need funds for that fight too.

Ljubimov: Moscow's rich, but we can't print the stuff.

Hippie: It's now that the battle has to be won. It's only a question of time before the PCE is legalised, so we've got to come from a position of strength. Otherwise the Socialists will run with the people. We're in a revolutionary situation.

Ljubimov: Moscow attaches importance to both the strike and the 1st of May. That's where the door to this rotten system has to be kicked in.

Hippie: I'm on the scene. Students and workers will be on the streets together on the 1st. Count on it.

Ljubimov: OK. Spain must be won.

Hippie: Then there are the Basques . . .

Ljubimov: Yes.

Hippie: My contacts say that they're prepared for a military offensive at the same time as the demonstrations and strikes.

Ljubimov: Yes.

Hippie: Chaos.

Ljubimov: Yes.

Hippie: The fascists will close ranks. The first wave of repression will be violent, but it'll be the final convulsions. Then the situation will be revolutionary for real . . .

Ljubimov: Moscow has decided that the correct strategy is to enter into the transitional phase in such a way that the PCE can be made a legal party.

Hippie: Ah-ha.

Ljubimov: The plan is to smuggle Carrillo in first and let him be here illegally as a symbol, and then when the time is ripe to let La Pasionaria return completely openly.

Hippie: They'll never go along with that.

Ljubimov: We think they will. We don't believe that terrorism should be a practical strategy in Spain's current circumstances. Moscow sees the correct strategy as a combination of winning over the workers at the workplace and the general population by participating in the parliamentary process which we believe will come. We must be there when fascism is replaced by bourgeois democracy. At least at first.

Hippie: My impression is that, as the situation stands, Berlin doesn't see the Basque struggle as terrorism, but as a legitimate armed struggle.

Ljubimov: We are possibly only partially in disagreement with the comrades, but at the moment we consider the legal course to be the correct one. There will be elections. The PCE must be in a strong position at those elections. If not, we will reappraise the situation.

Hippie: Misha thinks I should pursue my contacts with ETA.

Ljubimov: We have no quarrel with that.

Hippie: We're still training them, and we're linking up with the Czechoslovak comrades on a new consignment, but that means we've got to activate the cell in Pamplona.

Ljubimov: That's fine, but we'd like you to try to get more information about the student milieu and I'm also interested in names in the press who we can count on standing shoulder to shoulder with the working classes when the situation comes to a head. That's the assignment we think you should concentrate on. It's co-ordinated with Karlhorst.

Hippie: I'm on the job.

Ljubimov: Good.

I went out to the kitchen, got a can of beer and went back to my office to think about what I had just read. If you knew the sequence of events, a pattern emerged. The illegal, communist trade unions, *Comisiones Obreras*, had called a general strike and huge demonstrations for 1 May 1976, year zero after General Franco's death. In April of that year, Spain had been rocked by the biggest wave of strikes for 40 years, which had helped to overthrow the old fascist guard and pave the way for a more pro-reform administration lead by Adolfo Suárez.

The old communist leader, Santiago Carrillo, returned to Madrid concealed under a wig later that year, and in 1977 the Spanish Communist Party was legalised and the legendary leader from the Civil War, Dolores Ibárruri – known as La Pasionaria – returned home in triumph. It was typical of the communists that they considered not only the fascists as their principal enemies, but also the social democrats in the PSOE. The reason for this went right back to the 1930s and the Civil War, when the communists fought against the anarchists, who had always been dear to my heart, and also the socialists. The centre-right had won the general election in June 1977, but the PCE had made a strong showing, although not nearly as good as the PSOE. The communists' strategy had failed. Spain did not become a communist country, but a liberal democracy.

I understood the references to their Czechoslovak comrades. They were to supply the plastic explosive, Semtex, which ETA used in manufacturing its bombs. The GDR had trained and equipped terrorists all over the world. The Palestinians, the Red Brigades in Italy, the Red Army Faction in West Germany and ETA in Spain. Even though I knew this, reading the transcript still sent a cold shiver down my spine. This had been a European nation which had financed, trained and given shelter to terrorists from all over the world, while the GDR leadership had persistently claimed that they served only the cause of peace. Misha was, of course, Markus Wolf, who had been head of the GDR's foreign espionage until shortly before the Wall fell, when he saw which way the wind was blowing and left the service to join the democracy movement in East Germany. I had read that he had published his memoirs but still refused, even in the German courts, to disclose the names of his agents.

I switched on my computer, connected to the internet and did a search under "Karlhorst". A long list of matches appeared. Karlhorst was the KGB's old headquarters in the GDR. This was the real centre of power, where even the Stasi were controlled.

I went back to the papers while I drank my beer. It was completely dark outside now, and it seemed as if the warm night air had wrapped the cars down on the busy avenida in cotton wool.

The man referred to as Hippie in the surveillance report had mentioned a number of Spanish names. I recognised only one of them. Today he was a well-known television personality with a string of quiz shows on one of the privately owned TV channels.

I continued to read.

Hippie: I've heard about a Danish journalist and photographer who has good contacts with the Basques and the underground scene.
Ljubimov: Yes . . .
Hippie: He's travelled a lot. Bit of a nomad, but good at his job. So they say. Lebanon, GDR, Moscow, Basque Country. He goes where the pictures are.
Ljubimov: Is he right-wing?
Hippie: Progressive, liberal. Like everyone else he flirts with socialism, or rather the naïve Spanish version of Durruti's

anarchist ideas . . .

Ljubimov: But that's reactionary.

Hippie: I don't think it goes very deep, and he can be moulded. I'd call him progressive. I wouldn't call him reactionary.

Ljubimov: A potential contract?

Hippie: Maybe. Maybe more likely a source without actually knowing it. He's never got enough money . . . drinks too much . . . likes the ladies . . . so maybe later it would be worth pursuing the money angle. He's got a lot of contacts even though he's only in his mid-20s.

Ljubimov: Sounds promising. What's his name?

Hippie: Lime. Peter Lime.

Ljubimov: (laughter) Like Harry Lime. Well, rather symbolic.

Hippie: It's his real name, so they say.

Ljubimov: OK. Follow it up. You've had good results with a Dane before. They're usually naïve and guileless people. They often see that our convictions are right, even though they don't completely support the working-class cause. But don't forget the Spanish. They have top priority.

Hippie: OK.

Ljubimov: The money will be at the usual drop. Share it around.

Hippie: OK.

Ljubimov: And take care. It's a critical time.

Hippie: Isn't it always?


The subjects leave the room and conclude their conversation in the entrance hall where the electronic surveillance is not operative.

The surveillance group recommends that investigations continue and that surveillance of the named Peter Lime is implemented, and in addition that funds be allocated to establish Hippie's identity, that the unit in Navarre be informed and that cross-border surveillance be intensified.

I leant back in my chair and re-read the lines that described my youthful self. It was a very precise description, but it was still strange to have been the subject of a conversation between two agents. It was an encroachment on my privacy, an intrusion. It was as if a huge telephoto lens had been trained on me. It seemed like an act of violence to observe and divulge someone's secrets, be they political allegiances or love affairs. My hands were trembling slightly, not just because I had been mentioned in the report, but also because I was wondering who Hippie might be. I had pictured a young Oscar, but that didn't fit with the fact that I had met him – to the best of my knowledge by chance – in the spring of 1977, a year after this conversation had taken place. Wouldn't he have made contact with me almost immediately? And the impulsive, charming, fun Oscar hardly fitted with the cold-blooded East German who spoke of a supply of explosives as if it were a consignment of bananas. I could see that Hippie wasn't an East German agent, although maybe he was a double agent. His real employer was the KGB. Maybe the East Germans didn't know what his game was, but my knowledge of the world of espionage wasn't extensive enough to understand what was going on.

I thought again about myself and the agent's description of me. Maybe it was accurate, but who knows what they were like when they were young? We think we remember who we were, but every memory is rewritten and edited, every memory is full of holes.

My legs got twitchy, and I went to see if I could find anything stronger to drink, but Oscar and Gloria hadn't kept any of the hard stuff in the office for years. So I opened another beer and rang Don Alfonzo. He answered straight away, as if he had been waiting for my call.

"It's me," I said.

"Yes, my friend."

"I'd like to talk with the man who calls himself Don Felipe."

"That's not possible, my friend. But you can talk to me."

"I feel dirty," I said. "I know I'm not being rational."

"It's a very human reaction, Pedro. It's as if one has been molested."

"Did they ever find out who Hippie was?"

"No."

"Why not?"

"As is the case with so much else in this world, random factors spoiled the scheme. The French got tired of Victor Ljubimov's double game in Paris, blew the whistle on him and expelled him from the country. With his cover blown, he couldn't travel in the West again. He was of no further use as a handler. Hippie was assigned to another one, but we never found out where they met. That cover address was never used again. Do you know who Hippie was?"

"Maybe," I said. I paused. "What have you got on Oscar?"

I dreaded his reply, feeling the palms of my hands begin to sweat despite the artificial coolness of the office.

"I thought you might ask that. Nothing. Born in Hamburg. Left-wing journalist, very radical in his younger days. Today a solid and affluent citizen who pays his tax on time and contributes to the common good of the nation."

I was unbelievably relieved.

"What about me. What have they got on me?" I said.

"Nothing on you either."

"Nothing! Wasn't I under surveillance?"

"Perhaps, my friend. But we haven't got anything. That doesn't mean that you weren't under surveillance, but the intelligence services are bureaucracies and bureaucracies make lots of mistakes. Reports are filed in the wrong place, index numbers disappear, aliases are changed and there's no cross-referencing. The wrong files get destroyed or mislaid. Don't think of the intelligence services as organisations run by people of infallible genius. They are huge bureaucracies with their share of power struggles, drunkenness, slovenliness, stupidity, paper-pushing, little office dust-ups and love affairs, just like any other. We have your details, know that you fulfil Spanish residence permit requirements and don't cheat on your tax return, but otherwise nothing."

I could hear the mirth in his voice. It was one of the longest speeches he had ever made and it was clear that he took great pleasure in it. For some reason the pressure in my head eased and I laughed with him.

"So the game stops here?" I said.

His voice became serious again.

"Indeed it could, were it not for Amelia and Maria Luisa."

"Yes. Exactly," I said, and felt the familiar knot in my stomach.

"It puts a different light on the matter. Now it's more than a case of recording history, isn't it?"

"Exactly," I said again, and waited for him to play his hand. I realised that he had stepped into character as handler and that I was the one being handled. Without my being aware of it, he had quietly steered me towards an investigation. I thought I had chosen to do it myself, but somewhere along the line he had made the decision for me. As if he could read my thoughts, he said, "You reached that conclusion on your own. I'm just an old man who has a certain amount of experience. But it was your own choice."

"What does your experience tell you now?" I asked.

"Ring the woman in Copenhagen."

"Why?"

"Because perhaps the answer is to be found in Berlin, and she can help you get to the archives there quicker than I can. Take care of yourself, Pedro."

He hung up, as if he already thought he had said too much on the telephone. Old habits don't die easily. I lit a cigarette and found the numbers Clara Hoffmann had given me. It was Sunday evening, but I rang her home number anyway.

She answered, and a clear image of her came to mind as I heard her soft, cultivated voice.

"It's Peter Lime. I'm ringing from Madrid."

"Good evening, Peter. What a pleasant surprise."

"I've found something out about Lime's photograph," I said.

"Ah-ha."

"I've found another photograph and I've found a name."

"That sounds very interesting."

"But I don't think we should talk about it on the phone. It would probably be easier to meet face to face. Because I might need your help."

"One favour is always worth another," she said. There was the sound of faint music in the background and I could picture her sitting in a comfortable chair, reading a book. I felt myself becoming sentimental at the thought of such snug domesticity. She hadn't been wearing a wedding ring when I'd met her in Madrid, so I imagined her alone. Maybe she was having a quiet drink or a cup of tea. The living room would be snug. Danish women were good at that. Creating an atmosphere of cosiness, making the home a safe, warm and relaxed place. Danes spend so much of the year indoors that they use huge amounts of energy and money making everything as comfortable and attractive as possible. The home has to be an impregnable fortress.

I shook the feeling off. That time had definitively been and gone. I wasn't going to put down roots again. I wasn't going to risk such an intense and painful loss again. I thought of a line from an old Janis Joplin number. "Freedom's just another word for nothing left to lose."

"Are you there, Peter?" she said, probably for the second time. Had we been on first name terms before now?

"Yes. Sorry. I just got distracted for a moment. I didn't hear what you said."

"I asked if I should come to Madrid?"

"No. I'll come to Copenhagen tomorrow, if I can get a ticket. Otherwise the day after. Then I'll ring."

"I look forward to seeing you."

"You too."

"And your photograph," she said.

"That's a different matter," I said, and hung up.

# 15

There was an SAS flight the next day with plenty of spare seats, leaving
Madrid at 15.15, arriving in Copenhagen at 18.25. It was just as well
that it was an afternoon flight because that night I fell seriously off the
wagon. I stayed at the office drinking beer for another half hour and
then I went back to the hotel and downed most of a large bottle of
vodka that Carlos in reception fetched for me. Up until then I had
controlled my intake of alcohol, naïvely thinking that I could drink
like other people, but of course it couldn't last. I spent an evening
and a night filled with booze and self-contempt, sentimentality and
disgust. Fortunately I didn't have a gun. In the worst haze of drunkenness I realised that I didn't want to live, but I was too drunk to go
downtown and try to find a weapon that could end it all. Besides, I
probably knew that I wouldn't have the nerve when it came to it. But
life was shit. I looked at myself in the mirror above the bed and didn't
like what I saw. Unkempt hair, bloodshot, desolate and furious eyes,
the pain of missing Amelia and Maria Luisa as strong as the day they
had left me. At some point in the middle of the night I felt their presence in the room, and I talked with them, and they answered. In the
end I went out like a light.

Next morning I woke with trembling hands, a burning sensation in
my stomach and a splitting headache. The room stank of smoke and

booze. From down on Calle Echégaray I could hear the dustcart lumbering along the narrow street. Clanking and clattering, metallic grating and crashing like thousands of cymbals, the dustmen's warning shouts to pedestrians who had to pin themselves against the walls, all the morning sounds flooded in through the open window. I rolled up my bed linen and threw the clothes I had slept in into the wastepaper basket. The staff of the Hotel Inglés had undoubtedly seen worse. I drank a couple of bottles of mineral water and washed down two pills with cola. I didn't indulge in the empty promise of never doing it again. I knew my own weakness, but maybe self-contempt could be turned into something constructive. Would I want to look at myself in the mirror again? Had Amelia and Maria Luisa really been there during the night? What had they said? I seemed to hear their voices – "You mustn't kill yourself. You mustn't die and leave us!" But that couldn't be right. Because they had died and left me. They had been taken from me. That was the whole injustice.

I took a long shower, dressed in clean clothes from top to bottom and went down to a bar, where I ordered a huge glass of coffee with milk and another bottle of water. The street buzzed with normal, Monday morning activity. It smelled fresh now that the water truck had driven through and sluiced the weekend grime down the drains. I began to feel better and greeted acquaintances and the bartenders standing outside their premises in the lovely morning light. The air was fresh and invigorating and the heat had yet to take hold and cast its clammy mantle over Madrid.

I packed my spare jeans, last t-shirt, cotton shirt, socks and underwear into my bag along with my toiletries, and carried the suitcase of photographs down to reception. Of course they would store the suitcase for me. They could put it in the basement, and it could stay there for as long as I wanted. For as long as the Hotel Inglés continued to exist, and after all, it had survived both revolution and civil war,

Carlos reminded me. I rang SAS and booked my ticket, and got them to reserve me a room at the Hotel Royal in Copenhagen. That left me enough time to buy some clothes and have a lunch of vegetable soup and trout, plus more water.

Once I was on the plane I had a Bloody Mary and felt my jangling nerves settle down. After that I stuck to a quarter bottle of wine, suppressing my bad conscience and fell asleep. I woke when I heard the sound of the engine change and my ears registered the fall in pressure. Looking out of the little window I could see the Øresund, the strait between Denmark and Sweden, sparkling blue and speckled with a myriad of tiny, colourful yachts.

Copenhagen looked like its old self, lovely in the evening sunshine, with swarms of brightly coloured bikes and the traffic running smoothly and calmly. People grumbled about the heat, but after stifling Madrid it felt pleasant and fresh with a faint smell of salt drifting in from the Øresund.

I didn't ring anyone, but stayed in the hotel and avoided the minibar. I switched on the television, and was channel hopping, thinking about Bruce Springsteen's "57 Channels (And Nothing On)" when I came upon one of my old colleagues, Klaus Pedersen, on the News with a feature about Lola.

I had last seen him ten years earlier when he had been working for *Jyllands-Posten*. He had hired me a couple of times for assignments in Madrid, and on one occasion we had been together with the guerrilla soldiers of the Polisario Front, behind the front line in the Western Sahara. Following seasoned Bedouin soldiers on their raids against the Moroccan army hadn't exactly been a safe assignment. The Polisario had been fighting for the independence of the old Spanish Sahara for over 20 years. Yet another of the world's forgotten, hopeless wars, but my friend had written some good articles and my photographs had been given a prominent position in the paper. Oscar and Gloria had

been furious with me. There was no need to carry on accepting dangerous assignments now that the money was rolling in from my paparazzo
shots, but now and then I wanted to take "real" photographs.

Klaus Pedersen seemed to be a competent television reporter. Like
me, he had aged. I had lost quite a bit of hair, he had kept all his, but
he had put on at least ten kilos since our adventures in the desert in
those zippy jeeps that tore across the sand.

The item was about Lola's disappearance. The News referred to her
as Laila Petrova, but I knew it was Lola. It seemed that Lola's administration of a big art museum had cost the Minister of Culture her job.
They had looked at the books after Lola had vanished. The sum of
6.7 million kroner was missing. How much of that amount dear little
Lola had taken and how much was lost because the accounts were in
such a shambles wasn't clear. Copenhagen had been designated
Cultural Capital of Europe and, as also happened in Madrid, certain
creative personalities had taken this opportunity to milk the coffers of
the European Union, Denmark and Copenhagen. The News showed
pictures of a new museum of international modern art that had just
been built – a big greyish-white building that looked like a beached
ship. Klaus Pedersen gave a brief summary of what had happened. The
director, Laila Petrova, who claimed to be highly regarded in London
and at Moscow's Manége Exhibition Hall, had vanished. Inquiries
made by *Jyllands-Posten* and other papers had revealed that she did
not have the qualifications she had claimed. They had never heard of
her at the gallery she had claimed to have worked at in London or in
Moscow.

The Minister of Culture appeared on screen and made a statement,
surrounded by a forest of microphones and hand-held tape recorders,
and looking like she would happily be anywhere else but there. She
was a haggard woman, about my age, with a rather pursed mouth.
She defended herself, saying that her civil servants ought to have

checked Laila Petrova's references, and then she said she had no further comment. Passing the buck to the civil servants clearly hadn't worked this time. She had absolutely no comment on the Prime Minister having relieved her of her duties. No, she didn't know if there was another post awaiting her. Now she would take stock of her future. But none of this was her fault.

Klaus appeared on screen.

"Laila Petrova was appointed on the warm recommendation of the Minister of Culture, even though no prominent member of the Danish art world had ever heard of her. At the time of Laila Petrova's appointment, the Prime Minister called it a bold and visionary decision to bring her over from London, but today he laid the responsibility fairly and squarely on the Minister of Culture's desk. This tangled affair is not yet resolved – the story of how an elegant, charming woman fooled the Danish political establishment. This is a modern version of the Emperor's new clothes, and the real losers are the Danish taxpayers."

Klaus Pedersen's final words were accompanied by a shot of Lola in an extravagant crimson gown, walking with the Queen. It must have been at the opening of the museum. I could see the young Lola in her as she sailed through the imposing gallery, a tiny step ahead of Her Majesty, who looked insignificant and strangely out of place compared to Lola, who had managed to position herself in the Golden Section of the frame. It was as if the Queen had chosen an inappropriately plain gown for such a grand occasion, as if she was underdressed.

"Nice one, Lola," I said out loud, and rang the desk and got them to look up the number of the News.

At first the switchboard didn't know if he had already left or not, but then I was told that Klaus Pedersen was on the late shift, and I was put through.

"Hello, Klaus. It's Peter Lime."

"Peter, damn it! It's been ages. How are you?"

I could hear the News in the background. I could see on my set that they had started the weather.

"OK. And you?"

"Fine, fine. Are you calling from Madrid?"

"No. I'm in Copenhagen. I've just seen your item on Lola."

"Laila."

"Her name's Lola. It was fascinating. She stitched them up good and proper, didn't she?"

"Not half. And she could charm the pants off them. When she looked at them with her big blue eyes, all those Social Democrats who wanted to be oh so sophisticated just melted at her feet. Forgot to check her references. She didn't have a single qualification. Did you know her, Peter?"

"Yes."

"I'll be damned," he said, and I could hear the newshound in his voice.

"I'm at the Royal. Let me invite you for a drink and I'll tell you about her."

He went quiet at the other end of the line. The summer was set to continue, said the weatherman, and smiled.

"That's not really so good, Peter. I've promised to get home."

"What?"

That wasn't the Klaus Pedersen I knew. In the past he had never given his family a thought. He had lived and breathed foreign news, taking every opportunity to travel with the paper picking up the tab.

"Of course, you don't know. I got divorced a couple of years ago and then I married again. You know, a younger version. So I've got a new brood of kids, and the youngest one's got colic and screams all the time and if I don't get home to do my bit you could cut the air with a knife for the next fortnight."

"OK."

"You know what it's like, don't you? I sure as hell didn't want any more children at my age, but you can't just say no when a new wife wants a family, can you?"

"Not really."

"I gave up the foreign desk for the same reason. All that travelling did for my first marriage. So I applied for a job on the television news, home affairs. Fixed shifts and my own bed every evening. There's no damn way I could afford to go through another divorce."

"No problem, Klaus. It's none of my business, anyway."

"Haven't you got any children?"

"No," I said. "I haven't got any children."

"The same old lone wolf. Well. Right. I just can't, even though I'd like to. Couldn't you come out here tomorrow? I'm working."

"That sounds fine," I said.

"If you've got time then come about eleven o'clock. Ring just before you leave the Royal, then I'll go down and let you in."

"That sounds just fine. And give my regards to the new wife."

"See you. Good to hear from you."

I looked across at the minibar, but stopped myself and did some push-ups instead, until my shoulders and ribs ached. I read the *Herald Tribune*, starting with the front page news, on to what the leader writer had to say, then to sport and *Calvin and Hobbes*. I watched a late-night film on some satellite channel or other, before finally managing to get a few hours of fitful sleep. I woke up early and stayed in bed watching morning television. A succession of people came into a studio constructed to look as if they were in a living room, complete with both bookcases and a kitchen area. The guests chatted for five minutes about Danish topics that meant nothing to me and then they left the studio again. Now and then there was a bit of cooking and short news bulletins, and a woman stood gesticulating strangely in front of a weather map of Denmark and said that summer was set to continue.

I turned over to CNN and took a shower, waiting until I thought it would be all right to ring Clara Hoffmann. She sounded wide awake and breezy, and told me that her flat was just a few minutes' walk from my hotel, so she could come by on her way to the office, in half an hour.

I ordered a pot of coffee and two cups in the lobby, and sat waiting for her on a sofa in a corner where I could keep an eye on the door. There's something soothing about the sense of anonymity in an international hotel. You're alone and yet together with scores of other people, each going about their own business. When a hotel is run efficiently, everything is clean and tidy, buzzing with activity. A group of Japanese tourists stood waiting in the lobby and businessmen in dark suits carrying attaché cases and laptops were checking out, casting anxious glances at the clock and even more anxious glances at their mobile telephones. Mine was still at the Hotel Inglés back in Madrid. I enjoyed being incommunicado, a stranger in a strange place, which was just as familiar and recognisable as Madrid.

A lanky chap with a ponytail just like mine came out of the lift and walked across to the reception desk. He was wearing a pale, crumpled summer jacket, jeans and what was certainly a short-sleeved shirt with a loosely knotted tie. He was carrying a practical, cabin-sized bag in one hand and a heavy camera bag in the other. At first I thought I would pretend I hadn't seen him, but considering how many hours he had waited on our behalf and also with me when, for instance, Princess Di had gone to the gym, that would be have been ridiculous. He was an Australian named Derek Watson, who had stalked the jet set for 20 years and one of his photographs still brought in the money. A photograph of Diana with her children. She's wearing a long, flimsy summer dress and bending slightly at the knee as the wind catches her skirt and lifts it so that you can see most of one bare leg. It was a lovely picture of a mother with her two small children but, because of who she was, it was more than that. It was a sensation. Or as Oscar had put it when we got the photograph on commission, "There are lovely thighs everywhere, but not hers."

Derek and we had earned a packet from that photograph. A second time around too, when the Princess was killed in the car crash and the media all over the world went mad and we could sell any picture that had her in it. Derek's photograph had sold particularly well. It was perfect for the serious newspapers, accompanying their indignant leaders and articles on how outrageous it was to take precisely that kind of photograph.

So I got up and went over to him and tapped him on the shoulder as he stood fiddling with his credit card.

"Hi Derek. How's it going?"

"Lime, you old hound. Nice to see you."

"Join me for a coffee?" I said.

He looked at his watch.

"That would be nice, but I've got a flight to catch."

"OK."

"I've heard about it, you know . . . I met Gloria in London. I'm really sorry, Peter."

"OK."

He got his bill, barely glanced at it and handed his credit card to the receptionist. He wasn't paying.

"I hear you've called it a day?" he said.

"Well, I'm taking a break."

"I thought about doing that too, after the business with Di. You'd have thought that everyone with a damned camera was a murderer. Or worse. A paedophile. For a couple of weeks politicians were better placed on the shit-list than us journalists and photographers. Even my own newsagent wouldn't even sell me a paper because he held me personally responsible, but think about how much money he's earned thanks to you and me supplying pictures the readers want."

He flung his arms out.

"I tell you it was incredible. The crowds. The media. It was love and harmony and hypocrisy and bullshit across the board. All those flowers! It was enough to give you damned hay fever! Not to mention the BBC and the teddy bears. I don't know what was worst."

He signed his credit card receipt.

"Die young, then you're both martyr and saint," I said.

"And you have to be pretty. If she'd been 20 years older and not so damned photogenic it would have been a non-story. A tragic, mundane road accident. And our colleagues weren't even to blame, you know. But you can't say that to anyone. You weren't in London, were you?" he asked.

Even though I got the feeling that he had said all this many times before, I could tell that he welcomed an opportunity to get it off his chest again to a colleague who knew what riches lay unseen in photographs, knew the compelling fascination of the hunt and the satisfaction when the quarry was bagged.

"No. I wasn't, but Madrid went wild too."

"Even here in fair Copenhagen, they tell me. The whole thing was so over the top. When you think about how she used us, you know? When the dry stick or mummy needed a jab in the solar plexus or hungry children a bob or two. I still don't understand what came over the world. For the first time in my life I realised what it must be like to live in a dictatorship, be a citizen in a country like the GDR with thought police and enforced orthodoxy and all that shit. If you didn't think the woman was the greatest thing since the Blessed Virgin, you got the cold shoulder, and if it had been up to the people and sanctimonious editors, Britain would have set up its own Stasi to find anyone who didn't think Di was the incarnation of goodness, so they could be registered as enemies of the people for all eternity. Jesus Christ!"

"It's all forgotten now," I said.

"Precisely. That's the whole point," said Derek.

He looked nervously at his watch again, so I said I wouldn't keep him and asked him to pass on my greetings to Gloria or Oscar if he ran into them at one of the places in London where media types eat and drink.

"OK. It wouldn't surprise me if I saw them. How long are you staying here? If they ask."

"No idea. Maybe a week. Maybe until tomorrow."

"Called it a day, have you Lime? In my dreams. Well, ciao. See you around. Enjoy your break."

We shook hands and he doffed an imaginary cap on his way to who knows where. What he had been doing in Copenhagen was none of my business. He would never give up, he couldn't live without the hunt and the rewards, even if he managed to get a shot of Clinton with his trousers down and a young lady kneeling in front of him. A photograph like that would make him seriously rich, but he would still stand, rain or shine, in some city or behind a private beach or wherever, waiting as patiently as a sniper in Sarajevo. It was the chase that appealed to him. Just as it had me. The knowledge that anyone in this world could be brought down and exposed as merely human when they least expected it. His world was both enticing and awful. I had a choice: go back to the business and do something I was good at, or stay as I was in the void between oblivion and memory. I could go back to photojournalism and visit all the trouble-spots of the world, illustrating the horror for the morning papers. Or I could spare myself the decision and just carry on drifting with the tide. I stood in the lobby watching his retreating figure, the nonchalant way he lit a cigarette, the carelessness with which he slung his suitcase into the back of the taxi, his casual and appropriate greeting to the driver, the self-assurance of sitting in the front seat. I imagined his often-repeated request to be taken to the airport, his certainty that lovers and assignments were left behind and new ones awaited him, his loneliness, and his fear that age would catch him up and he would die alone. A portrait of my own state of mind. I saw all that as I stood, rooted to the spot, feeling both loss and relief.

I asked reception for the morning papers, went back to my corner, and tried to understand the strange Danish articles. I was glad that I didn't have to tell a Spaniard what was going on in Denmark. Not a lot it seemed, although pieces on growing xenophobia and how my old country was being inundated with fanatical immigrants were something new. When I looked up I saw the group of Japanese tourists, and then Clara Hoffmann came in through the door and stopped to look around.

She looked younger than she had seemed in Madrid. I remembered her as being in her early 40s. She was wearing jeans and a beige shirt which revealed the outline of her bra. Her body was youthful and slender, like Amelia's. She was carrying a large bag on her shoulder, which detracted from her stylish appearance. But of course she was on her way to work. Her hair had been cut since Madrid. Now it was short and curly. It suited her, making her face look younger. She wasn't wearing much make-up, just eyeliner and a touch of lipstick. Her bluish-grey eyes were alert and her lips shone slightly. But it was the way she walked that attracted me most. She came in with short, confident steps, as if she was dancing. A sensual, energetic saunter. She scanned the lobby with a confident gaze and I noticed a couple of men at the reception desk looking at her.

I was just about to catch her attention when, without thinking, I picked up my Leica, estimated exposure and distance, and took four quick shots of her. Two of them are lying here next to my computer. They could be used for an advertising campaign about a woman who keeps up with fashion, has well-groomed hair and a balanced, slim body. A beautiful, composed and efficient woman who is confident in herself and presents an open face to the world. I had instinctively framed a classic Golden Section. Clara is in soft focus, the fringes of a plant in front of her, and behind her are the reception desk and a man in a suit who has turned his head to look at her. It's one of my better photographs of a woman in the enterprising 1990s, mature and yet sexy. Self-sufficient, yet ready to take it easy should the occasion arise and there's a window in her diary.

I put the Leica on the table and waved to her and her face lit up in a smile as she walked over towards me. I realised that Clara Hoffmann was the first woman I had been attracted to since Amelia's death. It was the first time that I had looked at someone in terms of gender, not just as a person, but also a sexual being. Until then I hadn't thought about sex, apart from in grotesque dreams that resembled the paintings Amelia and I had seen in the Salvador Dali Museum at Figueres. Maria Luisa had cried at the sight of his paintings. She was inconsolable, and it wasn't until we were in a McDonald's later that we got her to tell us what was wrong.

"He must have been such an unhappy man, that painter," she had said. "I felt so sorry for him and then I got scared."

This is not what I felt when I saw Clara Hoffmann. What I felt was elation. That's how I remember it. I was happy, even though I had nothing on which to base my pleasure. I had a pang of guilt, but it was just so nice to see a summery, Danish woman walk towards me with a big smile, and put out her hand.

"Peter. It's good to see you," she said.

"Clara. It's good to see you again too," I said.

Her hand was cool and firm, she said yes to a cup of coffee and sat down opposite me; we chatted a bit about Spain and Denmark and, like every Dane, she talked about the lovely weather as if the good Lord had set aside these few days to bestow his favour on Copenhagen.

Then she leant forward.

"What can I do for you?" she asked.

The question surprised me. I had presumed she would ask what I had for her.

"First I have to tell you something, but it's a long story." I answered.

"I've got plenty of time," she said.

I gave her a broad outline of what had happened since we had last met, back when my life was utterly different. I had a strange urge to tell her something rather more personal, but it was a long time since I had been 20 years old. So instead, while we drank coffee, I told her about San Sebastián, Don Alfonzo, the suspicions of the Madrid police, the post-mortem and the surveillance report, which I showed her. She listened without comment, and read the report quickly, as if she was used to scanning that kind of document. I was grateful to her for not again expressing her sympathy. I couldn't have borne to hear it.

She listened attentively as she watched me and drank her coffee. When I mentioned the interrogation in San Sebastián without going into much detail, she reached out her hand and touched the healing wound under my eye.

"You look done in," she said. "You look older, and worn out. All the pain is in your eyes."

"That's a strange thing to say," I said. "We don't know one another."

"I think I know you," she said.

"I don't understand."

"If it makes you feel better, neither do I," she said.

I looked at her and she looked straight back, but I couldn't read her expression, so I carried on telling her about Las Ventas. Finally I took out the two photographs. The one she had brought to Madrid and the one showing Lola with the group of bearded men. She studied them carefully.

"Do you know him?" she asked, pointing at the man to the far left in the second picture.

"Yes. I'm not completely out of touch. He's a member of parliament today."

"He is, yes. But do you know the others?"

"Yes and no. I remember the woman," I said.

"I should think everyone does. It's a fantastic photograph."

"Not really. It's under-exposed and the composition's not great."

She laughed in a girlish and yet adult way.

"I don't mean the quality of your photography, Peter. It's the people. They're a big help."

I wasn't really interested in the significance of the photograph to the National Security Service, but the sound of her laughter and the expression on her face made me feel sexual desire for the first time in ages.

"OK. If it makes you so happy, you can repay me by saying yes to lunch or dinner while I'm in Copenhagen," I said, speaking without really thinking about it first.

She looked at me. She had tiny, attractive wrinkles in the corners of her eyes. Her eyebrows were rather more pronounced than was usual in a woman, but they gave character to the fine features below her curls and her even, soft mouth with its distinctive bow. Her skin was quite tanned, but still very fair and glowing, very Nordic. I wanted her in front of the camera in a studio in Madrid, with the afternoon light coming in from the left, a softened overhead lamp bathing her forehead, her soft eyes the focus of the composition, tricking the observer into being sucked into the midpoint of her face, and ignoring her slightly large ears.

"I'd have said yes please whether there had been a photograph or not," she said. "But before we discuss that, I'll need you to tell me more about the commune you lived in."

"Here?" I said.

"No. I'd prefer if you would come with me to Borups Allé. I'd like to go through the whole thing in more detail, in more official surroundings."

"Why?"

"Borups Allé, Peter."

"I'm meeting an old friend at eleven o'clock."

"May I take the photographs with me?" she said.

"Just as long as you remember who owns them."

"There's no risk I'd forget," she said.

"When can we see each other?" I said like a regular schoolboy.

"This afternoon. If you can."

"I was thinking about dinner."

"We can decide then."

"Borups Allé. Do I just say that to the taxi driver?" I said.

She laughed.

"Peter. It's Bellahøj Police Station. That's where the NSS has its offices. This isn't Spain or Russia. In Denmark the security service is in the phone book. Just ask for me at the desk."

"How reassuring," I said, and made her laugh again.

# 16

The television news was housed in a low-rise concrete building crouching under the giant tower known as TV-City. Since I'd last been there they had put a big red logo at the top of the tower, but the building still looked like it had been brought over from Karl Marx Allee in East Berlin, more like a place where the secret police were holed up than the headquarters of the television news. Klaus was waiting by the double glass door when I arrived. There was no one at the security desk. The message was clear: visitors were not welcome here. Any that did turn up would look pretty shifty talking into an intercom.

"This must be the only newsroom in the world where people can't come in off the street with a story," I said, when he had let me in and we had shaken hands.

"Write to the director general," said Klaus with an exasperated laugh. "The porter has gone as part of a cost-cutting exercise, so the punters just stand rattling the door. They sure as hell don't get in. God forbid. But it's par for the course. Come upstairs."

The offices were a row of small cages with glass doors. It was quiet on the editorial corridor. I knew the rhythm. The journalists would be either behind their glass doors talking on the phone, or already out recording. Klaus's office was tiny. He sat down at his desk that was dominated by a computer, surrounded by the journalist's organised clutter of newspapers, cuttings, magazines and tapes. CNN was running silently on a television suspended from the ceiling. He chucked a pile of newspapers off a low armchair and asked me to sit down. He fetched black coffee in plastic cups and sat in his revolving office chair. We started by chatting, mostly about old colleagues and what they were doing now and about the general folly of the world. He seemed tense, and I could see that the extra ten kilos had settled on his face and waistline. I told him about Lola and my connection to her. He made notes and asked if I would be willing to give an interview if he pursued the case. I said that would be fine, although I couldn't really see that it had the makings of a story. He was doubtful as well, he said, because it had gone cold now that political responsibility had been attributed. I asked him to tell me how it had come to light that Lola didn't have any real qualifications. He laughed, and I heard an echo of the old, reckless Klaus. He rummaged through the piles of papers on his desk and fished out a plastic folder full of cuttings.

"It's all in here, Peter," he said. "I can't take the credit. There was a reporter on *Jyllands-Posten*, Jørgenson, who simply sat on his backside and began ringing round. He was going to interview Laila or Lola or whatever the hell she's called, and the damned woman got really extremely pissed off when my colleague began digging into her Moscow days. Jørgensen speaks Russian, spouts all that stuff about the Russian soul and the rest of it, and he got suspicious. It seemed as if Laila wasn't really familiar with the arts world from the inside, as it were. She claimed to have been there during that extraordinary time in the 1980s when Gorbachev came to power – glasnost and all that. But Laila had gaps. There were things she ought to have known, people who ought to have been mutual acquaintances whose names didn't ring any bells for her. When my colleague read the interview to her, Laila refused to consent to *Jyllands-Posten* running it. Because the paper implied that Laila's knowledge of modern Russian art was maybe a little limited. That was her big mistake all right. Refusing to let the interview be published. You know how seriously suspicious that makes us reporters, don't you?"

"Indeed," I said, and began reading while Klaus went off to a meeting. Despite the mess in his office, his cuttings were in meticulous order. They were arranged chronologically and told the story right up to the point where Lola disappeared, with or without the money.

She had been hired just before the construction of the new art museum was completed. There had been much bewilderment in Denmark's art world. Especially in the circles that made a living from art – the administrators, reviewers, pundits, lecturers, professors. The Ministry of Culture had been delighted that someone from the outside had been found, and a woman at that. And Lola's CV was pretty impressive: studied at the Sorbonne, the Academy of Arts in Moscow and the Royal Academy in London, partner in a prestigious gallery in New York, contacts in every corner of the international art scene. I noticed she had knocked a couple of years off her age, and claimed to be the daughter of a Danish woman and an English lord. There were no children from her marriage to the Russian artist Petrov, from whom she had taken her surname. Petrov had gone to the dogs in St Petersburg, she had told a journalist, having just said that she never talked about her private life. He had found it impossible to exist as an artist in the materialistic atmosphere of the new Russia. Not an eye was dry.

She had got divorced around 1987. The photographs showed her to be attractive and well dressed, in a style that was both classic and modern – she had modelled herself on a certain Grace Kelly-type, appearing just a little dated, but maybe that was why she inspired such confidence. Lola spoke, according to the first profiles, an elegant, slightly old-fashioned, refined Danish not unlike that of the Queen. This description would undoubtedly have been intended as a compliment. It was obvious from the photographs that she cut a bit of a dash, and the older, male politicians, with their wide, loud ties and jackets a size too small, could be seen gazing at her in admiration. She had good press. They had swallowed her story hook, line and sinker.

Good press for the opening of the museum. Good press for the first exhibition, and then the critical articles began to appear. Staff resigned. Extra funding had to be provided. The travel budget was overspent. A lecture at the Academy of Fine Arts turned into a farce because the professors didn't think she knew her subject matter. Lola responded by saying that this was a typical case of the Danish tendency to knock success. And then finally the unmasking. A front page news revealed that Laila Petrova was not who she said she was, and that the selection committee had never seen evidence of her qualifications because they had never asked for it. A serious, full-page article, as exciting as a thriller, traced the journalist's investigation that led to the discovery that Laila Petrova had duped everyone. It was a simple, brilliant piece of investigative journalism. Hours spent on the phone making calls to Paris, where no one at *Le Monde* was aware of the fact that she had been one of their visual arts writers, and then via London to New York and Moscow. The same response everywhere: Laila Petrova had always moved in art circles, and plenty of people had positive things to say about her, but she didn't have any qualifications. At all. She had relied on the fact that people who know nothing about art, and possibly have no understanding whatsoever of modern art, like to appear to know an awful lot, since they can't afford to exhibit their ignorance; it's easy to bluff them if you have the nerve to play your hand ice-cold. She had gambled on the appointing authorities knowing little, but not daring to reveal their ignorance.

They had been easy prey for a skilled operator with the ability to show that she knew everything, even though she perhaps didn't know very much at all.

I couldn't help laughing. Lola had always been an actress and in the snobbish art world, where the definition of what is and what isn't great art is as ephemeral as a snowflake, she had found her star role, but she hadn't managed to see the show through to its finale. If the accounts hadn't been such a shambles, she would undoubtedly have ended up on the Queen's Honours List. Denmark is a tiny country, and the media always go crazy if a Dane, even a half-Dane, has made waves in the big wide world.

After the story broke, the politicians ran for cover, trying to pass the buck to the selection committee and civil servants. It was a case of trying to sweep the muck under the carpet, but the media storm intensified and then one day she was gone, along with a sum of money which, depending on which newspaper you read, was anything from two to 20 million kroner. Lola had vanished without trace. The pressure on the Prime Minister grew, but with the sacrifice of the Minister of Culture the crisis seemed to blow over.

End of story.

I put the cuttings back neatly in order. Klaus returned from his meeting. He stood in the door wearing his jacket, his tie loosened at the neck.

"I'm sorry, but I'm filming now," he said.

"I'm on my way too. Thanks for letting me see the cuttings. What about the money? Wasn't there a police investigation?" I asked as I got up.

"Officially, yes, but my sources in parliament tell me the police have been given to understand that they should use their resources elsewhere. She has, after all, fooled the entire system, so the system closes ranks and buries the issue. Yesterday's sacking was the ritual slaughter.

The purgative sacrifice. Now the museum must be left in peace. The concept of a new museum still holds good. In the future they should just concentrate on modern Danish art. One must look to the future and not the past. And so on and so forth, ad nauseam."

"So she'll get away with it," I said.

"Come on, I'll see you out," he said. "As long as she stays away from Denmark nothing will happen to her."

"Does anyone know where she is?"

"Some say London. Some say Tokyo. Others Moscow. No one really knows. She'll be all right. She'll probably add to her CV that she single-handedly got a new Danish museum off the ground, and then when it was up and running went looking for a new challenge. There's a sucker born every minute," he said as he took me down to the door.

We agreed that if he wanted me he would leave a message at the Royal, and we said that it would be nice to have a couple of drinks together one evening and talk about the old days, when the whole world was his playground, but I got the feeling that he didn't really want to. I didn't fit in with his life any more, it seemed. Maybe I knew too much about the old him, and he didn't want his new wife to hear any details. Who knows? We all change. I was probably just envious of his home life, his wanting to spend his free time with his family rather than with me.

I went for a walk in sunny Copenhagen and ate a hot dog while I watched the bike couriers weaving dangerously in and out between cars and pedestrians. A grilled sausage with a bread roll seemed to bring back the taste of childhood and teenage years. Eaten in the sunshine and cool breeze it tasted of the Denmark I wanted to remember, which had a place in my heart. An efficient, unostenta-tious country which made the best of the few resources the Lord had given it. The newspapers told me that it was a country gripped by a fear that foreigners would overrun the Danes and turn them into

Muslims and heathens, but looking around Copenhagen everything seemed as normal. On such a lovely summer's day you could almost forget that November and March existed. The city was smiling, and the slow tempo and lack of noise in comparison with Madrid were balm to my soul. I would find it hard to live there permanently, but having eaten the sausage, wiped my mouth with the paper napkin and listened to the hot dog man chatting with his customers, I felt better than I had for a long time. I couldn't explain why, but it was as if I felt a germ of hope that I would get through the crisis, not just survive it but also live life again.

Perhaps it had something to do with the fact that I looked forward to seeing Clara, her face and her smile, her melodious voice.

She was rather businesslike with me as I sat in a small conference room on the top floor of an ugly concrete building that housed the National Security Service, while downstairs the ordinary police dealt with local, visible crimes. We were in a plain, white-walled, slightly cool room with pale, functional Danish furniture. She had only, apart from my two photographs, a notepad and a tape recorder. There were a couple of pleasant abstract reproductions on the walls. I might just as well have been sitting in any other modern Danish public office of a certain status. There was a younger man sitting at the far end of the table, whom Clara introduced to me as Detective Inspector Karl Jakobsen.

The taxi driver who had taken me out to the meeting was a Kurd from Iraq who spoke rapid Danish with a heavy accent. He was in his 40s, and had the radio tuned to a local station playing old 1960s pop music, putting me in a pleasantly nostalgic mood.

"You going to see the spies?" the Kurd had asked when I gave him the address of Bellahøj Police Station.

"In a manner of speaking," I said.

"Big trouble, right."

"Trouble?"

"You Danish, aren't you?"

"Yes. But I don't live in Denmark," I said.

"Oh. Then you don't know. The National Security Service has listened in on legal political parties on the left and now big trouble."

"They've always done that, haven't they? Kept an eye on communists and Nazis and terrorists and Russians. That's what they're paid to do, isn't it?" I said.

"Well, now they've been caught at it. An agent told about it on television."

"Right. They've been caught with their fingers in the biscuit tin."

"No. Not biscuits. They've listened in and spied on legal Danish party. Listed legal Danish party in register. Spied on Kurds in Denmark. Kurds legal in Denmark, yeah? Big trouble."

"OK. I understand," I said, even though I didn't really.

I had intended to ask Clara about it, but the atmosphere was formal, so I didn't. Karl Jakobsen was wearing a grey-brown jacket and a muted tie. He stood up and we shook hands and he sat down again, studying me with his small, brown eyes. His eyebrows were in need of a trim.

Clara reached out to the tape recorder and switched it on.

"Peter Lime," she said. "I would like to begin by saying . . ."

I reached out, picked up the tape recorder and switched it off.

"Before we start recording or do anything at all, I'd like to know what this is all about," I said.

"A few questions," said Jakobsen, clearly annoyed. "That's all. Clarification."

"I wasn't speaking to you," I said. "Clara . . . ?"

"OK, Peter . . ."

Karl Jakobsen straightened up in his chair, looking surly, and cut her short.

"Just a few questions," he said. "No more to it than that."

I ignored him and turned to Clara.

"Is this your boss?" I said.

"No."

"Then I think you should tell him where to get off."

She smiled with her eyes.

"What would you like to know?" she asked, ignoring the fact that Jakobsen was looking rather pissed off. It was a very elegant way to put the jerk in his place. I didn't like him without really knowing why. He appeared trustworthy, but he had the cockiness of a typical cop who thought that his position gave him the power to do whatever he liked. He seemed to me to be the type who loved beating confessions out of people, not that I had any basis for that kind of misgiving.

I looked at Clara.

"What are you going to use this for?" I asked.

"Well, really all you have to do is tell me what I already know. That you took the photographs. That they are Lime's photographs, when you took them and if you can identify the individuals in the group photograph."

"That's not what I asked."

She took a deep breath and glanced across at Jakobsen who scratched his bluish stubble, which he undoubtedly thought was macho, but which I found repellent.

"No. It wasn't. Your replies will be entered into a report, several reports, in fact. Within a relatively short period of time we have to make a summary of the NSS's activities over the last 20 years. One report will be made available to the public, an expanded version will go to the Security Affairs Committee and an even more detailed report will be made to the Justice Department. Your information will be included in the latter."

"Why is it so interesting?" I asked.

Again she looked at Jakobsen, and I realised that he was her superior, but that they had some kind of arrangement for dealing with me. I was familiar with the manoeuvre from Don Alfonzo. These people were incapable of saying anything straight out.

"It just is," said Clara.

"Why?"

"Peter. You don't have any particular links to Denmark. You obviously don't keep up with what goes on here. One of our former sources has stated publicly that the NSS has kept legal political parties under surveillance. We want to tell our political masters that there was a reason for it. But it's of no concern to the public. We're not being put to the vote. We're not up for an election."

"OK. You've had a defector?"

She smiled.

"That's a splendid interpretation, Peter," she said.

"And now I am to tell you, so you can tell your political watchdogs, that you might well have monitored parties illegally, but there was a reason for it. Because this Lime chap, he's actually got proof in a photograph that a member of parliament, in his young revolutionary days, had coffee with German terrorists? So it was a good thing you kept tabs, even though nothing came of it. No bombs, at least. Is that how it fits?"

"We ask the questions, Lime," said Karl Jakobsen.

"I can just leave," I said. "Is that how it fits, Clara?"

"More or less," she said.

"OK. Last question."

"Yes, Peter."

"Is there a file on me?" I said.

Clara glanced across at Jakobsen before answering.

"No. There was nothing on you."

"You can switch on your tape recorder," I said.

254

"Thank you, Peter."

It didn't take long. She asked me straightforward questions: my name, why I had taken the two photographs, and about the identity of the people in the pictures. She was especially interested in the man who later became a left-wing member of parliament. Jakobsen took notes and stared at me. It was clear that he liked neither my ponytail, nor what I represented – which was everything he wasn't.

It didn't take long, and when we had finished Jakobsen got up and left with a brief nod. He took the tape recorder with him.

"Nice lad," I said.

"His manner possibly works against him," said Clara. "Can you come by tomorrow and give it your signature?"

"Maybe," I said.

"What do you mean?" She looked worried. "We're a bit pressed for time."

"I want you to do something for me," I said.

"I'd like to go out to dinner with you. That's got nothing to do with all this." She placed her hand on top of mine and looked me straight in the eyes, making me feel confused and nervous, as if I was 17 again. I didn't really know what I was getting into, but I knew I couldn't control my feelings.

"It's not that," I said.

"Then what?"

I told her that I wanted to see my file in Berlin, but that I didn't know how to go about it and that I hoped she could help.

"I'd be happy to try, Peter. But there's not much I can do," she said.

"Surely you could ring your colleagues in Germany and get me in."

"No. I'd like to, but I can't do it just like that. But you can get access yourself. The old Stasi archives are open to the public, but the demand is crazy. There's a huge waiting list. They've got 180 kilometres of shelves filled with files. The Stasi employed 280,000 people and countless numbers of informers. The whole GDR was one big nest of singing canaries. Everyone reported on everyone and a lot of people want to see what's in their files."

Clara paused and took her hand from mine.

"I can give you the address, I can help you write the letter. I can ring a couple of contacts and get them to try to speed up your right of access, but I can't promise to get you in ahead of everyone else. Why do you want to see your file?"

"Maybe there's an answer there, maybe there isn't. But I have to look," I said.

She tore off a sheet of paper from her notepad and smiled at me.

"It's Germany, right? Do you speak German?"

I nodded.

"OK. The place is called Bundesbeauftragter für die Unterlagen des Staatssicherheitsdienstes der ehemaligen Deutschen Demokratischen Republik. It's in the old Stasi headquarters on Normannenstrasse. The Stasi had the most enormous office complex sprawling over more than just one street. They tried to shred and burn as much as they could at the time the Wall fell, and angry demonstrators destroyed other material. But there are still millions of files open to the public. But – and this is the crucial thing – they're open to everyone and anyone, and people who are registered have first claim. Do you understand what I'm saying? It's not as if I can come along and get you in first, even though I work for the intelligence service of a friendly country. It's democratic but it's agonising."

I nodded again.

"That long, German name is colloquially called the Gauck Authority. They're the ones you have to write to. The whole idea of providing an insight into what went on has been named after Joachim Gauck. He was a priest in the GDR and now he's in charge of this colossal evidence of the GDR's paranoia."

"What do I have to do?"

"You write to them and say you think you're registered. They check to see if you are and if so, you receive a letter giving a date on which you can go along and read your file. It's as simple as that. But first they screen your case, to ensure that innocent third parties don't have their private lives exposed. It's unique. No democratic country or socialist state has ever gone so far in opening up their archives for anyone to look at as *die ehemaligen DDR*, the former GDR. In a way it pleases me. In a way it scares me."

"What if we got the chance to go through your drawers, you mean?" I said.

Now she laughed outright.

"Yes. Good grief. That wouldn't be at all pleasant."

I leant towards her.

"Have you got the addresses and everything?"

"I can write the letter for you, Peter. And then you can just sign it. If you're sure you want to, that is?"

"Why shouldn't I be?"

"People don't always come away from the archive in a happy frame of mind."

"Why not?"

"Because – and now I'm speaking against the very nature of my job – the truth isn't always essential. One doesn't have to lie, but sometimes it's not necessary to be free with the truth. Some things are actually better left unsaid. It's just like a patient's case notes. Is it really always best to know everything?"

I saw something else in her face. A shadow passed over it. In her job she was used to concealing her true motives, but I thought I could see exasperation or confusion in her eyes. I put my hand over hers.

"You want me to look, don't you?" I said.

"It's your decision."

"But you want me to, don't you?"

"It could be interesting."

"And if I find something that could be of interest to you and your review, then you'd like to know about it."

"Peter," she said. "Our review has to be submitted in a couple of days and the waiting time to be processed by the Gauck Authority can be several months. So it's not really a matter of urgency."

"But anyway?"

"But yes anyway," she said and smiled again.

I let go of her hand and looked into her eyes.

"OK. It's a deal. But on one condition."

"What time and where, Peter," she said and laughed aloud. I seemed to have that knack with her. I could make her laugh, and I got the feeling that she didn't really find all that much to laugh about. There was pain behind her confident bearing, but I could tell that she did everything she could to conceal the blow she had suffered at some point.

# 17

I went into town and bought some summer clothes, a shirt, a tie and a pair of shoes, got the hotel to book a limousine and picked Clara up at her address on Vesterbrogade, in the west of the city. She had changed into a light-coloured summer dress and was nicely made-up. She nodded with irony, but I could tell she was also a little flattered when I got out and held the door for her. She was wearing a simple gold necklace with a small snake charm on it.

"You look like a million dollars," she said in English.

"And you like a billion," I replied, making her laugh at my extravagant compliment, but the summer evening seemed to set a light and breezy tone.

I wasn't familiar with any particular restaurants in Copenhagen and had first thought about going to the Tivoli Gardens, but I followed the advice of the hotel and made a reservation at the Regatta Pavilion north of the city. It proved to be a good choice. We had a table in the corner of the restaurant, with a view across the lake. First we followed the waiter's suggestion and had a drink on the terrace. It was the kind of evening which the Danish Tourist Board could have sold all round the world. A beautiful, unusually warm evening with the scents of mellow, late summer drifting from the lake and mingling with the appetising aromas of the kitchen. Bagsværd Lake was as glossy as a old-fashioned silver platter, only the boats of various sizes being rowed back and forth broke the smooth, looking-glass surface. People were out strolling in couples, alone or with the ever-present canine companion, and you could hear laughter from the lakeside where a group of youngsters had installed themselves on a rug with their picnic hampers. It seemed that I wasn't the only one the Royal sent out there, because the other diners were mainly solemn men in dark suits talking business-English, but Clara and I sat undisturbed, facing one another in our corner, and continued the conversation we had begun on the terrace as the lake slowly turned red in the evening light.

We had got off to a rather awkward start, as if suddenly we didn't know what to say to one another, like a couple of teenagers on our first date. But it also seemed as though we both knew that silence didn't have to be uncomfortable. The lovely, summer's evening made it easier. And the fact that we were, after all, of an age where we didn't have to cover up our insecurity with words. When we got the menu, we chatted easily about what to order, the wine, how nicely the restaurant was decorated, and we invented stories about the businessmen in their sober outfits.

"Maybe one of them is a spy you once stalked during the cold war," I said.

"You don't have to say 'once'," she said. "I'm not out of a job. We have certain elements in this country, we still have a particular kind of Russian in the embassy, we have Kurds who are in the PKK, there are other risks to national security."

She smiled as she said those last words, as if they sounded out of place in the idyllic snapshot of Denmark we could see through the window.

"I wasn't trying to pump you for information about your job. I'm not terribly interested in that cloak and dagger stuff."

"It's not always that easy to be terribly interested in."

"How did you end up in the NSS?"

She broke off a piece of bread, put it in her mouth and chewed before answering.

"After police college I served on the west coast, in Esbjerg, but then I was lucky enough to get a job with the Copenhagen police. There weren't so many women in the force back then, so maybe that helped me a little. Then there was a chance of promotion to the national force and I took it. The job was interesting, and I got to learn Russian for free."

"So you caught the tail end of the cold war, the golden age of spying."

"Just the final breath. The KGB were the last ones to notice what was about to happen, and when they did notice, and tried to overthrow Gorbachev, it was too late."

"Three cheers for that."

"Yes. Three cheers for that," she said, but with no great conviction.

A further, lingering lull in the conversation was saved by the arrival of our starters, and we talked about countries and our travels as we ate. Then the main course came, and we finished our bottle of wine and ordered another one, even though all my warning bells were ringing. She had never travelled to the east for her job, but had often been to the US and to New Zealand, which she liked a lot. It was one of the few countries I had never visited. She asked me about my work. She didn't say so directly, but I could tell that she found it a bit sleazy. Lying in wait to capture the famous, as it were.

"I fulfil a need," I said.

"So does a prostitute," she said.

I couldn't help laughing.

"OK. Then the press must be the pimp, because without them and the people who buy newspapers and magazines, I'd be out of a job."

261

"You look at it as just doing a job?" she asked.

"I don't really know. Like so much else in life, it's more complicated than that. I've always enjoyed the hunt, the preparation, reconnaissance, planning, meticulous attention to detail . . . more than taking the photograph itself."

"I have to confess to that tendency as well," she said.

"Yes. The hunt can become second nature. Besides, we've got a sort of unwritten pact with the people we pursue. There are times when they use us. In a divorce, in a dispute over money, to get attention. Especially if they think their star is fading. But they want to call the shots."

"And they don't get the chance."

"No. They don't."

"It's not my place to judge you."

"It's fine," I said. "I think about it quite a lot myself. Lately, that is. We're part of the global village. We supply gossip to the people sitting round the global pond. Millions buy our photographs. And pay us handsomely. It's more the hypocrisy of it all that offends me."

She laughed again. She had a subtle, dry, ready laugh.

"When Diana died in the car crash, there was an editor on one of the Danish celebrity magazines who promised never to publish – what is it they're called – paparazzi photographs again. We learnt a brand-new word. It was an act of sheer penitence. As if he was personally responsible."

"I bet he didn't stick to it," I said.

"Of course not."

"Well, there you are. The world's full of hypocrites," I said. "There's too much money involved."

"The deity of our times."

"Money always has been, hasn't it?" I said.

"I only read those magazines at the hairdresser's," she said with feigned indignation.

"Don't we all," I said, and raised my glass and we drank to that.

I asked her about New Zealand again and, as she told me about a little rented house on the coast, she suddenly began referring to "we" and "ours", becoming aware of it herself when she saw my expression.

"It's not 'we' any more," she said, taking a gulp of her wine.

"Well there's no ring at any rate," I said.

"No, but you're still wearing yours."

Everything disappeared for a moment and the air seemed to grow cold, and she understood, and put her hand on top of mine.

"That was a stupid thing to say, Peter. I'm sorry."

"It's OK," I said.

"I flushed mine down the loo the evening Niels came home and informed me that he was moving out, but I won't bother you with all that."

"I'm happy to be bothered if you want to talk about it," I said.

"It's a thoroughly pedestrian, commonplace story. There are thousands like it."

"Most stories in this life are pedestrian, but it doesn't make them any less unique or painful if you're involved," I said.

Showing her good manners, she placed her knife and fork together on her empty plate where the sirloin steak had been and we lit cigarettes and smoked as she told me the story in a low voice. She was matter-of-fact, but I could see it still hurt.

She and Niels had started going out when they were students. They had got married when she was 21 and was about to start at the police college. They had met at a party thrown by one of her old school friends who was on the same course as Niels. He was 25 and reading political science and economics, having changed courses after a couple of unsuccessful years reading law. And that was fine, because as a trainee police officer she was earning a salary. They had been happy, she said. Very happy. Made for one another were the words she used. Like all couples, their relationship had its ups and downs, but it had survived her period of service in Esbjerg while he stayed in Copenhagen working at the Ministry of Finance; his first job, which he had been very pleased to get. When she looked back over the years, it seemed as if a lot had happened and at the same time nothing at all. They had moved from a small flat to a bigger one and eventually, through his political connections in the Social Democratic party in Copenhagen, he had managed to get them a cheap, sought-after flat in the upmarket Østerbro area of the city. They mixed with like-minded people, they saw more of his family than hers. Clara was an only child, her mother and father had her late in life and they had died within a few years of one another when she was in her early 30s. Her father had been employed by the state railway all his life and her mother had worked in a kindergarten. Niels's parents were grammar school teachers and, even though he never said so, she sensed that he found her parents a little boring and parochial. They had a few friends in common from the early days of their relationship, but as time passed they saw only his friends from the Ministry. She couldn't talk about her work, and in any case she had the impression that he thought most people in the police force were mediocre. She found him patronising to the few colleagues she did invite home now and then. He loved talking shop, but when she tried to talk about her job in a general way, as was necessary because of security considerations, he quickly lost interest. Even when he was promoted to the Prime Minister's office, and was given high security clearance, she still didn't feel he listened to her when she wanted to discuss difficult situations at work.

But she considered herself to be happy. She loved her husband. She felt loved by him. They liked travelling together, but they also had separate interests. She liked reading fiction. Niels never read anything except specialist literature to do with his work. They were both very engrossed in their jobs and worked long hours, but they tried to spend the weekends together. After he was given responsibility for EU-related legislation he travelled a lot, often staying in Brussels, but she trusted him, felt secure with him and never dreamt of questioning him. There were still aspects of her work that she couldn't talk about, and there were political deliberations within the Prime Minister's inner circle that he was expected to keep to himself. At the start of their marriage, which they regarded as an intimate friendship, they had agreed that they wouldn't have children. They had neither the financial resources nor the time for children in the early years. As they got older, there wasn't room in their lives. They lived well, had good friends, could afford to travel far away on holiday, surrounded themselves with beautiful things, were attractive and healthy and loved one another. Their friends thought of them as a golden couple. They had even received several offers to feature in articles about commitment in the 1990s, but they always declined – even though they felt they had things to say that would have been of relevance to others.

She emptied her glass and I refilled it and poured myself one as well. It had been a long story, and now it was getting dark outside. The waiter asked if we would like pudding, but she shook her head so I ordered two coffees.

"But Niels and Clara didn't live happily ever after," I said.

"What a penetrating mind you have."

"I didn't mean it like that."

"It's OK. You're quite right. We didn't live happily ever after. Or till death us did part or whatever the hell it is people still promise one another. We might very well believe that when we stand at the altar, but our brains must surely tell us what a hopeless undertaking it is."

"Let's hope not," I said.

"So, there's an old romantic behind that tough façade, is there Lime?"

"I was, at least."

"I forget about your loss sometimes. Please, I'm sorry."

"Don't worry about it. I have to move on," I said.

"That's probably easier said than done," she said, and of course she was right.

The waiter brought our coffee. It was in one of those peculiar jugs where you have to press the plunger down and suddenly I missed Madrid and a *café solo*, but Clara seemed to like the rather bland-tasting coffee.

"So what happened?" I said.

"It's not very interesting," said Clara. "He came home one day, terribly nervous and defensive, and said that he would like a divorce. Those were exactly the words he used. 'I'd like a divorce,' he said. As if he was asking me a favour. He'd found what men call a younger version. It's so damned trite. As if he was just changing the old car for a new one. She was a consultant in Brussels. They'd been having an affair for more than a year. Mostly in Brussels."

"At least it wasn't his secretary," I said.

"That's a pretty stupid thing to say. What difference would that have made?" she said angrily.

"You said consultant. So she's a lawyer or some kind of economist or something like that . . ."

"Lawyer, French, 32 years old, beautiful, charming – very feminine," said Clara.

"Well, there you go. It took a lot to win him over. Wouldn't you have felt worse if she'd been 25 and your husband's secretary?"

She looked at me.

"Peter. Sometimes you surprise me, after all. Yes, I suppose it would have made a difference, but I hadn't thought about it like that. I didn't think Niels could be quite so idiotic. Even though some men, when they reach a certain age, seem to cease to be accountable for their actions."

"So you took a lover, I suppose?" I asked.

She looked at me with an expression that said she had been expecting that question, but not quite so soon.

"I haven't got a boyfriend, Peter, if that's what you're really asking. I've had 'boyfriends' – as we say in Denmark like we're teenagers – since Niels, but not a regular boyfriend, which is how even women of my age refer to their partners when announcing that they've fallen in love."

"Then what?" I said.

"I threw him out, took him to the cleaners in the divorce settlement and was cool as a cucumber when a year later he said the whole thing had been a mistake. He'd got married by then. He was in a hurry to get married, and he was in just as much of a hurry to get divorced again and come back to me. If I hadn't thought he was such a stupid shit, I would almost have felt sorry for him. He'd been so in love, he said. She made him feel vigorous and virile again, and so on. But it didn't work out as he had expected, after the first passion had died."

"So he got divorced again?"

"No, no," she said with an almost gleeful laugh. "He's still married to the French woman and she's still unfaithful to him. As far as I hear. He's having a dose of his own medicine."

"And that makes you happy."

"Maybe not exactly happy, but satisfied. I know it's wrong of me, but it's what I feel."

"Why wrong? I don't blame you. Having a thirst for revenge and getting it satisfied probably saves a lot of pills or a lot of bottles," I said.

"Exactly," she said with a triumphant smile, but I could still see her pain. I don't know if it was pain from failure and loss and dashed hopes or the pain of rejection, but she hadn't got over it with quite the coolness that her account suggested.

I settled the bill and a taxi took us to her flat. I paid the driver and followed her to the door. Clara seemed momentarily to consider asking me in, but perhaps she thought that I wouldn't really want to – or maybe wouldn't dare.

Instead, she said in a very businesslike voice, "Will you come and sign tomorrow, and get your photographs back?"

"If you'll have lunch with me."

"I'm a working woman."

"Call it a meeting with an agent?"

"That's a deal, Peter Lime. But I'm paying," she said and kissed me on the mouth, light and fleeting, but erotic anyway, with a brush of her tongue, and I went back to my hotel feeling more buoyant than I had for ages.

My good mood held for the next few days. Signing the report was postponed, and when I rang we talked comfortably, but she was too busy to meet up with me. She said it in such a way that I believed her and it didn't spoil my mood.

I played tourist, going on a guided canal boat tour and lunching in a restaurant in Tivoli where press people used to hang out. I bumped into an old colleague there and we chatted just as though it was the old days. I wouldn't describe my state of mind as happy, but on hold. I didn't know what I wanted from Clara, and I didn't know what she wanted from me. I kept far enough away from the booze to be able to remember my dreams and they began getting erotic. But they were exciting in an uneasy way. I was in bed with lots of different women, but they never had faces, and now and then I would dream that Amelia was watching as I lay with a naked woman in a sterile room like a hospital ward. Then I would wake up feeling clammy, with a huge erection.

A few days later I signed my statement at the Security Service headquarters on Borups Allé and got my photographs back. Clara was there with two colleagues, both men. They were polite and pleasant, thanked me for my kind assistance and left quickly once I had signed.

My statement corresponded with what I had said, so I had no qualms in signing it. Clara stayed behind and gave me a letter addressed to the Gauck Authority in Berlin. That whole issue suddenly seemed rather remote. A few days in summery Denmark had turned out to be like a holiday. She had drawn up the letter, but without my address in Madrid. I wrote down the office address and she took the paper away and then came back with the address printed on it. All I had to do was sign. The letter requested access to documents on the basis of my assumption that, due to my work as a photographer and journalist, I had a file in the Stasi archives. Clara would enclose a recommendation from the NSS for speedy processing and send it, as she said, via the usual channels. We parted with a handshake.

Clara invited me to lunch three days later, at a restaurant called KGB, on the same street where the Danish Communist Party's head-quarters had been in the days before the collapse of the Berlin Wall and the disintegration of the Soviet Union. Back when the party could afford to pay the rent. The restaurant had a cool feel, the only decora-tion on the white walls was a square-faced clock. It matched the fresh, pleasant Danish summer weather which was very agreeable if you still felt the heat of Madrid in your body. Or knew that the unfortunates left behind in the Spanish capital were groaning under a humid heat.

The restaurant looked as though it had just been given a quick once-over with a spot of paint, and then a handful of tables had been scattered around casually. Some wiring had been left uncovered in the corners, a reminder of socialism's hopeless workmanship. In the toilets a looped tape played Russian language lessons. So while you were having a pee, you could entertain yourself with questions like – "Where can I buy a stamp? How much will it cost to send this letter to Denmark?" – first in Danish and then in Russian. The menu included borshch, various kinds of vodka, blinis and caviar costing several hundred kroner. The young waitress was wearing army trousers and an old Eastern bloc cap with a KGB badge on it. The borshch and the steak were first-rate. Clara drank a beer. I drank a beer and a vodka. We had espresso afterwards.

"An unusual place you've brought me to," I said, taking in the room and the waitress's outfit. "So this is how one of the most brutal and lethal organisations ended up – as kitsch."

"I still think it's strange," said Clara.

"The Berlin Wall?"

"That you have to search for the Wall in Berlin. That it's vanished. That it's as if it was never there, never cost lives, never sealed people in. That the Soviet Union doesn't exist. That the world has changed completely and it's as if no one realises it."

"Many dreams hit the rocks, maybe it ended up as nightmare, but I think originally those dreams were beautiful," I said.

"It was an evil system. I don't think that should be forgotten or turned into kitsch. Would you open a restaurant called SS or Gestapo?"

"That would be in bad taste, but you chose this place," I said.

"I thought you should see it."

"And, yes, it's amusing that even the KGB can end up as a joke." Her voice took on a serious tone.

"But that's just it, Peter. The KGB's OK. It's not considered bad taste. The whole of the old communist system is a joke today, even though it has got millions of lost lives on its conscience. I think that's really peculiar. It's as if the Gulags never existed and there weren't any Danes who supported the system. It's as if that world just didn't happen, and yet it was an inescapable part of our world too for almost half a century. Isn't that strange?" said Clara.

"Maybe it isn't so ludicrous that there are young people today who think that GDR is a deodorant. Maybe it's a good thing that an evil regime didn't fall in blood, but with a little whimper, while

270

the whole world watched with a broad, amazed grin."

"Maybe," she said. "I just don't think the past disappears so easily."

I took her hand.

"Can't you take the afternoon off? We could play tourists. I'd love to take you to Tivoli. Or the Deer Park or a walk through the city. Or to Paris. Or to Malmö. Or whatever tourists do in Copenhagen."

She put her hand on top of mine.

"I have taken the afternoon off, Peter. I've done more than my fair share of overtime recently and we submitted our report yesterday. I'm finished with it, thanks to you. So, yes, thank you. I'd love to."

"What shall we do then?" I asked.

"I'd like a trip to the beach. I think it's the last day of summer," she said.

I laughed.

"Good idea. But how do we get up north?"

"I've got a car. We'll drive."

"I haven't got any swimming trunks."

She looked at me.

"There's not a soul where we're going, not at this time of year, on a weekday. So I don't think you need worry too much about that."

# 18

She drove her blue Ford Escort fast and confidently. To my surprise we headed not north as I had expected, but west along the motorway in the direction of Holbæk, turning off towards Odsherred and Sjællands Odde. She had spent holidays there as a child and had more of an affinity with that part of the coastline than with the more fashionable areas of northern Sjælland. She had inherited a little holiday cottage on Sjællands Odde, but Niels had persuaded her that they should sell it. She didn't say so, but I guessed that he hadn't considered the location fashionable enough. It was a funny place, my old country. The casual spectator could be fooled by the seemingly perfect idyll of a nation united – the Danish people's cult of flag, royal family and national football team. But underneath it all, the Danes were a divided tribe who rarely spoke or mixed socially with anyone other than those who held the same beliefs, or those who lived in the same way as their particular group.

I explained these thoughts to Clara as we drove along narrow roads in the wonderful, mellow early afternoon light, the traffic on its way to and from the ferry streaming past, and the reaped fields looking like a golden carpet between the well-kept farms. The sun shone from a cloudless sky and the breeze from the half-open window snatched at Clara's hair, and the smell of straw and corn wafted into the car.

"I work for the police. You don't have to tell me about the contradictions of our society. I see the 'two-thirds' society every day. We've thrown a third away, but we're clever. We pay for our social tranquillity. We pacify them with welfare hand-outs. That's why the middle classes – people like me – put up with high taxes. So we can live our lives in peace, so there's enough money to keep the outcasts subdued."

"That's not actually what I meant," I answered. "You're making the forces of law and order sound quite revolutionary."

"No, exactly the opposite. The system's good for people like me. As Niels always said: deep down, every middle-class Dane is a social democrat, so you might just as well take that extra step and become a member of the party, thereby gaining some proper influence."

"Flats and the rest of it?"

"That's part of the package."

"So that's what you did?" I asked.

"No. I didn't. I'm not a member of anything."

She overtook a slow-moving car, swiftly but without much room, and gave an ironic wave of her hand at the oncoming car that flashed its lights angrily as she swung the Escort back to our side of the road again.

"On the roads, however, the Danes are real freethinkers," she said. "This is where we become bold Vikings again."

I laughed with her on that lovely day. We reached the top of a gently domed hill and suddenly, as if by magic, the sparkling blue Sejerø Bay appeared and soon we were driving with the Kattegat on our right and holiday cottages on our left. She drove past a general store and turned, first along an asphalt road and then an unsurfaced track, down to an area covered with heather where she parked. I could glimpse the sea between the trees.

"My parents' holiday cottage wasn't very far from here. One of the many things that I regret about my time with Niels is that he got me to sell it," she said, and took a straw basket out of the boot. I could see two towels, a blanket, thermos and a couple of plastic cups.

"And there's a pair of trunks for you."

"You had this all planned," I said.

"Not a plan. But a hope," she said. "I'd have driven up here by myself anyway, even if you hadn't come with me. I did tell you it's the last day of summer. It has to be enjoyed. It's a gift in a country with a climate like ours. Come on!"

I followed her obediently through the heather. She strode out briskly in her jeans and shirt, her bare feet in lightweight slip-ons, almost like ballet shoes. Secluded white holiday homes stood among the pine trees, but there wasn't a soul on the beach. The water in the bay was calm and blue and she spread out the blanket in a sandy hollow in the grass behind a large rose bush. The day had started out a little chilly, but it had warmed up again. It was an unpredictable climate. She turned her back to me, stripped off her shirt and undid her bra and put on a bikini top, then pulled off her jeans and briefs and put on her bikini bottom. I couldn't help but notice that she was tanned all over and had a trim body with the soft, gentle curves of a mature woman. We were adults, from a generation that considered nakedness quite natural, but I still looked away and she turned round and smiled ironically at me, pointing at the pair of blue swimming trunks.

"Come along," she said, sounding very like a gym mistress, and I couldn't help laughing.

"Yes, miss."

She went down to the water's edge, balancing carefully as she crossed the first couple of metres of stones until the water reached the middle of her thighs. Then she threw herself in and swam out with long, lithe strokes. It was a lovely sight, her tanned body breaking the surface and the drops of water sparkling around her. I turned my back on the sea, changed into the trunks and walked down to the water's edge. She had swum out past the first sand bar a short distance from the beach and was now treading water, snorting playfully like a dolphin. I walked out across the stones, enjoying the pleasant smell of seaweed and salt. The sun made the water gleam, as if the surface had been sprinkled with tiny, delicate stars. The stones were slippery and the water felt cold for a moment, then pleasantly cool. It was like the sea at San Sebastián, salty and invigorating, and my whole body tingled wonderfully as I plunged forward and swam out towards Clara. The water tasted clean, and when I dived under the surface I could see the clear, sandy floor and billowing green seagrass. It had been a long time since I had swum in the sea, and I felt utter delight. It was almost like being a child again when one day at the beach drifted imperceptibly into the next and you slept soundly at night, free from nightmares.

"There's nothing like having time off when everyone else is at work," said Clara when I swam alongside her. I trod water, while she rolled lazily over onto her back and floated further out, touching bottom on a sand bank where the water reached just above her waist. Her nipples pressed through the thin fabric of her bikini and her body glistened with goosebumps. I swam over to her and stood up, and she began splashing water at me and I splashed back. We were like children. We stayed in the water for 20 minutes, doing everything that adults stop doing: she dived between my legs and I dived between hers, she put her foot in my cupped hands and I flipped her over backwards, we dived for shells and swam idly side by side along the shore. The sun played on her tanned body, making the millions of tiny drops of water sparkle in all the colours of the rainbow. Her skin was smooth and supple to the touch and I was almost happy. After a while we felt cold, and swam in to the deserted coast.

I studied her smooth skin, as she turned her back and dried herself.

She had a little birthmark near her left shoulder blade that I noticed when she bent forwards and shook her short hair. She had kept herself in good shape, but wasn't unhealthily thin and angular like all those young women who look like the victims of eating disorders. She was gorgeous. I went over to her and began to dry her gently, first her back and then down the backs of her thighs. She stood completely still, but when I straightened up and massaged her back with the towel again, she turned round and looked me in the eyes and I kissed her, gently at first, then harder. Desire hit me like a hammer, recognisable but still surprisingly novel after months without physical contact with a woman. I had forgotten how desire could be so intense that it is almost painful. I pulled off her bikini top and felt her hands slide down my back and into my trunks, which she pulled down over my buttocks and with difficulty over my erection, and then we were naked in the sun, lying on the blanket on the warm sand behind the protective rose bush. Her skin was cool and smooth. I caressed her gently, but my desire increased and I slipped smoothly inside her, and then it was as if darkness surged through my mind and smothered my longing and my erection vanished and I slipped out of her and the air suddenly felt cold, as though it was blowing from the north. I rolled off her, my heart thumping as if I'd just had the world's most intense orgasm, but I felt empty, furious, desperate and tormented by a piercing, irrational guilt.

I sat up, half turned away from her, and then felt her hand run down my back and across my thigh. It didn't help and I hated my life and myself. I turned my self-contempt against her and pushed her hand away.

"It's all right, Peter," she said softly, but with some effort. Her breath was still coming in short gasps. "We've got plenty of time."

I didn't respond, but stood up and dressed quickly. My heart was still thumping violently, I had a bitter taste in my mouth and I didn't want to look at her, but that would be too cowardly, so when I had finished dressing I turned towards her. She was sitting unselfconsciously, leaning back and resting on her hands. Her breasts were rounded and her dark pubic hair looked almost obscene in the afternoon sun.

I turned and walked off towards the holiday cottages.

"Peter, for heaven's sake," she said. "Peter! Stay here, please, Peter."

I sped up and broke into a run without hearing what she said because the blood was rushing in my ears as if I was running in a strong wind. Where the track turned up towards the first row of holiday cottages, I stopped and looked back. She stood with the towel loosely covering the lower part of her body, watching me go, and that's how I remember her: a beautiful, naked woman holding a blue towel, bathed in a golden light, standing in front of a bush hung with heavy red rose-hips, and the tranquil, blue sea as glossy as a sheet of ice in the background.

I ran until I tasted blood and felt sick, and my lungs told me that either they had to rest or they would stop working altogether. I sat down, panting, on a tree stump. I had no idea which direction I had taken, but Odden is a narrow spit of land and I could see the Kattegat through a pair of tall birch trees. I sat for a while with my head in my hands. The back of my t-shirt was soaked through. When I had my breathing under control, I lit a cigarette and walked slowly towards the Kattegat. We had passed a general store on the way down to the beach. It must be possible to ring for a taxi and buy something to drink there.

Both were possible. I bought a half bottle of vodka and a bottle of cola and then went down to the beach in front of the shop to wait for the taxi, and drank the vodka straight and washed it down with cola until the cola bottle was half empty. Then I filled it up with vodka. I sat behind a boat, smelling seaweed and wanting to cry, but I drank instead. I thought I saw Clara's blue Escort drive past slowly, as if she was looking for me, but I wasn't sure if it was her.

The taxi driver was a young man with a trace of fair stubble on his chin.

"I want to go to Copenhagen," I said, and got into the back of the car.

"That's a long ride," he said, taking in my dishevelled hair, jeans and sweaty t-shirt.

"I'd like to see some money really. No particular reason . . . but I think I'd like to."

"The Hotel Royal in Copenhagen," I said, and showed him my credit cards.

"Fine by me," he said. "Missed the boat, have you?" he continued in that forthright, curious manner which some Danes take for granted.

"Right, listen," I said. "You'll get a hundred kroner tip in cash, but on one condition."

He turned round and looked at me with pale-blue, questioning eyes.

"You don't say a word until we get to the Royal. Not one," I said.

"I'm not quite sure where the Royal is. Is it the SAS hotel? By the town hall square?"

"It is. You don't say a word until we get into the city, then I'll give you directions. One word and zero tip."

"Fine by me," he said, and accelerated away from the store, the large Mercedes spraying gravel in its wake.

He kept his promise, and I had finished the vodka by the time he pulled up in front of the Royal. He got his hundred kroner in cash, on top of the credit card payment, and drove happily home to Odsherred. I went into the lobby to pick up my key and Oscar got up from one of the sofas and walked towards me.

"Well, there you are. I've been waiting for you most of the damned day," he said, and hugged me with his long arms.

"Hello Oscar. Is Gloria with you?" I said.

"She's up in the room. How are you?"

"Dreadful," I said.

"So I can see. And on the juice again, are we Lime? But easy does it. The Seventh Cavalry's arrived. We'll save you from the redskins, don't worry."

"I want a drink," I said.

"Go to the bar, I'll ring up to Gloria. She misses you, just so you ..."

"And tell her that if she's going to preach, she can stay away," I interrupted.

"Always happy to serve, old boy," said Oscar.

First Gloria kissed me three times in the Spanish way, then she gave me a hug and held me at arm's length while she looked me over and shook her head, but she kept quiet. She ordered a glass of white wine and merely cast a sidelong glance at the whisky Oscar and I were drinking. She was looking relaxed and very Spanish in a flimsy, brightly coloured dress which was most becoming against her black hair. She was wearing delicate gold sandals, and her nail varnish matched the colour of her lipstick perfectly. Their holiday had done them good. Oscar looked fresh and rested too, and I could tell that they were in one of their love-struck phases because they touched one another constantly and Oscar looked at her with an expression signalling both desire and possessive privilege. It was as if he was saying, "Look at my woman, isn't she lovely? And just remember, she's mine."

I told them the whole story. I was so very pleased to see them. They were the only fixed point in my life, the two people who knew me best, both my good and bad sides. They didn't judge me, but accepted me for who I was. They were my best friends and we didn't have many secrets from one another. They listened calmly and sympathetically and, when I got to my disastrous trip to the beach, Gloria leant forward and stroked my cheek.

"You poor thing, Pedro," she said.

I didn't like her feeling sorry for me, but I knew what she meant. I thought I had freed myself from Amelia, that I had got over her and Maria Luisa's deaths, that I had contained my grief, but it had only been skin deep. Deep in my subconscious, I was still married and incapable of being unfaithful.

Gloria lit another cigarette and Oscar ordered another round of drinks. I was aware of the alcohol, but I didn't feel at all drunk.

"I know it's not your thing, Peter," said Gloria. "But don't you think it might be a good idea to get some professional help?"

Once I would have taken offence and been angry, but now I didn't reply.

"I'm sure there's a good therapist back home in Madrid who you could talk to, and maybe come to terms with the things that are tormenting you. I know you're not a great one for talking, and you don't say much about yourself and your feelings, but perhaps that's exactly why a professional could help. I don't want to see you go to the dogs. I don't want to see you fall apart."

"No preaching, Gloria," I said.

"You're not getting off the hook," she said. "We're your friends, and friends are there to say the things no one dares to say."

"You know how it is with women today, Peter. They believe in the conversation like their parents believed in the Blessed Virgin. They are convinced that everything on earth can be solved through talking, no-nonsense talking," Oscar said.

"Do shut up, Oscar," said Gloria, but without anger. "Peter needs to talk. You and I forget what he's been through. We don't want to lose you."

"The problem is, I thought I felt something for her, or that I would

280

grow to feel something for her," I said. "It was as if I was alive again . . . as if suddenly there was light ahead. As if I could forget . . . do you understand?"

"We do. And maybe, in the end, it'll turn out for the best, Peter. But some professional help might be a good idea," said Gloria.

Oscar leant forward.

"There's something else," he said. "Have you considered that all this might actually have been planned right from the start?"

"What do you mean?"

"Listen. Clara Hoffmann from the Danish secret police comes to Madrid with a photograph, and since that moment everything's gone to hell. Somehow or other, that photograph got the whole roller-coaster ride going. What did she want with it? Why was it so important for you to come to Denmark and give evidence about some old story? What's going on in Denmark? Ask yourself that. What were the police going to do with Lime and Lime's photograph?"

It suddenly dawned on me. It was really quite simple in the light of what my old colleague Klaus had told me and what I had read in the Danish newspapers. The National Security Service was preparing some kind of report, but for whom? Clara had come to Madrid to ask about Lola and a German terrorist, but was more interested in a present-day Danish member of parliament who had lived in a commune with German terrorists 25 years ago. Why?

"Just a minute," I said, and went to the reception desk and got the number of the News. Then I borrowed Oscar's mobile phone and rang Klaus Pedersen. I was put through to a couple of different extensions, but finally got hold of him in an editing suite. He sounded harassed. I heard him giving instructions about a frame to one of the editing technicians.

"I'm seriously busy, Peter. Can we talk some other time," he said.

"What are you working on?"

"Busy, Peter. Stress. Deadline. Remember?"

"Is it anything to do with the NSS?" I asked.

He was quiet for a second.

"Who told you that?" he said.

"What's it about?" I asked.

"Briefly, the government has asked the National Security Service for an account of which legal political parties and trade unions they have infiltrated and bugged and kept under surveillance over the last 30 years. It's the first time we've had the chance to look through their books, get an idea of their working methods, and hear about their budget. The review hasn't turned up anything particularly new, but those on the left wing are furious and are demanding an independent inquiry. They don't like the idea of the police investigating themselves. The right is more or less satisfied, and the Minister of Justice says no to an inquiry, on the basis that national security can't be further compromised. It's a big story. Why do you ask?"

"What if I were to tell you that a secret report has been made, the Minister of Justice has received it, and it states that a current MP lived with German terrorists in his younger days, so the Minister is satisfied with a watered-down review, because he knows the NSS was right to use surveillance? That the government isn't going to explore the case because it is dependent on this particular MP's cooperation to keep its majority? But that it's very useful for them to have this knowledge, should pressure be required during parliamentary negotiations? What would you say to that?"

"Bingo! But where did you get your information?"

"It doesn't matter. Because it gets even better. The woman you call Laila Petrova lived in the same commune . . ."

"I'll be damned."

"Indeed."

"Can you prove it?" he asked.

"I've got photographs of them together. I lived there too. I took the photographs. I've made a statement about it to the NSS. A sworn statement. I'm one hundred per cent certain that there's another report, and that if the Minister of Justice denies it to you or parliament then he's lying. And you're still not allowed to do that in Denmark, are you?"

"Danish politicians can screw around, but they mustn't tell lies or they're for the high jump. You're quite right about that."

"Then he'll have to admit that he's received other information?"

"Maybe not to me, but I'll make sure questions are asked in committee. And if he tells lies there, he's finished," said Klaus.

"You're the source?" He asked after a brief pause.

"I don't know, I suppose you could call it that," I said.

"Well I'll be damned!"

"Join the club."

He paused again and I could hear him saying something to the editing technician.

"Where are you?" he came back to me.

"At the Royal."

"I've got to finish my 6.30 p.m. bulletin, so I could come with a crew just after that. Then we can do an interview and some cover shots, you can walk into the hotel and sit down, that kind of thing. Something quick. You know the score. And I can get it on the nine o'clock news."

"OK."

"Can I have the photographs?"

"No, but you can duplicate them."

"OK. And Peter? Why are you doing this?" he asked.

"My motives aren't important. You know what it's like. Where there's a secret, there's always someone ready to tell it to someone who wants to hear it."

"OK. See you," he said, and I could hear the journalist's dream of a scoop making his voice quiver in anticipation, excitement and delight.

I passed the mobile phone back to Oscar.

"What was that all about?" he said.

"Could you order some coffee? I'll just go and have a shower and get changed."

"Why?" Gloria asked.

"I'm going to be on television," I said.

Oscar laughed and slapped me on the shoulder.

"That's my boy! That's the way to get it out of your system. Excellent idea. Your little police lady won't like it either."

I didn't know what he meant. All of a sudden it was Clara's fault, and the strange thing was that I accepted the allegation against her as though I was a schoolboy who had been seduced. The desire and passion had been mutual. After all, that's why I felt so dreadful. I had wanted to make love to her. I would never admit it, not even to Gloria and Oscar, but not being able to felt like a blow to my manhood. And I hated and despised myself for it. It was primitive and not particularly intelligent, but feelings aren't located in the intellect.

"Is this really wise, Peter?" Gloria asked. She went into lawyer-mode when she realised what I was about to do.

"I don't know, but it feels good."

"It will be revenge," said Oscar.

Maybe it was revenge, maybe it was an ignoble way of making trouble for Clara, because I was furious with myself and with her. I despised myself and thought I might feel better if I took it out on her, because she had seen me humiliated. At any rate, that's what I felt. Maybe it was an attempt to rid my system of the agony that had been the last few months. To put it all put behind me. I had acted spontaneously when I decided to ring Klaus.

I got up.

"Check us out of the hotel and rent a car, we'll drive to Germany this evening and get a flight from Hamburg or Frankfurt. I'm not up to talking with the Danish reporters tomorrow. All hell will break loose when they run the story this evening. Let's get out of the country. Let's go home," I said.

"So you're coming home to Madrid with us, Peter?" Gloria said happily.

"Yes, I'm coming home with you," I said. "This story has gone on long enough."

# PART THREE

# OBLIVION
# OR REMEMBRANCE

We fought for a combination of socialism and freedom, a noble
objective that failed utterly but which I still believe is possible. I
hold to my beliefs, although they have been tempered now by time
and experience. But I am no defector, and this memoir is not a
confessional bid for redemption.

*Markus Wolf*

On everything we do, we stake our lives. Every moment is lived at the
gaming table, even though we may not know it.

*Carsten Jensen*

# 19

Summer turned into autumn, but the story didn't fade away quickly. Not that I had really expected it would, but there was no way I could have known that the stakes would be so high when we escaped Denmark in our hire car on the ferry to Puttgarten, like thieves in the night. We left behind a media storm which kept politicians and reporters busy for weeks. It didn't have any effect on me because I didn't respond to the approaches from the Danish press made via the office. Requests for interviews, in-depth profiles, magazines wanting to know about the photographer who had emigrated, publish a follow-up to my exposé. The press agency sent piles of cuttings from Danish newspapers and magazines about what was described as a scandal and the lack of a political will to set up an impartial commission of inquiry. The articles also described how, one by one, left-wing veterans came forward and demanded to know if they featured in the archives. It was as if it became a badge of honour, admission to a VIP list, to have been bugged and kept under surveillance. But then, as is often the case with stories in Denmark, the scandal died away when the media found other things to write about. This is symptomatic of the mass media all over the western world today, unable to concentrate on a single issue for long. Like distracted school children, they move on to something else when a subject bores them. The scandal was marginalised, appearing only on special-interest radio programmes and in the occasional small-circulation newspaper.

Most of the articles I received contained reports on the photographer Peter Lime, the cause of all the fuss. I was described variously as a mole in the Danish left-wing at the beginning of the 1970s, a fashionable paparazzo who rubbed shoulders with the wealthy, international jet set, a hard-boiled photojournalist who had been in all the trouble-spots of the world, a tax exile from Denmark and a drunken NSS agent who had suffered a breakdown after his wife and child had been murdered by Basque terrorists. I didn't know whether to laugh or cry, but mostly did the former as I translated some of the more extravagant articles for Oscar and Gloria.

One tabloid and two magazines sent reporters and photographers to Madrid. I refused to speak to them, even though they tried to appeal to me as a member of the profession. I was on the other side of the lens again. They took photographs of me as I arrived at and left the office, and they questioned the receptionist at the Hotel Inglés, having tailed me there. Carlos, of course, said nothing. My nerves were frayed. The long telephoto lenses were trained on me and I seemed always to be looking straight back at them, just as Uncle Sam's finger in the "I Want You for the U.S. Army" poster is always aimed directly at you, whatever angle you look at it. They found the site where my home had been and took photographs. But they didn't stick it out for long and went home after a week, and soon things returned to normal.

Oscar and Gloria tried to persuade me to start working again, but I had lost my appetite for it. Finally they gave in and bought me out of the firm without any drama. They wanted me to find my own lawyer, but Gloria had always seen to my affairs and I decided she could sort this business out too. If I couldn't still trust my two old friends then there was no point in anything.

With the help of one of Gloria's contacts, I rented a small, furnished flat in my old neighbourhood. Mostly I kept to myself, strangely empty and dark inside, as if someone had switched off my soul's light. I trained at the karate institute and started going to AA meetings again. I really had to force myself to walk through a room full of strangers again for the first time, strangers bound together solely by their struggle with the inner demons they tried to numb via the bottle. But in time it became almost habit to stand at the lectern once or twice a week and look out at all the faces with their understanding eyes and utter those therapeutic words: *Buenas tardes. Soy Pedro. Soy alcoholico.* It kept my drinking bouts in check, but it didn't prevent me from falling headfirst off the wagon now and then, and waking up after a blackout. More often than not I was in my flat. I seemed to have a homing pigeon's ability to navigate my way back there even though I could never remember how I had managed it. On one occasion, I came to in the gutter without a peseta in my pocket, all papers and money gone. And on another occasion I found myself with a very young prostitute who looked at me with pity and contempt, demanding payment even though her heroic efforts had apparently come to nothing. I lived, but wasn't really living. I often thought about Clara and while in the process of getting tanked-up, before losing it completely, I would put my hand on the telephone to ring Copenhagen, but my courage failed and by later in the evening I'd be too drunk to do it.

Autumn came early to Madrid that year. An icy wind from the mountains swept over the Castilian plain and chased the inhabitants of the cold city round every corner. There's no city as freezing as a Mediterranean one. The wind found every hole and crack, and the inadequate radiators and red-hot electric heaters fought a losing battle against an iciness, which seemed to bring out the worst in people. They shivered in coats that were too thin, elbowing their aggressive and bad-tempered way through the streets. We had a day of snow and the roads were in chaos, then the weather changed again and was mild and pleasant, until a new cold snap and torrential downpours made the city which never slept become almost comatose. Rain poured down on the empty café tables and Felipe loitered in the doorway of the Cerveceria Alemana, flicking the cloth in his hand, with his back to the almost empty café, perhaps dreaming of bulls in an arena bathed by the sun. Madrileños stayed at home and lolled in front of the television, refusing to go out.

On the early November day that it snowed, Don Alfonzo died. If a death can be pleasant or easy then his apparently was, but how could I know what the last seconds of his life had been like? If they had been accompanied by intense pain or terrible fear as his heart gave out in the greenhouse where he was preparing for winter? Or if, in his religious way, he had prepared himself to greet the God he had cursed, yet believed in? His neighbour found him next to the potting bench with a trowel in his hand. His face was peaceful, as if he slept. The greenhouse was tidy and well organised as usual. The light was subdued and soft because of the unaccustomed snow on the roof.

I buried him next to Amelia and Maria Luisa. I often visited the cemetery, with its white crosses, doves frozen in marble and cool, immaculate headstones. Sometimes just to sit and read a book. Other times with a bottle. I held long conversations with Amelia and she told me that I should get my life together and start living again. That I mustn't forget her, but that she should be part of the luggage I took with me as I continued my journey, and not a ball and chain. I argued with her, saying that this wasn't possible, and I could hear her voice among the crosses, saying my name in full, the way she had when she'd been exasperated or even occasionally angry with me – "Pedro Lime. Just don't you dare be awkward!"

I would cry when I heard her voice. It was as if she came alive, but then when I opened my eyes all I saw was headstones and the occasional elderly widow dressed in black, tending a grave in the distance.

Don Alfonzo had left everything he owned to me. He had a small fortune in shares, but his best gift was the house. I had Gloria sell the motorbike for next to nothing and the house in San Sebastián for a little under market price to Tómas, and I moved into Don Alfonzo's beautiful, well-kept house, surrounded by his classic furniture, extensive book collection, shimmering red geraniums and the cultivated orchids, which I accepted were bound to die. I didn't know how to keep them alive. In the spring I would remove his greenhouse and build a little studio with a darkroom, and go back to my portrait photography again. And I also had plans to take up landscape photography. I imagined myself standing at my tripod in the wide-open Spanish countryside, waiting for a fighting bull to come down from the hills somewhere in Extremadura and move lazily towards me in the changing light. Large and ponderous, it would walk with its ears cocked and its curved, sharp horns pointing in my direction. It wouldn't be aggressive, because its companions were right behind it, and these big dangerous beasts are placid and docile when in a herd. It would lift its head and the light would fall at a very particular angle through the olive tree and filter through the horns and down onto a parched tuft of grass next to a red desert flower. The moment would last a thousandth of a second. I could see myself growing old alone, standing at the tripod, waiting for the precise light that would produce the perfect photograph. Since I knew the perfect photograph couldn't exist, I would be forever seeking it out, and I would always have something to do with my time.

In the middle of November Clara Hoffmann rang. It was evening, the weather was rotten, and the rain that had begun early in the afternoon was still hammering down on the roof and beating against the windows. I was sober and sat reading one of Don Alfonzo's books on the Spanish Civil War, and the brutality and lack of mercy people are capable of manifesting. I had a fire burning in the hearth, made with logs from the old man's carefully stacked woodpile, and I was warm and composed. The melodic Danish voice threw me off balance at first, making my heart thump.

"It's Clara. Clara Hoffmann from Copenhagen," she said.

"*Si*," I said.

"Is that you, Peter?"

"Yes. Sorry. I was lost in a book."

"Please excuse me for disturbing you. I got the number from your office. A few days ago actually. I hope you don't mind?"

"No. No. How are you?"

"Fine thanks. And you?"

"Yes, thanks. OK, I mean."

There was a brief silence.

"I've often thought about ringing you," she said.

"Me too. You, I mean. Why didn't you?" I said.

"I don't know. Perhaps I was nervous about being rejected. And why didn't you ring me then?"

"I was probably nervous too. And a bit ashamed," I said, surprising myself.

She laughed gently.

"A tough guy like you!"

"I'm not as tough as I look."

"No. That's just what you're not. Not only tough, anyway. That's what I like about you," said Clara.

"And you still do? In spite of, I mean."

"Actually, I've missed you," she said.

"And me you," I admitted – to myself as well.

"It's hard to believe we're both adults," she said.

"Perhaps that's exactly why," I said.

294

Then there was another pause. The connection was excellent. Her voice was clear and there was only a little hissing sound from the digital signal.

"How come you got brave?" I asked.

"I had an excuse," she said, and her tone became more businesslike, but her voice was having an effect on me and I could picture her. I remembered her smile and her naked body in the sand by Sejerø Bay and conflicting emotions filled my mind again. She told me that she had received a letter from the German authorities. I was welcome to see my old Stasi file in Normannenstrasse whenever I wanted. They had sent a letter to me, but her colleagues in Germany had notified her too. Would I do it? Would I see my file?

I had put the whole case behind me, seldom thinking of it any more. I didn't feel anger at the culprits, just grief at my loss, and certainly no anger towards Clara. My thirst for revenge had vanished just as quickly as the harsh Spanish morning sun burnt the dew off Don Alfonzo's flowers in the summertime. Oscar and Gloria were right. Raking up the past only caused pain. Chasing ghosts would only cause pain and anxiety, and I told Clara this. I could tell from her quick "OK" that she was disappointed. And then, without thinking and without a rational explanation as to why, I said "I want to go to Berlin, but then you've got to come down from Copenhagen too. Otherwise I'm not going."

"When?"

"What about tomorrow?"

She laughed again, in a way that made me happy and relieved.

"What about the day after tomorrow?" she said.

"That's OK," I said. "The day after tomorrow would be fine."

"That's settled then. Ring me when you've made your travel arrangements. I'll probably drive."

"Will do. And Clara . . ."

"Yes, Peter."

"I look forward to seeing you."

"Same here, Peter Lime. Same here."

"I'm sorry if my speaking to the television news about the other report caused you problems."

"Don't think about it. I'm a big girl."

"All the same."

"I'll tell you about it in Berlin," she said, and hung up.

The rain in Berlin was icier than in Madrid, and now and then it turned into sleet, but this northern city was built for the cold, and Berliners behaved like a people who didn't concern themselves about rain, as their city marched towards its new importance. I had only been to Berlin a couple of times since the Wall came down, and the rapid process of change had continued. The newspapers might write of Germany's great economic crisis and the mental wall still dividing East and West, but Berlin gave the impression of being a city which hadn't read the bleak words of its own press. Huge cranes towered above the centre, where glass and concrete blossomed like a symbol of the unified capital to which the German government would soon relocate. The streets were full of people with their collars turned up and umbrellas tilted against the cold and rain, struggling through the dismal afternoon like small, flustered sailing vessels. I was surprised again at how early it got dark in northern Europe. I loved the Mediterranean for its warmth, but also the light. The dismal, northern darkness made me melancholy, but the Berliners looked as if they lived with it without any problems. There were lots of people in the well-lit restaurants and cafés that emitted a rush of heat and food smells as the doors opened and closed. The streets were packed with new cars that slipped slowly through the rain gleaming in the beams of their headlights. Now and then a little Trabant appeared in the stream of Mercedes and BMWs, a small reminder of a recent past, when the city had been split in two. But mainly, with typical German meticulousness and efficiency, the last ten years had been an attempt to erase all signs of the emblem of a sacred communist peace that had divided the city, creating two completely different worlds.

My travel agent had made me a reservation in a smallish, but luxurious family hotel near Kurfürstendamm, and booked a room next to mine for Clara. I had rung her at the National Security Service in Copenhagen to tell her where we should meet, but learnt that she was no longer employed there. I was put through to various extensions before I got hold of someone who knew me and was willing to tell me that Clara Hoffmann now worked in the fraud division of the Copenhagen police. I rang and left a message with a secretary, and next day I caught a flight to Berlin.

I didn't expect Clara to arrive until late, and as I waited for her I felt like an insecure young man. My heart thumped and the palms of my hands were sweaty, and there was a peculiar pressure in my chest that I had to take deep breaths to control. I was more than nervous about meeting her – I was terrified. To pass the time I did 50 push-ups, had a shower and went down to the bar and drank two whiskies even though I knew I shouldn't. Then I went back up to my room. It was a good-sized double room with a wide bed beneath a gold-framed mirror. Only a faint hiss of tyres on the dark, wet streets outside penetrated the heavy red curtains into the warm room. There was a door between my room and what was to be Clara's room. It was locked. I watched some television, but couldn't settle and went down to the bar again, this time ordering a cola.

Finally I got the *Herald Tribune* from reception and went back upstairs, starting on page one, and when I got to *Peanuts* on the back page I heard a sound from the adjoining room. A door slammed and I pictured Clara shaking the rain from her coat and her hair. I got up to go out into the corridor and knock on her door, then sat down again with the paper on my lap, but neither *Peanuts* nor *Calvin and Hobbes* made any sense. Words and drawings blurred in front of my eyes. I was over halfway through my life and yet I felt like an adolescent again. I was here to see my Stasi file, but I knew that Berlin would also test whether I could love another person again. It couldn't be like it had been with Amelia, but I had to discover whether I dared let myself go, which is an inextricable part of falling in love, and risk being hurt. Deep down, I had known this all along, although I hadn't articulated it to myself before I sat there in the hotel room. I had no way of knowing if Clara Hoffmann looked at our meeting here in the same way.

I heard the shower running next door. She had said she was going to drive from Copenhagen. It was a good thing I hadn't knocked on her door, of course she would want to freshen up after the journey. This gave me a few more minutes before we met, thank goodness. When she was ready we could have a drink in the room and then find somewhere to have dinner, and I would just have to see how it turned out. I took some more deep breaths and felt a little calmer.

I was sitting with the paper when I heard a key in the connecting door, and when it opened Clara was standing in the doorway looking at me. She was wearing the hotel's white bathrobe, but the belt was only loosely tied so I could see her breasts and a glimpse of the black, thick hair between her legs. She didn't say anything, but looked at me with a little smile, and I stared back. Then she stepped into the room and closed the door behind her, locked it and walked across to the door of my room and opened it, hung the Do Not Disturb sign outside, closed the door and locked it and put on the chain. It took no time at all, but it was as if I was watching her in slow motion. As if time ground to a halt and the world slowly ceased to exist. I watched her buttocks sway gently under the white towelling, the mature curves of her hips and the glimpse of the inside of a smooth thigh as she took a step forward. Her hair was damp and curly. The nape of her neck was pale and I had an overwhelming desire to kiss the little patch of neck below her ear. She turned round at the door. I stood up and the paper fluttered to the floor. My heart was pounding and the blood was roaring in my ears as if my head would explode. Clara looked me straight in the eye as she undid the belt of the bathrobe and stripped it off with an easy flourish and a little twist of her body, making her breasts swing gently. Her naked body was slim, but with a rounded belly and softly contoured hips. Her skin still bore the slight golden glow of summer. Her nipples were small and dark and not quite the same size. There was a little birthmark below her left breast. It was almost heart-shaped, like the one I remembered she had below her left shoulder blade. Her legs were slender, but she had small veins showing at the top of her thighs, making her even more attractive. She had painted her toenails the same muted red colour as her fingernails, and her lips glistened slightly. She stood completely motionless and let me look at her. It was as if she was saying, "Here I am. This is me. This is my body."

She took a few steps and I took a step towards her.

"Clara," I said.

She took three quick steps forward and put her finger on my lips and hushed me as if I was a little child. I could feel her breasts against my t-shirt and her nakedness against my erection. Her eyes were open and moist, as if she was frightened or just about to cry.

"Clara," I repeated and she hushed me again.

"Don't talk, Peter Lime. Don't talk. Words mustn't spoil it."

# 20

After we had made love the first time, I began to cry. I don't see myself as an emotional "new man". Before Amelia and Maria Luisa died, I couldn't remember crying as an adult, and I thought it was embarrassing when men bared their souls in the 1970s, and with tears in their eyes talked about how terribly difficult they found all that stuff with women. *Fuck them and leave them* had been my arrogant motto. But in that hotel bed in Berlin I couldn't keep back the tears that started out as one, then two, then three sobs, until finally Clara, even though I struggled, pulled my head against her breast and stroked my hair as if I was a little child who had hurt himself. I cried for all the wasted opportunities and the injustice of life, and because I would never get over my dreadful grief, but making love with Clara had also been a release. It was as if my subconscious – or, using that old-fashioned but fine word, my soul – had, at least temporarily, been set free from its anguished past. Perhaps that's how people feel when they go into therapy and are surprised when they come through as more of a whole person, reaching an awareness of what had made them break down. Amelia and Maria Luisa would always be the most powerful memory of my life, but it seemed that I might start accepting that a bandage could be carefully wrapped round the wound, and I could move on.

My weeping subsided, to be replaced by a feeling of shame, and I tried to pull free. Clara leant over me and began to kiss the tears from my face. Drop by drop, she cleared the streaks of tears from my eyelids, cheeks, throat and chest, and then her tongue tenderly and carefully stroked my lips before her mouth closed over mine. Her tongue against mine rekindled my desire with a force that I didn't think I had any more, and I pushed her onto her back and entered her with such intensity that she gave a little scream. But she quickly twined her legs round me, pressing me even further in and the world around us disappeared again.

I still hadn't spoken a word to her.

But we did afterwards. We lay in bed talking and drinking red wine which I fetched from the minibar. We didn't talk about us, but about ourselves before us. I did most of the talking, first about Amelia and Maria Luisa, but also about my childhood and my adolescence and my problems with alcohol. Clara lay in my arms and asked a few questions, but mostly she just listened. She didn't tell me much about herself. She said she couldn't remember her childhood very clearly. Perhaps because it had been so happy in that nice, orderly home? She had the usual memories of puberty and senior school. Her life had been rather straightforward until her marriage. She didn't think it was particularly interesting, maybe because there are never stories to be told about the happy times only the unhappy ones. Perhaps she felt that it actually wasn't any of my business, or perhaps she just didn't want to talk about herself.

"I bet you were the sweetest girl," I said.

She sat up and leant against the headboard, stretching her arms above her head, and arousing me again.

"I was very spotty," she said. "And now I'm hungry."

I was too, ravenous; I wanted meat and mountains of potatoes and hearty German gravy. But it was past midnight, and when I rang room service all they could offer was vegetable soup, sandwiches and omelettes, so I ordered some of each plus a bottle of wine and some mineral water.

Clara got out of bed and, still naked, went out and came back with her clothes and a little suitcase.

"I think we can cancel the other reservation," she said. "If you want to, that is?"

"Why did you do it?"

"I've wanted to ever since I first saw you, even though that's not quite how I thought about it. You were married and . . . I'm sorry. I shouldn't say it like that."

"It's all right, Clara."

"There haven't been all that many men in my life, Peter. I have needs like everyone else, but it just didn't seem worth the effort after the divorce. I didn't really have anything against bringing men home to my bed, the problem was getting rid of them afterwards."

"I'm glad you made the first move. I don't know if I'd have dared."

"I'm sure you would have. Anyway, I was sure you lusted after me. I remembered seeing it in your eyes this summer. I could see you wanted me. And standing in the room next to yours I suddenly thought 'I'm mid-way through life, and I've already seen people my age dying. There's no reason to waste time. All that can happen if you take a chance is that you get your wings singed again. But the first burn is always the worst.'"

I got up, walked over to her and kissed her tenderly, my hands gently caressing her breasts.

"I'm glad you did it," I said again.

She pulled away gently and pointed at the bathroom door.

"Don't you think you should make yourself a bit respectable before room service arrives?"

We ate as if we hadn't seen food for days. And although I usually get full rather quickly, now I ate until there was nothing left.

"You haven't told me why you changed job," I said to her when we had finished.

"When there's awkward business in Denmark, someone always ends up carrying the can, otherwise it won't go away. It was my turn this time."

"Because of me?"

"Yes. Because of you, Peter."

"I'm sorry."

"Well. Don't be. Give me a cigarette – although I've stopped smoking," she continued. "I needed to get out of the NSS. And it's Denmark, after all, so they don't fire you. They find you another job, further down the ladder. A blot on your record, same pay, but a sign in neon lights that your career is no longer running according to plan. Denmark doesn't like to see blood spilt, but we cleanse just as clinically as everyone else does. Only we do it without leaving too much blood on the carpet."

She was smoking furiously and I could tell she was angry and hurt.

"I was angry, Clara," I said. "Angry and ashamed and hurt and drunk."

"I've told you not to give it a thought. I quite understand. It's just that . . ."

"What?"

"I'm in the fraud division, in a junior position. I get all sorts, asset-strippers, tax evaders, the sort of fiddles that are virtually impossible to convict people for. And it doesn't look good, does it? What does that Hoffmann woman actually do? She's not securing too many convictions. We'd better give her something else, something even less consequential, to do. Still, this time I carried the can, but I'd probably have been given the elbow anyway. Lime or no Lime."

"What do you mean?"

"The service is under the spotlight after the recent revelations. The politicians have realised that while every other intelligence service has cut back since the end of the cold war, the NSS has increased its staff by 60 per cent. And what the hell are they all doing now the war's over? There'll be cuts, no doubt about that. So maybe I got out just in time."

"You sound bitter."

"I am bitter, Peter. About a lot of things. A lot of things in my life. It didn't turn out as I'd expected. I'm halfway through it. I've got a job I don't like, and in which I see no future. I'm on my own. I've got a large, pleasantly decorated, empty flat, where I talk to the pot plants. Maybe I should get a cat? I'm on my own, and it scares me."

I took her face carefully in my hands and kissed her. Now it was Clara's turn to have tears in her eyes. I kissed her and held her tenderly.

"Make love to me again, Peter," she said.

We went to bed and made love, this time slowly and gently. Afterwards she lay on her side with her back to me and I remember feeling happy and sad at the same time as I listened to her slow breathing and felt her heart beating through her soft skin against the palm of my hand. I thought about how banal love is, and yet how different and new it is for every single person who is lucky enough to experience it. And, for the first time in a very long while, I slept without waking and without being able to recall my dreams.

Even so, I woke early, and could tell from the sound of the traffic that it had stopped raining. It was strange to wake up next to someone again. For a second, between sleep and consciousness, I thought it was Amelia's naked, soft belly that my hand was resting on, that I was breathing onto her neck, but then the morning came into focus and I was momentarily torn between shame and pride that Clara was lying beside me.

When I came back from the bathroom, she was sitting up in bed.

"What an early riser," she said, looking at me with no hint of shyness.

"Sleep," I said.

"No. No," she said, swinging her legs out of the bed. "Go down to breakfast. I'll join you in a minute. You've got an appointment with the past."

"So soon?"

"Ten o'clock in the old block on Normannenstrasse. They're very busy. Lots of people would like to forget the past, but first they want to re-examine it. I had you squeezed into the queue. I forgot to tell you last night," she said, smiling at me. "I had other things to think about. But now we must get down to business."

We took a taxi to the eastern part of Berlin. It was a cold, clear day, with a pale November sun shining through the forest of cranes, their long arms swinging whole sections of buildings into place in what seemed like one gigantic construction site. It was hard to imagine that the city had once been divided, even though it was obvious from the change in the style of architecture as you crossed the now invisible border. In what had been East Berlin, concrete blocks were arranged like soldiers on parade, lined up in serried ranks, but the people wore the same kind of clothes and shivered with cold in just the same way as those in the west. You had to remind yourself that there was a mental boundary dividing the two Germanys. It was hard to imagine the astonishment and euphoria when, on 9 November 1989, the spokesman for the East German regime, Schabowski, told a press conference in an almost off-hand manner that the border crossings between East and West Berlin were now open. I had heard it in the afternoon on CNN in New York, and had jumped on the first available flight back to Europe, wanting to be there to see a new world being born. I had taken a whole series of photographs, but had never sold any of them. They were good photographs, but mine were no different from those of my competitors. I had been elated, and returned to Madrid with adrenalin pumping, convinced that the world had changed fundamentally and would never be the same again. It was a miracle that I had never expected to witness in my lifetime – people all over East and Central Europe had changed the world, just as we had dreamt of doing in the late 1960s. Gloria had been elated too. Unable to stand still, she had paced back and forth, kept returning again and again to the incredible footage being shown on Spanish television. Oscar was bad-tempered, drunk and surly He kept repeating that it would soon all be forgotten, and the Ossies would rue the day that they had thrown themselves into the arms of West Germany. Gloria and I had danced round the room to the glorious music surging from the crowds, laughing at Oscar sat there looking like a crotchety old man. A year later, when the two Germanys were reunified, Oscar got drunk again. At first I thought it was from pleasure, but the evening ended in a violent quarrel between him and Gloria, in which I had to intervene. He accused her of having betrayed their youth. She accused him of living in a past that was irrevocably over. It all ended in the usual scene about their mutual infidelities, and I had to put Oscar to bed and then sit and listen to Gloria's complaints. Oscar had a violent side to him, especially when he drank and took speed at the same time. Gloria was afraid that he was getting into it again. He had hit her in the past, after all. The next time I saw them they were stiff and polite with one another, but a month later they went to Hawaii and fell in love again.

I hadn't thought about it since, but sitting in the taxi next to Clara with my arm round her, I remembered that time, and told her about it. She would have taken her car, but I suggested a taxi. We sat close and I felt calm, composed and light-hearted. I didn't want to drink. All I wanted was what I was doing: to sit close to Clara and talk, the memory of our lovemaking fresh in my mind.

"I was in the kitchen ironing when my husband said I should come and look at the television," she said, taking my free hand and caressing it. "I can't remember ever having been so moved by pictures as I was by the sight of all those people standing on the Wall, dancing. I remember one thing in particular. A young man was sitting on top of the Wall, holding up an umbrella as protection against the water cannons which the Vopos had trained on him to get him down. It was fantastic in itself, but I don't think I'll ever forget his smile. When the water stopped, he lowered his umbrella, and when they turned the jets on him again, he just raised his black umbrella and smiled. That little, wry grin sums up the moment for me. One frail human being, smiling in the face of impotent authority."

"It's history," I said. "Young people today think the GDR is kitsch, just like that restaurant we went to in Copenhagen."

"Yes. And that's the beauty of it," she said. "Europe came through that period without what would have been a devastating conflict. That young people see it as the distant past is actually a miracle. And it's not very easy to try to explain to them what the GDR was, why the partition of Europe had lasted so long and why we didn't do anything – but also that it was the people themselves who sent their regime packing. We did nothing because we were afraid of jeopardising our stability. And we've been trying to forget about it ever since."

"But the GDR and the Stasi existed. And we're on our way to bear witness to that fact," I answered.

"Yes. That's the strange thing about these totalitarian regimes. Whether they were Nazis or communists, they were so convinced of their infallibility that they kept records of everything. They were convinced of the justice of their cause and of our approaching destruction, that everything had to be written down. They did so because they were completely paranoid – that peculiar mixture of megalomania and an inferiority complex. You never knew what the next purge might entail, so it was best to write everything down, cover every eventuality. The most criminal regimes in the history of the world have had the most conscientious clerks and administrators."

She turned towards me and I leant over and kissed her soft lips and suddenly I wasn't afraid of the future. I felt wonderful, in a taxi stuck in a tailback in a Berlin streaked with rain, the morning already shrouded in a grey hue that announced the onset of northern Europe's grim December darkness which devoured the light, making your soul dreary. But nothing could lower my spirits as I sat next to Clara on the way to discover that part of my past catalogued by meticulous servants of the defunct GDR.

The Stasi had occupied an enormous building in the Normannenstrasse complex in East Berlin. Today, part of it is a museum where you can see the office of the last director, Mielke, with all his telephones, so typical of the communist regimes, arrayed on his glossy desk of that dark wood favoured by leaders from Vladivostok to Berlin. Telephones for secret conversations, for top-secret conversations, for ultra-secret conversations. Direct lines to the armed forces, the Politburo and the KGB out in Karlhorst. Other parts of the building are now used for normal activities. In the museum, medals, busts of Lenin and red flags bear silent witness to the demise of an epoch. And then there is the reading room, where people can study their files. There's no lack of reading material. Every third citizen of the GDR was registered. How did that tie in with the fact that every third citizen was also an informer? Grasses endlessly grassed on one another. It's a monument to human perversity, a time when every trace of trust vanished from a society.

The taxi stopped in Ruscherstrasse, on the edge of the complex, and waited while Clara explained the ropes to me. It looked like an ordinary street in an eastern Berlin neighbourhood. Advertisements for Sony and Ritter Sport. A supermarket and pedestrians hurrying past without giving the sombre buildings a second thought.

"You have to ask for a Herr Weber," said Clara.

"Aren't you coming in with me?"

"No. I'll go back to the hotel. Go for a walk. Read. What's your German like?"

"I can get by," I said. "But come in with me, please."

She put her hand on my neck and gave me a quick kiss.

"You have the authorisation. It's your file. Take all the time you need, but come back soon. Out you get!"

I stood watching the taxi drive off. Clara didn't turn round, just gave a little wave. I went into Haus No. 7 and asked for Herr Weber at the reception desk. The floor and the lighting appeared to be new, but the place still had that particular lignite and low-octane fuel smell that encapsulated the essence of communist regimes. It was quiet in the building, but you could still imagine the long corridors, the hushed, dusty rooms with their millions of documents, the mute screams and the large rotary files spinning round and spitting out dossiers. Files which had been kept by diligent clerks so that the State and the Party could monitor each individual citizen's activities, invading their souls to discover their innermost thoughts.

Herr Weber was a small, stocky man with an expressionless face, but he smiled pleasantly when I gave him my name and his grey eyes were friendly and full of life.

"Ah, Herr Leica," he said with a look that momentarily made me think he was flirting.

"Leica?" I asked.

"Yes, Herr Lime. That's your code name in the Stasi archive. In there you're known as Herr Leica and it is under that name that I have scrutinised you. I think that I know you, just as I know others with whom my duties bring me into contact via the harsh memoranda of the past."

"Scrutinised me?"

"Sit down for a moment, and I'll explain the regulations before taking you to the reading room."

We sat at a little table in two uncomfortable, nondescript muddy-green armchairs. There was an ashtray, and I was told that I was welcome to smoke. He ran through the procedures as if he was a teacher repeating a syllabus for the umpteenth time. But he was also animated, as though the task of overseeing the passing on of the secret records of a dead nation was a calling to be discharged with responsibility and precise solicitude. The building had once housed a ministry of fear more diabolical than Orwell could have imagined. Now it was the world's most impeccable ministry of truth where people could examine the recent past and discover who had grassed on whom. Husbands and wives, friends, brothers, sisters, parents, colleagues. A large proportion of a population deployed as informers. Billions of words that had once spelt imprisonment or freedom. Words contrived and written down by individuals, and therefore unreliable and subjective, but of vital significance to other's lives. Words written in secrecy and seclusion and thus not open to appeal. A regime's inventory of a nation where no one trusted anyone an inch.

Herr Weber spoke, in his slow and clear German.

"Herr Lime. Our operations are based on a law which defines certain guidelines. It follows special legislation passed by the Federal Diet of reunified Germany in 1991. It regulates admission. Your request for access to documents has been processed and approved. Your documents have been located. I have read your file and, in accordance with the rules, blanked out names with no specific connection to you, in order to avoid innocent victims of the Stasi being harmed. The archive houses great tragedies. With my own eyes, I have seen people break down when they discover that a beloved husband could go for a Sunday walk with the family and then on Monday make a report to his handler. But everything of relevance to your case is of course available for inspection. You can request photocopies, but the original material is not to be removed. Do you understand?"

"I understand," I said.

What I understood was that it all seemed absurd and somehow very German. First the Stasi spends years collecting and cataloguing the most intimate and personal details of people's lives, and then new administrators take over and start re-cataloguing the mountains of material, with new classification numbers and new secrets, in an endless ritual that would continue for as long as there was someone who wanted to look at the material.

"Good," said Herr Weber, brushing a non-existent speck of dust from the sleeve of his tweed jacket. "Your file is not thick, Herr Leica. Just a few pages in a ring binder actually. Not like the 40,000 pages we've got on the singer Wolf Biermann or the 300 ring binders the author Jürgen Fuchs can come and study. You didn't work very much in the former GDR. You didn't let yourself be recruited, you didn't inform, so the material, I'm afraid to say, is not extensive. I apologise."

"You apologise? As if having a thick file is a status symbol?" I said.

Herr Weber gave a brief, dry chuckle.

"The human being is a strange creature, sir. Some break down when they see what is written about them. Others break down when they find out that they were never of enough interest to get into the archive. Today we can speak of a kind of archive-envy. There are those who have had to seek the assistance of a psychologist due to this new ailment, induced by reunification. For example, we have no body odour samples from you."

"Body odour samples?" I said. At first I thought I must have mis-understood his slow, precise German officialese, but then I realised that it was part of his presentation for foreigners. He took a jar from his briefcase and put it on the table between us. It was marked with a number and the lid was tightly screwed on as if it contained pickled gherkins. There was a piece of dirty yellow cotton-wool at the bottom of the jar. And nothing else. I picked it up, inspected it and put it down again looking at Herr Weber expectantly.

"The Stasi operations manual refers to bottled smells," said Weber, unable to suppress a smile. "There are thousands of jars like this one. Samples of people's body odours. We all smell different, sir. And by keeping samples of a person's body odour, sniffer dogs could be quickly and efficiently sent in pursuit of the relevant party, should he or she attempt, for example, to flee the republic."

I started to laugh. I simply couldn't help it, even though I could see that Herr Weber found it inappropriate.

"Perhaps one should laugh. It would have been a comedy, had it not been a tragedy," he said.

"Herr Weber. You have an interesting job. May I take the liberty of asking what you did before the Berlin Wall came down?"

He gave another of his tiny, ironic smiles.

"You may. For many years I looked after the monkeys in the Zoo. Before that I taught German literature, but after a particular lecture about Goethe, and certain private remarks found unsuitable by the Party, I lost my job and became that singular creature whom, on this side of the Iron Curtain, we called a non-person. Officially I did not exist. I was the living dead. But the monkeys were splendid company."

"And who informed against you? A student?"

"No, Herr Lime. My wife."

I didn't know what to say. It was a comic tragedy and a misery that wouldn't disappear until two or three generations had passed, and children and grandchildren could look back on the insanity of the 20th century and attempt to understand how it had been possible to get people to do what they had done.

"I'm very sorry, Herr Weber," was all I could say.

He nodded.

"Shall we go in?"

"Yes. Thank you."

"You don't have to thank me, Herr Lime. Or Leica. Not many of those who go through that door come out again in a happier frame of mind. Quite the contrary."

# 21

Herr Weber placed a pink cardboard folder on the brown, laminated square table. A number of similar tables were arranged side by side in a high-ceilinged room with pale, yellow walls and a worn lino floor. It looked like an exam room. You sat next to other people and yet on your own, unable to look over your neighbour's shoulder. We weren't sitting looking at exam papers, but at secrets. Most of the tables were occupied by people poring over documents, black and white photographs and microfilm, a tiny fraction of the hundreds of thousands who had looked in their brown case files, made of imitation leather or dingy cardboard. The covers of the files were of the same poor quality as their contents. Small, sturdy women wearing plastic sandals fetched and carried documents, placing them on the tables in front of the visitors. Each sat on their little island reading their life story. The grey November light glimmered faintly through the high windows, but was no competition for the cold glare of the fluorescent tubes. I could see from the heavy drops streaming down the window that it was raining again. The fluorescent lighting made a humming sound, but I could hear the rain pounding against the double glazing.

The cover bore a series of numbers and a code, OPK-Akte. MfS. XX, 1347/76–81. HVA/1249, which looked as if they had been printed on the cover with an old-fashioned rubber stamp. Below the numbers and codes a diligent clerk had written, in a well-formed, meticulous hand, *Leica*. I studied the cover. MfS stood for Ministry of State Security, Stasi. HVA was an abbreviation for espionage abroad. The letters stood for Hauptverwaltung Aufklärung, directly translated as "Main Division of Information". But information about what and from whom? The HVA was under the direction of Markus Wolf and didn't have quite such dark connotations as the Stasi, but it had still been part of the operation. It didn't take much to guess that 76–81 were the relevant years, and the other numbers just part of an indexing system.

I opened the folder, and saw a picture of me as a young man. It had been taken somewhere in Spain, from the background I thought it was the old bullfighting arena in Valladolid. It was a good, amateur photograph. But it had been taken with a cheap camera, and both the foreground and the background had that slightly blurred focus that looks sharp but isn't, because the lens wasn't good enough. A political rally of some sort is underway. There are red flags in front of the archway into the arena, and two Guardia Civil Landrovers are visible. I'm in my 20s and I'm looking straight at the camera, a cigarette jammed in my mouth and my hair blowing round my face. My Nikon and faithful Leica, which I took with me everywhere, are hanging on my shoulder. I'm wearing a light-coloured, short-sleeved shirt, jeans with a wide belt and the Spanish boots that I loved so much at the time, with high heels and pointed toes. I look like exactly what I was – a cocky, arrogant photojournalist on an assignment.

I could see where this was heading, but I stayed calm and started to read the smooth, new photocopies that Herr Weber had taken from the original, old and undoubtedly by now yellowing reports. They were marked for the attention of a Lieutenant Colonel Schadenfelt who was head of II/9, a division that must have had the task of countering Western intelligence services through the infiltration and recruitment of agents.

The reports were a mixture of truth and falsehoods. There was a short description of me, my date of birth, my background, my rootless nature. I was described as progressive, but not a member of any party. I had the potential to be an unofficial informer at first, and then later became a proper source, once I had been made aware of the importance of the struggle against imperialism and American militarism. I had voiced criticism of the American war in Vietnam and, seemingly, when I had been covering one of the euphoric rallies for the Spanish Communist Party, I had said that if I were Spanish I would have been a communist. The subjunctive suppleness of the German words leapt at me off the closely written pages. There were trivial, but obviously significant, descriptions of my preferred style of clothing, the authors I read – Hemingway and the Danish writer Rifbjerg – my girlfriends, my work assignments. My various addresses were recorded. Periodically it stated simply that I was travelling and not under observation. There was a note recommending a visa for Moscow. There were ongoing evaluations of my political views. They became slowly less progressive and no increase in my awareness had been observed.

Each page was littered with numbers and codes and aliases and cross-references. My commentator described how we started as colleagues and later became friends. He described how I drank too much and had difficulty in establishing a steady relationship with the opposite sex, preferring casual liaisons and affairs. There were descriptions of meetings and conversations, of trips and articles, of attitudes and views. As the years between the first report on me in 1976 and the last one in 1981 passed, my commentator made it clear that I wasn't as progressive as first presumed. I was open to right-wing propaganda and the enjoyment of a bourgeois lifestyle, and I had no great admiration for the results being achieved by the Soviet bloc, but increasingly expressed criticism of this implementation of socialism.

In 1981 I had expressed divergent opinions on the Polish counter-revolution and even went so far as to announce that I was going to Warsaw to follow and support the counter-revolutionary, CIA-financed, Solidarity movement. It was then that I was abandoned as a prospective agent. My bourgeois consciousness was too fixed and I was, wrote the commentator, uncompromising. Even though my life-style couldn't be considered proper in the normal bourgeois sense, I didn't care about my reputation and therefore couldn't be coerced. A work visa for the Polish Republic was not to be recommended.

So that was why I never got to the war tribunal.

Leica was not cut out to be an East German agent. File closed. File placed in the archives. A completely inconsequential case file which only a paranoid system would have bothered to keep at all, and which I could have forgotten, had it not been for the fact that the pen had been wielded by Oscar. That wasn't the name used. That was the name I knew him by. When Oscar had written to Lieutenant Colonel Helmut Schadenfelt, he signed himself Karl Heinrich Müller. First he was Lieutenant, then Captain and finally Major in the HVA, reporting directly to Schadenfelt and Misha Wolf. I had known as soon as I saw the photograph and immediately remembered the first trip Oscar and I had taken together. We had gone to cover the communists' rally in the bullfighting arena in Valladolid where Carillo was to make a speech, and I had translated Oscar's questions for him and our ostensible friendship had begun. He had never been a great writer – neither as a journalist nor in his reports to his ultimate masters in the Stasi – but he had been my friend for 20 years and all the time he had been playing with his cards face down.

There wasn't much on me. It didn't take long to read, even with my German, but I think I sat for another hour just staring into space, not really thinking, as if my surroundings no longer existed. My thoughts went round and round in circles. Oscar. Karl Heinrich Müller. Amelia.

Maria Luisa. And a photograph showing a young woman together with German terrorists somewhere in Denmark, a photograph Oscar had seen and which somehow had become a catalyst.

I felt horribly nauseous and went to find a toilet where I threw up violently and painfully. I splashed water on my face and sat on another toilet and smoked a cigarette. Then I went back to the reception and asked for Herr Weber. He appeared 15 minutes later, with his briefcase in his hand and several of his infamous folders under his other arm.

"Yes, Herr Lime? How can I be of service?"

"Can I see the file on Karl Heinrich Müller?"

Herr Weber studied me with his intelligent, friendly eyes.

"You look rather pale, Herr Lime. Do you need a doctor?"

"A drink and the file on Karl Heinrich Müller."

"I can't help with the drink, but if you would be so kind as to return to your seat, I'll see what I can do about Karl Heinrich."

I had a throbbing headache and my hands were trembling. I only had to wait for another 15 minutes. A younger woman was weeping silently. A stream of tears poured down her cheeks, as she seemed to read the same sentence over and over again. But no one took any notice of her. In the Stasi's reading room everyone minded their own business. You were all alone with information you had wanted, but which you would perhaps rather have done without when you got it.

Herr Weber placed a couple of sheets of paper and a photograph on my table.

"Thank you. That was quick," I said.

"There isn't much. His file was one of those shredded when they tried to remove the evidence just after *die Wende*. The Ministry's largest shredders were on overdrive. We are trying to reconstruct some of the documents, but it will take years. Perhaps a never-ending job."

"OK."

Herr Weber hesitated.

"Others have benefited from talking with a handler. Most of them live where they've always lived. Some will talk. Others won't."

"Thank you, Herr Weber."

"Not at all, Herr Lime. Not at all."

He was right. There was hardly any information about Oscar. Just that Karl Heinrich Müller was put on the service's permanent staff in 1967, when he was recruited via the border troops where he was doing his military service. He had been an unofficial Stasi informer ever since he was 14. As a 19-year-old he had been smuggled to West Germany with a new identity and life story. He had worked as a journalist on several small magazines partially financed by the GDR or Moscow. There was a photograph attached to the documents. It showed a young, clean-shaven Oscar wearing the Vopo's ugly uniform. He has a crew cut and is looking straight at the camera with his unwavering eyes. Part of the Wall can be seen in the background. I read it all through twice, but there was no mention of his ever having left the service. All it said was that his last rank was that of Major and that he was recommended for the Order of Lenin for exemplary and long-standing service. The recommendation for an Order of Lenin had been made in October 1989 in conjunction with the GDR's 40th anniversary. A month before the Berlin Wall came down. Hadn't these people had any idea what was about to hit them?

I felt like throwing up again, but I wrote the name Schadenfelt and the number of my file in my notebook and just left the documents on the table. They could burn them for all I cared. The reading room's dust and my despair at the nature of betrayal made me nauseous. I had to get out.

Herr Weber was standing in reception.

"Goodbye, Herr Lime," he said. "Will we be seeing you again?"

"No."

"In that case, I shall deposit your file as read and closed."

"Read at least," I said.

"Undoubtedly it will never be closed for those involved, but for us it is one more file which can be put away with the others. One more piece of grief that can go back to the archives."

"Goodbye, Herr Weber. Say hello to the monkeys from me."

He chuckled.

"With pleasure. I often visit my old friends when people get too much for me. God be with you."

It was a relief to get out into the fresh air. I zipped up my leather jacket and walked aimlessly through the wet streets of Berlin, letting the rain wash me clean. I don't know how long or where I walked, but suddenly I recognised the wide expanse of Alexanderplatz, with the statue of Karl Marx and Engels sitting all alone in the middle of the paved area in the shadow of the television tower. By now it was evening and dark, and the lights played in the puddles. My hair was soaked, but it had stopped raining. I looked around and spotted a bar. It was a stylish café. I went into the toilets and dried my face and combed my hair, and then went and ordered a coffee and double schnapps. I sat by myself at a corner table. There weren't many other customers in the café which was ugly and had cold lighting, horrible plastic tables and a mock steel counter. It made me long for Madrid and a proper café with loud, familiar Spanish sounds, heavy hams hanging from the ceiling and the smell of garlic and wine. A clean well-lighted place.

I finished my schnapps, ordered another double and asked if I could borrow a telephone book. The bartender slung it across to me without a word and I looked up Schadenfelt. There were only three called Helmut. One of them lived on Karl Marx Allee. It led straight down to Alexanderplatz so I decided I might just as well start there. I drained my schnapps, drank my coffee and left with my head spinning. Alcohol was rough on an empty stomach.

The housing blocks were arranged in East European-style rows of concrete, but the entrance looked freshly painted and well kept. There was an intercom. Helmut Schadenfelt lived on the ninth floor. I pressed his bell. Nothing happened. I tried again. Still nothing. I waited, and after about ten minutes the street door opened and an elderly, well-dressed woman slipped out and I slipped in with a courteous greeting. She glanced at me, but then walked off.

The lift smelled of boiled cabbage and fresh paint. Schadenfelt's door was brown like all the others. I rang the bell a couple of times, but nothing happened. I put my ear to the door, but I couldn't hear any sound inside. I didn't know if I had come to the right Schadenfelt, but I had an intuitive feeling that I had.

I waited for just over an hour. Every time I heard someone on the stairs, I pretended that I was either on my way up or on my way down. The old East Berliners had grown up in a paranoid system and I knew that it wouldn't be long before they rang the police about a dubious individual seen loitering on the stairs.

Then he arrived. He came out of the lift. He was a stout, red-faced man of about 60, wearing a pair of wide braces to hold his trousers up over his large beer gut. He had powerful shoulders and hands and a drinker's thin little legs, and he was drunk. He managed, with some difficulty, to put the key in the lock, and as the door swung inwards I stepped forward into the light and said in German.

"Lieutenant Colonel Schadenfelt? Have you got a moment?"

He turned round and swayed, but his eyes were amazingly alert even though they were swimming.

"Fuck off, foreigner!" he said in English, and started to close the door.

I took another step forward and jammed the outstretched, rigid first and middle fingers of my right hand into his solar plexus and up under his ribs, and all the blood drained from his face as he doubled up. I grabbed his shirt and pushed him backwards into the flat, and once we were inside I put my foot behind his and thrust him against the wall. I gave him a sharp right to the jaw and held onto him as he slid down the wall and then lay motionless, but I checked that he had a pulse in his throat. I looked out into the landing. There was no one in sight. It had all been over in a few seconds.

Helmut Schadenfelt's flat was quite spacious. It had a living room and three other rooms. He had obviously stayed in the flat that the Party and the Stasi had provided for him. The kitchen was cluttered with dirty dishes, the rumpled bedclothes smelled of unwashed man, and two of the rooms were empty, as if he had pawned or sold the furniture. The place was littered with empty schnapps bottles. The only thing that seemed cared for was a photograph of a younger version of Helmut in full Stasi uniform. He was being presented with a medal by Markus Wolf. Oscar was standing behind them, also in full uniform. I looked at the date and inscription. "For faithful service, 16 April 1985."

So Oscar had sneaked back now and then to strut the Stasi's prohibited zones wearing his smart uniform.

I smashed the picture on the edge of an ugly, brown tiled table, prized the photograph out from behind the broken glass of the frame, and put it in the inside pocket of my jacket.

I heard Schadenfelt groaning out in the corridor. When I got to him he had raised himself onto one knee. He was drunk, but he was also a large man, and I wasn't taking any chances so I kicked him in the side and he collapsed again, and then I took hold of his Adam's apple and squeezed and spoke in English, as he had sworn at me in that language.

"Helmut, my friend. It's only information I'm after, nothing else.

If I keep on doing this you're going to die. If you promise to behave, I'll let go, and then we can have schnapps together. Blink if you understand what I'm saying."

He blinked and I let go of his throat and let him finish coughing and belching before I got him onto an ugly green sofa next to a table covered with overflowing ashtrays and dirty glasses.

"Schnapps, in the kitchen," he said hoarsely. His eyes were scared, but not scared enough.

"Now we're not going to try anything, are we Lieutenant Colonel?"

"Schnapps," he said.

I went and found a bottle in the fridge and when I came back in he hadn't moved, but sat rubbing his jaw and his Adam's apple. I passed him the bottle and he took a swig and held it out towards me, but the surroundings had taken away my appetite for drink.

"Who are you and what do you want?" he said. "I haven't got any money."

"I want to talk about Karl Heinrich."

"Fuck off," he said, and I struck him on the temple with the edge of my hand. I didn't follow the stroke through, but he toppled off the sofa onto the floor. I kicked his knee and he screamed.

"I'm in a very bad mood, Lieutenant Colonel. As a matter of fact, my life's just been shattered yet again. So I'm feeling really ratty. Pissed off. Karl Heinrich?"

"Who are you?" he said, and crawled back onto the sofa again. He was tougher than he looked. I removed the bottle when he reached out for it.

"Who are you?" he repeated.

"Peter Lime."

He started laughing, but stopped because it hurt. He reached out for the bottle again.

"Peter Lime. You could just have said."

He spoke in Danish. He had a heavy accent, but the words came easily and were grammatically correct.

"How come you speak Danish?"

"Danish, English, Russian, German. It was my job. It was my job for 40 years. But tell me, how's Oscar?"

I looked at him, and he held up his hands defensively.

"Easy, easy, Peter!" he said. "I'm finished. I'm an old man. I surrender. I know about your karate. Let's have a schnapps, then we can talk. I know you like a schnapps. I know everything about you. You're Karl Heinrich's best friend. He loves you like his own brother."

He started laughing and, to make him stop, I passed him the bottle. He took a long swig and he began to speak. It was as though he needed to talk with someone. As if he had just been waiting for me.

"Peter Lime. Looking at me now, you can't understand. Power, influence, the feeling of being and doing something crucial. Of making a difference. Of building the first socialist state on German soil. Of thwarting the capitalists' intentions. But mostly it was the operation. Running agents, the most exciting game in the world. Don't see me the way I look now. This is what losers look like, and we lost the war. Without blood, but we lost it. But I was there when we were major players. We had 90,000 employees in the Ministry. We had 200,000 informers and there were over 5,000 of us in the HVA, the cream of the Ministry under the great Wolf. We were the most successful espionage network in the world. We knew everything that was going on in Bonn, in Copenhagen, in London, in the Vatican. We were a fucking success and I'm proud to have been part of it."

"But you lost, as you say yourself."

"We lost, but if you want an apology from me, you can forget it. I believed in socialism and I still believe in socialism."

He took another swig and I could see the anxiety evaporating from his eyes, so I got ready to put him back in his place with force. I was both angry and despairing and part of me wished he would make a move so I would have an outlet for my aggression.

"What about Karl Heinrich? Did he believe too?"

The stout man leant forward and found a cigarette amongst the filth on the table, lit it and leant back on the sofa again.

"He was born into the faith. His father was held in captivity by the Soviets and when he returned in 1948 he was a communist. Karl was born in 1950, the year after NATO was formed and West Germany became a nation. It was a betrayal. Karl Heinrich received the faith at the breast. Only a socialist German state could prevent the return of fascism. I recruited Karl Heinrich when he was 14 and already chairman of his school's *Freie Deutsche Jugend* group. He made the pledge of loyalty that he would never betray his country or talk about his work for MfS. And he's kept his word."

"Then what?" I asked simply.

"He was good and we were confident of the strength of his ideology, so we sent him across to the other side with a new identity. We already had two agents in Frankfurt, a couple who were the right age to have a son like Karl Heinrich, so he became Oscar. We moved them to Hamburg and the rest is history, as the saying goes. He was one of our best. I had the honour of being his mentor. I'm proud of that. He grew to be like a son to me. He never wavered. That's all there is."

"Not quite," I said. "Not quite."

"*Was meinst du?*"

"What did Oscar do?" I asked.

"Work in the field. It doesn't matter."

He scowled and turned his head away, so I stepped towards him and hit him twice on the face with the flat of my hand. I didn't want him to forget his fear. He had to be more frightened of me than of the promise he had once made not to talk. He tried to protect himself, but he was just a drunk old man. A punch-drunk remnant of the cold war, and he didn't stand a chance. I took the bottle from him and kept it in my hand.

"I asked you what Oscar did, Helmut," I said.

He held up his hands in front of his face again.

"Recruited agents, influenced public opinion."

"A Danish woman by the name of Lola, for instance."

The colour drained from his face. He wasn't a good liar, even though he had been a servant in the land of lies.

"That name doesn't mean anything to me."

He had expected me to hit him with my right hand again, but I jabbed him hard on the nose with a short, straight left and he rocked backwards on the sofa, blood trickling slowly from one nostril.

"I warned you, Helmut. I'm in a bad mood. You were his handler right from 1964. I mentioned a Danish woman called Lola."

"OK, Lime. OK. No more. Don't hit me any more. Just give me the bottle . . ."

"Lola," I said.

"She was one of his best agents. She came on in bed like men want it and in a way that makes them talk. Karl Heinrich recruited her. I took her over."

"Why?"

"It's not a good arrangement to have a man overseeing his wife."

I must have looked completely dumbfounded, because he laughed scornfully. His laughter turned into a coughing fit. Once he had got over it, he continued.

"Yes. You heard right, Peter Lime. The best couple I ever had in the field. They each had their special talents and they were willing to use both mind and body. They were exemplary servants of the State."

"When did they get divorced?"

"Divorced? As far as I know they're still married, under the law of the GDR, at least. They both had others. So what? Do you think they would live by other people's norms or bourgeois morality? They had each other, even at a distance. They were bigger than you and me."

"Where is she now?"

"I don't know. I'm on early retirement. I don't know anything. I am nothing."

I took a step forward again.

"You can't afford this flat," I said. "Oscar and maybe Lola help you out, so I'll ask again: where is she?"

"She's in Moscow. Contacts from the old days. It doesn't matter, Lime. We worked for a sovereign, recognised nation. We committed no punishable offence. Over there on the other side they've tried to have Misha convicted I don't know how many times. They haven't succeeded. Give me that bottle, will you."

"Supposing Oscar and Lola were the link between the GDR and the terrorists in the Red Army Faction, in ETA, in the IRA and the Red Brigades in Italy. Supposing these two, each operating under a cover which gave them every legitimate reason for trips and meetings across national frontiers, were key figures of red terrorism? What then, Herr Lieutenant Colonel? Would time have run out on that statute, or would it not still be a punishable offence in the Federal Republic of Germany? Or in Rome or in London? What is the Lieutenant Colonel's opinion of that?"

"I don't know what you're talking about."

"Wouldn't they be willing to go to great lengths to make sure it didn't come to light?" I said. "Would they be willing to murder in order to hang onto their comfortable lifestyles now that the war's been lost? And peace has settled? I'm afraid that's what has happened."

He reached for the bottle again and I felt sick at the sight of his face smeared with snot and blood and the smell of his sour, alcohol-soaked body. I realised that he had pissed himself too. There was a pool at his feet.

"Wouldn't they go to great lengths?" I said again.

"Even if you were right, it could never be proved. Everything that recorded the brotherly assistance in the struggle against imperialism, fought at the very heart of imperialism, was destroyed before the rabble seized power. In Moscow they've closed down those archives. The Russians are shrewder than we are. There are no documents. It's all gone. Burnt or chopped into tiny pieces. Shredded to nothing and stuffed into big sacks. It's as if it never happened. Like the Wall. Who knows if we just dreamt that we built it. It's all in the past, and now give me that bottle for fuck's sake."

I wasn't going to have to prove anything in court, and he had just confirmed what I had said, so I held out the bottle to him, and when he reached for it I grabbed his hand and snapped it backwards so he pitched to the floor in his own piss, and then I emptied the contents of the bottle over him while he howled in pain from his broken fingers.

"Cheers, Lieutenant Colonel," I said. "When you ring Madrid in a while, say hello to Oscar and tell him that Leica is on his way to take his photograph."

# 22

On the plane to Madrid next morning, I tried to follow Clara's advice and think everything through, but I thought more about the past than the future. A film played in my mind, episodes from all the years I had known Gloria and Oscar, a stream of good memories, and I wondered if Gloria had been aware of her husband's double-dealing, or if she had been as much in the dark as I had. Is it possible to keep a double identity hidden from your spouse for so many years? What do we know about one another when it comes down to it? Had Oscar, as I kept on calling him in the film, in effect been using infidelity as a shield when he worked for the Stasi? A cover to conceal his real identity? Was the same true of Lola? Had she felt the earth begin to crumble under her feet when the reporters began to ask questions about her qualifications? She knew that her life was a myth manufactured in Normannenstrasse. And what about Gloria? Was she part of the whole operation? I didn't know. It was a jungle of mirrors. I didn't know if I was looking at a true reflection or a reflection of one. It was like the hall of mirrors in Tivoli. You know what you look like, but the mirrors show something quite different. They alter the shape of your body, just as the intelligence services could alter entire lives and identities. A masked ball with no guarantee that you would be any the wiser at midnight when the masks fell, only to reveal new ones. All I knew was that I wanted to know for certain. I wanted to bury the whole business and Oscar too. But could I, when all was said and done?

Clara had been waiting for me in the hotel room and looked anxious when she saw my face. I had told her everything in detail, slowly and subdued.

"So you beat up an old man?" she had said.

"Yes," I said with a pang of conscience.

She had put her arms round me and whispered.

"Poor, poor Peter. Poor Peter."

I had held her at arm's length and looked her in the eyes.

"Did you know about Oscar?"

"I had my suspicions. We've kept an eye on Lola, and so have come across him a couple of times. And we got a tip-off from the British."

"Why didn't you tell me?" I sensed that both my anger and my aggression could easily be turned on her.

"There wasn't anything concrete to go on. And would you have believed me?" She looked alarmed. She had realised that I had a violent streak and that scared her. As if it wouldn't take much for me to hit her too. But what do we know about one another when it comes down to it?

Would I have believed her? I wondered on the plane. Probably not. We had made love frantically that night and she had driven me to the airport and now she was on her way back to Copenhagen. I hadn't promised her that I wouldn't do anything rash. We had parted with a hug, but made no promises

"Ring me, and don't get like those you're up against," she had said.

I hadn't promised anything.

A velvety darkness lay across Madrid as the plane prepared for landing. I thought of ringing first, but instead took a taxi out to Gloria and Oscar's penthouse flat. I couldn't bring myself to call him Karl

330

Heinrich. With Gloria, he was Oscar. As we drove into the city, through the heavy traffic and with the lovely sound of Spanish on the driver's radio, I didn't think about what I was going to do. Because I didn't know. I wondered whether Oscar would be there with Gloria, or if they would both have taken flight, or Gloria would have been left behind on her own. How much did she know? I was certain that the old man in Berlin would have rung straight away. They must have agreed on a kind of signal that meant run for it. Even Oscar, with his self-confident arrogance, would have prepared an escape route. It was part of his training, and also his nature. Being the sly fox that he was, his life must always have had many back doors.

Gloria saw it was me and slapped my face so hard that my whole head rocked, managing to land one more slap before I could get hold of her arms and push her into the flat. I pulled her towards me and held her tight. She was a large woman and there was strength under her ample curves, but I held on to her until she had stopped scream-ing arsehole, son of a bitch, pimp, ball-less faggot and a whole series of curses from the bountiful Spanish vocabulary. Eventually I could feel her relaxing in my arms and she began to cry. I stood holding her for a while, stroking her lustrous black hair and, when her tears began to abate, I led her into the living room and sat her down on the sofa, poured us both a whisky and lit her cigarette. She was a wreck. Her mascara had run and her face was streaked and haggard. Her elegant, silk blouse was crumpled and her little black skirt had crept right up to the edge of her briefs.

"Why the hell didn't you ring me, Peter?" she said.

"I was anxious to know if you'd be here. I wanted to see if there's one or two of you in on this."

"In on what, you arsehole? The telephone rang yesterday. A man's voice says something in German. I call Oscar to the phone and his face goes completely white. Then he puts on his coat and leaves. It's like he's

331

seen the devil himself. He turns at the door and says 'We won't be seeing one another again. You can thank Peter for that.' I dash after him, but he gets to the lift first, and when I get down onto the street he's gone. He's disappeared before, but I could tell that something was seriously wrong. And we were having one of our good patches. I've rung everyone and anyone. Even some of his old flames. He's gone. He's emptied our joint account and taken some money from the firm's account. Where the hell is he? What the hell have you done, Peter?"

She was on the verge of tears again, but took a gulp of her drink instead. I could tell it wasn't her first that evening. The big, airy room suddenly felt dark and cold, and Gloria seemed to shrink before my eyes.

"I think he's in Moscow," I said.

"Moscow? Whatever for? What's my husband doing in Moscow?"

"He's not your husband and it's a long story, Gloria."

"And might you take the trouble to tell the recent widow the story? Do you really think I believe what you're saying? We might be old friends, Peter. But what is all this?" she said.

I placed the photograph of Oscar in uniform in front of her and she picked it up and stared at it for a long time while she smoked another cigarette. She was a tough woman and a veteran of the business world's negotiating tables and exhausting courtroom battles, and the emotional storms she and Oscar had weathered. She wasn't easily thrown, and she seemed to be pulling herself together, so I told her the story of Karl Heinrich and Lola, and she listened without interrupting, without dramatic outbursts. She revealed her agitation only by smoking one cigarette after another as I described the bigamist's double life over almost a quarter of a century.

Gloria took it amazingly calmly. Other people might have broken down, but I could see that his betrayal didn't provoke tears, but the same ice-cold anger that I felt. In many ways we were cut from the same cloth. I could use violence without guilt, and I could see that Gloria's legal mind had taken control.

She excused herself politely, left the room and returned looking well groomed. Her mascara was where it should be, she had put on a fresh blouse, her hair was combed and her skirt no longer revealed the edge of her briefs. She returned with a pot of coffee and two cups and put them on the table. She removed our glasses and emptied the ashtray, playing the hostess. I didn't speak. I could see that her incisive mind was at work. I felt that I knew Gloria. Her life may have been coloured with infidelity to Oscar, but there had never been a single instance of deceit in relation to me. She wasn't a double person. She was Gloria. Once she had tidied herself up and arranged the room, she sat down opposite me with straight back and an almost formal manner and poured coffee.

"Well that's quite a story, Peter. What's your plan?" she asked.

"I'm going to pay Oscar a visit."

"Where?"

"In Moscow."

"Indeed," she said. "I've never been to Moscow, but as far as I know, over ten million people live there."

"I'll find someone who can find him," I said.

"OK. And why do you want to find him?"

I sipped my coffee. It was hot and strong like Gloria always made it, the coffee we three had drunk countless times at meetings about our joint business and our joint lives.

It was a good question. Why did I want to find Oscar? To hear from his own mouth why Amelia and Maria Luisa had to die? But was that the whole reason? I chose to be honest with Gloria.

"Yesterday I wanted to find him and kill him. Preferably twice. An eye for an eye. I thought that if I could throttle him, then I'd be released from the prison I'm in. It felt right to be set free through revenge. Now I'm not so sure. Now I think really I just want to look him in the eye one last time and hear him admit it. But, quite frankly, I don't know. Maybe I'll just thump him one and leave."

"Thump him twice," said Gloria. "One from you and one from me, but let him live."

"Surely you don't want him back again!" I exclaimed in amazement.

Gloria sipped her coffee and crossed her long legs and leant forward and spoke as if we were having a perfectly ordinary conversation.

"No, Peter. I don't. We've each had our lovers, Oscar – Karl Heinrich – and I. But we were like hand and glove. There were times when we couldn't get enough of each other, and I know he didn't fake it in bed. There's no doubt that he loved me and I loved him. But there's one thing the old communist can't do without. And that's the sweet life. And I have a plan to take that away from him. The champion of the proletariat will become a proletarian himself. And Oscar won't be able to cope with that. He loves the sweet life. So just don't kill him, OK?"

It was an absurd conversation, but it made sense anyway.

"I can't promise," I said.

"You've got to. Because of everything we've shared. So there's something left from all those years. So it doesn't all end in the sewer."

"What are you going to do?"

"Me? I'm a lawyer. I hold the keys of power in this modern society. I'll close the bank accounts; he can't get at most of them anyway without my signature. I'll have the marriage dissolved and then he'll lose everything we own jointly. I'll file an action against him for fraud. Tomorrow I'll cancel credit cards, accounts, the right to transfer money, you can complete the list yourself. I'll send a bad credit profile all over the world. I'll inform all our clients and their clients that Oscar's signature isn't worth a hundred pesetas. He ran off with some money, but with Oscar's consumption it'll be spent in a week.

And that's even counting the money he's bound to have put aside. I'm going to do what he can't bear. I'm going to make him poor and I'm going to disinherit him. I'll make him a non-person in the global village we live in. I'll transform him from a Spanish gentleman into an East German loser. And I don't want you thwarting that revenge, but you're welcome to kick him hard in the balls from me."

I couldn't help smiling. Gloria could be strong medicine, but she had been a fighter all her life, and while she might sit and weep again once I had gone, no man was going to see her on her knees, especially not a man she had loved.

"OK, Gloria. You're a tough old girl."

"I am. And I still look good, and when I get my second wind I'll activate some old lovers. He's not going to get the better of me. That's one triumph he's not going to enjoy. I know him. In a month's time he'll be missing me like mad and his current squeeze will get the heave-ho. A double person is no person. Correct or incorrect, Pedro?"

"Correct, Gloria. Will you be all right by yourself? Shall I stay here?" I asked.

She drank the last of her coffee and put the cup down a little too forcefully. She was still fragile, but she straightened herself.

"Either you go now, Pedro. Or you come to bed with me."

I went over to her and kissed her on the lips, like a brother would, but pulled my head back when her tongue found its way greedily into my mouth.

Gloria smiled and pushed me gently.

"Is it the Danish woman?"

"Maybe."

"If you find love again, Pedro, welcome it. Don't be a fool and let it slip away. Love's the only pure thing in this world. And now be off with you and ring me every day."

"Gloria, you know I think you're gorgeous . . ."

"Hop it, and ring me."

"You'll be all right?" I said.

"Either I'll get drunk or I'll get on the phone, but that's none of your business. So be a good boy and clear off!"

I took a cab home and rang Clara, but either she hadn't got back yet or she had unplugged her phone. There wasn't even an answering machine to leave a message on. I drank the better part of a bottle of whisky, but the image of the Lieutenant Colonel's battered face was a little too clear in my mind, and I stopped myself before it got out of hand. I staggered into bed with one of my favourite Danish poems running through my mind. It was a verse from Tom Kristensen's first collection that I had fallen for as a young man because of its title, *Buccaneer Dreams*. The line was "The world has turned chaotic anew" and I became desperate when I found I couldn't remember the next line. In my drunkenness I couldn't remember where I had put my few volumes of Danish poets among all Don Alfonzo's books. They had got lost in the disorganised, teeming shelves and after a while I gave up trying to find the next verse and maybe the meaning of the poem, even though in actual fact I understood it all too well.

Derek Watson in London helped me make my next move. I knew that he had done a lot of work in Moscow and when I rang him and said that I needed a contact, or more precisely a fixer, he knew what I meant. He asked after Oscar and Gloria and I said that they were fine. I was fine too, and he was fine, everything was fine. Once we had got through that ritual dance, Derek asked me what I needed.

"Someone who can find a man for me, point him out and then keep away."

"OK. You're back on the turf again, Lime," he said.

"That's exactly what I am."

"I know there's no point asking who the target is, but I'm going to anyway."

"The Second Coming in Moscow," I said.

"OK. Just the picture for you, but you might need a partner."

"You know I always work alone, Derek," I said.

"OK. There's a guy I've used a couple of times. He's really good, efficient, a bit scary and he costs . . ."

"The money doesn't matter," I said.

"OK. He'll probably want a couple of thousand dollars a day plus a bonus for finding your target."

"That's fine. What kind of guy is he?"

"Lime! He's a new Russian. He's a former Spetznats or KGB or something. They're all over Moscow. Most of them are small fry, but this one's good. He delivers the goods. Maybe he's Mafia, maybe he's just a businessman. The borders are a bit hazy in Moscow. Like all the others, he owns what he refers to as a security and consultancy company. What do I know? I don't know what that means, but he's always come up with the goods."

"Fine, Derek," I said. "Give me his number."

"He's a bit particular too," said Derek. "He's very cautious with his clients, so I'll have to ring him and then he'll ring you when he's checked you out, and he's not always easy to get hold of."

"OK, Derek. Ring him. Tell him it's urgent. Say it's a contract that's got to be wound up now. And then I owe you one."

Derek's husky smoker's laugh was loud and clear.

"Forget it, Lime. You got me started. I've got a lot of debts to you. You don't owe me a damn thing."

"Say it's urgent," I said.

"Pronto. And say hello to Oscar and Gloria and thank them for a great evening in London."

"Will do," I said. "I'll certainly say hello to Oscar and Gloria."

I spent a couple of days in Don Alfonzo's house, which I didn't really feel I could call my own yet, struggling to keep off the booze. I tried to put the books in some kind of alphabetical order and I ate the food which Doña Carmen prepared for me dutifully every day. She had carried on coming to the house after Don Alfonzo's death and I didn't have the heart to say she should stop. I didn't ring Clara again, but spoke on the phone with Gloria a couple of times a day. There was a frailty hidden in her voice, but she was businesslike, and talked about extricating herself from her life with Oscar as if it was an important and challenging assignment she had taken on by choice. It was a case of getting a marriage annulled in a Catholic country, legally closing various accounts and procuring documents from Herr Weber and others in the dusty rooms full of files of the former GDR. The work kept her going, but she sounded like she might collapse once the process had reached a meaningful conclusion. We were a sorry pair.

Sergej Sjuganov finally rang one morning. He spoke English as if he had been to one of England's top boarding schools, but it was more likely the result of time spent at Moscow's diplomatic school and perhaps a posting at the embassy in London.

"Mr Lime. You want to do business with me," he said.

"I'd like you to find someone for me. It's to do with . . ."

He interrupted abruptly, but politely.

"Excuse me, Mr Lime. But I never discuss business on the telephone."

"Then let's meet," I said.

"Frankfurt airport, the VIP lounge in the central hall, next to the duty free shop, tomorrow afternoon. The are flights from Moscow and Madrid arriving almost simultaneously."

"Fine. How will I recognise you?"

"I'll find you, don't worry. Tall, slim, leather jacket, ponytail, jeans. Be reading tomorrow's *El Pais*."

"Pretty accurate," I said.

"And bring a photograph of the target. Until tomorrow, Mr Lime."

Most people use the airports of Europe and the rest of the world as points of arrival and departure, but for modern businessmen or researchers working internationally, airports are practical meeting places. You can hire meeting rooms and you don't waste time getting into the city and finding a hotel. You can work between an arrival and a departure and never see anything other than the airport. I had used airports as meeting places myself, so I wasn't surprised by his choice. And Frankfurt was situated conveniently between Madrid and Moscow.

I bought a cola and sat at a table with the day's *El Pais*, and waited. The airport was swarming with travellers, many of them carrying parcels as if they were going on an early Christmas holiday. The transit hall of an international airport is one of the safest and most anonymous places in the world. You're just one among many, and unless you're on some wanted list or you're being shadowed, no one notices you.

A chunky, athletic man of about my age sat down opposite me and we shook hands.

"Sergej Sjuganov," he said. He was wearing an immaculate, dark suit with a dazzling-white shirt and a smart tie that was held in place by a gold tie pin sporting a fine little diamond. He had a Rolex on his wrist and smelled of an expensive cologne. His face was covered with tiny, delicate lines and he was tanned, as though he went on expensive holidays or perhaps used a solarium. His eyes were very blue and he had a little scar near one corner of his mouth. His handshake was firm.

"Coffee, Mr Sjuganov?" I asked.

"Please. We have a little under half an hour, Mr Lime. I'm taking Lufthansa back."

I went to the bar and got a coffee for him and another cola for me. I had brought along a couple of recent photographs of Oscar. Photographs I had taken. There was a full-length picture, a full-face portrait and one where he was seen more in profile. I passed them to the Russian and he studied them.

"He's a tall man," said Sjuganov. "About 50. Well-dressed. Self-confident. Money. Keeps himself trim, but with a tendency to a slight paunch. He'll stick out. Language, nationality, background?"

I told him about Oscar. That he was a German national, but his past was a bit murky. Besides German, he spoke English and Spanish, perhaps a little Russian. He was well travelled. He'd been trained by the Stasi. I explained the background.

This brought a gleam to his cold, blue eyes.

"Ah-ha. That of course somewhat complicates the matter."

"In what sense?" I asked.

"It's a little more difficult to find a man who has learnt to cover his tracks. It will make it slightly more expensive for you, Mr Lime. And what exactly do you want me to do?"

"Find him. I think he's in Moscow. He went there just over a week ago. That's all I know really," I said.

"I charge one thousand dollars per day. You transfer ten thousand dollars as a deposit to an account in Switzerland. You cover all expenses incurred during the operation. And you pay a bonus if I find him, of ten thousand dollars."

"And if you don't find him?"

Sjuganov smiled.

"A six-foot German who has been in Moscow for only a week or so? We'll find him. We have our contacts. As with so much else in the new Russia, it's just a question of money. If the target has left Moscow, it will be somewhat more complicated, but not impossible. If the target is still in Moscow, then it's unlikely to take more than a week. If we don't find him, you just pay the actual expenses, but that won't happen. We'll find him, dead or alive."

"Good," I said.

340

Sjuganov leant across the table.

"What do you want us to do once we have located the target?"

"I'll need a guide. I don't speak Russian."

"That goes without saying, but do you want us to do anything regarding the target? I don't need to know why you want to find the target, whether it's personal or business. But usually there's a reason that someone goes to ground and someone else wants to find that person. So what do you want us to do once we have located the target? An active response necessitates separate fee negotiations. If you understand me."

He was businesslike and detached, as if discussing a small issue in a standard commercial contract, but I had no doubt as to what he meant.

"No," I said. "You lead me to the address, I'll take care of the rest."

"And if the target has protection?"

I thought for a moment.

"If I think it necessary that someone keeps an eye out in case there's an attack from the rear, then I'd like to engage your services," I said.

"No problem," he said, getting up, and we shook hands. "I know you pay your bills."

"So it's a deal," I said. "You'll find Oscar."

"Consider it done. Stay by the telephone. It's been a pleasure doing business with you, Mr Lime. Have a good trip back to Madrid. See you in Moscow," he said, and faded into the crowd. The back of one more well-cut suit among all the others.

# 23

Russia looked like her old self. I hadn't been there since it was just one of 15 Socialist republics within the Soviet Union. like the GDR, it had disappeared from the map, not with blood and violence, but signatures on a piece of paper, signed by three half-drunk presidents in a hunting lodge in Minsk. Seen from the air it looked as I remembered it. As the plane broke through the heavy cloud cover and began its descent, I could see the landscape speckled with snow and small, deserted villages where only smoke from the chimneys of the snow-clad houses gave any sign of life. The countryside with its frozen lakes looked timelessly Russian and flat, as if the huge changes hadn't washed over it.

As soon as we were in the buildings of Sheremetyevo Airport, the new began to mingle with the old. There were still long, winding queues at passport control, but the airport was full of advertisements and promises of quick returns at the casinos. There were advertisements for computers and Russians of all types were chatting on mobile phones. They had mountains of luggage. The halls were still dimly lit and strangely oppressive and they smelled just as I remembered. A mixture of frost outside, heat inside, black tobacco and low-octane fuel. A grating female voice announcing take-offs and landings in incomprehensible English sounded as if it were the same woman who had been there for years. The customs officials worked in the anarchic way they always had done, either casually letting people through without a glance or laboriously checking everything. Russians returning home mingled with business people and tourists, and they were better dressed and more arrogant than I remembered, but there was absolutely no mistaking that I had arrived in Moscow.

Sergej Sjuganov had kept his word and phoned ten days after our meeting. The target had been located, observed, and a reservation had been made for me at the Hotel Intourist near the Red Square. It was below my usual standard of hotel, but it was less conspicuous than the renovated Metropol or National. Sjuganov hoped I would understand. He gave me a fax number and asked me to notify him of my time of arrival. I would be met at the airport.

I rang Gloria and told her that Oscar had been found and that I was going over to talk with him. Gloria wanted to come too, but I said no, and she let herself be persuaded fairly easily. I got the feeling that she didn't really want to confront him, that she would rather conclude the divorce and total dissolution of their union under cover of unemotional writs. Everything was going according to plan, she said. Accounts had been blocked; business went on as usual. She had asked if I would rejoin the company, and this time I hadn't said no outright, but I knew in my heart that I wouldn't do it. I had thought about it again on the plane, and also thought about Clara and the possibility of starting a new life. Just before I left Madrid, I had sat by Amelia and Maria Luisa's grave and was overwhelmed by as intense a feeling of grief as if they had died the day before, but they hadn't spoken to me. The feeling of loss was as strong and I still felt anger, which was really desperation and frustration over what had happened. A feeling of impotence. Rage against the injustice of life.

The female customs officer in her dreary, grey uniform glanced briefly at my currency voucher as my travel bag went through the screening apparatus. She had painted her lips and nails bright red, and her face was sullen as she stamped my passport and papers with a heavy hand and pushed them towards me. Without so much as looking at the next person in the queue, she pulled his papers across her desk. I walked into the dark arrivals hall and saw a young man in his late 20s. He was wearing a leather jacket, and stood in the throng holding up a cardboard sign on which was written in large, black letters: Lime. He was clean-shaven, and looked like the type who spent hours in the gym, but I could see that his physique wasn't pumped up, but was genuine muscle. I wouldn't like to take him on.

He greeted me with a nod, took my bag and with a movement of his head indicated that I should follow him. His black Mercedes was parked right outside. The cold hit me like a sledgehammer. I was wearing only jeans and my leather jacket over what I thought was a thick sweater. It was a dry cold, and the air was dense with diesel and petrol fumes. The car's engine was running and the exhaust swirled in the breeze. He held the door for me and I was grateful to get into the back of the warm car. The man who had met me got in beside the driver and the car pulled away from the kerb with hardly a sound, just the rumbling of the studded tyres on the asphalt. The man keyed in a number on his mobile and said a single sentence in Russian. Sjuganov was expensive, but you couldn't complain about the service.

We drove at speed, but not irresponsibly, into the city. The road was uneven, making the car vibrate. We drove past the memorial shaped like one of the twisted spikes used to derail tanks. I remembered having seen it before, but the modern, well-lit service station with a McDonald's attached was new, and all the old hoardings depicting the over-achieving socialist worker had been replaced with adverts for Sony and IBM. The traffic was heavy, but moved steadily until we got near the centre where we slowed to a snail's pace. The street we were on had once been called Gorky, but I could decipher enough of the sign to see that it had been renamed. The old Socialist countries had replaced everything from attitudes to street signs with such ease that you feared they might swap back again in the same casual manner. The pavements were packed with pedestrians, their breath like white fog. There were Christmas decorations and imitation fir trees in illuminated shops that hadn't been there before, but still looked insignificant among the massive buildings. It was both Western and yet still Soviet in its solidity. There were piles of snow along the kerbs, but the traffic lanes had been cleared. A smattering of snowflakes swirled in the headlights. Then the edge of the Kremlin appeared ahead, bathed in light, brooding and elegant at the same time. We pulled up in front of the Hotel Intourist, where I had stayed twice before, on the two occasions I had been in Moscow at the beginning of the 1980s. It's a large, solid, concrete skyscraper on the edge of Revolution Square. In the past there had been traffic crossing back and forth, but now the Square looked like a park with people out for a stroll.

"It's a shopping centre, Mr Lime. Eight floors underground," said the young man, in English with a heavy accent. "My name is Igor."

"Hello Igor," I said.

I noticed that an archway had been erected leading in to Red Square.

"Yes, Mr Lime. The old Kremlin Gate has been rebuilt. Stalin pulled it down to make way for his tanks during military parades. Stalin has been buried, the archway has been rebuilt and the Cathedral of Christ the Saviour is back in place. A lot has happened in Moscow since your last visit."

"I can see that," I answered.

We got out of the car and entered the lobby. Nothing much had changed. It was teeming with people. A group of tourists were waiting to be checked in. Two of the women behind the desk were having what was obviously an important private conversation, a third woman was listening, while a fourth was trying to sort out the paperwork for a large group of French people who were waiting for the keys to their rooms. It looked like an operation that could take all evening.

"Your documents, please," said Igor, and I gave him my passport and visa. He went over to the reception desk and spoke to the two chattering women. They ignored him. He said something else in a sharper tone of voice and they immediately broke off their conversation and one of them took my documents and gave him a security key with an apologetic smile.

We took the lift to the 19th floor and walked down a long corridor. Igor knocked on a door, stepped aside and ushered me in. We entered a large living room with a desk and an oval table. I could see a double bed in the adjoining room. It was an attractive suite, and it looked as though it had been renovated, but it was still decorated in red and brown, which seemed to have been the preferred colour scheme of the Soviet Union. There was a minibar and a television and a notice saying that satellite telephone was available. And Sergej Sjuganov.

He was wearing his immaculate suit. We shook hands.

"Welcome to Moscow, Mr Lime. Have a drink and let's get down to work. You are undoubtedly just as busy as I am," he said.

"Without doubt," I said, and went to get one of the miniature bottles of whisky from the minibar, but Sjuganov shook his head and picked up a bottle of Russian vodka, poured some into a schnapps glass and raised his own.

"To a well-executed operation," he said, emptying his glass, and I did the same. It had a good, biting and very Russian taste of grain and alcohol.

"We've got a job to do," said Sergej Sjuganov. "Please, come and look!"

Igor, who must also have been Sjuganov's bodyguard, had taken his place in a chair by the door. Sjuganov was standing next to the oval table in the middle of the spacious room. Some photos and a map of Moscow and its outskirts were lying on the table.

The photographs showed Oscar and a woman I recognised as Lola, although she had dyed her hair black. There were pictures of Oscar on his own, of Lola on her own and of the two of them together. I could see from the grainy prints that they had been taken with a tele-photo lens, some with a 1,000 mm lens, others with a 400 mm. They were at some kind of market where stout women wearing headscarves and shapeless coats were selling vegetables and what looked like pickled cucumbers. There was also a series of photos showing the two of them in front of a large red house in a birch wood, the snow lying thick on the branches and the ground. What looked like surveillance cameras were attached to a wall that seemed to encircle the building, and in one of the pictures I recognised the big Irishman with the cosh from the house in San Sebastián. Oscar and Lola looked as though they were having an argument and the Irishman was watching them, with his coat open revealing the edge of a shoulder holster. Lola looked just as she had on the television pictures I had seen in Copenhagen, but Oscar looked haggard and angry.

Sjuganov let me study the photographs. I don't know what I felt. I had engaged him to find Oscar, and he had. Now what should I do? I wasn't surprised that Lola was there, and this didn't make any differ-ence, but what was my next move to be? I had just arrived in Moscow. I guessed that Oscar had taken refuge in Moscow because Lola was here and he thought he would be safe until it had all blown over. It was a country where money could buy both influence and security.

"Are you ready to hear what we know?" asked Sjuganov in his strange upper-class English.

"Yes," I said simply.

"OK, Mr Lime. The target is living in a newly built villa outside

Moscow, in an old dacha district. A dacha, if you don't know, is a Russian holiday cottage, but today it can also mean a large brick villa, built outside the city by very rich people. The Party elite used to stay in that area, but now it has been privatised and developed by – how can I put it – enterprising people who want peace and quiet and maximum security. Do you follow?"

"I do," I said, and he continued in the same neutral tone of voice.

"The target has problems. Over the last two days the target has tried to cash a cheque, draw money by Visa, Eurocard and American Express, but the cards have been stopped. The target has become furious each time. However, the target does have some cash and he uses it. The target goes out now and then, but mostly stays in the villa. The target drinks too much and argues a lot with the woman. They sleep together, even though they each have their own bedroom in the villa. At least we think so."

"Do you know who the woman is?" I asked.

Sjuganov put the photographs aside.

"Checking her identity was not part of the assignment, but we know what she is in Moscow at the moment," he said.

"And that is?"

"She's rich. It's her house. She has connections in the Ministry of Culture and I know whom she bought it from. In record time, she has been certified as an art dealer. She is authorised to buy and sell Russian works of art and to export them, including works that are more than 50 years old. This licence has been expensive for her, but she will quickly capitalise on it. My country is selling off its assets, one way and another. One can deplore it, or help oneself to a slice of the cake. This is just a statement of fact. Once, Lenin talked in this city. Now money talks. Each, in their time, have held the keys to power, and if you have access to them, you can do pretty well what you like."

"What does she call herself these days?" I asked.

"Svetlana Petrovna. She's good. She's already been admitted to circles close to the President, thus she is regarded as being untouchable. I have the impression that she is a woman who could sell sand in the Sahara."

"Or snow in Moscow," I answered.

I looked at the photograph of the black-haired, but still beautiful Lola, and the scornful way she looked at Oscar, as they stood in the snow outside the villa. Gloria's tentacles had already reached far. It seemed that Oscar was now financially dependent on good Lola, and their curious relationship had undoubtedly never encountered this before. It wouldn't be long before Oscar would have to borrow pocket money from her. Oscar hated playing second fiddle.

"It looks like a very new house, Mr Sjuganov. Did she have it built?"

"All of that kind around Moscow are new, Mr Lime," said Sjuganov, looking at the photograph. "It was built by a director of one of the first private banks. Apparently he had connections with the Mafia, but his business partners became dissatisfied. He was shot outside his bank. The villa was taken over by a boy of 22 who moved in with his two wives and 14 bodyguards. He had the swimming pool built. The boy was one of the most popular producers and studio hosts on the new private television channel, but his two wives disagreed about which of them he loved the most, so they killed him. Got him drunk and high on cocaine and drowned him in his own pool."

"What a house," I said.

"It's Russia," said Sjuganov, and continued.

"The owner before Madame Petrovna was a well-known Mafioso who controlled the vegetable markets in Moscow. He had problems with his business partners too. One day he vanished. Madame Petrovna bought the house through a front man I know. She got it cheap and other prospective bidders were given the hint that they should stay away."

"Who was the front man?"

Sjuganov looked at me. I couldn't read anything in his strangely dead eyes. He poured himself another vodka and one for me.

"I am not obliged to give you that information, but Derek's a friend from earlier days, from before my business grew, so I'm willing to give you a bit of leeway. The front man was a colleague from the KGB era, Victor Ljubimov. Considering Madame Petrovna's past history in a sister organisation, I think he was merely repaying an old debt. There is a certain honour between comrades. In some matters money takes a back seat."

"But this won't compromise your loyalty to me?" I said.

"You are my client and I have nothing to do with the woman. She is not part of my assignment or of my current or earlier life."

"OK, Sjuganov. Then where do I find the happy couple?"

Sjuganov permitted himself a little smile and spread the map out on the table. He showed me the Hotel Intourist, on the edge of Red Square, and led me with his finger westwards out of the city, along a wide boulevard called Kutusovsky, and then to the right into what looked like a big forest and an area with lakes and little side roads leading up to a narrow highway. The map showed a multitude of small villages. Sjuganov explained that during the Soviet era it had been a prohibited area, but now it had been opened up and the families with new money were building houses out there on a grand scale. The thought that Oscar was in one of those houses, not quite 40 kilometres from the city centre, made my heart beat faster.

"OK," I said. "Let's drive out there tomorrow."

Sjuganov folded the map and cleared his throat. His bodyguard was still sitting calmly by the door with his hands on his knees, alert and relaxed at the same time.

"The choice is yours, Mr Lime. But the target has protection. There are two Irishmen, possibly ex-IRA, staying at the villa. Lola has two bodyguards who live in the old wooden dacha in the grounds. There are surveillance cameras, so access is tricky. May I ask how you propose getting in?"

"I intend to ring the door bell," I said.

He hadn't been expecting that, and looked taken aback. He straightened his perfectly straight tie.

"I would advise against that," he said. "I have an alternative suggestion."

Sjuganov produced some more colour photographs. They had also been taken with a long telephoto lens, but you could see Oscar and Lola quite clearly. They were walking in the snow in what looked like a birch forest. It was a very Russian, attractive scene, like a picturesque postcard, with the sun sparkling in the trees and on the deep, white snow. In one of the photographs they looked like they seemed to be having another furious argument, in another one they were walking side by side. Oscar looked rather strange, in a long, thick coat with a brown fur cap pulled down over his ears. Lola was elegantly dressed in a full-length fur coat and a fur cap covering her dyed black hair. Oscar was carrying something that looked like a golf club. Possibly a long 5-iron.

"Does he think he can play golf in the snow?" I said.

Sjuganov laughed.

"He takes it everywhere. Golf hasn't yet arrived along with the market economy. The season is too short here in Russia. I think it's a lucky charm or perhaps he has it for protection. Look at this."

He placed a new photograph in front of me. The air in the suite was hot and dry and I began to sweat. It was the big Irishman. He was walking a few metres behind the couple, his hands deep in the pockets of his black leather coat. He was wearing a knitted hat. He looked freezing cold and bored.

"The target seldom goes out alone. So I have to ask you again, Mr Lime. What do you want me to do? What are you going to do? My assignment is finished. I have located the target for you."

"Does he go for a walk every day?" I asked.

"He usually goes for a walk in the morning. We haven't had him under surveillance for long enough to be able to establish a fixed routine, but that seems to be the case. He stayed indoors on the day of the snowstorm."

"What's the weather forecast for tomorrow?" I asked.

"Fine. Frost and sun, snow later in the afternoon. A winter day of the kind we Russians prefer. A good day to go for a walk in the forest," said Sjuganov, and looked at me as if to say that the ball was in my court and either we concluded our business now or I should start things moving.

I thought for a moment.

"OK. Let's drive out there tomorrow. If I could hire you to keep the heavies at a distance while I talk with my former friend and hear his explanation, then I would be able to say that it has been a pleasure doing business with a man as efficient as yourself, Mr Sjuganov."

"Shall we provide you with a weapon?" asked Sjuganov.

"No. That won't be necessary. There will be no shooting. Just an amicable conversation."

"That's what I'm afraid of," said Sjuganov.

"Let's do it tomorrow," I said.

"That's fine with us. The client decides. That's the fundamental law of the market economy. Please be ready here at eight o'clock tomorrow morning. But we'll have to get you some more appropriate clothing at the very least," said Sjuganov.

He looked me up and down, almost as if he was appraising a woman.

"I think I've got something that will fit. What size shoe do you wear?"

I told him.

He held out his hand formally, and I shook it. "Will you be coming?" I asked.

"I don't go into the field so much any more, but yes, for Derek's sake and for your sake I'll come along, with Igor here. We know one another from the old days."

"And when were the old days?"

"Way back, to the days of the hammer and sickle. More recently, a couple of years serving the new Russia. Igor was on my last team, working for a new President in a new nation, but our work was the same – gathering intelligence, carrying out sabotage, infiltration, and elimination of the enemies of the State. He's one of the best I've had, but the State could no longer provide us with the pay we had a right to, so I allowed myself to be privatised."

"Well, it's a good thing that the new Russia needs your skills." I said. I meant it ironically, but the irony was lost on this sturdy Russian.

"I'm unlikely to become unemployed for the time being," he said, nodding to the silent man by the door and they went on their way, leaving me in the hotel room with its view over the snow-clad roofs with hundreds of tiny pennants of smoke rising from their chimneys and a feeling of emptiness which I didn't understand. I should have been either frightened or tense, but I was neither. I was tired, but as I looked at the photographs of Oscar and Lola, I could feel anger creeping up on me again. It wasn't that Oscar had lived a double life for all those years, that he had served a totalitarian state. That was past, and it wasn't an issue between him and me. It wasn't my place to judge him for having planned terrorist operations, or at least being the one who took care of the logistics. That was an issue between him and the countries that had suffered the consequences.

But he had let Amelia and Maria Luisa be murdered, whether he had done so himself or got others to do it. I wanted to know why the two people who had meant more to me than anything else in my life should have been the innocent victims of his egotism and lust for power. Of his desperate attempts to bury the past. He had gone to great lengths to wipe the slate clean, but *Lime's photograph* had shown him that he would never be able to. Because there is always someone who remembers and there is always one more photograph.

# 24

Sjuganov knocked on the door just after 8 a.m. I had slept badly. The room was hot and stuffy and it didn't seem possible to turn the radiators down. I had been sorely tempted to visit one of the many bars or casinos in the hotel. But I didn't. Instead, I drank the best part of a bottle of wine and watched CNN. I lifted the receiver of the American AT&T telephone to ring Gloria and Clara, but thought better of it. I looked out across the rooftops and watched the wintry city slowly settle down for the night, and finally I fell asleep in the early hours.

Sjuganov stepped briskly into the room, dressed in black from top to toe. He was carrying a sports bag that contained a thick pair of trousers, a warm undershirt, a sweater, socks, a ski jacket, a stout pair of winter boots and a pair of lined, expensive gloves, plus a blue woollen ski cap.

"It's a cold day," he said. "And the snow will arrive earlier than the meteorologists anticipated. Put these on and then we'll go. I've got two men out in the field. They'll inform us when the target makes a move. If he doesn't, we'll have to repeat the procedure tomorrow."

The clothes and boots fitted. Outside the hotel it didn't seem all that cold. The air was damp and felt like snow. A huge thermometer on the building next door read minus six and the road was a swamp of slush and grit. Pedestrians had to jump for their lives as cars sent a cascade of muck and water across the pavement. I had given up on breakfast, which consisted of a dry bread roll wrapped in plastic, a slice of cheese with turned-up corners and a little packet of butter which was yellow with age, making do with a bottle of mineral water and a weak cup of instant coffee.

We got into the back of the black Mercedes and Sjuganov handed me a large plastic mug of coffee and a fresh cheese roll. Igor was sitting in the front, next to an Igor clone, with the same crew cut, thick leather jacket and blank expression.

We drove through Moscow and left the city via a broad boulevard. The traffic was heavy and traffic officers in black jackets and body warmers were everywhere. They stood in the middle of the swarming lanes, misshapen in their bulky uniforms, batons swinging, their breath hanging round their faces like fog. At one point we were waved into the side of the road. Sjuganov ignored the policeman who came over and addressed his fur cap. I saw the driver give him a document and a green note. The document was returned to him and we drove off.

I drank the hot, sweet coffee and felt strangely normal. It was as if I was on one of my usual assignments, had hired someone to find a celebrity somewhere in the world. As if I had prepared myself for the assignment and days, weeks or months of research and investigation were about to bear fruit. The celebrity was unaware that I was on my way to take the photograph that would earn me a great deal of money and cause that other person problems, even change their life. It was as if I had done it all before, that this was a repeat performance. I was on my way to a hit as I had been on my way to so many. I was tense, but it was in anticipation of the hunt. I would take my photograph, leave the scene and deposit the money in the bank. That was the normal routine. But this time I wasn't carrying my Leica or my Nikon with its long telephoto lens.

When we had driven for ten or fifteen minutes, the car slid up towards a large triumphal arch and further along on the left I could see an enormous area with cannons, an obelisk rising into the sky, a little church and at the far side a monument like a big Roman wall with columns and arcades. It looked very Soviet.

"What's that?" I asked Sjuganov.

"Two memorials. The triumphal arch is for the first great patriotic war. The victory mound over there is for the second one. In 1812 we beat Napoleon. In the second we defeated the Germans. We are a nation built on blood and bones. We don't have so much to be proud of, so we cultivate war. Our victories in war. Our victory over Hitler in particular unites us. It is the only purity we have left. The only thing we share, Mr Lime. My father's brother died. My aunt starved to death during the siege of Leningrad. My wife's uncle died, my wife's grandmother died of starvation in the Ukraine. My wife's grandfather vanished without trace during one of the large-scale purges. Russia equals suffering – 20 million died in the great patriotic war. In this accursed land, there is not a single family that does not have a story of death to tell."

He spoke in his elegant upper-crust English, but I could tell he was moved. I couldn't help saying "I've heard the number was 26 million. But that the extra six million were murdered by comrade Stalin and the good Chekists."

Sjuganov turned to face me.

"That is undoubtedly correct. Blood and violence and terror are our heritage, but from 73 years of communism, the Second World War is all we have which is not tainted. So the extra six, along with the other hundred million who have been murdered in this century alone, are just a footnote in my country's grim history, and we don't talk about them. Every family has enough to weep about already. We labour under a legacy of brutality. We don't include human life in our calculations. Look at our latest military enterprise in Chechnya.

How many were killed – 50,000, 80,000, 100,000? No one knows and only a few are interested. We concern ourselves with those we are closest to. Strangers are strangers."

We turned off to the right and drove alongside some large blue blocks of flats, then the road narrowed and there were birch trees on either side. Oscar sprang to my mind, but I wanted to repress all thought of the approaching meeting.

"What do you think about the change? The collapse of communism. The new Russia?" I asked Sjuganov.

He turned his head towards me.

"The old regime foundered. I served the State. I didn't ask questions. We are mid-stream, Mr Lime. We live in a ruthless capitalist society where criminals occupy the Duma and the Kremlin. But it's a period of transition. I served socialism, not from great conviction, but because I am a Russian patriot. I remain so. Now I advocate democracy and a market economy. The latter because it has made me wealthy. The former because that is the future. And if one has children, one also has to consider the future."

"You've got children?"

"A boy of 17. A girl of 14. The boy is at boarding school in England. The girl goes to an English private school here in Moscow. They are the new Russia. They will forget the bloody legacy. I believe we are on the right track, but it will be up to the next generations to lift Russia out of the darkness."

"What do the children think of their father's work?"

He looked at me with his cold, blue eyes.

"The children are not acquainted with the nature of my work. I am a businessman. I have worked 18 hours a day all my life. For most of my life the State and the Party gave me pocket money and scrupulously handed out privileges in response to my contribution. Today I earn it all myself. I have a comfortable home, my wife is able

358

to shop in the new supermarkets. She can buy whatever clothes she wants. We go on holiday to Florida. My life is almost as it has always been. I no longer receive medals, but money as a result of my own endeavours. I have given up considering the moral implications of my life. It revolves around the welfare of my family and the satisfaction of my client. I can't imagine anyone would condemn that principle, would they?"

"It would never even cross my mind," I answered.

We drove in silence and the traffic thinned out as the road meandered further into the birch forest. I hadn't seen so much snow for a long time. The road was clear, but snow lay thick on the trees and the little wooden houses we passed. There were carved wooden bears dotted along the roadside, sometimes together with a deer. It looked very odd – little toys covered in powdery snow in a landscape you could imagine extending thousands of kilometres eastward. We drove through a smallish town and passed a café and a vegetable market. There were big Western cars parked in front of the café and expensively dressed men and women wandered around looking at the market stalls. I thought I recognised it from the photograph and Sjuganov looked at me and nodded.

"We're nearly there," he said.

We turned right and drove up a road full of pot holes, with more little wooden houses on both sides, then big, red-brick villas surrounded by high fences, and drove deeper into the forest. Out here the road was white and compact, with a solid surface of ice, and despite its studded winter tyres, I could feel the Mercedes skid now and then. We pulled into a clearing in the forest and the driver turned off the engine. Igor and Sjuganov got out of the car. They each took a pair of white overalls, like a boiler suit but with a hood, from the boot. They put them on. Sjuganov spoke quietly in Russian into a walkie-talkie and received a brief, crackling reply.

"The target hasn't left the villa yet. You'd be better off in the car, so you don't get frozen. I'm sending Igor to a location along the route; he'll be between you and the villa, I'll lead you, OK?"

I wasn't freezing at all, although it was biting cold. I was too tense. It was completely silent in the forest, which seemed untended and natural, despite the little footpaths running off a broader path that disappeared into the woods. The tracks of cross-country skiers ran back and forth between the trees.

Igor put on a pair of short skis and set off smoothly and effortlessly into the forest. In his white outfit, he soon vanished and became one with the yellowish-white bark of the birch trunks. I got back into the car. The driver switched on the heater and Sjuganov gave me another cup of coffee. It was like being at work. You got there, you had done all the preparation, you were ready. Now there was nothing else to do except wait.

But compared to other occasions, when I'd lain on my stomach or stood in a doorway waiting for a victim for hours, this time my patience wasn't tested for long. After half an hour, Sjuganov's walkie-talkie crackled to life and he answered briefly. I got out of the car. There was snow in the air. The clouds were heavy and grey and a plane could be heard not very high up in the cloud cover, as if we were under a flight path. Perhaps I had flown in over these very trees, streams and lakes.

"The target is on his way," said Sjuganov. "The woman is with him and the big Irishman is acting as bodyguard. As usual he's walking 20 metres or so behind them. Even though they speak German to each other, they obviously want him kept a little out of earshot."

"OK," I said, putting on the gloves and woollen hat. I wasn't used to the cold, but fortunately Sjuganov had provided me with practical, warm clothes.

"Do you ski, Mr Lime?" he said.

"Not at all," I said.

"I had not anticipated that you would. I shall lead you to a position ahead of the target. Then I will go back a little way and step in between the bodyguard and the target and leave it up to you. How much time do you need in order to conclude your business?"

"Five minutes. I just want to ask him about one thing."

Sjuganov looked at me as if he didn't believe me, gave brief instructions on his walkie-talkie and off we went. We followed Igor's ski tracks and soon were deep in the forest. We were only a few hundred metres from the road, but I quickly lost my bearings. Everything looked the same. Snow and birch trees and low bushes. There was no sun to navigate by, and we turned first to the right and then to the left in order to get round fallen trees. At one point we took a parallel path and then another one; I could no longer tell where the road was. If Sjuganov had abandoned me, I would easily have become lost. I was used to hunting in cities. I wasn't a child of nature who could cope out in the wilds.

Sjuganov walked with steady, gliding strides. In his white camouflage he would disappear easily. The only sound was the faint squeaking of his army boots in the snow. He placed his feet effortlessly and surely, while I stumbled constantly over holes and fallen branches. I was reasonably fit, but I wasn't used to walking in snow. After ten minutes or so, we came upon a broader path which was hard-packed with ski tracks. The path curved downwards for a few metres and then gently swung up again. We were standing on a sort of little hill looking down the trail.

"I'll wait here," said Sjuganov. "You go a bit further along the path and conceal yourself behind a tree. The target and the woman will walk past me and I'll detain the bodyguard."

"Won't they be able to see you?" I asked stupidly, and he didn't bother to answer, but pulled out a long-barrelled gun from inside his coat and with a toss of his head told me to get going. I walked up the track. Just where it curved there was a large, bare tree with a thick trunk and I stood behind it. I looked down the path for Sjuganov, but all I could see was snow and birch and bush. It was as if he had sunk into the ground.

I heard Lola and Oscar before I saw them. They were arguing. Lola spoke rapid and fluent German. It sounded as if they were arguing about money. I squatted down and looked out from behind the trunk. Oscar was wearing his long leather coat and had his big fur hat pulled down over his ears. I had noticed that Russians didn't pull down the ear flaps. Maybe that was why the hat looked so ridiculous on Oscar's huge head. Lola was wearing her fur coat and now had a matching muff for her hands. She looked very elegant. Oscar slashed snow drifts and branches with his golf club as he argued with Lola. It looked completely insane to be running around a Russian forest carrying a golf club. I wondered whether he had gone mad.

They walked past the spot where I thought Sjuganov was concealed and came towards me. When they were about five metres from me, the big Irishman appeared and Sjuganov seemed to spring out of the snow behind him and I saw the Irishman stiffen as he felt the barrel of the gun in his back and heard Sjuganov's muttered warning.

"This country is just unbearable," Oscar shouted. "I'll rip Gloria's head off. What the hell am I supposed to do? She's bleeding me dry. I can't operate, and if you won't lend me anything more than peanuts, then . . ."

"Be patient, Karl Heinrich. Reach a settlement," said Lola. "May I suggest . . ."

"I'm tired of your fucking suggestions," Oscar shouted, and pounded the golf club into a pile of snow, making the white powder fly all around him. Lola stepped aside and raised her well-plucked eyebrows in mild irritation at his childishness.

I stepped out in front of them and said in English.

"There aren't many golf courses in Russia, Oscar."

He stood stock still as if the cold had turned him to a block of ice in an instant. I had dreamt about this confrontation, and now I felt nothing but contempt. Oscar looked in a bad way. His face was sallow and lined under his ugly fur hat, and his eyes were watery and blood-shot, like they were when he drank heavily and took amphetamines or another kind of speed. I knew that then he didn't sleep and got cantankerous and aggressive. He had once beaten up Gloria when he had been in that state and she had left, for good I had thought, but she had gone back to him after he promised not to take drugs again.

Oscar pulled himself together quickly and looked over his shoulder, but there was no one there. He looked back at me and then over his shoulder again.

"Your friend is otherwise engaged," I said.

"Fuck you, Lime," Oscar hissed like a snake.

"Peter Lime. How nice," said Lola in Danish. "My goodness, it's been so many years."

"Shut it, Lola," I said.

"Same bad manners," she said in her affected voice and I looked at her, which was a mistake. Oscar swung the golf club into my unpro-tected knee and the piercing pain made me howl and double up and try to protect myself as he pounded the club into my side. The thick jacket spared my ribs, but the pain went right down through my spine. He had aimed for the back of my head, but Lola had pushed him and in doing so she had saved my life. It hurt so much that I could taste stomach acid in my throat. I tried to straighten up as Lola tried to get her hands out of her muff to stop him. Oscar turned to her, livid with rage, and smashed the club straight into her face, which shattered with a scrunching sound and a shower of blood.

"Sjuganov!" I bellowed, as I clambered to my feet with burning barbs of pain in my knee and hobbled off into the forest. Oscar looked at Lola, lying half on her side turning the snow red, and then at me. His eyes were mad and vacant.

"Sjuganov," I shouted again, but it was the big Irishman who came running. One side of his face was smeared with blood and he looked exactly like the murderer he was. Oscar turned round and raised the golf club, but when he saw it was the Irishman, he turned back to me.

The Irishman had a gun in his hand. It had all gone horribly wrong. I ran as best I could into the forest and heard a shot and then another one and a zipping sound passing me a couple of metres away.

"Stay here, Lime!" I heard Oscar shout, in Spanish now. "Stay here you arsehole. I'm not finished with you, you ball-less son of a bitch. It's your fault I'm in this mess. You've wrecked my life, you fucking bastard. Come back!" And then in English. "Jack, get him. But don't kill the motherfucker!"

I limped faster into the forest, my fear overcoming the pain. I could hear the Irishman lumbering like a clumsy animal behind me. My face was getting wet, both from tears of pain and because it had started to snow with small fierce pellets carried along on the rising wind. I ran through the trees, but after a couple of minutes my mind began to clear. Where the hell were Sjuganov and Igor? I heard a shot and then another, but in the forest it was impossible to hear how far away they were. I came out onto a narrow track where the snow was more compact. It might have been an animal track during the summer. It meandered in an s-shape. Once I had got round the first bend, I pulled off my gloves and leant against a tree. The big Irishman came running round the corner. His cheek was covered with blood, but I couldn't see any wound. Maybe it wasn't his blood? He was running with difficulty, holding the gun in his right hand against his thigh. I stepped forward, spun round on myself and tried to hit him in the face. Pain shot through my knee and I was thrown slightly off balance, but he was used to fighting and managed to move his head in time. My fist struck him on the shoulder and the gun flew out of his hand and vanished in the snow. He quickly regained his balance and positioned himself, ready for combat, his arms moving agilely in front of him and his knees slightly bent. He was panting.

"So you want to fight, Lime. All right by me. Come on then, motherfucker, come on, come on," he said.

I could hear Oscar crashing through the forest, roaring like a furious beast. I feinted with my left and the Irishman laughed at my all too obvious manoeuvre and effortlessly shifted his weight. I kicked out, a stabbing pain went right up to my neck, and I struck the tree next to him, shaking the snow-laden branches and sending a cascade of powdery snow over us. I was prepared, he wasn't and he was dazzled by the whiteness and lost his balance. I hammered my foot into his crotch and, with the edge of my rigid right hand, as Suzuki had taught me and warned me never to do, I struck him as forcefully and precisely as I could and heard the sickening dry crunch of his neck breaking.

Oscar appeared, wielding his iron. I ducked away from his wild swings that were so powerful he lost his balance and just carried on running out of control. I stuck out my leg and my knee protested as I tripped him up and his huge body fell into the snow. But he was like a madman, with a madman's insensitivity to pain and the strength of the deranged. He got up and attacked me again, still roaring, trying to crush me in his arms and squeeze the breath out of me. I punched him twice in the face with my left hand and tried to hit his larynx. His eyebrow split open and blood spurted from his nose, but he carried on charging at me and forcing me backwards, while he tried to get his arms round my back. I slipped away and rammed my elbow into his kidneys and he roared again like a wounded animal. He should have collapsed, but he staggered clumsily, looking for his golf club, and I belted him again with my right hand, so hard that the skin on my knuckles split. Oscar flew backwards into the tree and his eyes glazed over.

"Damn it, Oscar. I just want to talk with you," I said. "I just want an explanation."

I was having difficulty speaking.

"Why Amelia? Why Maria Luisa?" I said, trying to get my breathing under control. It was snowing heavily now and the lashing snowflakes landed on Oscar's battered face and mingled with the blood streaming from his nose, lips and eyebrow.

Oscar spat out a tooth and attempted to attack me again, but his demented rage had made him completely uncoordinated and I was able to step aside and let him charge past me. He stopped, glowered at me like a wounded fighting bull that had been tricked by the cape, but now knew there was a man behind the flapping cloth. He didn't attack again, but ran off into the forest. It surprised me for a moment, but then I ran after him. There was nothing else to say, but like a dog can forget its training and instinctively go for a cyclist, a moving target, I set off in pursuit of Oscar without thinking.

I could hear him ahead of me, and now and then his black leather coat appeared in the swirling snow between the birch trunks. I don't know how long we ran for. I lost both sense of direction and time. My lungs were screaming and my knee was hurting, but I didn't care. The snow made it even harder for me to get my bearings in the white, uniform landscape. By now it was falling so heavily that footprints were as good as obliterated the moment they were made.

Suddenly I was out of the forest. It stopped abruptly at a steep slope and I rolled forwards and lay flat out in the snow. I got to my feet. Oscar had fallen over too, but he had rolled further out on the brilliant white tract of ice. He got to his feet, but fell over again, stood up again and hung on when the ice covering the river we had run onto

366

broke up under him. Over on the far side of the frozen expanse, I could just make out the slope of the opposite bank and trees barely visible in the swirling snow.

Oscar managed to pull one of his legs up onto the ice, but then it vanished again and I heard another cracking sound. Both legs were stuck and he sank in up to his waist. He looked back at me and I began to walk cautiously out towards him. The ice was creaking. I could see fear and desperation in Oscar's face. He tried to pull himself up with his arms, but merely succeeded in breaking off a piece of the ice, which I could see was rather thin. The snow was lashing into the black water and the hole in the ice was getting bigger. There was a creaking sound under my feet, but I took a step forward anyway. Oscar tried to pull himself up again and the ice split in a long crack that ran towards me and between my legs, but held. I stayed where I was, a few metres from him.

"Why did they have to die, Oscar?" I shouted above the wind whipping snow into my face.

"Help me, Peter," he said in Spanish. "Help me. I'll freeze to death."

"Why, Oscar?"

"It was a mistake. Jack and Joe were just meant to get that fucking photograph and some other negatives. They were meant to burn the fucking negatives. It was meant to look like an ordinary break-in, but Amelia put up a fight instead of keeping quiet. And the fucking Irishmen went too far. I thought everything was burnt and gone and then that fucking photograph turns up. I thought it had been shredded. Everything. I thought I'd got rid of the past. Why the hell couldn't you just let it rest? You couldn't bring them back anyway. Done is done, you stupid fool. You were my friend. I meant it. I mean it."

He continued in English.

"A fucking mistake, Peter. Help me, please. A fucking mistake."

There was no remorse. It was just a mistake. An unfortunate

mistake. Like when a deal doesn't come off. It's unfortunate, but you have to carry on. He was more callous and immoral than I had imagined. I had no right to pass judgement on other people, but Oscar, my friend, was incapable of feeling for anyone other than himself. My anger evaporated. I even felt a bit sorry for him, but it was too late. I walked slowly backwards in to the bank, the split in the ice widening in front of me. Oscar watched me go.

"A fucking mistake, Lime," he said, and vanished into the hole, down under the ice, and the current took him and I didn't see him surface again.

I reached the bank and tried to get my bearings. The cold was biting my face and hands. The forest behind me looked dark and impenetrable. I thought that if I followed the river bank then at some point I would come to a house or a road. I had no idea whether I should go to the right or the left, but I decided on the left and began to walk through the snowstorm in the same direction that Oscar's body was floating under the snow and ice. I was frozen on the outside and within. My mind was a complete blank and I had no sense of time or place, and Igor said later that I had seemed to be very far away, even surprised when he found me. As if I was sleepwalking. I had reached that stage when you are just about ready to lie down in the forest and go to sleep under its quilt of snow.

# 25

I rang Clara from Moscow. She answered on the third ring. She sounded out of breath and her voice had a metallic edge from the satellite.

"Clara, it's me," I said.

"Oh, Peter. It's good to hear your voice. Are you well? Where are you?"

"Moscow. I'm flying home this evening."

"Is everything all right?"

It was in her blood. She wouldn't say anything straight out on the phone.

"Everything's all right. There's nothing more to be said. It's all over."

"In a way you can live with?"

"Maybe not always. There will be nightmares, things I regret, but I can live with that. I have to. Especially if you'll share it with me. Come to Madrid."

"Why, Peter?"

"I need someone to carry my tripod."

She laughed.

"Why, Peter? Come on, say it."

"I need you."

"That was a step forwards," she said.

"You know what I mean."

"Possibly. But sometimes it's good to put things into words."

"Will you come?" I asked, almost forcing myself to plead with her.

"What am I going to live on?"

"I've got plenty of money."

"Be serious. What will I do?"

"Carry my tripod."

She laughed again, but I could hear the uncertainty in her laughter. I sensed that she was just as uncertain as I was, but I had the advantage. The stakes were lower for me. The connection sizzled in my ear. Modern technology, the hotel's satellite system sending the signal thousands of kilometres up into the atmosphere and down again to Clara. There were a couple of thousand kilometres between us, but our voices travelled 40,000. I sat quietly and let the moment tick by in the faintly whistling silence. Looking down at the traffic far below, it seemed that the entire population of Moscow was on its way somewhere or other, as usual. A thaw had set in and the streets were awash with slush. The biggest and most lethal-looking icicles I had ever seen in my life were dangling from the building opposite. Pedestrians in Moscow lived dangerously in many ways. I missed Madrid and my house.

"I don't know. I don't know if I dare. I'm thinking about those delicate wings," Clara said after a long while.

"You said yourself that the first burn is the worst."

"I can't give you an answer. At least not now," she said.

"I need you, Clara. Come to Madrid."

"We'll see. Perhaps I'll visit. Perhaps I won't. Perhaps it's best to let it stop here. I just don't know. But take care."

It sounded like she was about to cry, and perhaps that's why she hung up. I couldn't really tell what I felt. I sat for a long time just holding the receiver and looking out of the window, suddenly not able to see anything. My life seemed meaningless, and I was as exhausted emotionally as my aching body was tired. But at the same time I felt liberated. I didn't quite know why, and I had absolutely nothing to base it on, but the conversation with Clara had given me hope.

"Funny old language, Danish," said Sjuganov.

He was sitting in my suite, vodka in hand. One of his arms was strapped up and he had a large plaster on one of his temples. He had also arranged for a doctor to see to me. My knee was badly swollen. I only had two small patches of frostbite on my face, so I had got off lightly. I had been lucky. I had chosen the right direction, and an hour later I had been intercepted by Igor. Despite the snowstorm, trained soldier that he was, he had been able to read the tracks and follow the route Oscar and I had taken down to the river, and the snapped branches and shallow indentations I had made in the snow as I walked and walked along the bank. Sjuganov had called in reinforcements and got a search underway, but he had not alerted the police or any other authorities.

It turned out that Sjuganov had underestimated the big Irishman, who had a knife in a spring-sheath strapped above his wrist. The knife had sunk into Sjuganov's upper arm and the Irishman had knocked him out with his own gun. Igor had got there too late and had exchanged shots with the second Irishman. Igor had shot him in the leg and then at close range in the head. Lola's two Russian body-guards had not been worth their pay cheque. They had legged it, but we weren't complaining.

"It was carnage," I said, picking up my drink.

"No one regrets it more than I. It goes without saying that the fee is waived," he said. "I made the inexcusable error of underestimating the opposition."

"What about the police?" I said.

He rubbed his right-hand thumb against his index and middle finger in a universal sign.

"Surely that's not enough," I said.

"The target will be blamed. There were enough drugs in the villa to get half of Moscow stoned. He killed the woman. He paid the two Irishmen for their services. They, of course, tried to defend her, but were killed whilst discharging their duties. Thus the target chose either suicide or flight across the river and was dragged down under the ice. The river is deep and the current is strong. The gun has disappeared, the golf iron has been found, smeared all over with the woman's blood. He had only recently arrived in Moscow and was unaware that we had a thaw a couple of weeks ago. The ice was weak. We have on average 20 murders every day here in Moscow. The police are overstretched. They are happy to file a murder case as solved. It earns them points in the media."

"And Oscar?"

"He'll surface when the ice breaks up in March. By then everyone will have forgotten about it and we'll bury him in an unmarked grave."

I sat thinking for a while.

"Could you arrange for him to be cremated and have the urn sent to me?" I asked.

He looked at me, astonished.

"It will require some paperwork, but it can be arranged. Do you mind if I ask why?"

"There were many sides to Oscar. I know a woman who, in the course of time, would like to remember some of the good ones. I think she would like to have a grave to visit in Madrid. I know that from my own experience. A grave doesn't put an end to the anger at the injustice of death, but it's a comfort to be able to berate or talk with those who aren't here any more. I think she'd like it, even though I'm not going to ask her. She'd only say no."

"That's settled then. If the body turns up, it will be arranged. I'll have a memo sent out to the police districts along the river. Bodies can float a long way, but they usually appear in the spring. Anglers, a suicide . . . targets. Consider it a favour."

"Thank you. So I can leave this evening without any problems?"

"You can go home without a worry."

He raised his glass.

"All the best on your journey, Mr Lime," he said, and drained his glass.

I did the same. The vodka was strong and good. I poured him another and one for myself.

"Happy Christmas," I said.

"And may fortune smile on you in the new year," he said earnestly and formally, and I was happy to raise my glass to that.


Spring came early, just as winter had come early. It was only late February and the sun was lovely and warm and some of Don Alfonzo's flowers had begun to bud. I sat in the garden in short sleeves, reading a biography of Hemingway by Kenneth S. Lynn that I had found among Don Alfonzo's books. It was early afternoon.

I heard a taxi pull up, and Clara got out carrying a little suitcase. She paid the driver and walked towards me. She was wearing trousers and a shirt and sweater, and even had a coat over her arm, as if she had brought the cold, Danish winter with her. She smiled and stopped a few paces from me. I put the book down on the table, got up and walked over to her. The mild spring breeze ruffled her hair.

"Hello, Peter," she said.

"Hello, Clara. You look fantastic."

"What wonderful weather you're having. It's snowing in Copenhagen."

"It's good to see you. But you took your time," I said.

She glanced away for a moment, but then looked me straight in the eyes again.

"I decided to take a chance. I didn't want to phone in advance. I put my chips on the roulette table. If you were home, then it was fate. Winnings, maybe. If you weren't home, then maybe that's how it was meant to be. I haven't got a rational explanation, that's just how it is."

"A risky thing to do," I said. "But I'm usually home these days."

She smiled, moving close to me and I put my arms round her. I tried again to tell her how lovely she looked and how happy I was to see her.

"No more words just now," she said. "Keep them for later. Kiss me instead!"

I did and much later, in bed, I said, "You haven't brought much luggage. So you're maybe not counting on staying very long?"

Her head was on my chest.

"That depends on how long I can stand carrying your tripod. For the time being, I've got leave of absence and I've sublet my flat until the end of the summer. I'm not a complete fool. We'll have to see."

"It's a beginning, at least," I said.

"And at our age we can't really ask for much more. And I'm famished. So you can start by showing me the fridge."

*Harvill Crime*
*in*
*Vintage*

# Henning Mankell

# FACELESS KILLERS

'Wallander is among the very best fictional crimebusters'
*Daily Telegraph*

One frozen January morning at 5am, Inspector Wallander
responds to what he expects is a routine call out. When he
reaches the isolated farmhouse, he discovers a bloodbath.
An old man has been tortured and beaten to death, his wife
lies barely alive beside his shattered body, both victims of a
violence beyond reason. The woman supplies the only clue:
the perpetrators may have been foreign. When this is leaked
to the press, it unleashes racial hatred.

Kurt Wallander is a senior police officer. His wife has left
him, his daughter refuses to speak to him, and even his
ageing father barely tolerates him. He works tirelessly, eats
badly and drinks his nights away in a lonely, neglected flat.
But now, Wallander must forget his troubles and throw
himself into a battle against time and against mounting
xenophobia. *Faceless Killers* is the first in a series of Kurt
Wallander mysteries.

'Mankell is one of the most ingenious crime writers around.
Highly recommended'
*Observer*

VINTAGE

*Harvill Crime*
*in*
*Vintage*

# Henning Mankell

# THE DOGS OF RIGA

'Mankell is in the first division of crime writing'
*The Times*

Sweden, Winter, 1991. Inspector Wallander and his team receive an anonymous tip-off. A few days later, a life raft is washed up on a beach. In it are two men, dressed in expensive suits, shot dead.

The dead men were criminals, victims of what seems to have been a gangland hit. But what appears to be an open-and-shut case soon takes on a far more sinister aspect. Wallander is plunged into a frozen, alien world of police surveillance, scarcely veiled threats, and lies. Doomed always to be one step behind the shadowy figures he pursues, only Wallander's obstinate desire to see that justice is done brings the truth to light.

'The real test of thrillers is whether you want to spend more time in the detective's company. I certainly do.'
Sean French, *Independent*

'Mankell is a powerful writer'
*Independent*

VINTAGE

Harvill Crime
in
Vintage

# Henning Mankell

# SIDETRACKED

'Inspector Wallander has touches of Dexter's Inspector Morse about him, while remaining an original and highly likeable creation'
*The Times*

A girl commits suicide in baffling circumstances. Three vicious murders shatter the tranquillity of the Swedish province of Skåne. Is there a connection? Inspector Wallander must find out.

Midsummer approaches, and Wallander prepares for a holiday with the new woman in his life. But his summer is ruined when a girl commits suicide before his eyes, and a former minister of justice is butchered in the first of a series of apparently motiveless murders. Wallander's hunt for the girl's identity and his furious pursuit of a killer who scalps his victims will throw him and those he loves most into mortal danger.

'Another terrific offering from the talented Mankell'
*Publishers Weekly*

'Inspector Wallander is one of the most wonderful creations in contemporary crime writing'
*Le Monde*

VINTAGE

Harvill Crime
in
Vintage

# Henning Mankell

# THE FIFTH WOMAN

'Mankell could turn you to crime'
*Daily Telegraph*

Four nuns and a fifth woman, a visitor to Africa, are killed in a savage night time attack. Months later in Sweden, the news of the unexplained tragedy sets off a cruel vengeance for these killings.

Inspector Wallander is home from an idyllic holiday in Rome, full of energy and plans for the future. Autumn settles in, and Wallander prays the winter will be peaceful. But when he investigates the disappearance of an elderly bird-watcher he discovers a gruesome and meticulously planned murder – a body impaled in a trap of sharpened bamboo poles.

Once again Wallander's life is on hold as he and his team work tirelessly to find a link between the series of vicious murders. Making progress through dogged police work and forever battling to make sense of the violence of modern Sweden, Wallander leads a massive investigation to find a killer whose crimes are the product of new realities that make him despair.

'The real test of thrillers is whether you want to spend more time in the detective's company. I certainly do'
Sean French, *Independent*

VINTAGE

DAVIDSE

Davidsen, Leif
Lime's photograph

$ 12.00